Legends Of Shimrah

Saffrodel Silverstream

Nadha Zar

I dedicate this book to my parents for providing me with the education to make this possible. Especially to my mother, N. Who was my rock then, now, and forever! Also to my siblings for supporting me, however and whenever they can.

Thank you to my King, R. For his never-ending support and faith in me. I adore you and I wouldn't be able to do this without you. I am extremely grateful to all my darling little Princesses and Princes for helping me in whichever way they can to make Legends of Shimrah, a reality. Especially my eldest, V, Who is my first editor and reviewer. I love you all, Bubblecakes!

Contents

Alaq the Dragon

The Vision

Queen Debriar stirred uneasily as she slept. It was close to midnight and the dark shadows loomed outside her windows, thrown into sharp relief by the light of the rising full moon. The soft breeze swept the drapes into the room and the ghostly rustle of the stiff therin made her more apprehensive, even asleep. The gentle lapping waters of the Crystal Lake which she usually found peaceful, couldn't ease her disquiet this night.

Her long fingers caressed her swollen midriff protectively as she tried to ease her mind with the thoughts of the little shimling, moving peacefully within her. She sighed and stirred again, restless and agitated.

'No...! I don't want to know! Not now...!' she cried as she felt herself slipping into a Vision. Queen Debriar tried to snap her eyes open desperately but it was in vain. They moved rapidly behind her delicate pink lids as her fingers clutched at her heart, her breath shuddering and cold. The shimara who had been asleep with her head on her arm, on the floor beside Queen Debriar, snapped awake as she felt her Queen move restlessly.

'Your Highness...?' She whispered as she stared at her Queen's beautiful face in dismay.

This shouldn't happen, not now! The shimling isn't due for another three moons and if the Queen is to be upset by a Vision, it would mean an imminent birth! She thought. The shimara grabbed a cool towel, torn between wanting to stay by her Queen and running for help. She gently wiped the beads of moisture on Queen Debriar's ashen forehead.

'Please awake, my Queen, please...' She panicked as she shot a burst of red stars through the window with her centient, to alert the healers.

Queen Debriar moaned softly. The flashes were starting, vivid, painful and she knew she wouldn't be able to snap out of it even if she used up all her core and centient powers. She held on, lips pursed and tense. *I would have to see it through.* She thought.

The darkness engulfed her in a cold mist as she transported far, far away to a blood-sodden battlefield. An impressive figure with a vast mane of golden hair flying behind him, raised his ornate sword victoriously, high above his head. Sounds of cheer and mirth filled the air as he smiled, sunlight glinting off his gold armour and the fierce dragon on his crown. Queen Debriar calmed a bit.

This does not look too bad! Then why did the essence of this vision feel so ominous?

The handsome, golden-haired leader looked exhausted but the triumph on his face and the infectious laugh was catching. The tzars ran towards him from all corners of the field, waving and cheering, their shining silver blades raised high in victory. An elegant, brown-haired tzar stood beside him, Jaraadh, the Lord Protector, beamed through the trickle of blood at the corner of his full lips. The three-winged dragon, the Alaqwa, pinned on the back of his head snarled in the sun as he effortlessly blocked an enemy straggler who dared to point his sword at his Sovereign.

Lord Jaraadh sent him flying with a quick open-palmed blow. King Dunyazer grinned at him, his startling green eyes, soft and mellow. His King placed a hand on his shoulder, nodding at his swift response appreciatively. Lord Jaraadh bowed his head, the affection he cherished for his King, apparent in the warm sparkle of his eyes and his graceful movements.

A sudden resounding crash in the far end echoed through the fields. He glanced momentarily towards the sound, his javelin shielding King Dunyazer protectively. A brilliant flash of steel, a whirl of golden hair and black robes, a gasp of pain as a sword pierced flesh with a dismal thud, Lord Jaraadh's howl of anguish; Queen Debriar awoke with a tortured cry, tears streaming down her cheeks.

The shimara stood over her Queen, petrified but still trying to remain calm and stabilize her Queen's centre with her own. Her palm pulsed red, changing to a pale lilac as she held it over her Queen's left shoulder. A wave of desperation washed over her as she felt her Queen's massive centient forces, ebbing swiftly and closing in dangerously to her core. She huffed.

I need help, I cannot do this alone! Where are they?

The shimara was one of the ancient healers who often worked in the main remedial rooms, situated right at the back of the citadel. She was standing in for Mistress Afra, the head healer who was taking a break from caring for the Queen. The shimara concentrated as she poured more of her centient into her

Queen but it was no use. The Queen's centients had already drained and her core was rapidly depleting too, spent due to the vision and the growing grief gnawing at her heart. The lilac aura around her paled swiftly as her being ebbed.

Queen Debriar drew a quivering breath, her long fingers splayed over her unborn, trying hard to regain control over her core and focus on the shimling. She trembled with the strain but it was too late. A flash of jagged pain racked her slim body and a low, piercing scream escaped her lips.

The door flung open and a stunningly handsome, young shimratzar swept in. He looked about fifteen Shimran years of age. He glanced quickly at his Queen. She was white with pain and her being, drained almost to exhaustion. He swung back the lengthy sleeves of his robes, exposing his fair hands and slid a finger swiftly over his eyes, obscuring his vision with a thick silver sliver of his centient.

He moved his hands in rapid, fluid movements collecting his centre within them in a graceful circle and focused a steady silver stream on his Queen's left shoulder. The shimara beside the Queen panted with effort as she tried to maintain her own centient flow.

'You! You can't! We need the healers...!' she stuttered. Jaraadhrin quelled her with a stern and cold tilt of his fair face.

'Why didn't you send a yishin?' He inquired quietly. She stared at him for a moment, speechless then shrugged.

'I panicked...' she replied, tremulous. Jaraadhrin nodded. He understood. He had too. Queen Debriar convulsed weakly.

'No, Jaraadhrin! We will need you before the end. Do not use your centre...!' she murmured, sighing as the pain faded. Jaraadhrin's fair face tensed in concentration, his strong, attractive features turned pale as the meaning of his Queen's words sunk in.

'Stay still, my Queen' He whispered, his voice soft and enchanting as a cool spring breeze. He tilted his head at the shimara beside him, questioning her. He could feel her nodding, confirming his suspicions. She was on the verge of tears and her aura bleak with despair.

One of his Queen's many Royal Shifrs was the Visions. It was a formidable one that often drained her when it chose to make an appearance or when it was summoned. More so, if it was dark or bore bad news. Usually this wasn't such an issue. The Queen had a vast central core of some thousand years and her centient was twenty-five times that. But today, with a shimling on the way and the Queen already worried sick for her King in the fields of war faraway, it threatened her very being. It had exhausted her core to a minimum and his charge would soon make an appearance. He sighed softly, focusing more of his centient on the Queen.

'Everything is ready?' Jaraadhrin asked, his full lips hardly moved, fair forehead furrowed with concentration. The shimara nodded, busy with her preparations. Queen Debriar stirred again.

'Jaraadhrin, stop! Just get the healers, they have enough. Just get help!' she whispered urgently.

'I know my Queen, I have' Jaraadhrin answered her, gently turning his palms inwards and closer to his Queen's slim shoulder. He tilted his head away from her even though he was blindfolded. The silver shimmer emanating from his palm brightened and pulsed faster towards Queen Debriar, shimmering lilac as it entered her. His Queen's eyes darkened in confusion as she struggled to make sense of his words through the cloud of pain tormenting her.

'You have...?'

Jaraadhrin nodded, smiling tenderly. The heavy doors banged open at that moment and a stream of Shimran healers poured in, at the head of whom stood a translucent version of himself. It smiled at the Queen, sank into a quick salute and vanished.

Jaraadhrin had projected a part of himself to summon the healers when he had seen the red stars. He could have sent a yishin too but he had been anxious for his Queen, just like the healer shimara beside him. Queen Debriar's gentle smile flashed for a moment at the real Jaraadhrin beside her.

'You are quite accomplished with the projection. Thank you, Jaraadhrin.' she murmured as her eyes slid shut again. He wasn't. He was sure he had destabilised his core, ripping himself apart and made it worse by giving away his centient power, in his projected state. Jaraadhrin felt drained but smiled warmly at his Queen. He felt her aura reaching up to him as she raised her arm. She gasped as pain flooded back, her hand falling on the bed, too weak to continue.

'My Queen!'

'That's enough... young shimratzar!' An ancient healer grabbed him by the elbow and pulled him away. Three other healers took over and replenished their Queen with threads of shimmering colour. Jaraadhrin stumbled and caught himself quickly as he was ushered through the door. He vanished his blindfold as he went. The healer was Mistress Afra and she followed him out, grabbing his wrist roughly to check his life force.

Shimran folk never stumbled. She thought. *They were graceful and lithe on their feet. Especially young shimratzars in the prime of their youth and trained in combat like this one. They were accomplished soldiers, excellent at martial skills and was always full of grace and dignity. This senseless tzar must be close to exhaustion! He certainly looked pale.*

The head of the healers was very old in core years indeed, nearly six thousand, possessed a substantial experience in healing and eons in centient powers. She was also Jaraadhrin's mentor who oversaw his training in the Shimran arts of healing when he was younger. She looked up at him, concerned. She was right, his pulse was very faint.

'Idiot of a tzar! You have exhausted over a half of your core!' She said angrily. Her face smooth and young but her aura strong and ancient. It throbbed around him, hardly contained in her irritation. 'What would we do if the shimling is born now? Or if the citadel is sieged? Have you any idea how damaging this is?' Jaraadhrin shook his wrist free from her grip calmly, his face stern and cold.

'She is my Queen and I will not just look on until you take your time to arrive, Mistress!' He sighed at her outraged face, his expression changed to thoughtful and mellow 'And I think both your qualms might come to pass before the night is done.' he added, his face reverted to cold and aloof again. The face of a soldier, ready to do anything for his King and Kingdom. The healer stared at him, her anger abated and her face softened at the determination etched in every delicate line and lift of his spectacularly attractive face.

No! It couldn't be. Jaraadhrin was hardly even fifteen. He hadn't entwined yet; he had no dragon. He had hardly any control of his Shifr and he wasn't even sworn in as the next Lord Protector.

'Young shimratzar...' She questioned, quietly. Jaraadhrin drew a sharp breath.

'Mistress Afra, hard times may be ahead. Stay with my Queen and keep me informed of everything. I must see to the citadel's defences. Her Highness had a vision, her reaction does not abode well.' He spoke quickly and Mistress Afra gazed at the change in his voice and features with admiration.

'But your core, it's almost – ' she started.

'It's enough!' He replied, stern and impatient. 'Keep me informed.' He turned away from her abruptly and his white robes swung in a rapid circle, caught in the stiff breeze around his heels.

Mistress Afra shook her head exasperated, centred her immense, ancient centient in one swift swish of her long-fingered hands and slammed her palms with unnecessary force against Jaraadhrin's shoulder blades. She thrust a huge bolt of power into him, replenishing his core almost to the brim. She did it very roughly indeed, unlike the gentle manner in which he had streamed into his Queen.

The sudden action jolted Jaraadhrin. He inhaled sharply as it stopped him in his tracks. It paralysed him as the mists surged through. He closed his eyes as his lips lifted in a small smile at her way of showing how displeased she was with him. Mistress Afra withdrew her hands with a flourish, letting the therin of her sleeves flow over them as she crossed them at her slim waist.

'Now you may go wherever you fancy, young tzar. You will need to replenish the balance yourself. I will need the rest for the Queen and your charge, should he or she make an appearance.' She said curtly. Jaraadhrin turned to face her still smiling and relieved that she had not clicked on to his unstable core even though it was replenished.

'Thank you, Mistress Afra' he whispered. He inclined his head elegantly down to her, his hand on his heart, the tips of his long fingers reaching to his right shoulder and his brilliant blue eyes cast down. It was the Shimran salutation, a sign of respect and Mistress Afra's sternness dissipated.

She had taught Jaraadhrin all he knew about healing and he had always been such a respectful, enchanting little shimling. His transformation overnight from that youthful, carefree little youngling to this stern, proud shimratzar, carrying the cares of the world on his shoulders, astonished her. It was like he did everything else, elegant, efficient and effortless. This transition was just so, too. She stood on tiptoe, reached up and slid the long, wavy length of hair free from behind his ear, to hang unrestricted against his chest as he usually wore it. She patted the side of his face gently.

'Stay safe, young tzar, you are not alone.' She sighed. Jaraadhrin nodded. His eyes glittering with determination and courage as he held her hand on his face, lightly in parting. He turned and walked away quickly; his tall, white-robed frame, magnificent against the darkness. Mistress Afra gazed after him with her heart heavy, lost in thought.

Why is Shimrah in this state now? Where was the time when young tzars like Jaraadhrin enjoyed their fledgling lives without a care in the world, laughing and bright eyed with their families and friends?

Jaraadhrin is so special! Ever since he lost his mother, he had been a favourite of all the shimaras in the citadel. The Queen loved him as her own and everyone had always been enchanted by his mannerisms even as a shimling. His piercing blue eyes, wavy bronze hair, high forehead and chiselled cheekbones made him very charming indeed. Jaraadhrin's smile was so captivating that none could resist him. She shook her head, her heart heavy.

A smile that has been missing ever since his King and his father, Lord Jaraadh, had departed for the war, leaving him in charge of the citadel's defences and the protection of the Shimrans.

It was very late and the palace's white stone walls glimmered dimly in the pale moon as Jaraadhrin reached the citadel's enormous main doors. He stepped into the white marble courtyard, inlayed in gold. It was dotted with plinths and chairs arranged in circular flowers and was often full of shimrans in the daytime. The moonlight glinted off the tips of the petals that made the backs of the chairs and glimmered against the gold cushions of the seats.

Jaraadhrin flipped his wrist in a quick circle and summoned his centient. It swirled in a silver globe before him with a crystal sheet within. He waved it away and in disappeared with a flash. He tapped his right foot against the stone courtyard. He harnessed the wind under his robes in a swift twirl and flew into the air, arms outstretched to maintain his balance. He took another light step against the tower, the therin of his long sleeves, billowing behind him in a white cloud as he soared over and alighted gracefully on the topmost parapet. The guards sprang to attention, saluting his arrival.

'Summon the second-in-command to my presence, immediately.' Jaraadhrin ordered to no one in particular. 'Activate the citadel's defences, all eight levels. Inform the shield-maras to be ready for an imminent attack. Flood the moats with the waters of the Crystal Depths in battle formation, Denisthar. Maze layout, Drystwitch.' He continued as he walked swiftly among them.

'Get the archers in position within all eight levels of fort walls and turrets. The blade-Shimrans in the inner courtyards. Send word to the sentinels and relay back anything, anything at all even if it be a bird in the skies. Power up your centients and use martial yishins!' Jaraadhrin continued his orders.

His voice quiet but so stern and full of authority that his soldiers flew left and right to obey his commands in a whirlwind of motion. No one dared to ask him what happened as they flew off the parapets to action his orders, an unspoken communication and division of tasks so efficient, there was no delay at all.

A flurry of sounds rumbled through the night as with thuds, clanks and gushing of flooding waters in the moats, the citadel raised its defences to high alert. Huge beacons of light flared up along the fort walls and turrets, illuminating the speeding shadows of the soldiers. They flew like pale, blue ghosts as they assumed battle position, cloaks spinning in fans as they soared between the tiers.

Jaraadhrin heard a quick rustle of soft therin and a gentle thud as a skilled soldier alighted behind him. He could tell just from the sounds that this tzar was exceptionally light footed and elegant. A soothing, sweet scent wafted in the night air. It smelled of warm honey and the freshness of a breeze after a rain. Jaraadhrin closed his eyes taking in the scent, trying to calm himself and did not face the stranger. He guessed that this tzar was his father, Lord Jaraadh's chosen second-in-command for him and he did not want this tzar to see any doubts on his face.

'Ahem...I am Quinzafoor. How may I be of service?' he said, his voice was strong, serious and yet hid traits of laughter. A voice that could break into mirth at any moment and fill everyone else with jollity around him. It sounded very comforting.

Quinzafoor...? The name stirred a memory, almost from a past life. A young tzar blindfolded in a clearing, lazily fighting three other tzars at once, each more skilled than the other and yet not a single blow fell on him, not a single strand of his locks were out of place. He had a pair of very strange, ornate, gold headpieces clipped on to either side of his head. They had looked majestic, blazing in the sun against the brilliant bronze of his tresses.

He had twirled and pirouetted, blocked blow after blow with his gold inlaid, three pronged, double daggers. His long, straight bronze hair flying in sync with his light blue robes, graceful and elegant. His laughter infectious and filled with mirth, echoing around to where Jaraadhrin had stood, far away with his father as he pointed out this young tzar.

He was the son of Lord Jaraadh's own second-in-command and after his untimely passing, almost an adopted son. His father had explained that someday he would be Jaraadhrin's second-in-command. That day was probably today.

At that point, Quinzafoor had blasted all three of his attackers with a quick and powerful blow, ending the fight early. He had then turned in mid-air towards where they had stood and waved, his sleeves flying around him, the glint of his brilliant teeth visible even from afar. His father had laughed at Jaraadhrin's frown of confusion at the absurd scenario, only commenting that Quinzafoor had a lethal Shifr. He was already a master of it, even without entwining with his dragon and that it was a secret. Jaraadhrin had thought he was quite the show-off!

'Ahem....' Quinzafoor cleared his throat delicately, muffled by the sleeve of his robes as he covered his lips with his fingers. It sounded oddly as if he was laughing. Jaraadhrin drew a sharp breath.

'Quinzafoor, the Queen has had a vision. We know not what it was but she is unstable and with the healers. We should be ready for the worst. The King and my father....' Jaraadhrin paused to stop his voice breaking, his heart cold. '...we have no news of. I have sent them a yishin but they have not answered. Alert the soldiers under you and see to it that everything is being monitored. I need you to command them from here. I will project to you for updates.'

'You have already efficiently covered all grounds within the few moments, it took me to come to your presence.' Quinzafoor chuckled in awe. 'Denisthar and Drystwitch, I had forgotten those formations. Excellent choice and for-midable together. I see the great Lord Protector, Jaraadh, in you. I shall stand by you as I was trained to be by my father and the Lord' Quinzafoor's voice floated to Jaraadhrin, soothing and calm. It seems to strengthen him from within. Jaraadhrin nodded as he shook himself internally. His core must still be more unstable than he thought. Jaraadhrin closed his eyes as he steadied himself.

'Forgotten...? and yet, you recognise the lay immediately. We are dealing with Ibreeth and Ifreeth here. Don't forget they used to train within the eight tiers. Do not get complacent!' He reprimanded, his face stern.

'The healers think a Prince or Princess is due soon' Jaraadhrin continued 'I will need to be by the Royal shimling as the Lord Protector of the 4th generation.' He could feel the slight excitement of Quinzafoor's aura behind him, tainted with concern.

'Her Royal Highness is early' He observed. Jaraadhrin frowned, his centre shivered a little as his long, white fingers tensed on the cold stones of the parapet. His father's voice echoed in his mind from another, far away mem-ory from a happier time.

'You have to train harder and be more patient if the heir is a Princess.' Lord Jaraadh had said, laughing at the look on Jaraadhrin's face at the suggestion.

'Shimaras are more powerful in general, their Shifrs' are fuelled by their emotions. But those of Royal blood have a lot more power than the shimratzars and can be highly volatile when very young. It all depends on the number of Shifrs they have

accessed. *Royal Shimrans can access any number they want. It's what makes them Royalty and the Protectors of our world. You will need to be detached and mentor them from a distance. You cannot get involved with them emotionally which is very easy to do, especially with shimaras. Remember that you are their Mentor and Protector! Nothing more. They make the most powerful, influential rulers and you help shape them!'*

'Her Royal Highness?' Jaraadhrin repeated. 'What makes you think that?' Quinzafoor cleared his throat again, answering hurriedly.

'It is just an assumption; I may be wrong...'

'Do not assume! It does no one any good!' Jaraadhrin replied, abrupt as his being unbalanced and raged. 'You may leave.' He could feel Quinzafoor incline his head with respect, his fingers against his right shoulder. He stepped towards the parapet beside Jaraadhrin and moved his long, slender hand above the white stones, half covered by the thin blue therin of his cloaks. He wore an ornate ring made of black metal, probably Siyan, on his fore finger. It had a large, flaming stone set in it. An auburn mist swirled and hardened into the solid form of a decorative vial, holding some fiery, red-gold liquid.

'It is a very cold night' Quinzafoor observed 'I hope you will have this warm drink...' Jaraadhrin moved his head to look at the vial and as he did, Quinzafoor leapt lightly on to the parapets without waiting for a reply. He sailed off, his blue robes spread around him in a large, fluttering circlet. Jaraadhrin sighed.

Oh wonderful! Quinzafoor probably thinks I am unsuitable as his leader, leaving me a drink like that and why did he have his drinks in vials? He wound his fingers around the vial and brought it to his lips. He sniffed, frowning slightly. *This isn't any drink....* thought Jaraadhrin, his eyes narrowed. He sniffed again trying to place the scent which was vaguely familiar....

Jaraadhrin's eyes snapped open in disbelief. He stared after the diminishing blue spec in the sky. The fiery liquid was a tincture. The elusive Javnoon! Incredibly difficult to make and highly treacherous if made incorrectly. An elixir to stabilize the internal energy core of Shimran folk and lend eons of centient power to the drinker. Mistress Afra had taught him this many years ago but he had never mastered it. This Quinzafoor had just magicked it into his presence out of nowhere.

Dare I take a sip...? Shimrans trusted each other with anything and everything they had, anyway. We could trust each other with our lives even as complete strangers. Quinzafoor is personally known to and highly thought of by my father.... but how in the Crystal Depths did he know that my core was so unstable? Even Mistress

Afra had not picked up on it? Another assumption.... a guess? His father's voice echoed from the past.

'A lethal skill.... a secret...'

Jaraadhrin inhaled, bracing himself. He raised the cup to his lips and took the tiniest sip. Immediately, he felt his core bubble and froth, rising in strength and stability, well above its full level. It spilled over and increased his centient by years, much more than he was used to. He jerked away from it, breathing hard. It was very potent indeed! It had matured for many years.

He set the cup back down swiftly and performed the six-point, core stabilizing movement. His sleeves swung and swished against the vigorous aura of his bubbling core and the grace of his manoeuvre. He closed his eyes, calming and dispersing the powers of the numerous years he had just consumed within his body. His core felt strong and rock solid. He had three hundred and seventy-five centient years over his fifteen-year-old core as each of them added twenty-five years of power to his centient. It now felt ancient, at eight hundred and seventy-five years.

He lowered his arms slowly to his sides, confused. That vial would give him many hundred, thousand centuries of centient power! He would need to take it a drop at a time and meditate to mediate it within his body.

Such a priceless gift and Quinzafoor just left it...? Jaraadhrin frowned, his eyes narrowing to mere slits. *What is this strange tzar playing at? Where did he even get it from? Could he have made it himself?* Jaraadhrin moved his fingers in a circular motion above the vial, lost in thought. It shrunk to the size of a small flower with the power of his silver centient. He picked it up and slid the lengthy, crimson trinket ribbon, knotted over his belt from within his robes and clipped the vial on it.

The Shimran trinket ribbon allowed them to carry important items within their person. The ingenious innovation had voided the need for carrying huge weapons and shields since the revolt began. Objects could be minimised and clipped on the enchanted ribbons which stored them infallibly till it was needed. It had enabled the shimrans to remain as elegant and as graceful as ever without being weighed down by heavy arms. He arranged the many weapons on his ribbon delicately, deep in thought. His slender fingers slid from one to another, positioning each one precisely before slipping it away to the left, at his slim waist. Jaraadhrin shook his head and his bronze waves flew out behind him.

I have more important issues to deal with. Quinzafoor and his oddities can wait!

As he stepped lightly over the parapet and launched into the night, back towards the palace, he realized that the sweet scent of warm honey and the rain drenched freshness had been missing from the air for a while.

The Soul-Light Crossfire

Jaraadhrin made his way to the Queen's chambers. It was quiet outside her door but he could sense the buzz of activity within. There wasn't much he could do now. He might as well try distributing his surging centients in to his central being properly. The six-point, core stabilisation was just an emergency measure. Without proper meditation, he was in danger of his centre being overwhelmed, destabilizing again or causing serious internal injuries. The more organised he was with it, the more powerful he could be in a fight.

Jaraadhrin moved over to a low pedestal beside the Queen's door. He lifted the robes off his legs and sat down cross-legged, letting them fall back around him naturally. Placing his hands on his knees with two fingers in each hand extended, he closed his eyes, concentrating on his core. Jaraadhrin had a hard time keeping his thoughts blanked out. His mind wondered incessantly to his King, his father, the Queen and the little shimling.

Would she be a Princess? Is Quinzafoor right? He worried about what his future held in store for him. The ceaseless opening and closing of the doors beside him weren't helping either.

Jaraadhrin took a deep breath, blocking everything out with effort. Somewhere far above him, the gentle strum of a harp sounded in a haunting tune. Jaraadhrin's fair brow tensed at the temples. He recognised that tune. It was the one for relaxing and sleeping that Mistress Afra often played in times of troubles or unrest, amplified over the palace's many towers, minarets, turrets and terraces. This melody was very different, however. It had more intense notes and the harmony of it struck very deep in to his being indeed. Whoever was playing it was highly skilled and had modified it to cater to a lot more than just to relax.

Maybe Mistress Afra is adapting? She did know that I depleted over half my core and she did replenish me. Jaraadhrin sighed as the melody surged around him, feeling himself relax physically. The tensions slid away from him in rivulets.

He sat up straighter, broad shoulders square. The peace surrounding him, lifted the corners of his lips in a slight smile and his eyes stopped moving behind his pale, thick lashed lids.

Jaraadhrin didn't know how long he had been there in that state of peace. No one disturbed him and his centre merged, moved and flowed seamlessly within him, depositing the extra years he had consumed, smoothly within his slender frame. The soft melody from above was all that weighed on his conscious mind, flowing along with him.

He was vaguely aware of his surroundings, beyond his aura which felt very busy but not threatening or near enough to warrant his attention and so he continued. The many centient years added to his own, now gave him a beautiful, shimmering, silver aura which looked tangible as it spun around him. He had never been able to see that before. There was so much that he didn't know about his own existence that ancients like Mistress Afra knew as common knowledge.

As his mind unconsciously focused on the silver around him, Jaraadhrin could feel another, pearl-pink one just outside of his, regarding him inquisitively. His smooth forehead creased as his conscious mind made the connection. The pink aura needed his attention and it was very happy.

Jaraadhrin let go of the calm with a soft sigh and opened his long-slanted eyes, gazing straight into Mistress Afra's beaming face.

'Pink...?' he chuckled, his voice filled with mirth. She raised her eyebrow at him.

'Yes...? Good, you can see. Where is the half century from then? Oh and be careful...you are floating!'

Jaraadhrin glanced down at himself. He was many paces above the pedestal, held up by his aura still swirling in circles. His hair spread in a cloud behind him and long tendrils swished over his eyes. He smiled. *That is new!* He moved his hand in a slight flourish and floated, light as feather, back to the pedestal on his centient. The silver subsided, settling his long waves. He stood up, sweeping everything back to its place with the refinement that only a Shimran could possess.

'You didn't answer my question?' Mistress Afra looked up at him, rather stern. Confusion flooded Jaraadhrin's face for a moment.

The melody is still playing...? If it isn't my Mistress, then who is it? He lifted his eyes to the ceiling, answering her question as he wondered.

'Quinzafoor...'

'Yes, that's him playing ...but about your centient years?' Mistress Afra pressed impatiently. Jaraadhrin's eyes flashed back to her even more confused but just as stern.

'... gave me the Javnoon tincture.' He continued, swinging back his white robes to reveal the miniaturised vial on his crimson ribbon and pointing to it with a long finger for emphasis.

'Oh!' said Mistress Afra as she understood. 'That shimling was an expert potionist even then! I am glad he has made your acquaintance at long last. That is a lordly gift, indeed!' She gushed. Jaraadhrin rolled his eyes and curved the finger pointing to the vial, back to the ceiling, slow and deliberate. He raised his brow at her. Mistress Afra grinned at his confusion, her expression rather mischievous.

'Quinzafoor is also a master in melodies especially those that help with healing.' She wiggled her brows. 'I am guessing, this one was for your benefit as its right after he gave you the tincture.' Jaraadhrin's eyes narrowed, prodding her to continue. Mistress Afra shrugged. 'His Shifr is very powerful, a lethal skill! You will know about it soon enough, young shimratzar! Now come, the Queen has summoned you! Your charge is here!'

She grasped the top of his arm by the therin of his sleeves and pulled him to the door, jolting it as she skipped off in front of him. Jaraadhrin glided after her, shaking his head and smiling. Shimaras often behaved in such childish manner. They were strong, formidable and immensely powerful than tzars due to their emotions and Shifrs but they were also adorable, mischievous and downright endearing when they wanted to be.

No tzar ever dared to cross them in anger and no tzar could resist them at such times. The maras were well aware of this little fact. It was why they never misused their powers and it was also why Jaraadhrin respected them so. His Mistress was eons old yet she behaved like a shimling at times, though Jaraadhrin was quite sure it was entirely unconscious. It stemmed from the playful nature of a shimara.

Mistress Afra led Jaraadhrin to an alcove with a large window, within the Queen's chambers.

'Wait here, I will be back soon' she said. She made to turn away and stopped mid turn. She gazed back at Jaraadhrin, her green eyes sparkling. Reaching up on her toes, she placed her palms against the sides of his broad shoulders, patting them affectionately then drew her hands together in clasp under her chin.

'Oooh! Young Lord Protector!' She beamed up at him. 'My disciple is finally going to be the Lord Protector to the Royalty of Shimrah!' she sang, head tilted comically to the side, gazing up at him in pride and affection. She placed the tips of her right fingers to her left shoulder, kissed them lightly, touched them to the middle of her brows with her eyes down and waved them towards his face!

Jaraadhrin chuckled. It was a Shimran sign of affection and Mistress Afra looked adorable doing it, like a little shimling who had been given her favourite toy. With a soft sound of adoration, she spun on her heels and disappeared, her long pastel pink robes, sailing around her.

Jaraadhrin glanced out of the window, still smiling. The sky was lightening and the huge towers, turrets and forts stood, tall and imposing. Long, white flags and their gold ribbons curled and soared from the high masts of the parapets. Semi-circular terraces with ornate banisters of white marble, dotted the main palace and gleamed in the morning light. Shimrans loved curves in their architecture and huge sculptures and pillars, incorporating the design, rose like streamers wherever possible.

Harp music swelled in the same haunting tones as he had heard before. He glanced up quickly around the walls trying to find the source. Even with his piercing sight, he could barely see the hidden archers and blade-Shimrans behind the main siege walls.

On the very edge of the tallest turret, sat a lone figure in long, pale blue robes contrasting against the darker skyline. His silky mane flew with the wind behind him. He was sat on one heel, supporting a harp on crook of his bent leg, strumming away merrily. He perched precariously at the very edge but seem to be very much at ease. Jaraadhrin leaned forward, his hands splayed on the cold, stone sill.

'Quinzafoor...?'

The figure stopped playing abruptly, rose to its feet with the grace of the wind itself and turned in his direction. It raised a hand and waved. Jaraadhrin frowned in confusion.

Again, with this...?

Quinzafoor whipped around, swift and sudden, facing the opposite direction. The harp disappeared from his hand as he reached into his robes. Jaraadhrin guessed he must have stowed it away in his ribbon. He tried to see what had caught Quinzafoor's attention but the skies were clear. Quinzafoor whipped back to face Jaraadhrin for brief moment then turned and launched himself away in the opposite direction. He harnessed the full forces of the winds and spun rapidly. His tresses and mantles spiralled around him in a violent whirl-wind, exposing his long, white clad legs and heavy war shoes as he shot away, straight as an arrow to its mark. Jaraadhrin leapt lithely on to the sill to follow him as Mistress Afra returned.

'What on Shimrah are you doing?' she exclaimed. 'Can't leave you tzars for a moment alone, can I now?' Jaraadhrin caught himself, staring after the rap-idly diminishing speck in the sky.

I am right here, Quinzafoor would have informed me had it been an actual emer-gency, wouldn't he? he thought with uncertainty, still gazing after his second-in-command. Mistress Afra rustled her robes impatiently. Jaraadhrin sighed, turned and alighted beside her. He smiled at the exasperated expression on her face and followed her through the door as she led him to the Queen.

Quinzafoor is certainly odd, odd enough to make the effort to get to know better.... oddities are intriguing. He thought, chuckling to himself. After all, Jaraadhrin did have to thank him twice within the short space of time, they have been acquainted.

The large room felt very different to the last time he was here. It was light and an air of happiness veiled the apprehension underneath. His Queen sat up against the large pillows with a bundle in her arms, covered in beautifully worked therin. It had been made from a stunning, late evening, violet cloud, worked with the gold of the early morning light. The therin Shimrans who had immersed these from the clouds and the sun at exactly the right moment, were indeed skilled in weaving them.

However were they able to combine that colour clouds with gold beams? Unbeliev-able! He had always admired the art.

Tinctures, elixirs and potions littered his Queen's bedside plinths. Brilliant, coloured crystals lay at the corners of her magnificent four poster bed, placed there to help stabilize her centre. The lush draperies around it were pulled back and tied away with long, tasselled bells. The breeze blew in gently, jan-gling them. Healers stood around or moved quietly, busy tending to their Queen. One stashed an abnormally large bundle of crimson drenched, white therin sheets, hastily into a basket as he approached. Jaraadhrin pursed his lips in concern. It looked like it had been a very difficult birth. Queen Debriar replaced an oddly shaped carafe from which she had been drinking, back on the plinth beside her bed as he approached her.

She glanced up and smiled but all he saw was the despair and agony in her eyes. She was heartbroken, in anguish and very weak. Mistress Afra positioned herself behind the Queen, relieving a healer and core sharing with Her Highness. She placed her palms delicately against the back of the Queen's shoulders, streaming her many eons in. It pulsed as a pale pink haze away from her and turned a shimmering lilac as it streamed into his Queen.

'Your Majesty....' Jaraadhrin inclined his head and saluted her, his eyes clouded with worry.

'Jaraadhrin' Queen Debriar breathed with such pain in her voice yet smiling so radiantly, that Jaraadhrin's felt pure torment. He shifted his gaze to Mistress Afra behind her. His Mistress's face looked ancient and solemn, compared to how it was moments ago. She shook her head slightly. A single tear clung to the corner of her thick lashes, confirming his worst fears. The facade wouldn't last long in the face of such grief.

Jaraadhrin drew a long breath and sank slowly to his knees beside the bed, unable to look up at his Queen. He felt cold and hopeless. Shimran folk were immortal if they chose to be but they were not invincible. They could live eons if they wanted to but it did not stop them from dying of unnatural causes, such as being killed in battle or fading due to a broken heart. They could also perish, simply because they have lost the will to live. Queen Debriar laughed. It sounded hollow and wrought with pain.

'Why so forlorn, young Jaraadhrin? Today is your swearing-in-ceremony, my young Lord Protector. Your charge is finally here.' Jaraadhrin nodded, torn between his duty to the shimling and the grief for his Queen, his King and his father. His emotions threatening to overwhelm him at any moment. He drew a deep breath.

'I, Jaraadhrin, Son of Lord Jaraadh....' he began, forcing his voice to some semblance of normality. How many times had he practiced this oath with his father, never imagining it would be in such situations? His King gone, his Queen dying, his father...? And an orphaned Royal shimling as his charge!

How many lifetimes ago was it? How many times had he laughed and dawdled around as his father tried to train him? Jaraadhrin drew a sharp breath through his teeth. He had always imagined his father beside him when he said the oath, tall, fair and elegant, smiling proudly down at him. He shook himself and straightened. He was Jaraadhrin, Son of Lord Jaraadh, Lord Protector of Shimrah and he would see it through!

'...solemnly swear...'

Queen Debriar's chuckle interrupted him as he knelt before her, his head bowed and his long locks sliding against the sides of his face in a sleek curtain.

'You haven't even seen her yet, young shimratzar' She whispered. Jaraadhrin closed his eyes and pursed his lips.

Her? Quinzafoor was right...could this situation get any worse? He sighed, forcing a smile and raised his head as Queen Debriar moved the bundle to her left arm, closer and facing him. The shimling was asleep, her long lashes curled against her rosy cheeks. Her hair was of the darkest red, Jaraadhrin had ever seen and had strands of brilliant gold through it. It made her skin almost translucent. Shimaras usually had red hair and green eyes but this shimling wasn't any regular shimara. She is a Royal. Her hands curled in tight little fists against her full pink lips, pouting in her sleep. Jaraadhrin's forced smile warmed into a real one as his eyes softened. She was exceptionally delightful.

As he gazed at her enthralled, the shimling stirred in her sleep, lifting her tiny arms above her and towards him. Jaraadhrin shook the sleeves off his fingers, remembering that he had to place the shimling's hands on his eyes as he said the oath. It was an age-old Shimran tradition, signifying him protecting his charge as preciously as he would his eyes.

As he made to take her little fists in each of his hands, the shimling moved again and nudged his long fingers. Her mouth curved into a circle as she yawned and her little fingers wrapped tightly around his index ones. Jaraadhrin chuckled as Queen Debriar's laugh, tinkled above him. The shimling was exceptionally strong too. He pulled his fingers gently, trying to free them. She wouldn't budge! She stirred again and with another loveable, little yawn opened her eyes, looking straight in to Jaraadhrin's glittering, blue ones.

Jaraadhrin gasped, trying to steady himself on his elbow against the bed. He felt a physical jolt from deep within his core, a shattering that knocked his breath away. The fingers, the shimling still held, burned as if on fire. His mind drifted in a sea of raging thoughts. Her eyes were a brilliant emerald, shimmering with floating specs of the brightest gold. She held his gaze inquisitively as he struggled to regain his composure. Jaraadhrin drew a long, shuddering breath, his heart hammering against his chest. He felt tremulous, quivery and he could no longer feel the auras of anyone around him. His surroundings didn't exist anymore. His hands shook as he tried to control his tumultuous centient powers, as it roared deafeningly in his ears and maintain a calm exterior.

All the meditation he had done with the help of Quinzafoor's melodies undid themselves in rapid succession, shaking his core and his centients viciously.

It displaced everything, rattling and tousling his very being with alarming briskness. He couldn't break away from this little shimling! The specs of gold within her eyes, seemed to dissolve and escape as a mist into the air around them. It thickened, swirled and turned, enclosing them in and blocking everything except the pure golden aura surrounding him. He couldn't remember the Oath! Was he sad about something before? He couldn't remember his name! He swallowed hard trying to make sense of the jumbled mess of his thoughts and emotions.

Jaraadhrin's eyes clouded with moisture as he fought against himself. He had feared a Princess would make his duty more difficult, worried about their nature and the power of their Shifrs. He had been uncertain and had doubted whether he could be an adequate Protector and Mentor but as he gazed into her eyes at this moment, unable to break free, not wanting to either! He could feel the resolve forming so tangible and solid within his heart and mind, that it hurt. It was the only thing that made sense.

He would do everything he could do for her! She will always have him, as her Mentor, her Guardian, her Friend, her Protector, always with her and yet away from her. His existence was for her and it will end with her. He will swerve his Princess with every essence of his strength, spirit, being and whatever else he was made of or had to offer.

Jaraadhrin shook his head, eyes still locked, trying to think. He needed to bring her hands to his eyes but he couldn't break away. He was no longer in control of anything, anymore. He felt himself leaning closer to her, his long hair cascading around her. He brought her little fists to his lips, still wrapped tightly around his fingers, her tiny face, a hair's breadth from his. He pressed his lips against her hands gently. The golden glaze around them infused back into their eyes, hazing them over in a shimmer as his lips touched her little fists.

Jaraadhrin heard a collective gasp and blinked, the connection fading. His surroundings snapped back to him and he leaned away from the shimling slightly. He stared down at her.

What just happened......? The shimling let go of his fingers and rubbed her gold covered eyes. They reverted back to the brilliant green they had been as she blinked. She seemed suddenly interested in his bronze waves flying around her, still caught in the invisible breeze of their auras. Her little arms swung around and finally grabbed a large tuft of his tresses with both hands. It effectively stopped him from moving away further. She gurgled and cooed in glee. His hands free, Jaraadhrin steadied himself as discretely as possible, a palm flat on the bed and the other pressed against his racing heart under his robes, trying to calm his quick shallow breaths.

'I ...The Oath...my Queen...' He couldn't remember it! Jaraadhrin had never felt this raw and vulnerable. His core was more than full, his centients well over his years and yet he felt as if he had projected to a hundred different places at once. He raised his eyes to his Queen in fear.

What punishment would my actions warrant? What did I just do? Surely, I have already failed as the Princess's Lord Protector? He thought desperately.

If there was anything more unexpected and shocking, it was the expression on his Queen's face. Jaraadhrin stared at the change in her eyes. The despair was gone! The pain and torment, non-existent yet her eyes swam with tears. A smile lingered around her full lips. Behind her, Mistress Afra's face beamed with pride and joy, tears falling unceasingly, thick and fast into her pale pink robes.

Jaraadhrin, fighting his own from falling, shifted his gaze back to his Queen, adding confusion to the list of emotions, already wreaking havoc within him. Queen Debriar smiled and lifted her hand towards Mistress Afra, shaking the thin therin of her sleeves, off of her delicate fingers. The Alaqain – the Ring of Royalty, glittered gold on her slender middle finger in all its five-coiled, dragonesque glory. Without looking away from Jaraadhrin's' pale face, she slid off the little sceptre trinket from the crimson ribbon, Mistress Afra handed her.

Queen Debriar tossed it gracefully into the air. It spun and expanded to its full length. She caught it deftly. She swung it over Jaraadhrin's head and landed the elaborately decorated head of the golden sceptre, on his right shoulder. She tapped him gently, thrice as it blazed a brilliant lilac, warming him. Jaraadhrin looked up in astonishment. Her Highness was accepting him as the Lord Protector for her daughter and he hadn't even said the oath yet!

'My Queen, I haven't ...' He struggled to whisper. Queen Debriar smiled at him radiantly, her eyes glimmering with hope and affection.

'You have... I heard...I have seen and it's enough.' She murmured, nodding at him. Queen Debriar raised her voice higher.

'And I, Queen Debriar, daughter of King Dheriyadhar accept you, young Jaraadhrin, Son of Lord Jaraadh of the 4th generation as the Lord Protector of Saffrodel, daughter of King Dunyazer,' Her melodious voice cracked slightly and a flash of pain crossed her perfect features as she mentioned her King. 'The Princess and the future Queen of Shimrah! May you be her Mentor, her Guardian and her Protector!' she paused still gazing at Jaraadhrin. Queen Debriar twirled the sceptre up and over his head, pointing it at the open window.

With a graceful prod, she shot a large cloud of brilliant lilac dust which fluttered away rapidly into the night air.

Queen Debriar spun the sceptre once again, shrinking it and clipping it back on the ribbon. She moved her hand in a swift motion so that the therin of her sleeve slid over it and leaned forward. She laid her hand, gentle and soft, against the side of his head, lifting his face higher up to her as her eyes glittered with authority and love.

'May you be her Friend, her Beginning, by her at her End, Everything and Anything you can be for her and…. More!' she whispered. A tear escaped the corner of Jaraadhrin's eye as his Queen echoed his thoughts. She wiped it away surreptitiously, with the tip of her finger.

She slid her hand to the back of his head, holding him in as she kissed him between his brows. Jaraadhrin closed his eyes. He felt the warmth and love flood through him at her touch, comforting him, strengthening him from within. It wasn't just an action of affection; she was streaming in her blessings into him.

'Rise, my son!' she breathed tenderly as she released him. Queen Debriar leaned back, trying to free the large tuft of Jaraadhrin's mane still clutched in Princess Saffrodel little fists.

The shimling was falling asleep again. Jaraadhrin raised his trembling hand quickly to stop his Queen. His lips lifted in a smile even in his confused state as he gazed down at her. He used his centient to carefully sever off his locks above the shimling's fists. Mistress Afra tutted in disapproval as his Queen's sweet laugh tinkled above him.

'Princess Saffrodel' He whispered, guiding her tiny hands back on to the blanket as it fell, his long-severed locks still clutched in her fists.

Jaraadhrin glided swiftly off the floor and bowed his head, still weak and heart racing. He needed to get out of there! He needed to right his tumultuous principle being yet he couldn't bear to leave! He stood torn, unable to move. The healers around him stared with varying expressions of shock, disbelief, affection and bewilderment. Queen Debriar smiled, ever radiant, lightening his heart.

'Rest. Young tzar' she said. Jaraadhrin nodded. He glanced at the Princess; he didn't want to leave but knew he had to. He took a deep breath and strode off to the door, pausing briefly to steal a final glance at his adorable little charge before disappearing behind it. Queen Debriar sighed, closing her eyes and allowing exhaustion to catch up with her at last. Mistress Afra stood up, helping her.

'Leave us' said Queen Debriar to the other healers who bowed and glided away. She shifted Princess Saffrodel on to the bed. 'Was that...?' she inquired quietly as she glanced up at Mistress Afra.

'The Soul-Light Crossfire.... yes' she confirmed, her eyes shining 'The first time I saw that was in the first generation as a ten-year-old shimara.' She continued. 'And the second... well, as you are aware my Queen, some five hundred years ago. It's incredibly rare and it is for all eternity!' She ran her fingers along Princess Saffrodel's hair. 'It's the oldest and strongest of Shimran magic. It will see the Princess through anything!'

'What was the nature of it? Could you tell?' Queen Debriar wondered, gazing at Mistress Afra with hope. She nodded, thoughtfully.

'I do not believe it was the friend crossfire of The Dhawasath or the sibling one of The Javaahath. Gold mists signify the other three types - The Marshadath which is The Mentor, The Jafath which is The Twin and then of course that of Love, The Ashaqath.' Mistress Afra paused, eyes shining. 'I would rule out the Jafath, my Queen. A tzar cannot usually be the twin of a mara. It has to be the Marshadath or Ashaqath!' She giggled. 'With the mist that thick, I would say it's a combination of both which would fit as Jaraadhrin is the Princess's Mentor!' Queen Debriar smiled at her.

'He doesn't know...? Does he?' she said. Mistress Afra shook her head.

'Jaraadhrin would have learned about it within the Shimran history lessons when he was a shimling but no. I don't think he would have made the connection. He is still very young' she sighed.

'And an astounding young shimratzar' Queen Debriar added, her eyes tender. 'He was confused, his years completely out of sync, both core and centient. His very being shook and he was drained! He was struggling and yet outwardly he showed no signs at all. Being caught in one Crossfire is challenging enough but in two at once...?' She paused, reflecting back at his composure and her own experiences. 'Let him know as soon as possible, Afra.' She said as Mistress Afra bent her head respectfully. 'There is still hope for Shimrah'

Three Auras.... two cores....

Jaraadhrin stepped out into the courtyard. The air felt cool on his flushed face. He inhaled sharply and covered his eyes with his long fingers. He traced along the length of his brows, down the sides of his face, till the tips rested on his lips which still burned red hot.

He sighed heavily as he turned towards the stone wall. He pressed his forehead and palms against the cold stones, eyes shut tight as he tried to placate his centre. His robes quivered around him in tense waves as he breathed deep. The cold felt good on his skin as he stood fighting his core's surges. The emerald eyes of his little Princess were all he could see, imprinted on the back of his lids.

What on Shimrah is happening to me? My father never said anything about this! The more he tried to understand what happened, the more it all eluded him. Jaraadhrin wished Quinzafoor would start playing again.

Quinzafoor...!

Jaraadhrin whipped around, thankful for something else to think about. *Where did that odd tzar fly off to? Had he seen anything important? Had he returned yet? Are we going to be attacked soon?* He leapt into the air to fly up to the ramparts only to land back down again, some distance away. Jaraadhrin looked down at his hands in disbelief. Why couldn't he harness the wind? He felt weak but this was ridiculous! Jaraadhrin swirled the long sleeves of his cloaks as he tried again and alighted back down in chagrin.

Fine! He thought angrily. *I'll walk!*

He probably wasn't calm enough and it wasn't an option to harness nature when one wasn't at peace with himself. It was at times like these that he envied the maras. They were boiling, bubbling cauldrons of emotions and it made them so powerful. If a tzar lost their cool, they were woefully weak.

That is so unfair! He scoffed and leapt against the wall beside him. He ran up vertically and maintained his balance with much difficulty. Jaraadhrin nearly lost it at the very top but managed to swing himself over with one hand, at the very last moment. As he alighted lightly within the circle of the highest tower, Jaraadhrin called, sharp and stern.

'Quinzafoor...? Is he back?'

'Not yet' One of the soldiers answered with promptness. Jaraadhrin clasped his hands behind him and gazed in the direction, he had last seen Quinzafoor.

Where is he? Should I send him a yishin? He knew that his second-in-command would never leave his soldiers unless it was genuinely necessary. As he stared far away lost in thought still trying to calm himself, a chorus rose among his soldiers, started by the tzar who had answered Jaraadhrin, initially.

'Long Live, Lord Jaraadhrin, Son of Lord Jaraadh. Lord Protector of the King, Queen and Princess of Shimrah. We bow before you, our Lord! We swear fidelity to the King and Kingdom, in immortality and demise. Accept our sword and service, our Lord!'

Jaraadhrin turned to face them in astonishment, realizing he was on the topmost tower below the great, horned dragon of his ancestors. The first one ever to have entwined with a shimratzar, from the great mountain range of the Ice Spikes.

It towered over them, its neck, mid back and tail wings, spread in three ascending tiers behind it, each visible above the other. Its right foot raised and its claws spread, sharp and menacing. Brilliant, shining eyes glistened, wise and stern on either side of its long, ornate entwinement horn which sparkled with the large cone shaped diamond, encased in its tip. Its lengthy serpent like tail curved behind it, fluid and graceful as a ribbon even in its stillness.

Queen Debriar's sceptre sparks had formed large, pale lilac banners, informing the birth of the Princess and his swearing-in as her Lord Protector. It adorned the main walls of the citadel, the fort walls, turrets and the tiers. This tower was the ceremonial position for accepting new command. The heart of the fortress and in full view from every point of the citadel. The central focal point of the courts, the terraces, the turrets, the minarets, the fort walls, the moats, the tiers and even the defences. The soldiers were officially accepting him as their commander!

But what kind of ceremony was this? There was no Royalty gracing the high pedestal seats beside the winged dragon and his kindly father wasn't smiling down at him. He was being accepted under Emergency Martial Etiquettes of the Shimran army. Jaraadhrin sighed. Nothing was as he had imagined or expected.

The archers, the blade-shimrans, soldiers, shield-maras and defence Shifr Shimrans down in all eight tiers, turned to face him in a whirl of pale blue robes and glimmering bronze or brilliant red hair. Their movements spectacularly graceful, their fair faces upturned as they repeated their allegiance, thrice. Their voices blended melodiously, accompanied by the fluid movements of their weapons as they saluted him, in the standard but impressive flourish of the Shimran Martial Forces. Their graceful movements ended in a smart click of their heels, sinking to their right knees, their hands over their right or left shoulders as required and heads bowed low.

Jaraadhrin's centre trembled but he held his head high, a stern cool gaze on his face. He really didn't need this right now. The cold emphasis on reality of the extent of his duties to the King and Kingdom. He lifted his right hand high, the therin of his sleeves blowing gently in the breeze.

'Rise! Warriors of Shimrah and may the Kingdom serve you well!' He called loudly as he channelled his centient to his voice, to amplify it over the eight tiers. It rang out, crystal clear, strong, confident and in sharp contrast to what he felt.

The soldiers spun to their feet, centring their centients mid spin and shooting a minimal bolt of it into the heart of the dragon's chest as they faced it again, immediately above Jaraadhrin as per Shimran traditions. Thousands of bolts flashed and crackled, activating it. His long, bronze waves lifted off his slender waist as all their oaths, loyalty and patriotism poured in to the massive Shimran insignia behind him.

The gigantic creature shook its colossal form and spread its enormous wings majestically, high above them, the tips grazing the dawning sky itself. It raised its huge head and roared deafeningly, breathing a vast plume of fire and ice! It crackled, hissed and burst into stars and dust above them as it rained down on everyone in all eight tiers. It flapped its wings once, then in one swift flash, the huge serpentine tail swung around Jaraadhrin!

Once, twice, it swung fluid and rapid, forming thick rings of scales, gently enveloping his tall, stately figure. His white wraps, bronze waves and crimson ribbons, swirled around him in the stiff wake of the wind under the dragon's massive tail. The tail wing swished to the back of Jaraadhrin's head and flashed open, forming a huge mantle behind him, rising high above him like some majestic canopy. The magnificent, dragonesque beast held its position for a moment more before unwinding its massive embrace from Jaraadhrin, stretching up high and solidifying back to its original position. He drew a sharp breath through his teeth as his soldiers stared up at him, bewildered beyond belief.

That isn't supposed to happen! Alaq is just supposed to acknowledge me with a roar! thought Jaraadhrin in confusion. It had never shielded another tzar with its body and crowned him with it tail wing protectively as far as he knew. His much beloved world seemed to have turned on its head overnight.

The moment he had decide to take a leisurely stroll down in the courtyards before seeing the Queen's emergency signal, felt eons away. He dismissed the awestruck soldiers with quick salute, nod and a wave of his hand. They broke from their trance, clapping and cheering him loudly with more colourful blasts of their centients as they swept off to their various positions.

Jaraadhrin turned to face the majestic creature, standing still as if it had never moved. He gazed into its large, life-like eyes, sighing softly and inclined his head to it, his hands clasped behind his back.

Great Alaq, the most Ancient of all Dragonesque beasts. I thank you for your blessings today, though I am unsure what all this means. Jaraadhrin looked up at its eyes again. *Is this your boon to me for the absence of my King and my father at my initiation?* His centients moved weakly within him, still tumultuous and chaotic. He nodded slightly.

Then grant me the will and strength to complete my duties to my beloved King and Kingdom and make me worthier to accept one of your descendants on my sixteenth. If am still alive by then! He thought. Why was he having such an impossible time managing his own being and centient powers, it felt unrestrained and riotous. A soft whisper of therin and a thud sounded behind him, accompanied by a waft of warm honey. Jaraadhrin rolled his eyes and pursed his lips.

Why does he have to always appear before me at my most vulnerable! ... Every time...Aaashh!? He thought, irritated. Mastering his calm as best as he could, he straightened, pretending to study the dragon closely to avoid facing him.

'Quinzafoor...' Jaraadhrin said calmly.

'Congratulations! That was indeed glorious to look upon. That vison will always be the freshness of my eyes! I had the best view from the sky of the great Alaq embracing and crowning you with its tail wing and I paid my allegiance as I flew here ...' Jaraadhrin frowned. Quinzafoor was talking too fast, something was wrong.

He whirled around and leapt up gracefully, flinging his long robes behind his lean legs. The fortification behind Quinzafoor were almost as high as his shoulders, an easy spring for any Shimran but he nearly lost his balance as he caught his toe on the edge.

Aaashh! For the Love of the Shimran Core! Are my emotions affecting my very balance now? This is outrageous. He thought in chagrin as he righted himself.

He searched the skies and grounds with urgency, combing them for anything unusual. He flashed a silver bolt which split in to fourteen yishins. It soared off to the shield-maras at the turrets, behind the citadel and by the massive lake. It contained his thoughts and orders to activate the shield defences for each tier.

Yishins were the usual forms of mail in Shimrah but martial yishins were faster, they transcribed the thoughts, moods and orders of the sender with much accuracy and delivered them to the intended recipients, almost instantly. Jaraadhrin could see the grey shimmer of the eight shields of the tiers, rising even as the silver trails of his yishins vanished.

'What did you see?' He demanded, stern and cold again. Quinzafoor drew a quick breath.

'A firehorn! It was almost burning up. Friend or foe, I do not know. I couldn't read them; they have a protective field. Two auras other than the firehorn but only two, with less than quarter of their cores. Three auras, two cores!' He reeled off, speaking so fast only another Shimran could understand him, his voice puzzled. 'Three beings, three auras and two cores...? Doesn't make sense!' Jaraadhrin frowned.

'What more did you want to read from them...?' *What more was there to read anyway...?* His thoughts flashed forward to a plan of action.

'No...!' yelled Quinzafoor as Jaraadhrin swung his arms in a large circle and a brilliant silver glow traced his movements. He flashed his arms apart forcefully, splitting himself into three silver projections.

One of his silver duplicates, flew down to a group of blade-shimrans and with a barked order, soared into the palace with a few dozen following it. They were off to guard his Queen and new-born Princess. The other sped around to different parts of the citadel, alerting his soldiers while the third disappeared to scout ahead, outside the eighth-tier defence shields.

Jaraadhrin felt himself sway forward momentarily as his core unbalanced, the effort of the projections, destabilizing it even worse than before, in its already vulnerable state.

'Aaashh! Of all the Absurdities in Shimran History, my Lord!' exclaimed Quinzafoor as he leapt up behind Jaraadhrin with serpentine swiftness. He wrapped an arm firmly around his Lord's waist over the many layers of his robes, preventing his fall. He spun his other wrist in a swift flip, summoning an auburn cloud of his centients and slapped it against the back of Jaraadhrin's right shoulder. He rotated his wrist inwards gently as he propelled his years in.

Jaraadhrin chuckled. He hadn't heard that exclamation before. Shimrans were rather inventive with their quotes of exclamations. This was the first he had been addressed as a Lord too. Quinzafoor's aura surrounding him, felt ancient and glimmered a radiant, golden auburn. It felt at least a few thousand years old.

How in the Crystal Depths had he stowed it within his elegant, slim stature? Drawing a deep breath, Jaraadhrin shrugged his shoulder, displacing Quinzafoor's hand.

'Enough!' He snapped. His soldiers were armed and ready, waiting for his signal to fire. Two of his projections were already feeding back to him, positioned at the entrance to the Queen's chambers and at the head of the defence moats in the lowest tier. The last swished back into him and disappeared, having completed its order.

'But ....' Quinzafoor objected in exasperation. Jaraadhrin shook his head sternly, a slight smile on his lips. He extended his hand, palm up, towards Quinzafoor behind him. He tilted his head backwards as his locks soared, in the aura of Quinzafoor's frustration.

'Fly with me...?' he requested, trying not to show how exhausted he felt. Behind him Quinzafoor sighed and nodded. He grasped Jaraadhrin's hand and spiralled him high into the air. Together they flew, the wind harnessed in Quinzafoor's robes alone still holding his Lord firmly and battling against their combined weight. They could barely see the long plume of fire approaching them. Quinzafoor suspended them with his centient as the wind gave up, his hand raised to signal the archers, waiting for Jaraadhrin's command to fire.

'My Lord...?' he whispered as Jaraadhrin shook his head.

Something isn't right! He thought. *Why is it just a single firehorn at the end of its tether...? Why the protective shield...? Why such a direct approach...? Why is there an absence of a third core yet a distinctive third aura?*

'A decoy, perhaps? A trojan?' Quinzafoor whispered behind him. Jaraadhrin frowned and tilted his head to the side towards him still trying to pierce through the firehorn's flames, his mind in a turmoil.

Couldn't read them.... read them how, exactly? Is he reading me...? Is that how Quinzafoor's answers seem to harmonise to my unspoken questions? He thought. Quinzafoor cleared his throat.

'Ahem...My Lord, they are getting too close.... they will incinerate if they hit the shields, their cores are too drained to pass through.'

Jaraadhrin took a deep breath and doubled his focus. Something felt very wrong, deep within his rapidly draining core, about shooting this firehorn down. The first golden rays, bursting over the horizons, were not helping either. Jaraadhrin felt a warm shock around his midriff. Auburn mists pulsed around the arm at his waist, rapidly turning silver as it absorbed into him. Quinzafoor was replenishing his core...! Again...!

Of all the stubborn little .... and this time I can't shrug away! Jaraadhrin gnashed his teeth in exasperation as Quinzafoor chuckled. He refocused, zooming in and narrowing his eyes to slits. *This isn't working!* He changed tactics and closed his eyes completely, reaching out with his senses, testing and tasting the essence of the beings approaching them. Quinzafoor made a soft sound of admiration behind him, increasing the flow of his centient, pulsing in at his Lord's midriff. Jaraadhrin gasped suddenly as his eyes snapped open.

This was no enemy. Three auras.... two cores.... Of course!

'Shields down, let them in! Healers, element and creature Shifr Shimrans' to the courtyard with stretchers for two. Soldiers to stand down. Secure the perimeter beyond the unisus with stronger shields. Allow no one in after them and watch for any pursuit!' Jaraadhrin's orders poured in a torrent, faster than thought and Quinzafoor, shot bolt after bolt of yishins. His free wrist whistling as it swiftly delivered Jaraadhrin's orders to the respective sectors within the citadel below them. Jaraadhrin reached for the tincture on his red ribbon that Quinzafoor had given him earlier.

'My Lord, that may not be the best – '

'Fly over!' Jaraadhrin cut in sternly 'Warm drink? Was it? You have some explaining to do later!' he said, simultaneously thanking him as he took a quick sip from the now expanded vial. Quinzafoor's quiet laugh rang in his ear. An immense bubble of energy erupted within him. Jaraadhrin barely managed to clip it back in before he hurriedly stabilised his core in mid-air as they soared towards the flaming firehorn.

His centient bubbled and churned as his central being expanded. Jaraadhrin couldn't feel how many years he had added but the solidity was enough for now. He could feel Quinzafoor's ancient aura, glowing with admiration and pride. It surrounded him as they shot towards the firehorn together, spinning rapidly. Their pale blue and white cloaks billowed behind them as they sped, trying to reach the unisus before its core gave up.

They were close enough to see two soldiers in Shimran martial gear. One bronze- haired tzar holding on to the other with every ounce of his being, almost nearing oblivion. The other figure lay across the firehorn, unconscious, his long golden hair, singeing in the firehorn's flames. Shimran hair didn't burn in unisus flames!

'The King!' Jaraadhrin whispered, tapping Quinzafoor's strong hand at his waist as they got closer.

'Careful, my Lord!' Quinzafoor replied and released him, spiralling swiftly to the left of the firehorn as he positioned himself opposite his Lord. Jaraadhrin reharnessed the wind and stayed afloat. They moved their arms, mimicking each other in perfect sync, their long sleeves swishing around in the wind. Together, they broke through the feebly glimmering, blue centient shield which had protected them thus far. Jaraadhrin spiralled in, pulled his King off the firehorn and supported him as Quinzafoor had done, moments before. He laid his King's head tenderly on his shoulder, his pale face trapped against the crook of his slender neck. He placed his hand on His Majesty's chest and shot a bolt of his raging core, directly into his king's heart.

Jaraadhrin choked against a surge of energy within his head. His core was expanding too fast, the centients brimming over. It needed to be controlled as quickly as possible. He knew Shimran folk could go insane or explode their fragile bodies if the centre of their beings were not properly maintained. He had never needed to worry about it till this very long night. He took a deep breath, trying to placate his centre temporarily.

Jaraadhrin flashed a quick glance at Quinzafoor who had taken care of the other bronze haired soldier, his father, Lord Jaraadh and whose cool blue essence he had felt. He would know his father's essence anywhere. Quinzafoor's arm around Lord Jaraadh's waist, pulsed a brilliant auburn and his other palm on the neck of the unisus, glowed against the flames. Jaraadhrin chuckled to himself.

How many hundreds of years had Quinzafoor given away tonight? Not that he would miss them with his centient overflowing above capacity yet contained and vials of Javnoons appearing out of thin air at his will. Quinzafoor's lips curled in a comical smile as his brows rose. He shook his head slightly as he tended to Lord Jaraadh.

The unisus blazed brighter between them, flames bursting from many parts of its huge body as it maintained the effort to keep flying. It neighed in pain. Fire horns were rather dangerous at the end of their lives and could burst into flames, destroying themselves and much of their surroundings. Jaraadhrin summoned a large bolt of his overwhelming centient swiftly and enveloped the unisus in the silver mists. He cooled it right down to just above freezing. He pulled the shield tight around the firehorn as Quinzafoor kept reviving it. His cold centient shield should keep it from bursting into flames until they alighted in the courtyards below and the creature Shifr Shimrans could tend to it.

Jaraadhrin glanced back to ensure they were not being pursued by any foes and caught sight of his soldiers, closing behind them in a defensive line protecting them, their cloaks flying with the swiftness of their movements. His glowing silver projection at their head still held the citadels defences. He could see through its eyes. There was no sign of an attack and the Shimran skies and plains, stretched peaceful in the serene light of the morning.

Jaraadhrin changed his stance slightly in mid-air, streamlining his stature to move faster, in order to keep up with Quinzafoor and the unisus. He soared smoothly trying not to jolt his King as they made their way to the inner courtyards. They alighted on the white stones with unparalleled grace as the healers rushed forward. They relieved him swiftly and laid their King on stretchers while the element and creature Shifr shimrans, tended to the firehorn.

It crumbled to the ground and promptly burst into flames, the blaze contained within Jaraadhrin's shields. The creature Shifr shimrans battled to douse the firehorn, water and ice shooting from their hands, encasing it so it couldn't hurt itself anymore. Jaraadhrin withdrew his centient as the blaze quieted around it and patted its smoking muzzle gently.

He moved towards his King, not sparing a thought for his father. Lord Jaraadh still lay in Quinzafoor capable arms, being tended to by him and the healers. Jaraadhrin's head clouded again as the activities drawing on his centient decreased. It surged through his conscious thoughts, threatening to overwhelm him. He knelt by his King as the healers worked around them.

Jaraadhrin caught snippets of anxious conversation among the healers through his haze. His central being was too full and even with everything he had used up, it was seething out of control. His head spun and his heart hammered against his chest. He realised he was more anxious and fearful for his King than anything else. Jaraadhrin steadied himself, trying to think.

'Its deep....'

'All the way through his right shoulder....'

'A mortal injury...!'

'Can't stop the bleeding...!' Jaraadhrin shook his head, blinking his eyes rapidly.

Three auras .... two cores.... three auras.... two cores....three auras ...! Quinzafoor's words were repeating again and again in his power sodden mind like some strange litany. It was so clear before. What had he forgotten again? What piece of fact eluded him in his energy infested mind? He could feel a hopelessness and despair descending in the auras of the healers around him as they worked feverishly on their King.

The right shoulder.... A mortal injury...! He thought, through the haze as Quinzafoor called out from behind him, his voice anxious. He was probably going insane with his surging core unmanaged and the years streaming into his head. Jaraadhrin shook it hard from side to side, his hands on either side of his temples. His bronze waves flew off his shoulders and he slid his fingers down on his eyes as he squeezed them shut. He huffed. A bolt of lightning shot behind his lids as he struggled to think straight.

A mortal wound....?

'No, it isn't!' He panted, louder than he intended as his eyes snapped open. With a tremendous effort, he focused his surging thoughts. He spun both his arms around rapidly to centre his massively, uncontrollable centients, between his palms. The mists gathered, silver and angry within his tense hands as he wrenched his years out of him. The surge made a resounding crash and lightening like bolts crackled within the sphere of silver, writhing and swirling as he moved his fingers quickly, round and round to maintain it. His hand flipped and twirled around with elegance as he kept the shape of the angry, thundery sphere of force, contained within them with difficulty.

Three auras. Two cores. The healers are streaming eons into my King to revive his core. My King never had a principal core. They are killing him. Jaraadhrin clenched his teeth as he focussed hard on his unconscious thoughts. *My King is not a Shimratzar! He is.... human...! His life elongated with the repair of his physical body. His spiritual being is non-existent compared to the Shimran folk.*

His core capacity is insignificant in comparison. He is alive because of the borrowed centient of my Queen, this past five hundred years. King Dunyazer is a human! The only one in Shimrah!

Jaraadhrin leaned over. The massive forces churning within his tense white hands, blasted the healers away from around him. His King had moments of life left. His aura was fading rapidly. Jaraadhrin floated the sphere of pulsing energy on to the bleeding right shoulder, laying it over the wound instead of forcing it in. He let it heal the actual, physical body of his King. The actual injury... the sphere pulsed as it pulled the skin, muscles, tissues and bones together, searing around the jagged edges and closing in on itself.

King Dunyazer groaned in pain. Jaraadhrin rotated the wrist of his other hand in a quick spin, recreating another smaller version of the crackling, lightening sphere. He pulsed it into King Dunyazer chest, quickening his heart. His brilliant blue eyes hazed over as his brain moved, indolent and sluggish. It swamped and drowned in the eons of centients the healers had poured into his King as he absorbed them. He drew a shuddering breath trying to clear it as he dredged up bits of information.

The Silverines, the small, intricate, colourful mark nestled deep within the dimples, under the edges of their collarbones, housed the life force entryway of Shimran folk. They were private, unmentionable and unexposed, found on the right shoulders of the tzars and on the left for the maras. They were personal and sacred to the Shimrans and held the secrets of their beings. The human's life force was housed in the heart and the mind. He didn't know if they were taboo but he couldn't care less right now. A large book bound in ornate leather. A memory of his father chiding him because he wouldn't read it! Another flash, The King's diary!

Heart and mind.... heart and mind.... Jaraadhrin repeated to himself, blinking against the flashes of silver, blinding his brilliant blue eyes. The healers, rather younger than Mistress Afra, stood around, uncertain and dumbfounded. They could feel the difference in their King's aura as Jaraadhrin worked which held them back from interfering.

Where is Mistress Afra anyway? He thought. *There were very few Shimran folk who knew of the King's heritage and those who knew, often forgot due to King Dunyazer long life and the camouflage of Queen Debriar's centient on him.*

The wound on the King's shoulder had closed completely, the skin smoothed over clear and unblemished. With a tortured breath, Jaraadhrin swung his wrist, scooping the large, thundery sphere and shifting it to King Dunyazer's forehead. He let it float above it, instead of driving it in.

Again and again, Jaraadhrin pulsed the lightening spheres into King Dunyazer chest till he could feel the King's aura strengthening. His body jolted up with every sphere and curved gracefully back down to the stretcher. The silver sphere at his forehead was turning a chilling crimson. With one final pulse, Jaraadhrin reabsorbed the swirling crimson globe, the sphere from his other hand and the eons that the healers had streamed into King Dunyazer.

Centient energy couldn't be just released. It would drain the life forces of everyone present like a magnet. Jaraadhrin had never extricated his centient out of his body nor did he know how he was able to pull it back in to himself or out of the King. Core sharing was a specialist skill in itself, only known to healers and highly trained tzars and maras of the Martial Force. Core and centient power extraction were a formidable and dangerous skill, taking much practice. The practitioner could kill the victim unintentionally by absorbing the whole of their lifeforces.

Jaraadhrin flashed his arms around, collecting everything within it as the centients crackled and stormed violently. Palm over palm he forced the raging silver sphere back into his blazing right shoulder through his white robes. A flash of lightening, a bolt of thunder and ripping, searing pain gouged through him as the mists disappeared.

Jaraadhrin gasped, clenching his teeth against the agony as his head blanked out in a silver mist, too heavy to hold up. He withdrew his hands from over King Dunyazer. It fell lifelessly to his sides, eyes closing as he sank back on his heels. He was rapidly losing consciousness. Utterly exhausted yet crammed and brimming over with unmediated power.

Am I going to explode and release my being? My head certainly feels like it! Aaashh! The eruption would probably kill the whole of the courtyard anyway. All that was in vain! Why did I even bother? How did I do it? What did I do, anyway? It doesn't matter anymore. Jaraadhrin sighed. *I just have to find the Crystal Depths and then I can rest....* Two strong hands caught him as he swayed on his heels.

'Jaraadhrin! Not so fast. Jaraadhrin! Not as my Lord...! Jaraadhrin...! Dhrin!' cried Quinzafoor on his right. His voice urgent, distraught and melodious in his ear.

He has been behind me all night. Jaraadhrin thought with a tired smile. *Literally!* His mind unhinged in the silver clouds as it carried him to darkness. Even Quinzafoor couldn't help him now. He was too full and he knew no one who had the skills to extract his centient except Mistress Afra and she was nowhere to be found. He hoped they had the sense to move him away from the other Shimrans or may be even lay him in the waters of the Crystal Depths in one of the moats.

That should help absorb all my energies without too much damage to the Shim-rans. It could save me the trouble of finding the Depths too as the moats flushed to it at the end. May be I would even meet a Crystallite. Jaraadhrin's lips curled in a small smile at his mind's parting attempt at humour. A cool blue split the icy silver in his mind. He knew that essence, it encircled him from his left in a comforting embrace. He turned slowly, staring up at Lord Jaraadh's twinkling, concerned eyes and warm smile, fully revived by Quinzafoor and the healers.

'Father...I....' he murmured as Lord Jaraadh's eyes glowed with pride.

'Glad to see you were so worried about me too, son' he lilted, his pearly white teeth flashing in the early morning light. He nodded urgently at Quinzafoor in an unspoken command. Jaraadhrin chuckled, his stunning eyes sliding shut. Lord Jaraadh shook him, gentle but firm, making his long locks flutter over his pale face. Jaraadhrin couldn't hold on anymore. He had seen his King again. His father held him. He was content. He regarded Quinzafoor as his friend. He had everything he needed around him.... At least, it was a better parting than most had endured in the fields of war....

Reunion

A flash of emerald-green. A shudder of pain in his chest and Jaraadhrin leaned forward, clutching at the therin of his robes as his eyes flew open. Princess Saffrodel...smiled gleefully up at him! The green vanished. He choked, his breath caught as his core fought to stay within his body, bound inside him by an unexplained force...surging out and clinging on at the same time.

A gentle hand gripped his right shoulder firmly from behind and to his utter amazement, his overwhelmed core and centients began to ebb swiftly out of him. Jaraadhrin glanced at it, moving his head as if in a dream. The shock cleared his hazy mind as the silver pulsed out, turning to a brilliant auburn as it streamed away from him. It was Quinzafoor's long, slender fingers. The large, glittering, auburn stone of the black ring on his fore finger glowed as the mists swirled around it. Quinzafoor siphoned off the excess rapidly and efficiently into himself. Jaraadhrin sighed and placed his hand over Quinzafoor's, his heart overflowing with gratitude and amazement.

'Recall the projections, my Lord' he whispered, his strong voice, soft and gentle. 'The danger has passed.' Jaraadhrin swept through the eyes of his silver twins before summoning them back into himself, one from the door of the Queen's chamber and the other from the frontlines.

Quinzafoor is proficient. Mistress Afra is right. He is her star disciple. But how is this even possible? Core and centient extraction took years to master. thought Jaraadhrin.

He could feel the tenderness, admiration and profound devotion to him in Quinzafoor's aura, the depths of which sunk into him, warm and comforting. He understood the rest but the admiration was truly misplaced. Quinzafoor was the hero of the night, constantly saving and supporting him. Jaraadhrin had barely been in control. He didn't even know what he was doing, half the time. Quinzafoor scoffed quietly behind him and withdrew his hand from under Jaraadhrin's with a mild, momentary pressure. He left Jaraadhrin's centient precisely over his core!

His hands moved up over Jaraadhrin's head, catching the stray tendrils on his young Lord's face deftly and positioning them neatly back behind him. He picked up a thick lock of hair, shorter than the rest with a jagged, severed edge. Quinzafoor slid the tuft between his fingers and as they passed the rough edges, the strands regrew back to their normal curly length. Jaraadhrin's temples tensed.

Why had he cut it off again? His mind felt like a sieve. Quinzafoor sighed behind him. King Dunyazer stirred weakly and everyone rushed to take care of him.

'Quinzafoor, you know what to do...I believe...go with your King and stay by his side' Jaraadhrin commanded, his voice strained with the effort.

He is good with healing and has an insane amount of control of his being and its centient. No doubt he would have analysed what I had done and would understand it better than myself. Jaraadhrin reasoned. Quinzafoor saluted him quickly, rose and followed King Dunyazer behind the healers. Jaraadhrin watched him till his tall, slender figure disappeared into the palace.

How many years of Quinzafoor's short life had he practiced core and centient extraction to withdraw with such precision? Jaraadhrin frowned. *How did I manage it then? I have never practiced. I could have killed the King easily!* His heart iced over at the thought. He had an inclination of what Quinzafoor lethal Shifr maybe but he was also sure that he had barely scratched the surface of understanding its potency. If he was right, Quinzafoor was a deadly weapon. He sighed.

Yet another responsibility that takes a lot of will, patience and work. Quinzafoor is only about thirteen or fourteen at the most yet his spiritual being is far more advanced than any I have seen at this age. It would be a disaster if he defaulted from the right path.

Jaraadhrin felt it was his duty to protect him. An unknown tie had formed between them that night. He didn't try to comprehend or make sense of it. Jaraadhrin just accepted it. He had learned more about the spirit and formation of their beings in this night, than he had bothered to learn in his whole fifteen years. He shook his head smiling at his father who sat observing their communications silently and with a satisfied grin. His father helped him stand, ever gentle, as the courtyard emptied.

Jaraadhrin walked in silence beside his father, who held him up with an arm around his shoulders. It had been a long and hectic night but the sun had finally risen, warm and bright, bringing hope and life with it. His King had returned and his father was beside him, hale and hearty. His Queen would soon get better and his Princess...? Jaraadhrin's lips curved into a tender smile, she will grow up, happy with her parents.

Everything was righting itself and the nightmares of the night before were diminishing in the brightening light of the day. He would train harder with Quinzafoor at his side. His father and his King would guide him for a while longer. He would love to train with Quinzafoor. He hadn't even spoken to Quinzafoor face to face all night. He had been trying to hide and yet if he had guessed right, Quinzafoor probably 'read' him and knew what he felt. There really was no other explanation for the Javnoon tincture, his unspoken reactions and replies at various moments throughout the times, they had been together.

Lord Jaraadh smiled at his unusually quiet son. He could feel the severe disturbances in his aura. He had been through a lot; He was no longer the playful shimling he had worried to leave behind. He was a shimratzar, a soldier and he had aged to a thousand Shimran years in one night. Lord Jaraadh felt immensely proud of his son. He reached up as they passed under one of Queen Debriar pale lilac banners, trailing it between his fingers.

'So, young Lord Protector? How was the swearing-in-ceremony?' he inquired. Jaraadhrin raised his eyebrows.

'Eventful' he replied shortly. Lord Jaraadh laughed.

'Then it can wait' he said. They were outside Jaraadhrin's chambers. 'I think some rest would do you good, your aura is all over the place. Freshen up and rest, it will help' Jaraadhrin nodded and left his father's presence, rather hesitant.

He slipped through his lavish bed chambers and entered the vinnerry, a spacious set of rooms tastefully decorated and filled with sweet scents, salts and incenses. His bath was ready for him, steaming in the middle of the floor. The warmth felt good against his sore centre as he disrobed and slid into the scented waters, Incareth had prepared for him.

She was the shimara who often served himself and his father, after his mother had passed. Incareth had been his mother's newest and personal server and she had efficiently taken over, looking after them, when her mistress had died. She was never seen but her presence was always felt in their chambers. Her aura left a pale, creamy essence in her wake.

The water swirled around Jaraadhrin, pink tinged. He inhaled deep, letting the fragrance diffuse within him. Incareth had infused it with the remedial salts from the healers. She already knew what had happened to him and had taken the initiative to help him heal. She was very thoughtful indeed and kept their chambers stocked with everything and anything they would need. He really needed to search for this elusive shimara and thank her personally someday.

His body was immaculate, unblemished, its skin smooth and glistening yet he felt as if he had been stabbed through with numerous daggers. He lay back, closing his eyes with a soft sigh, his wavy tresses floated around him as he let the healing waters, wash away the discomfort. The soothing powders in the waters dissolved into his very centre as the liquid swirled around him. Jaraadhrin lay still, it wasn't his movements that caused the waters to ripple but the subtle powers of the restorative powders itself.

The shimrans who served them, hardly showed themselves. It was almost an unspoken rule. It was also highly unfair to them. He made up his mind to see if he could change that. They needed to be rewarded and praised for the excellent manner in which they tended to their charges. Everything they did were tinged with affection, care and warmth.

Finishing his bath and feeling much better, Jaraadhrin dried quickly and slid into fresh, white nightrobes, laid out neatly for him. He passed his hands through his long locks, drying them quickly with the warmth of his centient and re-joined his father as soon as he could manage. Lord Jaraadh had already set the low plinths in the outermost hall for him, with his favourite foods. Incareth's pale centient swarmed over as it warmed it. It was almost a celebration. He sat down beside his father on the low, thick cushioned chairs.

'You come in from the battlefield, core spent, dragging your dying King on an unisus on fire and are sprightly enough, father.' He teased. 'And I stay safe and sound within these walls and I am asleep on my feet!' Lord Jaraadh laughed.

'Looks to me like you fought a more difficult battle than the war.' He said smiling gently at his son. 'Fighting with one's own spirit and powers is much more draining than any physical battle, son.' he continued. Lord Jaraadh reached over and flicked his son's straight nose, affectionately. Jaraadhrin grinned at him. His father often channelled his mother's endearing ways of showing her affection. It wasn't a regular habit for tzars but he liked it, it helped keep his mother close.

'Hmmmm.... Let me see?' Lord Jaraadh folded his hands in front of him and tilted his head to the side. 'You ripped your core, destabilising it. Shared your centient in that state then re-stablished it somehow. Added more years, mediated the extra's within a short space of time.' He frowned. 'Something else transformed your centre, it's no longer your own essence. Ripped it apart again, took in more years but didn't mediate properly. Saved the King by absorbing eons and nearly exploded. Finally, Thanks to Quinzafoor, back to an unstable but manageable core!' He finished with a chuckle. 'You have tortured that poor centre, son.'

Jaraadhrin stared into his father's wise blue eyes. It was as if he knew everything he had been through and understood. But then, his father was always that way with him. Ever since his mother's death, Lord Jaraadh had made it his mission to be there for his son and to cater to all his needs even through his demanding duties to the King and Kingdom as the Lord Protector of Shimrah. He smiled as he shook his head.

'It was necessary.' Jaraadhrin replied.

'Of course, I don't doubt that.' said his father, passing him a drink. 'The years and expanded core were probably Quinzafoor? he questioned. Jaraadhrin nodded, raising his eyebrows in exaggerated amazement as he tapped at the ribbon at his waist.

'Javnoon......a whole boggling vial of it' he said briefly. Lord Jaraadh chuckled.

'But the alteration has me puzzled; I must admit. Something unexpected happened. When?' he glanced keenly at his son. Jaraadhrin hesitated then sighed. He had never hidden anything from his father before. They had always been the best of friends.

I might as well get it over with. Jaraadhrin began to recount everything that had happened, going in to detail to try make sense of it. Lord Jaraadh did not interrupt him but listened to him attentively. He frowned slightly as his son recounted the gold mist and the involuntary kissing of the Princess's hands at the swearing-in-ceremony and again, at the incident with the dragon, Alaq. He offered no explanations but Jaraadhrin could see the light of wisdom in his father's eyes as he explained. Lord Jaraadh had a good inclination of what happened but he was not saying it just yet. As Jaraadhrin finished, his father sighed.

'You have surpassed yourself at the cost of your wellbeing, young Lord Jaraadhrin and I couldn't be prouder of you! You proved to me today that I have indeed succeeded in raising you right.' Lord Jaraadh reached across the table, pulling back his long sleeves from overturning the large flask on it. He lay a gentle hand on Jaraadhrin's head. 'When your mother ....' he paused, smiling. 'She would have been overjoyed to see how you have turned out'

41

Jaraadhrin beamed. His father slid his fingers down his son's handsome face. 'I know you want me to explain those that you do not understand and I promise I will, just as soon as I am sure of the answers.' He continued as he patted Jaraadhrin's cheek lightly.

A flash of auburn appeared between them and Lord Jaraadh deftly plucked a thin crystal sheet out of the glowing yishin sphere. Jaraadhrin caught a faint whiff of warm honey.

'Quinzafoor...?' he said. His father glanced up at his with a grin as he read the message.

'You recognise his essence. Good. I picked the right tzar then. Your auras are quite in sync with each other.' Lord Jaraadh stood up. 'The King has woken; I have to be by his side...' Jaraadhrin leapt up.

'I am coming too! Let me...' he swayed suddenly. His father darted around the table towards him and grabbed him by the top of his arm.

'No. You are resting and getting that core right. I have to relieve Quinzafoor too. From what you have told me, he could use some time to himself as well' he said firmly, marching Jaraadhrin through the chambers to his bed. Lord Jaraadh helped his son lay down, arranging his white nightrobes around him. He pulled the sheets rapidly over him. 'Sleep!' he ordered as he straightened. His father wiggled a finger at him and strode off to his beloved king.

Jaraadhrin nodded, chuckling. It was a while since his father had treated him like a shimling, authoritative and ordering him about. He sighed. His mind dwelled on a pair of radiant, green eyes. He wondered if Queen Debriar had been informed about the King. Jaraadhrin frowned. What was it that his Queen had seen that had brought all this along? Maybe, Her Majesty saw the instance the King got hurt? Jaraadhrin sat up, flung away the covers and swung his legs off of the bed. The therin swishing angrily as he shook his head, vexed at himself.

Why didn't I ask about what happened in the field when I was speaking to my father all this while? How pathetic! We only talked about me. My troubles, my core, my centients. How immature! I hardly get time to talk to my father and when I do I talk about poor me. What idiocy! Jaraadhrin stood up suddenly, swayed and caught the post of his bed to support himself.

Aaashh! Of all the Absurdities in Shimrah! I just got off of my bed! He thought as his core growled again with his emotions. Jaraadhrin coughed, his hand on his chest as a flash of pain passed through it. A trickle of warmth escaped the corner of his lips. He dabbed at it in surprise and stared, brilliant crimson against the white therin of his sleeves.

What now? This is unbelievable! Aaashh! Well...there is a first time for everything, I suppose! he thought, annoyed as his surprise ebbed. *It looks like the instability is causing internal injuries already. I am not going anywhere before I fix it!* Jaraadhrin sighed, still gazing at his sleeve in utter annoyance and exasperation. He looked up suddenly as far, far above him, amplified over the palace, the haunting, melodious tones of a harp played, enshrouding everything in peace. Jaraadhrin's anger abated and his face softened into a smile.

'Quinzafoor!' he breathed gratefully. He drifted back down, crossed his legs under him on the bed and arranged his night robes around himself. He placed his hands on his knees and closed his eyes, still smiling. Jaraadhrin let the tunes escort him to peace.

The Prophesy

Lord Jaraadh flew through the corridors to get to his King as fast as he could. His pale blue martial cloak, swishing behind him in a large fan. The healing rooms were at the rear end of the palace, just in front of the large lake and the Icefalls, from the Icy Spikes Mountain range. It was the safest place in the palace as it cannot be attained from the back and had the many stretches of defences, of the eight tiers in front.

He remembered building this huge citadel with his beloved King Dunyazer. It was a stronghold and impenetrable by even the deadliest of Shifrs. It was built right in front of the large, deep Crystal Lake filled with the enchanted waters, falling off the Ice Spikes beyond which lived the dragons. They were the purest creatures in Shimrah and were full of light. They were eons and eons of concentrated essences, centients, cores and auras of Shimran beings which had accrued and sedimented into powerful, dragonesque beasts of pure light.

They bore the Dragonlight in their horns – a jewel that enclosed and stored their life forces. Some of them were attracted to living Shimrans and offered up their jewels in The Entwinement, a scared and ceremonial ritual, making such Shimrans very powerful indeed. They then resided within the Shimran's core forever or until they are released by the death of their Shimran.

The waters falling over into the lake, carried their light which made it impossible for any creature without the Shimran's pure core to cross, whether it be over, under or through. Any creature with darkness or malintent would be immediately vapourised or dissolved in great agony. The Crystal Lake separated in to two arms, the Western and Eastern Silverstreams which surrounded the two enormous land masses of Northern and Southern Shimrah, making the islands impenetrable to evil. This was the reason Shimrah had remained light and pure for centuries but now darkness had reared its ugly head from within.

The Silverstreams filled with the enchanted waters, from which the seven moat arms had been dug, lent its protection to the citadel as well. Each moat wall or tier had multiple gateways corresponding to its number which could be all opened, closed or partially used. They were rigged with weapons, arrows and other deadly objects apart from the Shimran Shifr enchantments. The moats, bridges, turrets and fort walls formed a maze. He and King Dunyazer had devised many battle formations combining the moat sections, defence walls, turrets and fort structures.

Between the many moats, stood large walls and forts, hiding secret passages, storages, armouries and supplies. The whole citadel was a mind-bending maze and only the tzars and maras of the Martial Force and Royalty knew the way through. They were stationed at every entrance so they could escort inhabitants in and out with ease. Each dike entrance only responded to a specific kind of Shifr and getting it wrong would be a hazardous mistake. The waters of the Crystal Lakes were often used in end level martial strategy.

Though the palace hid such a formidable outlay for an enemy, it also had the most elegant architecture and landscape of the entire Kingdom. Made entirely of glimmering white marble with gold inlay, it stood tall and majestic with its many minarets and turrets, flying enormous white and gold lined banners, with the Shimran insignia of Alaq, the dragon on it. Gold ribbons flew in brilliant streaks across the blue skies. The love of Shimran folk for elegance and sophistication was reflected in the many curving pillars, intricately designed, everyday furniture and the many decorative sculptures, dotted around the palace gardens and courtyards.

The lake was on high ground at the top of an elevated hill, therefore the water flowed naturally around the citadel due to gravity, flooding the network of moats without any effort at all when the sluices were opened. Barricades and sluices were stationed strategically to cut off the water flow to needed areas of the moat in an attack. The force of the water, when opened on to a dry moat was enough to wipe the tainted cores of all who were caught in it.

Currently the defences were still up and the palace was on red alert. Lord Jaraadh smiled proudly as he thought of how efficient his son was. He noticed the dry moat sections and fort entrances were in a layout that was very ancient battle strategy which he was sure Ifreeth had never bothered to learn. The Denisthar moat defence layout and the Drystwitch maze arrangement was a combination devised by the King himself who was a master in defence planning and warfare. He had yet to see a Shifr or Shimran who could surpass his King's talent.

Lord Jaraadh's handsome face darkened, eyes narrowing as he remembered the divination that had led him and his King, to build such a formidable citadel in this peaceful world, where the Shimrans were as one with nature and life. A prophecy predicted by his beloved Queens' great grandmother who had forsaken the palace, shortly afterwards.

Queen Thiloket was one of the strongest, most influential Queens in the history of Shimrah but as she hit her thousands, she had become oddly paranoid. Her Shifr's increasing powers had sent her reeling with visions and predictions. She had been against her granddaughter, Queen Debriar betrothing King Dunyazer and had left the palace immediately after the celebrations, leaving a deadly prediction in her wake. She had predicted the fall of Shimrah under King Dunyazer rule!

The actual words of Queen Thiloket's prophesy was unknown to everyone except Queen Debriar but it was enough to make the King plan ahead to try prevent such calamity. Unfortunately, no one imagined in their wildest dreams that the threat would be his beloved Queen's own elder brothers! Ibreeth and Ifreeth had always had an eye on the throne of Shimrah. They were stewards of Southern Shimrah but they wanted it all and was furious when Queen Debriar was assigned the throne with King Dunyazer by her side.

Lost in thought, Lord Jaraadh had already reached the healing chambers. He knocked and entered quickly as his King's weak voice sounded through the door.

'Jaraadh, my brother!' King Dunyazer rose with difficulty, his arms outstretched.

'My King!' Lord Jaraadh exclaimed, 'you shouldn't be up!'

'I am well… ' replied King Dunyazer quickly. 'Where is my saviour, our young Lord Protector, Jaraadhrin? Quinzafoor has been telling me all about it.' He beamed. Quinzafoor stood behind the King and it was evident he had been working on his Liege. He looked exhausted; His aura diminished. Lord Jaraadh smiled at his King, eyes glimmering with devotion and tenderness.

'He is resting my Liege; I am afraid he has sustained some internal injuries due to a destabilised core. I have instructed him to sleep and repair it.' Lord Jaraadh informed him. He looked at Quinzafoor who had glanced up at him, his face pale, when he had mentioned Jaraadhrin and now seemed to be concentrating very hard. He twirled one of the ornate clips off his head, rapidly within his fingers.

'Quinzafoor, clip that back on and take leave. You need your rest too.' Lord Jaraadh commanded. 'Oh and you are not to visit Jaraadhrin!' his voice softened. 'He is well. We can't have you giving away anything more today' he continued, his eyes twinkling. Quinzafoor snapped out of his thoughts 'Go recover first. That's an order.' He grinned, nodded quickly, bowed to his King and Lord and slipped away as silently and gracefully as a shadow.

Quinzafoor sped with the wind to his terrace. He felt rather spent himself. This was the first time in many years he had felt this fatigued. He landed lightly on his lavishly decorated, marble terrace and skipped into his chambers. He couldn't stay long. He was tired, yes, but he was too worried about his young Lord to rest. He needed to replenish quickly and be on his way again. He had to do something to help. Lord Jaraadhrin's internal injuries and his unstable core could give rise to further complications to his wellbeing. He had felt how unbalanced it had been when he had held his Lord on the parapet.

He glided over to a massive wall cabinet filled with potions, incenses, tinctures and crystals. He selected a few herbs, dropped them in an ornate, gold incense holder and lighted it with a gentle bolt of his centient. It blazed fiery auburn and went out. Tendrils of swirling golden perfumed mist, floated off of it and Quinzafoor breathed in deep. He sighed as he caught sight of his massive bed, richly decorated in beautiful therin, reflected off his large ornate mirror. It was ready for him, covers down, warm and inviting. He couldn't afford to nap just yet.

He glanced at his reflection and tutted in annoyance. His golden clips were already darkening again. He had only cleaned them last night. The power of his mind dulled them more often as he expended it. Lord Jaraadh had recommended that he make his headpieces with the black metal of Siyan for this very reason. However, Quinzafoor had felt, gold looked more fetching against the brilliant bronze of his locks. He chuckled as he remembered his adopted father's expression of amused exasperation when he had first worn them.

Quinzafoor pulled off the thin therin blindfold revealing a pair of brilliant blue green eyes, twinkling back at him from the mirror. *Tsk...Tsk...Aaashh! These are so strange.* He thought with increasing irritation. *Tzars' have brilliant blue eyes, why did mine have to be this, I will never get used to them.* He was quite glad that he wore the blindfolds half the time.

He slid the ornate clips off his head and his long locks fell around his broad shoulders in a silky bronze sheet. Quinzafoor inhaled sharply against the sudden heightened babble of voices within his head. He slid a soft piece of therin over the clips hastily, polishing them to an immediate shine. He fastened them back on, held in place against the gossamer of his hair by the many tiny combs, built into the back. He sighed as the loudness within his head, dimmed to a distant chatter. However one familiar whisper remained, murmuring from very far away.

'What now? This is unbelievable! Aaashh! Well...there is a first time for every-

thing, I suppose! It looks like the instability is causing internal injuries already.' It echoed in Quinzafoor's mind.

Lord Jaraadhrin! He thought as he whirled out to his terrace. He caught himself abruptly at the very tip of his banister as he made to leap off of it, towards his young Lord. Quinzafoor twisted the black Siyan ring on his forefinger rapidly as he thought He couldn't visit Lord Jaraadhrin. He couldn't disobey a direct order. His adopted father knew him well but Lord Jaraadh couldn't stop Quinzafoor playing his harp and healing his young Lord! Quinzafoor chuckled as he flew off the terrace to his favourite tower.

I could do with some melodies too. What a day it has been. That Lord Jaraadhrin! He made a soft noise of awe and exasperation. *The Shifrs he used are akin to my own and whatever is going on with his core? It was so unstable yet no one could have guessed it by looking at his face. So stern and confident. A natural leader! How did he even do it? How did he rip all that centient from his being? Extracted it out of the King? Put it back into himself? He had never practiced core and centient management. Jaraadhrin nearly sacrificed himself willingly. That was some courage and loyalty. And yet he was so humble. He never even spared a thought for his own father in his fidelity to his King.*

Quinzafoor alighted on the tip of a minaret and settled on his heel. He drew his harp, richly designed and elaborately decorated, from his trinket ribbon and slid his slender fingers across the strings. He imbued it with his centient to amplify the tunes over the palace. The delicate melody welled around him and dissolved into the cool morning air. Quinzafoor sighed, his brilliant blue-green eyes glittered with affection as his heart warmed within him. Jaraadhrin had won his allegiance and devotion irrevocably and forever with his actions that night. The bond forged between them was strong and unwavering. His loyalty and admiration for his young Lord, blazed infinite and incessant in his heart and mind!

Back in the healing chambers, King Dunyazer grabbed Lord Jaraadh's shoulder, pulling his Lord Protector with him to the door.

'My Queen...?' he inquired urgently. Lord Jaraadh steadied his King as he swayed.

'My Liege, you are not strong enough and the Queen...' he paused, pursing his lips and unsure how to continue. '...has been unconscious for a while now. Her Majesty is exhausted and has been put to sleep by the healers. Her core keeps draining no matter what the healers do. It's as if she has lost the will to.... They are taking it in turns to – '

'That's why I have to see her' interrupted King Dunyazer. 'Don't you see? She saw it happen! She thinks I am dead! Right shoulder? Remember? My Queen has forgotten my heritage in her worry and exhaustion!' Lord Jaraadh stared at his King as understanding dawned on him.

'The reason you wanted to return immediately even in your wounded state my King. Ahead of the Forces –?' King Dunyazer nodded impatiently.

'Yes, yes, come now!' Lord Jaraadh pulled his King's arm over his shoulders, holding him firm around his waist and moved as swiftly and as smoothly as he could, towards the Queen's chambers.

Queen Debriar lay against Mistress Afra as Lord Jaraadh and King Dunyazer entered her chambers. Her pearl, white face pressed against Mistress Afra's cheek, her long, red, silky locks trailed on the floor by her bed. Three more healers stood around her, replenishing Mistress Afra in turn who had refused to leave her Queen. She had her hand on the Queen's left shoulder, streaming her pale pink centient in a steady flow, directly into it. It was all that was keeping her Queen alive.

King Dunyazer limped over as rapidly as he could manage. His heart broke to see his strong, powerful Queen so pale and limp. Lord Jaraadh sighed by the door, his eyes on the floor, unable to look at his Queen. King Dunyazer sat on the bed and raised her on to his arm, gentle and delicate. Mistress Afra moved covertly; her face turned away. She slid her hand away from the Queen's shoulder, down her arm and tightened her grip around Queen Debriar wrist, still streaming her lifeforce into Her Majesty.

Queen Debriar's head slid back, lifeless and limp against the King's arm, exposing her pale, slender neck. Her locks gleamed crimson against her white robes in the brilliant rays of the sun, streaming through the large windows. The very ones through which she had shot the lilac banners, announcing the Princess's birth and Jaraadhrin's swearing-in, not too long ago. King Dunyazer stared at her, unable to think clearly. He pulled her closer to him as his arm encircled her slim waist. His head shot up as he realised the shimling bump was gone! The little one wasn't due for another three moons!

'The shimling...?' he choked out in a strangled whisper, pain raging in his voice.

'The Princess is well, my Liege' Mistress Afra hastened to set his mind at ease. King Dunyazer sighed in relief.

'Princess...?' He repeated. His breath fanned a few tendrils of his Queen's hair over her pale lips. King Dunyazer moved them gently off of it. He traced the line of her cheekbones and along the length of her stunning, heart shaped face.

'Debriar, my Queen...?' he whispered. Her eyes were still, behind her violet lids and her long fingers lay motionless in Mistress Afra's hand. The ancient healer increased the flow of her core into her beloved Queen, exhausted as she was. The other two healers gathered around Mistress Afra, surreptitiously placing their hands on her shoulders, replenishing her centient rapidly in turn as hers flowed into the Queen.

A lone tear slid from the corner of King Dunyazer eyes and landed with a splash on Queen Debriar's full lips. Drawing a shuddering breath, he wiped it away on the therin of his sleeve.

'My Queen, come back to me... I am here....' he quavered, his deep voice cracking as he cradled her against him. 'I came back as soon as I felt your vision, I saw what you saw. I knew you would not remember.' His handsome face tensed in agony and he pressed his lips,tender and gentle, to her cold forehead.

Lord Jaraadh turned away as he steadied himself. His hand clenched on the cold marble wall beside him, unable to witness his King's distress anymore. His heart ached. After everything, his beloved King and Queen had been through to be together, it couldn't possibly end this way. He remembered the struggles they had overcome when they were younger. The massive oppos- itions to their love. Their sacrifices for each other and the hardships they faced as they surrendered themselves for their Kingdom and the folk of Shim- rah. The relentless heartache, the pain of their family's disapproval and so much more. But through it all, their love persevered. Was it all to end in such an untimely manner like this?

He had always been with his King, defending, protecting, supporting, com- forting, always by his side but today he could do nothing to help. They were the most questionable couple involved in a Crossfire even so he knew neither would survive without the other. Eyes shut tight and teeth gnashed, Lord Jaraadh forced back the grief, threatening to overwhelm him.

'How long has it been?' King Dunyazer whispered, supporting the back of her head lightly, his lips moving against the smooth skin between her brows. 'Over five hundred years. It is easy to forget. I forgot my Queen till young Jaraadhrin and Quinzafoor reminded me.... I am not a tzar, I am a human. How easy was it to forget? Shoulder wounds aren't mortal injuries for me, my Queen.... Find the will to live. Find the way back to me. My Heart.... My Soul... My Light...!

King Dunyazer's green eyes clouded over as his tears fell thick and fast against his Queen's face. They slid down into her eyes, glistened off her lashes and ran down her cheeks. His long golden hair slid off his shoulder as his shaking breath moved his whole frame. Kind Dunyazer turned his head slightly, eyes shut tight to stop the tears falling and pressed his lips against hers.

'Come back to me....my love' he whispered as he kissed her gently. Long delicate fingers swept King Dunyazer golden locks away from his face and behind his ear, tracing the length of his strong square jaw. A soft sigh blew warm against his cheek.

'Hmmm.... water would have worked just as well, my darling. It didn't have to be tears. They are too precious...' He gasped and drew a quivering breath; his eyes flew open in joy. He chuckled involuntarily through his cries. Mistress Afra was no longer holding the Queens wrist. Queen Debriar's brilliant green eyes still half closed with exhaustion, gazed up in to his. Even in that state of utter fatigue, they twinkled with her bubbly humour. Her lips lifted in a gentle smile.

'My King...' she whispered tenderly. King Dunyazer half smiled and buried his face into her neck, holding her firm against him. His slender body heaving with silent sobs.

Lord Jaraadh who had whirled to his King's side at the sound of his Queen's voice, helped a weeping Mistress Afra, out of the chamber as quietly as he could, along with the other healers. His long-wet lashes clung to his cheeks and his heart throbbed with happiness. Of course! By the Miracles of Shimrah! The tears of the Crossed! His Queen made it. He should have had no doubts at all. Their love was too pure and too strong for anything to disrupt. Such was the power of ancient Shimran Pledges!

King Dunyazer lost track of how of long he held his Queen, their arms around each other. When he finally raised his eyes to hers, her face was grim. She still looked spent but her glittering eyes, flashed cold steel. He grinned down at her. Here was his Queen. Wise, brave and powerful. She laid her head against his chest as he gathered her to him, unable to let go. Queen Debriar sighed, running her hand over his right shoulder.

'I did forget' she admitted 'but so did you, my Lord' King Dunyazer looked down at her in confusion. She grimaced 'Ifreeth is not dead.' she said. He shook his head.

'He is, my darling, he drove his sword from the back and I killed him before I collapsed. I felt your vision and as I did, I knew I had to be at your side. I ordered Jaraadh to bring me here before I lost consciousness and we left ahead of the army on a stray firehorn' Queen Debriar sighed, shaking her head and repeated quietly.

'Ifreeth is alive,' her King frowned.

'But I drove my sword to the hilt –'

' – through his heart, yes' She finished for him. 'He is a tzar, my darling.' Her king stared at her as understanding flooded his face. 'It has been over five hundred years that you have lived a tzar. It is easy to forget that you cannot be hurt by a shoulder wound. But it isn't possible for you to forget that Ifreeth is a tzar. You fought so hard on the fields; you always targeted their life forces. Why the heart for Ifreeth?' King Dunyazer shook his head, frowning in confusion.

Why indeed? His Queen sighed against him and closed her eyes in resignation.

'We didn't just forget my King; It was the prophesy. Its fate. Ifreeth will be back. He has been heavily injured but he will be back. The threat is not over. Nobody noticed. Jaraadh was too worried about you, the soldiers triumphant in their victory. Ifreeth crawled away' Queen Debriar's pretty face darkened. 'His essence is different, my Lord. There is a darkness in his aura that I haven't felt before. He no longer has a pure Shimran essence. It has been soiled. How and by whom, I cannot place' King Dunyazer pinched the bridge of his nose with his fingers, deep in thought. His Queen slid his hands away with a soft chuckle.

'Do not hide that handsome face from me, my King and do not fret. My great grandmother, Queen Thiloket's prophesy will come true. It is a risk we took and we will see it through, my darling.' She whispered. 'We have been given more time for which we should be thankful and there is someone I would like you to meet too' she added, a hint of her cheeriness creeping back into her voice. She moved her fingers slightly and sent a glowing yishin through the door. King Dunyazer frowned gazing after it.

Tsk... tsk... tsk.... Why didn't I just get Jaraadh to send a yishin to my Queen? It would have prevented so much trouble. True, I did black out as soon as I commanded Jaraadh to bring me hither but I could have ordered the yishin instead? He sighed *'My queen is right, certain things are just not in our hands and there is no benefit in worrying about things out of our control.*

King Dunyazer smiled. His Queen had always been courageous. She was his strength, his sanity and his reason for forsaking everything he had known in the human world. She was the light of his eyes and soul.

The door opened and Mistress Afra brought in a bundle, beaming, her face radiant. She handed it to her King who stood up eagerly, his heart hammering in joy. He gazed at the little Princess, his eyes tender and a warm smile on his face.

'She looks just like you' he murmured, tilting his head.

She arrived last night? he thought. *The shimling looked like she was a few weeks old.* He knew Shimrah had many differences to his world, a world he had not thought of in five hundred years. Recent events seem to have reawakened old memories and he caught himself wondering if this was again, significant. There was no such thing as coincidence in Shimrah, it was always a plan, a destiny. His Queen always said so and she believed in it firmly too. He sat down beside his Queen still holding Princess Saffrodel and ran his fingers through his daughter's hair.

'She has streaks of gold. My hair?' he observed in astonishment. Shimaras had red hair in varying shades. The Princess's was different. Queen Debriar smiled up at him dazzlingly.

'She is special, my King' she answered him. 'Half Shimran, half human, she has inherited the strengths of both our kinds. If this part of my ancestor's prophecy is indeed true then the rest must be too.' He gazed into his Queen's intelligent eyes, seeing her strength gathering and her core reinforcing. His heart warmed as he felt her soothing aura, surround him once more.

'Then this is my first gift to my little Princess. She should have this and know everything about a world that she is a part of.' King Dunyazer reached into his robes, unclipping a tiny, ornate, leather book from the crimson ribbon at his waist. He removed the blankets around Princess Saffrodel and clipped it on to the long, empty ribbon, around her plump, little midriff.

'Your diary from hundreds of years ago' Queen Debriar whispered in awe. 'You were only five in human years when you came here....? I gave you that so you wouldn't be homesick. It looks so thick...? she looked at him questioningly. He grinned at her.

'Jaraadh helped me back then, to write everything I knew and could re-member about the world I was leaving behind. Just before the wedding. He expanded it and we made a sort of guide, comparing it to Shimrah. He even tapped into some latent, forgotten memories. It was a sort of a game. Never thought it might come in use....'

King Dunyazer's voice trailed off as his hands slid down Princess Saffrodel's red ribbon. It ended in two tassels made of thick, shining, bronze locks that felt strangely familiar. It was held in place by tassel holders, richly worked in golden Altheen. It wasn't the usual design for a Shimran trinket ribbon. King Dunyazer frowned.

'Is this a tzar's hair? It has a very familiar essence?' He puzzled. *What is it doing on my daughter?* Queen Debriar broke into a giggle, her long fingers over her lips.

'You aren't the first to give her a gift, my King' He gazed up at her confused yet thrilled to hear her sweet laugh again. 'Do you remember the day we met?' she asked.

'How could I forget that moonlit night?' King Dunyazer smiled, reaching for hand. 'You pulled me out of the waters behind the palace, I was a little boy of five, you were this enchanting young shimara. You stayed with me till I awoke and when I opened my eyes....' he kissed her hand, looking deep into her dazzling green eyes. He traced the line of her brow. 'Your eyes have never stopped haunting me since then!' Queen Debriar lowered her lashes shyly.

'Do you remember the gold mist?' she queried, her voice low and enchanting. King Dunyazer nodded.

'Afra told me about it, years later before the wedding, Soul Light something, ancient Shimran pledge...er... magic?' King Dunyazer frowned suddenly. 'Are you telling me that my Princess...?' Queen Debriar chuckled at his sudden anger and exasperation.

'Young Jaraadhrin at the swearing in ceremony, gold mist so thick it blocked them from view for a moment. Rattled his core quite a bit too. Cut the whole lot off just because this mischievous little thing wouldn't let go. We believe it is a combination of The Marshadath and The Ashaqath' She replied, grinning. 'Afra made it into a keepsake.'

'Aaashh! Of all the Absurdities in Shimrah!' King Dunyazer exclaimed to a peel of laughter from his Queen.

'You know it's not like that! I was your closest friend, a sister, even motherly till you grew up, all shimratzarry and attractive.' She giggled, wiggling her eyebrows at him mischievously

'You were the same, always hanging on to my robes, everywhere I went. I wore three belts and had to make sure everything was knotted on extra tight; You were so clumsy back then, tripping over my robes!' king Dunyazer's face broke into a smile and he roared with laughter at the memory. He sighed as he replaced the tassels and his daughter's little fingers grabbed it, holding it against her cheeks in her sleep. King Dunyazer shook his head, trying to remember.

'The Marshadath and The Ashaqath are for Crossfires for Mentor and Love?'
Queen Debriar nodded, smiling.

'The Ashaqath... like us...' she breathed, looking into his eyes. He placed his
hand on the side of her pretty face and she pressed her full lips into his palm,
still gazing at him affectionately.

'Jaraadhrin saved my life, this morning.' He recounted 'He is a fine young tzar,
full of courage, loyalty and devotion, almost released his being trying to save
me. He is just like his father, Lord Jaraadh.' Queen Debriar's eyes shot up, it
glazed brilliant lilac for a moment as she summoned the visions of the happenings of the courtyard and then cleared back to her usual green.

'Oh my...! She cried as she touched his face, her brow knotted in worry. King
Dunyazer smiled.

'I am well and Jaraadhrin is too. He is resting' He sighed heavily, shaking his
head. 'With all the uncertainty of the future and the prophesy, I am relieved
that my Princess will have someone to take care of her with that level of devotion. You are right my Queen, nothing in Shimrah is ever a coincidence. All we
can do is prepare ourselves for whatever the future holds for us. We have so
little time but we will make the most of it' He beamed into his Queen's moist
eyes.

King Dunyazer slid his arm around her and pressed Princess Saffrodel to his
heart. He was alive with his charming little family at this moment in time.
The future was uncertain and he would not be wasting what time granted
to him with such worries of it. If Shimrah was to fall to Queen Debriar's
brothers, it will be over his death. He would do everything in his power to
protect his family and his beloved shimrans. For now, He had the two beings
for which he existed in his arms and that was enough.

The King's Diary

Jaraadhrin stirred, opening his eyes and holding his hand up, to shield them from the warmth and light, filtering in through his window. The sun was quite high in the sky, it must be almost noon. He sat up glancing hurriedly at his moon maps. He had been asleep for a whole day and night!

How have I slept this long? Why didn't anyone wake me? He remembered Quinza-foor's melody, it had been different again. *Was it meant to make me sleep more to rest my core?* Jaraadhrin chuckled. *That mischievous little whelp is certainly capable enough!*

He stood up and felt his core move, fluid and solid, within him. He felt light footed and energised. Jaraadhrin washed up as fast as he could, eager to step out. He dressed rapidly in his long white breaths, shirt and socks. His under-garments secure, he reached for his robes and stopped short.

His usual white robes were gone. Instead, there was a fresh set of pale blue robes. The therin so floaty, it lifted in the breeze of his movements. He examined them closely. It was expertly made, the blue tinged clouds these came from, wouldn't have been easy to find. He let the soft, floaty fabric flow between his long fingers. This was martial grade flight therin for the Royalty and Nobility. The type that all high officials wore in the Shimran army. He strode over to his large, ornate wardrobe and slid the doors open. There were a few sets of them. Fresh and new!

Father. He thought gratefully as he caught sight of the richly worked, gold belts and the ornate headpiece, the Alaqwa of a Lord Protector of Shimrah.

Jaraadhrin picked up the Alaqwa and admired the exquisite workmanship. It was the dragon Alaq made of Altheen, a glittering gold metal. The three tiers of it wings open and bristled behind its slender neck, its crystal thin wings studded with brilliant jewels. Its eyes, a vivid blue, glistened up at him. Its long-coiled tail set with precious jewels, meant to slide over the wearer's head and over to nearly their right temple, shone brightly with its own light.

The Alaqwa glowed suddenly, warming between his hands. The heat slid through his fingers and deep within his core. Alaq bristled its wings, snarled up at him and stiffened back into a sculpture. Jaraadhrin chuckled. It looked rather annoyed. He couldn't blame it, he felt quite irritated himself.

How on Shimrah am I going to make it stay on my darned waves? My father wears it with such ease on his rod straight locks. I must wear it anyway now. Hopefully it would stay.

He slipped the robes on quickly, swinging and swishing the many layers around him in his haste. Jaraadhrin fastened the gold worked belt, securing everything in place. He turned to get the comb for his hair and the robes lifted quickly in the non-existence wind. It rustled with his movements.

He stared at the floaty material in surprise. The therin harnessed the breeze so well. He couldn't wait to fly in it. It was a masterpiece! Jaraadhrin did his hair up quickly and positioned the beautiful, ornate Alaqwa at the back of his head, scoffing at the waves at the ends of his locks and the sides of his face. He pulled at them once again, in the hope they would fall straight and long like the other tzars.

No such luck! None of the other tzars had such wavy hair. No matter what he did it always curled back up. He positioned the dragon's tail to the right of his head with precision and it promptly slid on the thick bump of his hair and hung by his ear.

'Aaashh! Tsk... tsk...!' he tutted in frustration. He stepped back, fingers on his chin, thinking. He moved the clip back into place tying it down to his hair with a binding thread from his centient. It stayed put. He grinned.

No one needs to know that!

He angled his head, gazing at himself in the long mirror. The robes suited him quite well. He moved his fingers slightly, his trinket ribbon flew off the bedside table and swished around his slender waist. It knotted itself, firm and elegant, on the left, over the gold worked belt and hung gracefully at his side. He looked stern and tall, his clothes flowing elegantly from his broad shoulders. Jaraadhrin grinned and his stern face lifted as his slanted eyes narrowed charmingly.

Apart from the extremely annoying hair, I don't look half bad, I guess. He thought with a chuckle.

He strode over to the terrace leading out of his room, his robes rippling behind him. The citadel's defences were still up but the day was so gloriously warm and beautiful, Jaraadhrin sighed with content. He gazed at the exquisite Shimran landscape stretching all round him. Its green-gold fields, gently rising hills, lush, flower strewn valleys and glistening, silver rivers and streams, glowed warm in the tantalizing rays of the sun. The great arms of the Silverstreams embraced the enchanted paradise of Northern Shimrah within it as far as the eye could see.

Jaraadhrin leapt off the terrace lightly, arms spread. The wind caught the cloudy therin of his robes and propelled him high into the air. He laughed with exhilaration. He really must congratulate whoever had made this therin. It took no effort all. He soared from tier wall to wall, light and graceful as a bird, his core singing within him, completely in harmony with his being. With a dignified spin he alighted on the third-tier fort parapets, his robes settling around his long legs in a shimmering blue cloud, just like the one it had been made from.

The citadel was bustling with activity. The King's return, the Queen's revival and the arrival of the Princess had made everyone excited and happy and there was an air of festive cheer in the atmosphere. Banners, streamers and lanterns extended in long lines, high across the cobbled streets and little ice boats and sculptures, decorated with flowers, floated lazily in the many moats. Shimrans bustled around in their best attire, celebrating, their laughter and mirth exploding in bursts of cheer everywhere.

Mead flowed and tzars and maras moved gracefully to soft melodies, swelling across gardens. They moved so exquisitely that it reminded him of the elegance of swirling pink petals and green leaves caught in the sweet, scented breezes of spring. Jaraadhrin smiled to himself as he glided down and walked along the waterways.

'My Lord' A couple of tzars saluted him as they passed. Jaraadhrin returned it and walked on. A group of stunningly, beautiful shimaras curtsied low.

'Lord Jaraadhrin'

'My Shimaras.' He inclined his head respectfully, hand on his heart and they promptly blushed, giggling. He realised his presence was causing rather a stir as more and more Shimrans waved, inclined their heads, curtsied or saluted him. Word of his exploits in the courtyard that morning, must have spread and his Lordly appearance today wasn't helping either. Another pair of very pretty maras waved their fans at him. He inclined his head again. They promptly placed the tips of their closed fans on their right cheeks, glancing up at him bashfully. Jaraadhrin tinged pink.

'Ahem!' he cleared his throat and turned away in embarrassment. *Darned accessory languages! Maras are so cryptic as it is. Why was it necessary and why did I have to learn them too as a part of my training? Probably wasn't for use in this particular scenario!* He chuckled.

Jaraadhrin leapt off again and flew up to the turrets, looking for his father who was nowhere to be seen. Far away in the middle of the clearing over by the training fields in the second tier, a young tzar practiced swordplay, blindfolded and against two others. He grinned as the tzar spun lazily away from his attackers and waved at him.

Quinzafoor.

As he was about to make his way over, a horn sounded loud and victorious. The main Martial Force was returning home!

Jaraadhrin pirouetted in mid-air excited but it was short lived. His face fell as he saw how little had returned. The palace's defences lowered as the spent soldiers streamed in through the many bridges and gates, their armour stained and soiled but thrilled to meet their loved ones. The tiers echoed with their reunions while others moaned their losses.

Jaraadhrin felt the pain and joy of each and every one of them, echo within him. War was devastating and some day he might have to command such a war.

How could I do it? How could I command an entire force of peaceful Shimrans in the knowledge that many might not make it home? How could I possibly order them to sacrifice themselves like this?

He drew a deep breath and alighted on a wall, hands clasped behind his back and frowned. The emotions of his soldiers blazed in brilliant colours over their base shades. This felt like when he had reached out to his father that night. Was it a new Shifr he was experiencing? He closed his eyes and in the darkness, he could see the coloured outlines moving around, below him. Their auras shone in different shades of glimmering colour; it was overwhelming.

He inhaled, long and deep, steadying himself and focusing on each, one by one. He tried to avoid those that looked red, their pain cut into him like daggers. A deep, cool blue shimmered amicably among the muddle of coloured mists, potent and familiar. Jaraadhrin's lips lifted at the corners and he opened his eyes in the direction of the blue aura. He could see his father helping the injured soldiers that were being brought in with the healers. He glided over to offer his help and as he landed, Lord Jaraadh smiled up at him.

'Hmmm... mmm.... Someone finally decided to wake up and grace us with their presence. Looking quite sprightly and polished too, I might add' Jaraadhrin grinned. He reached for the potion trays but his father stopped him at once.

'Oh no, you don't!' he said. 'I didn't get you those for you to help out here. You are needed elsewhere.' Lord Jaraadh said mysteriously. 'But let me look at you first' He stepped back as he admired his son, turning him by the arm. Jaraadhrin raised a brow.

'Acceptable?' he asked, a half-smile still on his lips. Lord Jaraadh stepped further back and folded his arms. He pursed his lips in mock dissatisfaction as if struggling to find something to compliment him on. He wiggled his fingers with fake disdain.

'Meh... good idea with the Alaqwa, though.' he tapped his own with a superior expression. 'Not everyone can imitate my refinement and elegance.' Jaraadhrin threw back his head, laughing at his father's amusing expressions and Lord Jaraadh joined in. His son hardly ever laughed and when he did, it was too infectious and difficult not to join him. Another horn of victory sounded, loud and triumphant, over the citadel and Lord Jaraadh's face sobered to seriousness. He sighed.

'What is it father?' Jaraadhrin frowned, despite the blanket of happiness, something still brewed dark. His father shook his head resignedly.

'Walk with me, son' he said, handing a large tray of potions and crystals to a healer nearby. They walked in silence till they reached a quieter path beside one of the gurgling waterways. Lord Jaraadh spun him around suddenly, holding his son by his shoulders.

'Jaraadhrin, the war is not over, Ifreeth is alive and he is amassing a sinister army.' He spoke quickly and to the point as he always did when he was serious and was the Lord Protector of Shimrah. His kindly father had disappeared. Jaraadhrin stared at him in dismay.

'We made a mistake, Ifreeth escaped and we have to reassemble, it is just starting!' He drew a sharp breath. 'Your charge is the Princess, let nothing sway you from your duty! Not your fidelity to the King, not your devotion to the Queen, not your loyalty to your soldiers and certainly not your affection for your father! You focus on the Princess alone!' Lord Jaraadh shook his son roughly. 'Do you understand...?' Jaraadhrin blinked and nodded, his hand flashed in a Shimran salutation to his chest.

'Yes, my Lord' he answered, gazing gravely into his Lord's cold, blue eyes, brimming with command.

'I need you to train as hard as you can with Quinzafoor. I had a word with him and I feel he is exactly right to be by your side. You will both need to be by the Princess' his father continued. 'But be warned, Quinzafoor is immensely powerful, very young and he has had a hard past. He will need work and patience on your end. You will be his closest. Your Shifrs are the only ones that can match him and even manage him!' Jaraadhrin scoffed and his father's stern face, mellowed.

'I know it doesn't feel like it now but that is the truth. You will know when the day comes. Pairing a second-in-command to a Lord Protector doesn't happen overnight. There was no one better for me than his father Zhafoor....' Lord Jaraadh stopped suddenly, his eyes glimmering moist. Jaraadhrin stared at him, stunned at the sudden crimson shoot of agonising grief within his father's essence.

'Ahem....' he cleared his throat, shaking himself. 'As you command, my Lord, on my honour, I give you my word' Jaraadhrin responded, his voice strong and serious.

What on Shimrah is going on? Why all this about the Princess? It is almost as if she is in mortal danger! Lord Jaraadh sighed, placing his hand gently on the side of his son's face and smiled.

'Good' said his father, satisfied. Jaraadhrin nodded.

'We have nothing to worry about father. The citadel is impenetrable' he added thoughtfully. 'We have tested its defences so rigorously; it will not fail!' Lord Jaraadh shook his head.

'There was something different about Ifreeth' he hissed in anger 'He feels tainted with something dark. The army of creatures we fought, looked like Shimrans but they didn't have the cores, Shifrs, essences or auras. They vanished in black smoke as we slashed at them but there was hundreds and thousands of them. The blades of his armies were black and it paralysed our dragons.' Jaraadhrin gazed at him in horror. Entwined dragons were the most powerful creatures of Shimrah. What could possibly subdue them? If Ifreeth could overcome their dragons, their prospects of winning were very bleak indeed.

'We couldn't use them for days after. The younger ones were killed. We lost many dragons, son. Barely two hundred entwined soldiers made it back, of which, half cannot summon their dragons anymore. They will need much time for their Dragonlights to re-glow and to recover from the evil that touched them' Lord Jaraadh continued, his blue eyes flashing as his hand tightened on his son's face.

'We have word that Ifreeth associates with strange creatures. We do not know what kind' he sighed again as his anger ebbed. he stroked his son's cheek with his thumb as he stared piercingly in to Jaraadhrin's eyes.

'Shimrah has never known to be this dark but it is said that a certain blackness is spreading, especially during the nights, from the far corners of Southern Shimrah. Scouts who see it, never come back; We know because we received a few hurried yishins before they disappeared. Be on your guard always and train your Princess. You are her Mentor. Teach her your skills and to fight as soon as she can hold her head up. Do not fail her...and me, son!' finished Lord Jaraadh, his voice low and urgent.

Jaraadhrin nodded dumbstruck, his hand over his father's, upon the side of his face. Lord Jaraadh smiled and exhaled heavily, looking back the way they had come. He tapped his son's cheek and withdrew his hand.

'I have to go; we will soon bid farewell to our fallen by the Western arm of the Silverstream. Here...' He turned back to Jaraadhrin, clipping something quickly into his ribbon. 'Learn and memorise that as soon as possible, guard it well. Quinzafoor has already done it and you should know it too' Jaraadhrin examined his ribbon, it was thick booklet.

'Their Majesties' have summoned you to their presence. They have been waiting for you for a whole day. They are very pleased with you.' His father continued swiftly, bursting with pride 'Hurry now, we shouldn't keep them waiting any longer.'

'Hmmm...?' Jaraadhrin looked up in surprise at his father, distracted, who made a funny face at him. He was still thinking of the booklet, the dire words and warning his father had just given him.

'Don't look so stunned, you senseless tzar! You will be summoned a lot from now on, being the Lord Protector to the Princess and all.' kidded Lord Jaraadh, chuckling. 'What do you think the new robes were for...? If you are lucky, they may let you babysit the Princess...!' he spread his stoles to the wind and soared off, still snickering at the look on his son's handsome face.

Jaraadhrin scoffed, shaking his head at the diminishing figure of his father. He was a soldier, not a minder for shimlings. He didn't know the first thing about shimlings. His father was surely jesting! He turned and whirled off to the palace at the very top of the tiers, feeling rather nervous. It was the first time he had been summoned to his King's presence and he didn't know what to do or expect. It looked as if it was the first day of his new duty.

He approached the King's terrace. A brilliant expanse of white marble, full of luxurious furniture and sculptures in the standard, curving architecture of the Shimrans. Rows of plants hung in little marble pots along the banisters and huge pillars held up the massive and highly decorated canopy as it sprawled above it.

Queen Debriar walked back and forth as lightly as a feather in the wind, holding his Princess in her arms while the King flipped through, what appeared to be a large book. Jaraadhrin landed on the terrace and sank to one knee, saluting them with a hand on his right shoulder and eyes to the ground.

'My Liege... Your Highness....' he greeted them.

'Aha! Jaraadhrin! Welcome' The King stood up and strode over to him. His King slid his right hand under his chin, the Alaqain on his finger glimmered gold as he raised Jaraadhrin rapidly to his feet and pulled him in to a firm hug. Jaraadhrin huffed in surprise, his eyes widening.

'My Liege....' King Dunyazer released him smiling, his eyes affectionate.

'How are you, young shimratzar? he inquired; head tilted to the side. His King gazed at him as if he was seeing him for the first time. Jaraadhrin inclined his head.

'I am well, my Liege – '

'I have something for you, young Lord.' King Dunyazer said patting his robes and searching for something. He pulled out a glimmering, ornate, golden medallion with the Shimran insignia on the Royal court of arms, exquisitely fashioned and encrusted with precious stones. It was the Alaqath. Jaraadhrin's eyes snapped to his King's wise face. This was identical to that of his father's. The high honour bestowed to the Lord Protector of a Royal.

'I had it made a while ago' said King Dunyazer as he gazed at him piercingly 'I didn't know when the time would come, only that it would be soon.' Jaraadhrin drew a quick breath, steadying himself. The Alaqath would affect his central being at its first touch. His King smiled warmly at him.

'Now ordinarily' King Dunyazer continued, sliding away the robes on his left and exposing his waist, where the crimson ribbon curled, above the gold worked belt. 'I would present this to you on the ceremonial tower in front of everyone' He clipped it firmly over the knot of the red ribbon. Alaq pranced around on it, bristled its wings and snarled up at him from it, its brilliant blue eyes, twinkling.

Jaraadhrin inhaled sharply as a scorching warmth emanated from it, flowing deep within him and into his heart. His core glowed as the warmth engulfed it. Shimran articles of power like his dragon clip, Alaqwa and the Lord protector medallion, Alaqath, were imbued with enchantments which bound the wearer to their oath. The depth of the reaction was directly related to the strength of the oath. Jaraadhrin shook himself. It felt so potent! King Dunyazer stepped back, looking into his dazed eyes, smiling with content at his reaction.

'But I heard, the great Alaq, more than made up for it at the allegiance…! That was very significant, Jaraadhrin.' He added, nodding at him.

'My King …I…' Jaraadhrin dropped to his knee again. The warmth brimmed within him and his King's graciousness and affection overwhelmed him.

'Aaashh!' Exclaimed King Dunyazer in amused annoyance. He raised Jaraadhrin by his chin again. 'I like my Lord Protectors' heads level with mine! Rise tzar, For the sake of all that's Holy in Shimrah!' Jaraadhrin chuckled involuntarily. That, according to his father, was the King's favourite expression coined from something his mother had used to say to him as a child in the human world. It kept her close to the King.

Everything in Shimrah was pure and light except recently that is. Apparently, the human world was very different to Shimrah.

Princess Saffrodel emitted a sharp cry from Queen Debriar's arms as she tried to placate her. King Dunyazer moved back to his seat in front of the book with a nod. The Queen sighed.

'She has been restless all day and night' she said. 'Here, Jaraadhrin hold her for me' he took a step back, looking rather worried. His Queen laughed. 'You don't know much about shimlings, do you?' she said.

'Erm…No your Highness…. except from when I was a shimling myself' he replied. King Dunyazer chuckled.

'Knowing Jaraadh, you were probably handed a sword on your first year' He jested.

'First full moon, my Liege' Jaraadhrin replied with a small smile.

'A month!' King Dunyazer exclaimed. He looked back at the huge book, flipping the pages quickly. 'Is that possible...?' he muttered to himself. Jaraadhrin peered at it. It looked oddly familiar. Princess Saffrodel let out another cry and Queen Debriar moved over to him.

'Hold your arm out like this....' she instructed '...and curve it towards you....' Jaraadhrin obliged hesitantly, his hands shaking. She placed the Princess into the crook of his arm. He drew a quick breath and held her. His Princess was a lot bigger than the last time he saw her. He stared down at her, her small face wrinkled up as if she was about to cry again. His Queen sank into a nearby chair with a sigh. She looked spent.

'She has been crying quite a bit and wouldn't calm down. The healers, the King and I, have been up all night.' She said, with her eyes closed and her head resting against the cushions of the chair.

Jaraadhrin shifted his arms slightly. Princess Saffrodel felt warm and comfortable in them. He gazed down at her beautiful, gold-streaked red hair, delicate brows and little button nose. The lashes curled, long and wet, on her plump little cheeks. He blinked slowly as warmth flooded his heart, the hesitancy, uncertainty and anxiousness left him in its wake. He gazed down at her mesmerized and her sweet little face twisted as if she was about to cry again.

Jaraadhrin lifted her higher against the soft therin of his chest, fluidly sliding his arm out from under her. He slipped the long sleeves over his fingers, dabbing gently at her wet lashes and soaking up the moisture on to the therin. He moved his feet in tiny steps, rocking her from side to side. His pale blue cloak floated in a gentle swirl around his heels as he replaced his arm back under her.

'Shhhhhh...Princess....' He murmured. Princess Saffrodel's lips relaxed into a smile as she snuggled closer to him. She slid her little hands within the folds of his robes at his chest and with a soft yawn, fell fast asleep! Jaraadhrin lips lifted in a tender smile at her peaceful little face. Quiet laughter sprinkled over the terrace and he glanced up at his Queen who had been watching him with half closed eyes.

'Jaraadhrin, you are a natural. We have been trying all night and you put her to sleep with a word.' She gazed at him, eyes twinkling. Jaraadhrin could feel the colour rising rapidly in his cheeks.

'Here it is!' King Dunyazer called suddenly still engrossed in the book.

'Shhhhhh!' Queen Debriar shushed him with a look of mock anger on her face.

Her King chuckled at her expression and pointed at the book. She leaned forward and started reading. Curious, Jaraadhrin moved closer too, careful not to jolt the Princess in his arms. King Dunyazer grinned up at him.

'We are trying to compare Shimran years to human years' He obliged at his curious look. Jaraadhrin recognised the massive book.

'This is the book about the human world that my father often chided me for not reading, my Liege. The record of the human world.' he whispered, keeping his voice low so as not to wake his sleeping princess. King Dunyazer raised his brows.

'Chided for not reading? I would say you read it well enough, young shimratzar. How else were you able to save my life the other day? His King replied, his brilliant green eyes moist. Jaraadhrin inclined his head, gazing at the floor. He was at a loss for words.

How does one answer such a gracious comment from his beloved King? He thought.

'So according to this...' Queen Debriar saved him from answering. 'You were five human years when you arrived in Shimrah, my Lord and you had the intelligence of a moon old shimling. You also looked like a two-moon old shimling.' she teased him.

'Aaashh! Jaraadh probably exaggerated that bit over there' King Dunyazer said with some frustration. 'I wasn't that bad, surely!'

'Oh, it is the truth alright' said his Queen, wrinkling up her nose and creasing her eyes at him. 'Don't forget, I found you, my Liege' King Dunyazer shrugged, grinning good naturedly and reached for her hand, distracted. Jaraadhrin smiled to himself, rocking Princess Saffrodel asleep, completely at peace in his arms.

He had always loved hearing about this part of his King and Queen. His father had often said that it was like looking after two shimlings, always bickering with each other over completely trivial things. They were so in love with each other and were soulmates. Today he had the fortune to see it for himself.

'Each Shimran year adds twenty-five centient years to a shimling.' Queen Debriar continued. 'I think the centient years are more like human years. Shimrans reach their permanent height and stature around the ninth full moon after their birth but their intelligence and spiritual being, develops faster than their physical form.' She looked up at Jaraadhrin. 'You are fifteen, Jaraadhrin, aren't you? That's three hundred and seventy-five centient years?' Jaraadhrin nodded. 'Of course, Saffrodel's human side might slow her growth.'

'Hmmm...' King Dunyazer hummed, deep in thought. 'If it doesn't? That means in about a month's time the Princess will look like a three-year-old human child who can speak and think well like a....er?

'...ten-year-old human child I believe...as shimrans grow faster mentally.' She finished for him.

'And she will look like you by the time she is eight full moons?'

'Well, I certainly hope so' she grinned mischievously. 'Though it would be a pity if her nose changed to look more like yours, my King! Don't you agree, Jaraadhrin?'

Jaraadhrin swallowed hard, his eyes wide in shock. He shook his head swiftly and took a hasty step back. His King and Queen roared with laughter at the look of utter horror on his face at being asked an opinion on such a matter, then promptly shushed each other as Princess Saffrodel stirred.

Queen Debriar sighed, her mirth subsiding. She pressed her palm to her heart. Jaraadhrin felt a glimmer of crimson flash over her pale lilac essence. He glanced at her concerned.

'My Queen, please rest' he said, regaining his composure. 'I will take care of the Princess for a while.' Queen Debriar nodded.

'Thank you, Jaraadhrin' she murmured, her eyes closing again. King Dunyazer stood up. He shrunk the book and handed it to Jaraadhrin.

'Clip that back on the Princess's ribbon for me, will you? I have to be with your father as we send off the fallen' he said, sombrely. 'Stay with the Queen, I will send the healers in, on my way out' Jaraadhrin bowed his head.

'As you command, my Liege,' he said, his head inclined as low as he could without waking his princess. King Dunyazer placed his hand briefly on the side of his cheek as his face broke into a tender smile. He kissed his Queen be-tween her brows and moved towards the door. He paused and turned around, his eyes twinkling.

'Oh, and that was a fine first present for the Princess, very....er...' King Dun-yazer tilted his head, searching for the word 'Unique....? But let's not keep doing that at every instance shall we? I rather like my tzars with a full head ... especially if they were as wavy!' His King chortled at the look of confusion on

Jaraadhrin face and left in a swish of robes. His Queen tinkled with laughter which twisted into disturbing cough. He turned to her distracted.

'Your Highness...?' Jaraadhrin queried, his concern growing. She opened her eyes and smiled warmly up at him. Though she was merry and laughed, he could see she was exhausted and she nurtured dire worries.

'I am well Jaraadhrin, do not worry about me.'

'If there is anything else I could do...? ' Jaraadhrin asked. She shook her head and gazed up at him piercingly.

'Just take care of Saffrodel' she said, Jaraadhrin nodded. He understood. She didn't mean just now. His Queen meant forever!

A healer appeared at that moment and helped escort Queen Debriar back to her chambers. Jaraadhrin watched her leave, her slender frame swaying and his heart weighed heavier. There was something below all the banter and merriment that was dark and worrisome. His King, his Queen and his father were hiding it from him. What could it possibly be that sparked such uncertainty and fear?

He had woken today, happy in the hope that the tide had turned and the world was righting itself. But the more this day waned, the less that feeling of comfort prevailed. Something was afoot, he could feel it in his core. Jaraadhrin sighed, his breath fanned Princess Saffrodel's little face. She let out a soft snore and smacked her lips together, loud and adorable. Jaraadhrin chuckled and sat down with his little princess in his arms, on one of the low cushioned chairs.

Trying not to wake her, he clipped the book back on to her crimson ribbon. It fell out as he did and his locks on their tassels, dangled at the ends. Jaraadhrin's face broke into a grin as he remembered the confusing words, his King had said to him when he had left. He tucked the tassels back within her robes and wrapped his Princess snug in her blankets. He stood up and started gliding with her in his arms, back and forth, on the terrace.

Far away, perched on the top of his favourite minaret, Quinzafoor sat watching his young Lord, head tilted to a side. He smiled affectionately as Jaraadhrin glided, to and fro, his Princess tenderly wrapped in his arms, his mantles swirling and trailing behind him as he moved.

It amazed him that any tzar could be this brave and courageous enough, to viciously plough through his own being with no thought for himself, to protect his King and Kingdom. Yet still be so pleasantly gentle and sensitive to care for a shimling. Jaraadhrin was a true shimratzar and his devotion to the crown knew no bounds. He sighed; something was brewing, his Lord was right. He could feel the ominous silence before the storm. He jumped lightly into the air to join Lord Jaraadh and his King with the farewells. His adoptive father's words rang in his ears as he soared.

'Stay by his side Quinzafoor and stay in the Light!' The first he vowed to honour with his life. As for the second, it may already be too late.

Ice Spikes Cupolas

Jaraadhrin left the terrace with a heavy heart later that day. The healers had come in shortly after his Princess had woken up and had taken her away. She had cried hanging on to his robes and not wanting to let go. She had only calmed after playing awhile with her tassels. Jaraadhrin had had to slip away quietly when she was distracted. He hated leaving his Princess. It was almost as if he had a left a part of himself behind.

Leaping nimbly from tower to tower, he made his way across to the Eastern arm of the Silverstream, where he was sure his father and the rest of the soldiers and their families were gathered, bidding farewell to their fallen brothers and sisters.

The light was already fading and he hoped he would be able to pay his respects to them. Jaraadhrin alighted lightly on the last fort, immediately to the side of river.

The Eastern arm of the Silverstream was an immense river flooding down from the large lake, fed by the three waterfalls behind the palace. It flowed the length of Northern Shimrah all the way to the Crystal Depths and then on again around Southern Shimrah. It was a massive river, flowing thick and fast. The Crystal Depths were the final resting waters of the Shimran folk, placed between the two land masses of Shimrah.

He could see the gathering of the soldiers in the high banks, their pale blue therin, shimmering in the fading light. His King, his father and Quinzafoor would all probably be there.

Floating on the river were crystal boats made of ice, glittering and sparkling like diamonds. Each one had an icy staff with a banner of water flowing over it, enclosing the solid, crystalized form of the Shimran dragon, Alaq, within it. The water Shifr shimrans had really outdone themselves. They looked majestic! A fitting tribute to the fallen heroes of Shimrah. The ice would not melt till it reached the quiet waters of the Crystal Depths, where it would disintegrate slowly to allow the Crystallites, the water nymphs of the dead, to accompany them to their final resting place. The Crystallites were often called soul-keepers and would only appear from within its deep nadirs when there was a death or an essence floated on the Shimran waters, close to the Depths.

The Shimrans avoided the Crystal Depths in life and often deemed the Crystallites ill-omened. It was widely believed that those who had the misfortune to meet a Crystallite, would face their death shortly. He wondered what they looked like. He didn't really believe in the tales. Shimrah was too full of light for malevolence or darkness.

And yet, there had been a deepening dread... a clearing darkness within its light. Ibreeth and Ifreeth were Shimran. How did such darkness envelope their cores to kill so many? War was unheard of in Shimrah till these two had started it. He slid to his knee in salutation, his head down and exhaled.

'You have served your Kingdom well, Shimratzars and Shimaras of my kin' he whispered. 'Your services and sacrifices will always be honoured and respected in the hearts of your King, your brothers and sisters gathered here. Rest now, be at peace and may you find you way back to your loved ones as Dragonlight'

It was a Shimran belief that the souls, centients, cores and essences of the dead often sedimented for centuries to be transformed into the dragons of the Ice Spikes. How they get there from the Crystal Depths to the enormous, cold mountain ranges, was an age-old mystery but it was the only way Shimrans could explain the uncanny attraction of some dragons to their owners. The only explanation for the way they often seemed to represent the traits of a much-loved, deceased family member, mentor, lover or friend.

He rose slowly, took a deep breath and closed his eyes. How many more were ordained to make their final destinations down the river before this war ends? The soldiers and the families glowed in varying shades of red over their base shades.

A brilliant, auburn essence, tinged crimson, caught his notice as he stood up. Jaraadhrin opened his eyes, a slight smile on his face. He gazed down at the group, who were all still watching the boats, except one lone figure who was gazing up at him, twirling something golden in its hands. It inclined its head to him, saluting him. Jaraadhrin's stern face broke into a smile.

Quinzafoor obviously! He thought. Tomorrow he would probably go down to the clearing to practice with him. He did need to train harder if they were facing another attack. Besides Jaraadhrin really wanted to see how good

Quinzafoor was in his martial arts.

Would I be able to match him? The crimson dimmed and the auburn aura blazed brighter in his mind as if reacting to his words. Jaraadhrin chuckled.

What Shifr of mine could possibly match that? he thought dryly. Jaraadhrin raised his hand in farewell, spun lightly and flew off into the night, towards his terrace and chambers. Quinzafoor's aura felt stronger, it was back to a few thousand years again. Maybe he should top up and use this night to mediate as much as he can into his body. After all, if an attack was imminent on the citadel, it didn't hurt to be ready.

Back in his chambers, Jaraadhrin washed and dressed, changing into his night robes quickly. Incareth had made sure he had a tub full of steaming water saturated with the healing powders again. He was immensely grateful to her. Her care reminded him of his mother. She had loved bath salts and healing powders too. He wanted to mediate the tincture and get some rest before it dawned. Tomorrow, he needed to be at his very best. He reached for the Javnoon on his ribbon and stopped short as his fingers nudged the booklet, his father had given him.

It must be very important for father to have given it to me so urgently! He sighed. *Hopefully it wouldn't take long.* He undid it from his ribbon, expanded it and lay it on the table. He flipped it open and gazed at the rapidly extending pages in dismay. It was a massive map and every single page stretched into a vast sheet of minuscule and very detailed drawings. Jaraadhrin flipped it back to the cover, reading the words in front, in his father's neat hand.

'Ice Spikes Cupolas'

He stared at it in confusion. What vaults were these? Plans for them to be built? Have they already been built? Why ever would they need strongrooms or vaults under the treacherous Ice Spikes Mountain range?

He flipped back to the first sheet and studied the minute markings with interest. The entryway to the vaults seemed to be in the cellars of the main citadel, locked by shield-maras Shifrs. It required four of them and was a complicated combination. It could only be sealed from within by Royalty. Jaraadhrin frowned, that felt like a rather severe design flaw.

What if there was no Royalty present? He shook himself sternly. *Why shouldn't there be? How pessimistic of me?*

He tapped it, lost in thought. His father would not ask him to memorise it if it was not already built. It must have been constructed when the citadel was erected but kept a secret. Does that mean there was indeed a possibility that they would lose to Ibreeth and Ifreeth? Was it a possibility or a certainty? He inhaled sharply as he remembered his father's and his Queen's many words and reactions that seemed to coincide. The incessant worry over the Princess. The warning and the need to be prepared. Did all this point at something definite? Queen Debriar did not have the power of premonition like Queen Thiloket but that did not mean, his Queen couldn't access it if she so chose to! Royalty could change Shifrs' as often as they wished.

Jaraadhrin placed his slender fingers on his temples, shaking his head, eyebrows raised. It didn't matter, none of it did. He would do his part and be ready for anything. If it required him to memorise this infernal booklet full of its daunting maps, he would see it done. He felt certain that his Queen hid something from him but it would be the right thing to do. His Queen was infinitely wise and no Royal had ever let a Shimran down yet. His fidelity and allegiance to King Dunyazer, Queen Debriar and Princess Saffrodel would remain even in the face of the impossible. Nothing could make him falter from this path. Jaraadhrin exhaled, bending over the sheet. It would take him a few days and he would need to work through the nights. No matter, he would see it through.

Fight, Flames and Fear

The next morning dawned, cool and grey. Clouds lay heavy and thundery below the blue skies as Jaraadhrin dressed. He felt rather tired but powerful, his core stable and solid with some seven hundred years that he had added to it from the tincture. He had memorised some of the map and caught up on some sleep as well. The harp had played its haunting tunes again, starting late last night, just as he lay on his bed to sleep.

Jaraadhrin made his way to the clearing, eager to practice. It was quite early and the soldiers may not be training there just yet. That suited him fine. He was sure, Quinzafoor would be waiting from him and he wanted an early contest before it got too crowded. Besides, he had a feeling he would be summoned to his Princess soon. His heart ached as he remembered how she had clung to him, the last time he saw her.

Sure enough, Quinzafoor sat on a little mound, twirling his three-pronged, ornate, double daggers, swiftly and elegantly between his long fingers. They were beautifully made, entirely of glittering silver metal. They were probably made of Elmas, the hardest, most durable metal found in Shimrah. The side prongs curved in sophisticatedly around the main blade. All three blades inlaid with silver and black lines. The same design etched into the hilts, made them both decorative and provided a good grip. Those would be rather difficult to dislodge from his hands.

Snarling dragon heads decorated the bases of the hilts. They looked handsome and deadly, not unlike their master. Quinzafoor was already blindfolded with thin, blue therin worked in gold like his belt. Jaraadhrin chuckled as he alighted, the therin flowing off his shoulders gracefully.

'Training early, are we?' he jested.

'Waiting for you, my Lord' Quinzafoor grinned. He leapt off the mound with a slight spin to his step as he saluted Jaraadhrin in mid-air. He landed exceptionally lightly, twirled his double daggers and caught them by the handles, proficient and neat. Jaraadhrin smiled at his elegance and skill.

'Aaashh! So, you got the message? It was to be a surprise!' he said in mock dismay. This was the first time he had seen Quinzafoor face to face. He was a stunningly handsome tzar with a high forehead, elegantly arched brows above his blindfold and strong, chiselled cheekbones below. Dimples blinked in his cheeks as he grinned. His face emanated power and radiance.

Jaraadhrin could make out the shape of his eyes and a dim blue behind the thin therin. It was thin enough to let him see through but not be seen by any who looked at him. Tzars had blue eyes and Jaraadhrin was sure, his would be piercing and attractive. Quinzafoor's long bronze locks glistened in the pale light, laying straight as silky rods around his face and behind him, unlike his. He felt a stab of annoyance. Quinzafoor face reddened and his lips pursed in a subtle smile.

'Thank you, my Lord. They are an odd blue-green though. You might find them rather strange and you have no idea how many tzars like waves... ahem... including myself.' He replied. Jaraadhrin laughed to himself but smoothed his face to a sternness again.

'Why the blindfold though? I don't feel comfortable fighting a blind tzar' he bantered, mirth still evident in his voice and in sharp contrast to his face.

'I have an unfair advantage in any fight, my Lord as you have already guessed and I can see through them anyway' Quinzafoor answered 'It is just dangerous to lock eyes with my opponent in a fight and it is Lord Jaraadh's orders as well.' Jaraadhrin nodded. He was right. The potency of Quinzafoor's Shifr was much deeper than he thought.

Jaraadhrin unclipped his staff, off of his ribbon and expanded it rapidly within his hands. It was almost a head taller than him and had a long, intricately worked handle, laid in with fine lines of brilliant silver Gumoos. The staff had a flat ornate circlet at its head which ended in two glinting sharp prongs. It looked lethal, sophisticated and ornamental with all the decorations on it.

'That's a handsome staff, my Lord' Quinzafoor chuckled. 'Very...er...delicate'. He hadn't seen his Lord fight either. Being the next in line for Lord protector and as per Shimran traditions, Jaraadhrin had trained privately with his father, Lord Jaraadh. Quinzafoor was sure his young Lord's martial skill was proficient but he had yet to see just how proficient. That staff though ....

It looked like it would snap with one blow of his three-pronged daggers. His Lord tilted his head at him, raising a brow at the stab at his staff.

'Thank you, Quinzafoor …I designed it myself, made from Elmas of course and inlaid with Gumoos' Jaraadhrin answered, rather stern but good naturedly. Quinzafoor grinned. Gumoos was a beautiful silver metal, previously used for jewellery! It was probably very flimsy.

Jaraadhrin twirled his staff in a rapid circle and slashed it at Quinzafoor who bent back with ease and blocked it with both of his daggers. The staff made contact with a resounding crash. It was very strong indeed. It reverberated against his daggers, sending waves of shock into his wrists and arms!

The staff is an extension of my Lord's own characteristics! thought Quinzafoor in wonder as the Gumoos flashed silver, nearly blinding him. *It is just like him. Elegant, ornamental and stronger than even a thousand-year centient!*

Jaraadhrin withdrew and swirled in with rapidity. His feet rotated around each other, nimble and light as he brought his staff down on Quinzafoor's head this time. He whirled away chuckling and blocked it with ease, once more. Again and again Jaraadhrin's staff clashed against Quinzafoor's daggers as they whirled around each other, trying to lay a blow on the other. Quinzafoor ducked, twirled and flashed around the clearing. His footwork and skill immaculate, matching Jaraadhrin's every move with efficiency and stability.

They were too well co-ordinated and completely in sync. Quinzafoor attacked fluidly as a sea serpent, his tall frame curving around Jaraadhrin, wraps soaring in the air as he whipped around, effortlessly blocking Jaraadhrin's powerful staff strokes. His attacks concentrated of blasts of force with the nimble, rapid strikes of graceful precision. His martial style closely resembled the rumbling power of thunder and the flashing majesty of lightening.

Jaraadhrin, lithe and agile as a dragon, swished and flashed under, over and around the double daggers. His robes and waves seem to channel his infinite elegance as they flowed around him, frothy and cloudy as he moved. His martial strikes resonated more of the delicacy of a dance than a fight, which made his attacks more powerful and fatal. He reverberated the fury and lethal beauty of tornadoes and tempests.

They flowed like rivers around each other, their training evident in their swiftness and the nimbleness of their movements.

The soldiers gathered around the clearing in droves as they heard the thundery clashes of Jaraadhrin's staff and Quinzafoor's double daggers. Stray rays of sun glistened down through the breaking clouds, flashing off their weapons as they reeled around in their masters' hands. The Shimran warriors cheered and whistled as the fight increased in ferocity, power and speed. They were familiar with Quinzafoor but their young commander facing off with him was a first and this was right after he was sworn-in as Lord Protector. It all made it even more sensational.

Jaraadhrin tried to keep his head clear as he fought, trying one tactic after another to catch Quinzafoor off guard. It wasn't working. He swished his staff high above his head, spinning it around rapidly, his mantles lifting in the wind as he slashed it towards Quinzafoor neck. He diminished it at the last moment and positioned his hands for the blow in mid-air instead.

Quinzafoor, who had already placed his daggers to block the staff, gasped suddenly. He flung his daggers away from him at a nearby tree, leaving his slender neck exposed. He whirled away at the last moment, his neck, a hairs breath from Jaraadhrin's sharp, slashing fingers. The crowed shrieked in awe and amazement. Quinzafoor's wrists smashed in to Jaraadhrin's, blocking the knife sharp attacks.

They fought with their palms and wrists, blinking around swiftly, trying to get a grip on each other. Their long legs, locked and unlocked as they tried to find a gap to overpower the other. They were perfectly paired, their skills as lethal as the other and it was impossible. They vaulted high into the air, their blows being blocked, hard and fast. Through the tumultuous motion, Jaraadhrin could see a brilliant, auburn haze, gleaming behind Quinzafoor's blindfold.

They moved away for a split moment and performed the exact same manoeuvre, The Coreblow! Their arms flashing around collecting a core bolt and driving it forcibly in to each other. Their palms slapped hard in the middle of the clearing, sending them spinning in whirlwind of leaves and dust, still joined at their hands, before their cores blasted them apart.

Jaraadhrin and Quinzafoor landed lightly. They pirouetted to the ground at the far ends of the clearing, therin swinging around them in a fan, chuckling and still in their defensive stances. Jaraadhrin straightened, adjusted his already immaculate cloaks and flipped a stray wavy lock over his shoulder. He clasped his hands behind his back and walked calmly towards Quinzafoor as if he was taking a stroll, his breathing easy and grinning away in exhilaration.

Quinzafoor summoned his daggers with a wave of his hand from the tree, where they were still lodged, eased up and diminished them smartly with a whirl and click. He strode over, pulling his tresses around his face, straight and sank into quick salute before rising, his eyes cast down, still blazing auburn behind the blindfold.

'That was a very risky move, my Lord,' he said seriously, as his smile disappeared and referring to the decoy with the staff. 'You could have maimed yourself.'

'Jaraadhrin' his Lord corrected him, 'We are evenly matched; I will not tolerate titles from you…Quinn.' Quinzafoor's head shot up.

'It is not one's prowess that entitles them to respect, my Lord' he said softly. Jaraadhrin tilted his head.

'What does, then?' he questioned. Quinzafoor drew a quick breath and pursed his lips.

'It is the devotion, loyalty and affection we place on one.' He answered, even quieter. Jaraadhrin took a step forward as Quinn stepped back.

'Then' Jaraadhrin whispered, his voice stern as he leaned towards him, the auburn blaze level with his eyes. 'You will address me as Jaraadhrin. We have been through too much for formality and because in my opinion, those things bring one closer, eliminating the need for titles.' He stepped back, tilted his head and tapped his chin with a slender finger. 'Or do you prefer Zhafoor?' Quinzafoor drew a sharp breath at the name of his father.

'Quinn…. if it pleases you, my Lord…. Quinn is good' He answered. Jaraadhrin nodded, his eyes gentle. He had touched a nerve.

'Jaraadhrin or Dhrin' he repeated. 'You have already addressed me by my name thrice before and there is no need to revert now….' A memory flashed across his mind, Quinzafoor calling his name, his voice urgent and worried as Jaraadhrin neared unconsciousness.

'Jaraadhrin! Not so fast…. Jaraadhrin…not as my Lord!… Jaraadhrin…Dhrin!!' Quinzafoor had cried while he had siphoned off the extra centients off of him, that morning in the main courtyard. Quinn shifted his foot awkwardly. Jaraadhrin chuckled and nodded. Quinzafoor probably 'read' that flash just now.

A movement behind Quinn caught his eye, deep within the shade of the trees. It was an unisus, a firehorn! Its mane, tail and wings, blazing in flames. The watching soldiers made excited sounds pointing at it, especially the shimaras. They didn't seem surprised at all, just thrilled to see it. They were used to it.

'Is that the firehorn..?' said Jaraadhrin, stepping around Quinn to get a better view. He turned, following his Lord's gaze.

'Yes, that's Ashoora.' Quinn answered, grinning widely at him.

'Ashoora...?' Jaraadhrin repeated in amazement as he stared at the wonderous creature. The firehorn stepped out of the shadow and cantered over to them briskly. It was an imposing beast, taller than the shimrans by at least a few heads. Its flaming mane, wings and tail flowed fiery and scorching against the glossy black sheen of its skin. The pair of wings at its midriff flowed over its rear in a blazing skirt of flames, dripping over on either side and stopped short of its tail on its back. They were thinner and more glazed than the rest of it, much like a sheet of shimmering, fiery crystals. They went all around its back in one fluid, tiered length before folding down neatly and settling on its rear. The elongated, red-gold horn on its forehead glittered in the sun, a glow of shimmering heat, enveloping it as it tossed its head, shaking its fluid mane and wings out in a fiery arc.

It stopped beside Quinn and nudged his head with a quiet whinny. Quinn chuckled and nodded at it. The firehorn promptly fell to its knees on its front legs before Jaraadhrin and bowed low with its horn to the ground. The grass around the place the tip of it touched, caught fire and blazed up. Quinn put it out with his cooled centient with a rapid flourish.

'What on Shimrah...?' puzzled Jaraadhrin as he stepped back from it with cool composure.

'She asked me if you were Lord Jaraadhrin who saved her that night. She is thanking you for not shooting her down and for making sure she was well looked after. She is very grateful to you.' Quinn explained gazing at the firehorn, his face affectionate. Jaraadhrin glanced at him in surprise, raising his brow.

'You speak unisus?' he inquired in amazement. Quinn chuckled.

'I can read them, yes but she offered her allegiance to me. We can read each other now.' Jaraadhrin's brow furrowed. He reached up to Ashoora's mane, running his fingers along it, thinking hard. The flames slid and wound around his hands and wrists. They felt warm but didn't burn him.

Unisi, like dragons, could offer up the jewels in their horns, binding themselves to shimrans they chose. They didn't disappear within the Shimran cores like the dragons though as they had physical bodies of their own. Dragons on the other hand were pure light and power, solidifying when, as and if required. Unisi were quite powerful and had their own brand of enchantments that were hardly known to the Shimran kind. Shimrans, however, hardly ever entwined with unisi, simply because they were fine with flying on their own. They had no need for these wild and majestic beasts. This firehorn was probably the only one in the citadel at this moment in time.

Had this firehorn entwined with Quinn? Dragon entwinement is a very sacred ceremony and very personal. It was probably the same for unisi. It isn't unheard of but it is very rare indeed. If it had entwined, it would have pierced Quinn on his right shoulder with its horn, wedging its jewel deep within his life force. I wonder if it hurt? Quinn does look normal to me. That is, if he could ever be called normal with his Shifrs! thought Jaraadhrin, glancing at Quinn beside him in some concern. Quinzafoor reddened slightly. His lips curved in a bashful grin and he kept his head down, avoiding Jaraadhrin's face.

'She did... with my permission.... erm...er...ahem...slight discomfort but I am completely well. She is very powerful and it infiltrates to me at times. I can also see through her eyes no matter how far away she is. I am still learning.' He explained quietly, still not looking at him. Jaraadhrin nodded, gazing at the brilliant auburn eyes of Ashoora.

She certainly matched with Quinn's auburn aura, all fiery, flaming blaze. Tsk.... tsk... I am glad that I don't have to voice such private and rather personal questions, yet they get answered anyway. He grinned as Quinn chortled at his thoughts beside him. He found Jaraadhrin's thoughts exceedingly humorous and rather awkward.

'You are very welcome, Ashoora.' Jaraadhrin whispered to the firehorn. 'Stay well and try not to burn down the citadel when Quinn isn't around, will you?' Ashoora tossed her head and snorted as Quinn snickered behind them. Jaraadhrin shook his head, his lips lifting in smile.

'She probably said something very mischievous now, didn't she? ...Anyway' he stepped away from her, facing Quinn. 'Well then...' he swished the therin off his feet, ready to fly off. 'Same time tomorrow for another contest?' Quinn nodded, his face brightening. Jaraadhrin leapt into the air with a quick salute to his soldiers as the crowd cheered loudly again. They flashed colourful sparks into the air with their centients. They were in awe of him and were already replaying his many moves to each other. Ashoora and Quinn inclined their heads in salute as he soared away.

Jaraadhrin sailed off towards the King's terrace wondering whether he dared to go there unsummoned but he wanted to see his Princess. Had she slept last night? Had she cried for him again? He thought he would just glide past but was met, mid-air, by a yishin. It was brilliant lilac. He smiled; It was the

Queen. He plucked the crystal sheet from within it; he had been summoned. He quickened his space and landed lightly on the terrace.

'That was very swift indeed' laughed Queen Debriar.

'I was on my way here, Your Majesty' Jaraadhrin admitted as he saluted her. Hearing his voice, Princess Saffrodel came crawling rapidly on all fours, giggling. Her hair was longer to almost her waist, braided up into her tiny tiara and her movements swift.

'What? The Princess crawls...?' exclaimed Jaraadhrin in surprised 'How many days has it been? Isn't that a little too fast for a shimling?' he wondered. Queen Debriar's face became serious.

'We have been watching her, she is growing a lot faster. Physically and mentally' His Queen confirmed. 'It's unprecedented. We thought since she has some human qualities, Saffrodel would be slower than a normal, full blooded shimling' She continued. 'But no, it's faster. It might be the combination of Shimran and human qualities. We have been looking through the book for explanations...but to no avail' She shook her head.

Jaraadhrin sat down on his heel as Princess Saffrodel approached him. She clambered on him, destabilizing him. He slid back, cross-legged swiftly, catching his balance and laughing at her antics. His Princess stared at him for moment, her little mouth a circle of awe, then threw her hands around his neck. She grabbed the back of his waves and loosened the Alaqwa on his head, which he had arranged with much difficulty as usual.

Jaraadhrin gasped at her warmth and sudden embrace. Holding her lightly to prevent her from falling off and gathering his composure, he lifted her off of him and placed her on his lap. He picked the loose Alaqwa off his hair, letting it fly free. He wasn't going to get that to stay now, anyway.

'Aaashh! Princess!' he exclaimed, handing it to her to play with, Alaq grimaced as he did. 'I was training for a while down at the clearing and not a hair fell out of place and you managed to dishevel it completely in moments' he said, smiling down at her. 'How will I ever face my soldiers again when a shimling Princess had tousled me so?' he teased. Princess Saffrodel giggled up at him, meeting his eyes with a clear, intelligent gaze, before playing with his clip. Queen Debriar chuckled.

'Well we can't have that now, can we?' she said, waving her hand in a slight gesture. Jaraadhrin's locks flew back the way it was, held by his clip. Princess Saffrodel let out an exasperated cry as it flew back into Jaraadhrin's hair, from her hands. Queen Debriar crafted another glowing one from her centient, much like his Alaqwa, for her daughter to play with.

'My Queen' he bowed his head in thanks, relieved that he didn't have to battle with the annoying dragon clip, to try position it, on his even more irritating waves. Queen Debriar nodded, her face solemn again. She sighed as she watched them play happily together. He, ever gentle and caring, immensely patient with the shimling's antics.

'Jaraadhrin,' she said thoughtfully. 'You have to learn more about Saffrodel if you are to fulfil your duties to her.' He glanced up at her.

'Of course, my Queen' he replied.

'No, I mean a lot deeper than just mentoring and protecting' she said, her voice hesitant. Jaraadhrin tensed at the tone. His Queen never wavered. She never did anything that would warrant an uncertain reaction. She was wise and always thought about something numerous times before she actioned on it. 'You need to learn about how the human side affects her, what she has, doesn't have, how she can be revived if she was to be harmed.' She continued.

'No one will harm the Princess if I can help it, my Queen' Jaraadhrin replied fiercely. Queen Debriar sighed again.

'I know' She looked away for a moment then turned back to him, gazing piercingly into his eyes. The reluctance was gone, she sure as ever. 'You need to know everything about her growth, her core, her physique, her silverine......'Jaraadhrin reddened as his hands shook with discomfort.

'My Queen, she is a Princess and a little mara, I cannot infringe on her privacy!' He whispered as he tried to maintain a steady voice.

'It's that or her death!' Queen Debriar's voice rang, cold and stern. Jaraadhrin stared at her, shocked. What on Shimrah was going on?! He had never heard that tone in his Queen's voice. It rang of fear, uncertainty and darkness. His mind wondered to the booklet on his ribbon, it certainly felt very significant at this moment. Her eyes softened as she saw how shocked he was. 'I know it is uncomfortable for a young tzar but try take it as a sibling, a close friend or even a father, however you see fit.' She said, her voice filled with gentleness but firm. Jaraadhrin nodded in silence.

'I will tell you everything I know about the Princess and you will find out as much as possible about her, in the time she spends with you.' Queen Debriar commanded. 'If she takes after the King, you may need to keep reviving her body against ageing as I do with the King. I will teach you how just in case, However, Saffrodel does have a core and I can sense it's a lot more powerful than a normal Shimran one. Her centient years do add normally as the days pass and I have been keeping track.' Queen Debriar paused. Jaraadhrin nodded, listening intently, still avoiding her eyes under the pretext of playing with his Princess. Queen Debriar smiled; she knew he would obey her command, no matter what.

'Her growth, both physical and intellectual is faster and the use of her limbs are more pronounced.' Queen Debriar continued her explanations in a steady voice. 'Saffrodel's silverine....' Jaraadhrin flushed a brilliant crimson, his head low and the clip in his hands clattered. Talking about any silverine, the Shimran life force entryway, was unacceptable as a norm especially that of a shimara. He picked it up quickly and handed it back to Princess Saffrodel, moving her slightly further away from him.

'.... appears to be a normal Shimran one on the left shoulder as is usual for the shimaras,' his Queen finished, her voice, hard and firm. 'As you know, the King does not have one. So Saffrodel can be harmed that way. However, she may still be harmed by her heart or her mind like her father,' Queen Debriar shook her head. 'That means she has more targets than Shimrans and therefore more vulnerable. You will need to guard her more vigilantly; you cannot afford to forget it' Jaraadhrin nodded again, still blushing but this time his eyes flashed cold steel as he glanced up at his Queen. Queen Debriar smiled, content and continued.

'Humans are prone to illnesses affecting their physical bodies. Usually due to uninhabitable things in their blood. You will need to detect them and remove them. They typically have these massive temperature changes, usually high when some such thing enters them, that they are incompatible with. They can get chills too. This is generally due to very insignificant little bugs. Other times it could be due to their deteriorating physical body. They don't do well with very cold or very hot external temperatures, unlike us. We can just heat or cool our centients. They need an external aid. These are easily fixed. Our centients are more than enough to accommodate for it.... hmmm....Humans are rather fragile.' She smiled tenderly and Jaraadhrin knew, she was thinking of her king.

'Saffrodel is only half human so she can do most of this herself after some time. You will just need to guide and aid her as and when she requires it. I can see Saffrodel's Shifrs manifesting already though, she will not be able to use them till at least five moons later. Again, that's uncertain considering how rapidly she is growing. Something about the combination of the Shimran and human blood is accelerating everything about her.' Queen Debriar paused, tapping her chin as she thought hard for any little fact that she may have missed out.

'Dhrin... Dhrin... Dhrin...!' Princess Saffrodel squealed suddenly, shaking with laughter as she clambered up to him again. Jaraadhrin's eyes snapped to her in disbelief. Queen Debriar rolled hers, comically at him.

'Tsk... tsk.... tsk.... naturally!' She scoffed, good natured but rather exasperated. 'How annoying! Those have to be her first words...Why Dhrin though... why not Jaraadhrin?'

'Quinn called me that once and I did ask him to address me as such today...' Jaraadhrin replied, perplexed. He shook his head, his smile tender as he gazed down at his little princess. This was going way too fast for him. What next? Would his Princess be fighting him? At the same time, it thrilled him that she was growing so fast and was so close to him. Soon he would have an exceedingly clever little Princess to have proper conversations with. He would be able to mentor her and teach her his skills. Princess Saffrodel's Shifrs, a shimara's volatile nature, emerging from their emotions and their powers, didn't worry him anymore. He was there for her as long as she existed and he will let no harm touch her.

'That is indeed strange...' replied Queen Debriar.

Jaraadhrin pulled his Princess off himself again, trying to sit her down. She tittered and wriggled as she snuggled deeper into his robes on his crossed legs. She yawned, raising her little hands high, pulled the tassels made of his locks at her waist to her cheeks and fell asleep promptly. Queen Debriar exhaled.

'She sleeps a lot too. She tires very easily; it could be because of the fast growth rate.' She informed him. Jaraadhrin covered Princess Saffrodel gently with his long sleeves, the day was still quite cold. He gazed up at his Queen. Her Highness was too worried and she wasn't telling him what was worrying her. He was beginning to think that it was not just the attack from Ifreeth but something more serious and sinister beyond everyone's control.

Has my Queen seen something that is happening now? Is that why she is this worried? Is it Ifreeth? Jaraadhrin pondered. *Or am I right in thinking that she has accessed a premonition?* Queen Debriar rose and glided over to him as he sat on the cushions on the floor, still lost in thought.

'You had better go when she is asleep, Jaraadhrin' she said wearily. She scooped Princess Saffrodel up from his arms, drawing her little fists from within his robes. Jaraadhrin rose and lowered his head.

'Come back tomorrow when you can' She smiled. 'I know you can't stay away from her. Has Mistress Afra spoken to you yet?' his Queen inquired.

'No, Your Highness' replied Jaraadhrin. 'I haven't seen the Mistress in a while now. She has been busy treating the dragons of the injured soldiers. Apparently, it takes much care and time for their Dragonlights to re-glow' Queen Debriar pursed her lips.

Should I tell him about the Soul-Light Crossfire? she thought hesitantly. He *already looked overwhelmed with everything so far.... May be tomorrow.'* she decided.

The Royal Imp

Jaraadhrin hardly saw his father or the King, in the days that followed. They were shut away in the council rooms, devising strategies and holding meetings. Scouts came in and out of the palace but no news reached Jaraadhrin or Quinzafoor. The citadel's defences remained on high alert and security in and out was tightened, further each day. The moat and fort defences rotated every few days in various battle formations. There was much confusion and fear in the air.

Jaraadhrin's days whizzed past him between the vault – map booklet, Quinzafoor, his soldiers and Princess Saffrodel as he did all he could to help, train and prepare for the uncertainty that hung over them. He trained hard, early in the mornings with Quinzafoor and the other tzars and maras down at the training grounds. He was often tired due to his late nights and lack of sleep but was always prepared. Quinn would be ready every time, when he arrived, blindfolded and with a different weapon of choice.

Ashoora often watched from under the shadows of the trees, seated daintily on her crossed hoofs. She shot little bolts of flames from her horn, whenever the shimratzars made a particular praiseworthy move. She was rather biased. She shot thicker plumes for Quinn than Jaraadhrin! But their soldiers, the shimaras in particular, more than made up for it. The first contest of the day had become something for the soldiers to look forward to and they would gather as early as Jaraadhrin and Quinn to watch.

The shimaras were usually the first to arrive even before the tzars and never in battle gear. They were always robed as if they were attending a celebration. Shimmering visions of loveliness they were too, making it impossible for most of the tzars in the clearing to focus on anything else. That was – until Jaraadhrin commanded that only martial robes were allowed in the fields. They had accepted his direct orders to them with blushes and giggles but still managed to look stunning and formidable at once, which just made them more appealing!

The only thing that made the tzars focus was, his and Quinn's match. They had still to see a win. The match always ended in a draw when Jaraadhrin had to hurry off to his Princess. No amount of tactics and planning was enough on either tzar's side, to nail a win. Nevertheless, the soldiers found their morning fights inspirational as each of them brought a new move to the arsenal. The soldiers would then practice whatever they learned from their Lord and his second-in-command that day. Engrossed in it for the whole day.

The Princess was growing at rather an alarming rate. By the time the full moon approached she was knee high, petite and an elegant little shimara. Her intelligence was beyond her years yet her centient added as normal. Queen Debriar and Jaraadhrin poured over King Dunyazer book. They made notes of her progress in great detail from the other end of it. Recording infinite comparisons between Princess Saffrodel, a regular shimling and a human child. They made sure to research anything and everything, irrespective of how insignificant it seemed.

They tutored Princess Saffrodel to read, write and basic skills, involving Shimran day to day life. Queen Debriar was relentless, training Princess Saffrodel, using her heightened growth and intelligence as an advantage. She made every moment with her, an entertaining and learning experience for the youngling. Jaraadhrin often felt confused as to the necessity of it all, even saddened at the persistent education but he trusted his Queen's wisdom explicitly and knew that there probably were significant justifications behind her actions.

Princess Saffrodel loved the attention and learned quickly. She never slowed and developed hobbies along with her gruelling education. She loved dancing and found time for it. She was already so proficient that she was considered the best dancer in the whole of the citadel. She would often pirouette around Jaraadhrin as he taught her, preferring to keep moving while she learned. She never needed repetition and never sat in one place for too long. Her attention was exquisitely precise even when she seemed to be otherwise engaged. Queen Debriar and Jaraadhrin learned long ago that this was her way of learning and catered to it.

As Jaraadhrin glided over after a particularly difficult training session with his soldiers, he saw them practicing down in the Palace gardens. His fatigue was finally catching up to him and the soldiers had been rather restless due to the constant uncertainty in the air. He had had to set them straight again. Fortunately, he had finished memorising everything in that infernal booklet last night and didn't have to worry about lack of sleep in the future. He would sleep earlier tonight and replenish.

It was a beautiful day, bright and breezy as it had been for the last two days. Queen Debriar was teaching his Princess to harness the wind and fly. His Queen had been trying for the past two days and Princess Saffrodel still hadn't been able to master it, which was a first as she usually needed no repetition.

As he alighted beside them and saluted his Queen, Princess Saffrodel stumbled on her long, pink therin robes and plopped down on the floor. Jaraadhrin gazed at her in surprise. The Princess never stumbled or fell. Even as a baby she had always been graceful and supple on her feet. Queen Debriar sighed in frustration.

'Saffrodel, for a shimara that was exceptionally clumsy, my darling....' It certainly was and his Princess was never ungainly, this was surely another first. Jaraadhrin frowned slightly. Was something ailing his Princess? He ran a quick centient check over her, looking for any human ailments. There was none. Her core and aura felt well and healthy. A beautiful, sparkling, rainbow glimmer of every colour, suspended in a transparent mist, swirled around her. It wafted of spring blossoms and summer fruits. He had never felt such a glow. It was special as was everything about her.

Princess Saffrodel stood up brushing off her robes. She grimaced, flicking her knee length, red-gold hair off her face, the long braids swinging behind her.

'I am not!' she pouted at her mother. 'I dance well enough and dancers cannot possibly be ungainly!' she turned to Jaraadhrin and complained loudly. 'Dhrin! The Queen thinks I am awkward, it's not my fault, Her Highness happens to be so dainty! Not everyone can drift around like my mother does now.... can they?' She raised her hands to her sides, exaggerating Queen Debriar's elegant walk and promptly stumbled, falling on her side.

Jaraadhrin hid a splutter of laughter as Queen Debriar exhaled in exasperation, shaking her head. His Princess was pretending and having a laugh, antagonising her mother! Princess Saffrodel pretended to be offended at his mirth as well, stood up with dignified annoyance and marched off with an indignant 'Humph!'

'I can't understand it' Queen Debriar shrugged. 'She should be flying in a day at most and it's been three days. She just does not want to learn this skill, for some strange little reason.'

'She will my Queen, she has done so well and I am sure she will master it eventually' replied Jaraadhrin, still trying not to laugh at his little Princess's pouty face and covert glances at him.

'It is not a matter for amusement' said Queen Debriar, glancing at him sharply. 'Every day is a boon, another chance to train and keep her safe. If she masters flight, she could at least escape. She would get nowhere on foot and she will never learn to defend herself without the fundamentals' Jaraadhrin tensed, his brow furrowed in confusion.

'Escape from whom, Your Majesty?' Queen Debriar shook her head.

'It doesn't matter. We need to train and be ready for every eventuality. It is not prudent to overlook anything.' Jaraadhrin gazed at his Princess, his eyes troubled. She was prancing along the thin, marble rim of the circular fountain as light footed as ever. She somersaulted, pirouetted and cartwheeled, the picture of elegance. Her pale pink therin cloaks, long sleeves, braids and ribbons fluttered around her. Her graceful movements made him think of mischief and mirth.

She is expressing her feelings through dance! He realised suddenly. Queen Debriar smiled beside him.

'She really does love to dance though, any moment she could spare, any emotion she has, she articulates them through her movements. Maybe you could teach her your fan dance? The one you used to practise when you were a shimling, Jaraadhrin? She does love accessorised movements. I caught her twirling around with a sword last night. Fans may be little less dangerous for now, don't you think?' Queen Debriar grinned at his discomfort, mischievously.

'Ahem...' Jaraadhrin cleared his throat in embarrassment and stared at her, astonished. 'My Queen, no one knows that, not even my father.... how?' He murmured. Queen Debriar laughed.

'Four moons, weren't you then? You should have kept it up, I thought you were exceptionally elegant. Not many tzars can master that level of daintiness and still wield a sword. Saffrodel would love to learn from a master like you.' She chuckled. Jaraadhrin stared at his Queen, puzzled and mortified, the colour rising quickly. Queen Debriar smiled at his discomfort, her eyes tender.

'I watched over you when your father and the King were working late, busy with the training of the Martial Forces, at that time. You and Quinzafoor, you are both Jaraadh's sons. I was concerned that you were all alone.' She explained. 'Obviously, I need not have worried, especially not about Quinzafoor' She added laughing. Jaraadhrin nodded his eyes moist. Of course, the Queen's visions. She could choose to see as well. He was touched that His Queen had cared so much and expended such power on his behalf. Queen Debriar laid her hand against the side of his face.

'Both of you have always been like my own, Jaraadhrin and always will be.' She whispered tenderly. 'Now!' Queen Debriar's tone changed, her voice full of laughter again. 'See if you can teach that naughty little Princess of yours how to fly' she said with a pat against his cheeks. Jaraadhrin smiled.

'I will try, my Queen' he replied. She laughed and sailed off towards the palace. Jaraadhrin walked over to Princess Saffrodel still cavorting on the high rim of the fountain. As he approached, she hopped off and sat down, running her fingers in the clear waters within. He sat down beside her, pulling his mantles in, to avoid getting them wet. He studied her with his head tilted, face stern.

'Are you going to give me a sermon on how important flight is as well, you old tzar?' Princess Saffrodel grimaced. Jaraadhrin arched his brow at her.

'Old tzar?' He repeated, condescendingly.

'Yes indeed' she replied 'How old are you then? I would say about one thousand six hundred and I am only two and a half?' She held up her slim, little fingers in emphasis. Jaraadhrin stared at her in astonishment. She was right. He had been adding centient years and mediating it, powering up for any eventuality.

How could she tell so precisely? He frowned. W*as it her Shifrs manifesting already?* He shook his head and chuckled.

'So, are you afraid of heights, Princess? He teased her.

'Of course not!' Princess Saffrodel answered him, flipping her hair back indignantly.

'Hmmm… well, it's unfortunate that you haven't mastered flight, I had hoped to take you down to the training fields to meet the soldiers, my Princess' Jaraadhrin feigned a disappointed sigh. She looked up at him with interest.

'Fly with you to the clearing, where you train every morning?' She contemplated. He nodded. She grinned back, her little face filled with mischief. 'I would like to fight like you, I watch you sometimes.'

'Well,' Jaraadhrin replied, his face stern but eyes tender. 'You do need to be able to use the wind to fight. Flight is the foundation for martial arts.'

'Hmmm….' Princess Saffrodel sat thoughtful, gazing in the direction of the clearing, a tier down from theirs. 'So, you know fan dancing?' Jaraadhrin choked and cleared his throat. She glanced up at him, a flash of guilt crossing her sweet face.

'I wasn't eavesdropping, I can hear over a great distance' she explained in a hurry.

'How great a distance?' questioned Jaraadhrin, frowning. *Another Shifr?* she pursed up her little mouth.

'I listened to you down in the clearing this morning' she said, her voice quiet.

'Aaashh! Of all the Inquisitive Little....' Jaraadhrin stopped himself, stood up and turned away from her. He had been grilling his soldiers extra hard today, telling some of them off for dawdling and not too gently either. It was bad enough she watched him, without hearing what he said to his soldiers too. Princess Saffrodel leapt up.

'Don't be angry, Dhrin I was just wondering what you were doing, just today.... just once' she said looking up at him, her eyes wide and her bottom lip pouting.

'Why do you call me Dhrin?' he questioned, turning back to her. He had asked Quinn to call him that, the day she had first said it. Could this Shifr have been manifesting that early? His Princess shrugged her shoulders and raised her hands comically.

'Your name is sooooo long!' she said rolling her eyes in sync with the elongated syllables of her speech. 'Why couldn't your father have named you something shorter? Lord Jaraadh is a lovely short name. Or did you want me to call you Master, now?' she widened her eyes, staring up at him in mock horror. Jaraadhrin chuckled internally. He couldn't help himself; she was so endearing. He sat down on his heel, facing her.

'Alright then, Princess' he said, trying not to laugh at her expression. 'I will forgive you this time, if you try and learn to harness the wind with me and who knows, I could even start teaching you to fight afterwards' She laughed and shook her head.

'Ah...ah...ah...I am the Princess and I set the conditions' she trilled. Jaraadhrin's lips lifted and his eyes twinkled as he fought back the laughter.

'Oh? And what does Her Royal Highness command?' Princess Saffrodel raised her chin, mimicking the Queen.

'I will learn this skill and you will fan dance with me, I don't need you to teach me, I already know the moves' she said. Jaraadhrin stared at her in exasperation as his mirth vanished.

'Please?... Please?... Please?... Dhrin? she squinted her eyes up at him, moving from foot to foot adorably, her hands clasped in front of her. Jaraadhrin could feel a smile creeping on his face again. He exhaled; he couldn't refuse his little Princess anything even if his life depended on it.

What a spectacle I would be if my soldiers saw me. Quinn would probably find it hilarious beyond doubt. He thought as he nodded at her.

'Agreed Princess' he consented hesitantly.

'Yaaay...' Princess Saffrodel skipped around in excitement.

'Now come, let's find a high place for you to leap off of ' said Jaraadhrin, half amused and half exasperated. Princess Saffrodel looked around. There weren't any high places here, just the fountain.

'There isn't any – 'she began.

'Oh yes, there is' Jaraadhrin replied firmly. 'Enough excuses, come now' He held his palm out, level with his Princess's head by his knee. She giggled and leapt up lightly, landing with both of her tiny feet flat on his palm. Jaraadhrin raised his arm high above his head, his many layers rustling around his tall frame. He was ready to catch her with the other if she lost balance which he knew was highly unlikely. The Princess was too sprightly and sure footed for that.

'Feel the wind in your robes, ascertain its direction, that will be the path of your spin, flow with it and rise up. Arms straight, palms up for balance.' Jaraadhrin instructed. Princess Saffrodel scrunched up her nose and lips down at him, then taking a deep breath, sprung straight up off his palm. Her robes swirled as she did a quick pirouette and landed back down on his hand, heels slightly lifted this time. Jaraadhrin nodded.

'Very elegant indeed, my Princess. Try again but spin in the other direction, winds that way' he encouraged. Princess Saffrodel nodded in concentration, positioned herself and jumped up once again. She rose higher this time and the therin swung around her in a soft fan as she spun. She dropped back on to his palm. Jaraadhrin felt a crackling jolt as she landed. He channelled his centient covertly to keep his palm steady against it. She was light but the force of her drops was rather high for her weight and the jolt as she landed, made him wonder if she could be channelling yet another unconscious Shifr. He was sure, the Princess addressing him 'Dhrin' was no coincidence.

'That was undeniably better Princess, try again' he encouraged. She frowned down at his palm.

'Am I heavy?' she inquired, a little concerned. She had probably caught the surge of his centient into it. Jaraadhrin grinned.

'Of course not, my Princess. Try again, the faster you master this, the quicker we can visit the clearing' he enticed, his glittering blue eyes twinkling up at her. Princess Saffrodel gazed down into them for a moment.

'I would like that very much' she said. She closed her eyes and drew a deep breath. Her posture changed drastically. She brought her slim arms in, elbows curved, fingers pointing down in front of her. She lifted right up on her toes and spiralled off, this time rotating her ankles around each other briskly. Jaraadhrin stared at her in amazement. That was not what he instructed at all. It was her own unique flight, a combination of a dance pose and a martial stance.

She already knew how to fly! What a Mischievous, Royal Imp she is! He chuckled. She had him hoodwinked as well, that time. *Probably to get me to perform the fan dance! Aaashh!* He thought, rubbing his fingers against his forehead, torn between irritation and amusement.

The skirts of her robes caught the wind as it flew off of her slim, white clad legs and she lifted a great distance above Jaraadhrin, swivelling up as gracefully as a feather, in the stiff breeze. Jaraadhrin vaulted into the air after his Princess, his palm outstretched in case she lost height and needed to stabilize. Princess Saffrodel squealed with excitement, repositioning her arms on either side, palms up to end the spin and slide into a glide. She performed the manoeuvre immaculately and soared away from him, giggling at his face.

'Wait Princess, not too fast. You could lose the wind' Jaraadhrin called after her, still chuckling as he flew around her, his cloaks swishing as elegantly as hers. She shook her head, her long red-gold curls and braids glinting and fluttering behind her as she twisted higher from his grasp. Jaraadhrin laughed, he remembered his first flight. It was exhilarating. Princess Saffrodel landed lightly on his palm with the toes of one foot, the other bent behind the crook of her knee, sleeves flying in the stiff breeze.

'Catch me if you can.' She chirped as she jumped off again. Higher and higher she spun and Jaraadhrin followed her, soaring around and around, under his gliding Princess. Every so often she would land on his palm, in her one-foot posture and fly off. Pink petals spun off the nearby trees caught in the winds of their flight as they whirled around each other, laughing and chuckling at the game it had become.

They were almost at the King's terrace and Queen Debriar glanced up at the sounds of mirth. She stood up in amazement and walked to the edge of the terrace. She stared at them, swirling around each other, robes and hair sweeping around them, like clouds caught in the winds. She shook her head, tapping her fingers on the banister. It had been mere moments since she left them! She laughed. Nothing was impossible for Shimrans in a Crossfire as long as they had each other. It was the oldest and purest form of Shimran magic.

Jaraadhrin saw his Queen gazing at them, signalled his Princess to alight as he landed on the terrace. Princess Saffrodel whirled in a final circlet before alighting but instead of landing gracefully on the terrace, she slid down on to Jaraadhrin left shoulder, her little hand circling his head and holding on to his right ear.

'Ahem.... Princess' Jaraadhrin cleared his throat, awkwardly.

'What? I want to fly again' Princess Saffrodel grumbled. 'You promised to come with me to the clearing to watch the soldiers training' she frowned.

'And he shall' said Queen Debriar, her laughter ringing over the terrace at his discomfort and her daughter's frolics. 'A shimratzar always keeps his word no matter what. Well done, my darling' she said to the Princess. Queen Debriar nodded at him. 'Jaraadhrin' He inclined his head to his Queen and turned to face the little Princess on his shoulder. He made a face and pulled her hand off his ear with an 'Aaashh!' of mock distress.

'Come then Princess' he held up his palm. Princess Saffrodel giggled with glee, stood up, twirled a couple of times down his shoulder, over his extended arm to his upturned palm and dived off of it nimbly. Jaraadhrin soared after her, shaking his head at her antics.

Lethal Shifts of Royalty

They made their way to the clearing where the soldiers were still training. They sank to their knees in salutation, excited to see their Princess and their Lord re-joining them. This was the Princess's first visit and everyone gazed at them eagerly, gathering forward to get a better view.

'Long live, Princess Saffrodel' They cheered her, shooting colourful hearts and flowers into the air from their centients. Jaraadhrin alighted at the top pedestal and his Princess flew down promptly on to his shoulder again, light as a bird, adjusting her skirts around her and crossing her ankles in a decorous manner.

'Princess, you should probably stand beside me on the ground' Jaraadhrin whispered. She shook her head vehemently.

'No! I am not getting my new, pink robes dirty.' she retorted, turning up her little button nose to the sky and folding her arms in front of her. Jaraadhrin rolled his eyes. The Princess acted so amusingly impish at times, that he had much difficulty keeping a straight face. The Shimran soldiers especially the tzars, chuckled while the shimaras gazed at Princess Saffrodel affectionately. Some even clasped their hands below their chins, making soft sounds of adoration.

Princess Saffrodel waved at them. She placed her hands palm on palm over her left shoulder then touched the tips of all her fingers of both her little hands to her lips, placed them over her eyes and waved them at the soldiers! The shimaras nearly melted to puddles around them as they applauded her, loud and awed. Jaraadhrin gazed at her in respect and mirth.

My Princess is already in love with the Shimran folk, she will one day swear to protect. That gesture is heartfelt, grown up and a very Royal one indeed! She is delightfully adorable too. She is the Shimrans' Princess!

Shimling childhood flashed so fast that most Shimrans cherished every moment of their youngling's infancy. They were ferociously protective of theirs and each other's shimlings, especially the tzars. Jaraadhrin stood tall and straight, gazing sternly at his soldiers while his Princess wiggled around in excitement as she sat on his shoulder, looking around everywhere at once.

Quinzafoor was fighting against two tzars at the far end of the clearing, back to his ornate, double daggers again. He inclined his head quickly in their direction between blocks and blows. He continued to fight as the tzars attacked him ferociously. They were trying to defeat him with this chance as he was distracted by the presence of his Lord and the Princess. His ornate, gold clips flashed in the sun, on either side of his head as he spun around them.

Princess Saffrodel watched him with an air of disdain as he fought, deft and light-footed. Quinn's locks and the therin of his robes, whipped about him as he swirled around his opponents with ease. His movements emanated a certain laziness that was both endearing and annoying.

'Humph! What a show-off, it's a disgrace really' she griped. Quinzafoor threw back his head, exploding with mirth, his eyes blazing auburn behind his blindfold. Jaraadhrin swallowed a burst of laughter himself, fighting to keep his face straight and stern, wondering what other silent admonishments, Quinn had heard in her head.

'I thought so too Princess, initially but he is actually quite good with his martial skill. I do have a hard time winning against him.' Princess Saffrodel huffed again, turning away from him in scorn. He glanced at her questioningly, surprised. 'What has made you so annoyed, Princess?' Jaraadhrin inquired.

'You won't defeat him, Dhrin!' she declared, gazing into his eyes. 'You can but you won't. You are too soft with him. You are all paternal and odd with him!' Quinzafoor roared, nearly being guillotined by a swishing sword. The crowd gave a collective gasp. Jaraadhrin choked back his mirth, concerned for Quinn's wellbeing.

Concentrate Quinn! You senseless tzar! Jaraadhrin thought sternly. *Stay out of the Princess's head and try keep your own on your neck!*

Quinn nodded, almost doubling up with his hilarity. His dimples looked permanently etched in, unable to control his infectious laughter. He twirled his daggers around the offensive sword that had attacked him and sent it flying between the trees. The tzar whose sword it was, grumbled and flew off after it, leaving Quinn to fight with the other. He turned to them quickly, exaggerating a low bow.

'As you command .... My Princess....' he chortled before turning back to block the other tzar.

'Hmmmm.... The nerve of him!' she scoffed again. Jaraadhrin stared at the Princess, keeping his face straight with difficulty. It looked as if she and Quinn were having some sort of mental bickering! She shook her head. His face sobered as he remembered her words. How long had she been watching him practice so early in the mornings? How did she know of his protectiveness for Quinn? Not exactly to the exaggerated extent she had just mentioned but still...? She smiled suddenly.

'You are the only one who can beat him, you know' Jaraadhrin frowned. Hadn't his father said something along these lines once? He shook himself. The more time he spent with her today, the more astute and perceptive she was.

'Time to go Princess, it's time for some food' he said, preoccupied. He nodded to his soldiers and leapt in the air at the same time as his Princess. They left the cheering soldiers and the still snickering Quinn behind, rapidly. Jaraadhrin flew back, deep in thought. Princess Saffrodel fluttered around him, then landed suddenly on his outstretched arm as he glided towards the palace. She sat, dangling her legs and staring at him.

'He doesn't fight fair you know; he sees you coming' she remarked, her voice loud above the sound of the wind. Jaraadhrin nearly lost his balance in shock, he switched to a slow glide and stared at his Princess in disbelief. She tilted her head watching him expectantly.

'How do you know that Princess?' he mused.

'I can see his Shifrs, yours too. You can beat him but you don't want to' she grinned at him. He shook his head.

'Quinn does blindfold himself to try make it fair sometimes and I can't beat his Shifr, Princess. We are equally matched' Princess Saffrodel scoffed again, rolling her eyes at him.

'Your Shifrs are far, far superior Dhrin. You should probably put down your weapons and fight him with your Shifr like he does. He uses weapons to compliment his Shifr, without it, he wouldn't be that deadly.'

'What Shifr do I possess that can counteract such a potent one, Princess? We are just even. Quinn's Shifr and skill against mine' Jaraadhrin replied.

What is this shimling princess talking about? Did she mean what she said? Does she even understand what she is saying?

'Ah.... ah....' She disagreed, shaking her head and sending her long braids flying around her. She swung one leg over his arm to face him 'It's his skill and Shifr against your martial skill alone. Why don't you use your Essence Shifr?' he gazed at her, astonished at her understanding and intelligence.

What Essence Shifr? Did she mean the glowing auras and essences I can see with my eyes closed? Talking about Shifrs, how many had my Princess exhibited today already? He shook his head, trying to clear it and think straight.

'I would like to see you win someday, Dhrin' she said, widening her eyes in earnest. 'Till then, I will not fly down there with you again' Her green eyes and button nose wrinkled into a smile and she sailed off suddenly with a 'Race you to the palace!' Jaraadhrin shook his head, chuckling and stunned as he sped after her. She was suddenly so serious and mature and then the next moment, the adorable little shimling she is.

They descended lightly on the terrace and Princess Saffrodel slid back on to his shoulder again, legs dangling on the side of his chest. It was becoming a frequent action for her. That was thrice in the space of a very short time.

'Princess, you need to go with them and have something to eat.' Jaraadhrin said sternly as the servers approached to take her way. 'You have been working very hard and have mastered flight. That would have made you ravenous' Princess Saffrodel sighed.

'Will you come earlier tomorrow, Dhrin?' he nodded, eyes softening.

'Nothing can stop me Princess' he replied, his voice quiet and gentle.

'What about Quinzafoor?' She demanded with a grimace. Jaraadhrin's laugh reverberated off the terrace.

'You certainly disapprove of him don't you, Princess? No, indisputably not!' he said, shaking his head. His Princess beamed at him and slid off. Queen Debriar glanced up; her brows raised questioningly.

'You do not approve of Quinzafoor?' she asked with interest, Princess Saffrodel shook her head.

'He is a show-off and no one matches my Dhrin' she groused, barely audible and skipped off with the shimara who held her hand out for the Princess. She paused for a moment and turned to Jaraadhrin.

'Flight is the foundation of martial arts; I have mastered it!' She dictated. 'I want you to teach me to fight now and I want to visit the armoury to pick my weapon, early tomorrow, then practice' Queen Debriar's eyebrows nearly disappeared into her red hair as the Princess broke into a quick smile and skipped away. Jaraadhrin stared at her in awe and amazement.

That wasn't the agreement, it was the fan dance. Could she have forgotten it? But start training to fight already? He felt relieved, frustrated and annoyed at the same time. *Why the rush?*

'I see it has been quite eventful' Queen Debriar gazed at him in amusement. Jaraadhrin shook his head, sighing heavily.

'This is nothing my Queen, many Shifrs manifested today, one quite lethal and I am still trying to understand half the things, my princess has said to me, in the last few moments.' He informed her, his voice weary. Queen Debriar strode over to him, her face sobering.

'The Princess can hear over long distances on focus and I believe she can see too. She heard me down in the clearing today. She can sense the Shifrs of others, she saw through Quinn straight away. She even commented on a latent Shifr of mine that I hadn't even realised as a potent one. My father mentioned something like that a while ago.' Queen Debriar inhaled sharply.

'One of Jaraadh's Shifr is to sense Shifrs in others. So he must be right about yours. Not only has Saffrodel's Shifrs developed quickly but she is already using them with accuracy. This is unheard of and dangerous' she mused. Jaraadhrin nodded in agreement. His Queen turned away from him staring out into the horizon, her slender white hands gripped the banisters, lost in thought. 'And the lethal one?' she queried.

'I am not sure, Your Highness' Jaraadhrin answered, rather apprehensive. 'But she may have the Lightening Foot.' Queen Debriar glanced back at him in amazement.

'That's a deadly, offensive Shifr, requiring a lot of practice and could deplete her core in an instant, if not used with restraint' she grimaced 'What makes you think so, Jaraadhrin?'

'Whenever she landed on my palm during the flight glides, I felt a little jolt and she lands hard. The weight is not physical, it's her core. I had to summon my centient to counteract the weight and for protection, just in case. I am not sure still but I have heard tell, that this is how it starts' he recounted. Queen Debriar sighed.

'We may have to bring in the proficients of those Shifrs to help Saffrodel control them as well. We cannot have them rage out of control especially the Lightening Foot.' Jaraadhrin nodded, lost in thought. 'You will take her to the armoury tomorrow and help her to pick her weapon. We have to trust the Princess on somethings. The look in her eyes tells me she is ready.'

'As you command....' Jaraadhrin answered her absently, his mind elsewhere. 'My Queen...?'

'Hmmmm? She glanced at him, wondering at his tone.

'Er...is there any indication at all that, all this swiftness... is harming the Princess in anyway?' he faltered, voicing a concern that had been keeping him awake at night. His Queen flashed him a radiant smile.

'No Jaraadhrin, I have had Afra check her every morning and night. She is as healthy as she possibly can be. Do not worry yourself.' She reassured him. He was probably more worried for her daughter than she was. 'We don't see any problems arising from her actual growth, only the ability to control them as she comes into them. It's too soon but she does seem to be able to handle them, especially if she was advising you on your Shifrs.' He nodded, relieved.

Jaraadhrin alerted the armoury, regarding the Princess's intended visit in the morning as he headed to his terrace that night. It was based within the mid-tier fort walls and ran deep underground. The Metallurgy Shifr Shimrans worked within the underground caverns, detecting and excavating the many types of metals and making them into arms of all forms, for the Shimran army.

It was a relatively recent skill born of need due to the building of the citadel and after Ibreeth and Ifreeth revolted against the throne. Shimrah had never needed weapons before that, nor did they have use for martial skill. Metallurgy Shifr was considered a trade and domestic talent to help with the making of cooking utensils, jewellery, ornaments and other homeware. The Shimrans who possessed these Shifrs were initially merchants but now a few trained to specialize in weapons.

Jaraadhrin alighted lightly on his terrace, wondering what type of weapon his Princess would pick for herself the next day. It was an important, coming of age decision and he felt it was rather early. She didn't even have the height or stature for it! He sighed, her little face flashing before his eyes. The command in her voice, the authority of Royalty etched into her features, made it impossible for him to disobey his Princess.

He should probably involve Quinn soon. His shimling Princess hardly behaved like a shimling anymore. She acted so grownup at times and they needed to settle their differences quickly if he was to stay by Jaraadhrin's side in protecting the Princess. He attributed these periods of maturity to her aggressive growth and development. They still did not know how fast she advanced mentally. It had become very difficult to trace as she kept blinking in and out of her shimling self with such rapidity, like she had done today.

His father had disappeared again and Jaraadhrin had no idea when he would be able to see him. Incareth had prepared everything for him as usual and he washed, ate and changed, deep in thought. Was he being the mentor he was supposed to be for his little Princess? These days it felt more like she was mentoring him. He sighed. He had hoped to catch up on the many sleepless nights, he had spent memorising the vault maps but it didn't seem possible. His head was too full and his concerns too potent. Jaraadhrin lay down on his bed, swinging his nightrobes restlessly around him. He closed his eyes and recalled the map perfectly in all its many sheets and details. He remembered it all.

'Aaashh!....tsk ...tsk' he tutted as he turned yet again, trying get comfortable enough to fall asleep. He stared up at the elaborately carved mantle of his four-poster bed, covered in lush, gold beamed therin. His Princess's stunning, green eyes smiled down at him. He closed his eyes again, pressing them down with his long fingers, sighing. *Maybe I should just try mediating more tincture.* Jaraadhrin was about to swing his legs off the bed when the slow, soft tones of the harp sounded above him. The notes struck deep into his mind, dissipating his worries and thoughts quickly. It was very potent and worked with alarming speed. His heart calmed at the gentle melody and his thick lashed lids grew heavy over his eyes.

'Thank you, Quinzafoor....' he breathed as he slipped into peaceful dreams. The notes jarred slightly in acknowledgement. It sounded oddly like Quinn's chuckle. He had played every night since Jaraadhrin started with the maps, usually very late. *Did Quinn ever sleep? .... Maybe he didn't need to? .... Is that another part of his Shifr...?* Jaraadhrin smiled slightly, as his mind slipped to oblivion.

Healing Melodies

Quinzafoor replaced the small, flat cup back on to the low plinth, covered in food and drinks beside him. The tincture was rather strong and he cleared his throat against it. It would help muffle the loud babble of everyone's thoughts and dreams and enable him to sleep. Quinn coughed as his throat seared. He poured himself a drink quickly and downed it, eyes shut tight against the burn. The discomfort eased and he lay back against the lush cushions of his chaise, gazing up at the fading light of the sky. He sighed softly. It glowed in gentle hues of pinks, auburns and lilacs as the sun slid down the horizon.

He hummed as the breeze swept around his face, lifting the long, bronze tendrils and blowing them over his brilliant blue-green eyes. He moved slightly as he buried deeper into the cushions and the therin of his robes, slid off the chaise, in an elegant arc to the floor. He closed his eyes with a sigh against the babble of voices in his head, pushing them out of focus. They dimmed with the tincture's effects but didn't go out. Quinzafoor had never known a quiet mind but at least he was used to it.

He had laid on his terrace every night since Jaraadhrin had started studying the maps of the vaults. His bed was too comfortable to keep awake in. He had tuned in to Jaraadhrin's thoughts at regular intervals to ascertain when his Lord was ready to sleep. However, Quinn's mind had now become so attuned to his young Lord's thoughts, that it filtered him involuntarily when Jaraadhrin needed him. He had then played his harp to aid his Lord to rest and fall asleep so he had the energy for the next day.

Jaraadhrin was doing too much. He was exerting his being again and his fatigue had been almost at breaking point today. Fortunately, Quinn knew that the maps were now done and his Lord could finally get a full night's rest. He meant to unleash the complete relaxing power of his melodies tonight so Jaraadhrin would recover entirely. They would be rather potent.

The many details of the extensive sheets of the maps, flashed within his mind. Memorising them were a daunting task and he shuddered to think how much effort went into learning things the conventional way, even with the heightened intelligence of Shimran folk. He was immensely lucky in that respect. He crossed his arms over his chest snuggling down deeper. It was peaceful on his terrace and he inhaled deeply. The chaise with its cushions was still comfortable and he was already falling asleep.... maybe a quick nap....

Something soft grazed his cheek and a mild scent of fresh ocean winds, sharp and salt laden, wafted down to him. Quinzafoor's brows relaxed and his full lips curved into a slight smile. He knew and loved that scent, it belonged to the one Shimran who could sneak up on him without forewarning. A Shimran who had meditated extensively to obtain such control of his own mind and emotions, that he could empty it to silence at will.

'My Lord...' he murmured as he opened his eyes to gaze deep within the glittering blue brightness of his adopted father's. Lord Jaraadh grinned down at him from behind the chaise he lay on, his arms folded over the top of it and leaning towards him as the bronze locks at his temples, hung down to Quinn's face. He brushed them away and slid upright as Lord Jaraadh chuckled and took a seat before him. Quinn stood up with a quick salute and poured him a drink. His Lord's visit was always much welcomed.

'You look rather spent, son' he observed as he sipped from his cup, his long fingers curving around it gracefully. He tilted his head. Quinn grinned as he settled back on his chaise.

'I have been helping Lord Jaraadhrin to rest, he has been exerting himself again' he replied. His adopted father raised his brow at him from above his cup.

'Hmmm... hmm, by forfeiting your own rest? Jaraadhrin is not a shimling, you know. He should be able to fall asleep without your lullabies.' Quinn chortled at his Lord's words.

'I am not too sure if that's true, my Lord. He is a handful and has no sense of his own being or self-preservation.' Quinn's face mellowed to admiration. 'His fidelity to everyone and everything is greater than to his own being.' He ended in a quieter tone.

'As is yours to him....' Lord Jaraadh added, his eyes tender. Quinn smiled as his Lord replaced his cup and stood up with a sigh. He strode over and behind him, facing the long bronze locks at the back of Quinn's head. He ran his fingers through his silky tresses and Quinn closed his eyes at his Lord's touch.

'You need to be strong in yourself to support him, Quinn. If Jaraadhrin is wrong then you are making the same mistake. You need your strength first to strengthen others. Keep that in mind, my son.' Lord Jaraadh gathered his locks behind him into one thick tuft at the nape of his neck and held it in place with a sliver of his centient. 'Have you taken the tincture tonight?' he asked. Quinn nodded, his mind peaceful. His Lord had a very calming, cool blue aura that enveloped and relaxed him. The absence of senseless chatter within Lord Jaraadh's mind, also helped.

His Lord slid the gold clips off the sides of his head, again dulled to almost a dirt colour, with the power of Quinn's mind and placed them on the cushion beside him. He slipped a couple of black Siyan clips, similar to the ones he had just removed, off his ribbon. He expanded them and tapped Quinn's shoulder with them. Quinn sighed and turned to glance at the reason for the tap. His eyes widened as he gazed in amazement at the glinting black clips in his Lord's hand. He took them with reverence and examined them with awe.

They were very similar to his own but much more ornamental and magnificently decorated with thin silver lines of Gumoos. They glittered and sparkled in the fading light and the curving lines of the design, flowed sophisticated and elegant within his hands. The edges were studded with brilliant silver jewels that flashed iridescent as the light caught it. The face of a silver dragon snarled at him from the middle of each clip. It matched the dragons of his daggers exactly. They looked very Princely indeed, fit for Royalty. Lord Jaraadh chuckled at his expression.

'Yes, I thought you would like them. I know your love for exquisite workmanship in your accessories, not unlike that other, rather particular son of mine. Its time you had a spare with all the power you have been expending. I did warn you that you Altheen clips may dull. I noticed that they were indeed dimming, that day when you tended to me...' His voice trailed. He remembered Quinn's face as he had healed him in the courtyard. It had been ashen and wrought with agony. His eyes dampened as he recalled his adopted son's anguish at his state of weakness, when he had arrived at the citadel with his King.

'These are magnificent. How can I thank you, my Lord...?' Quinzafoor whispered, his voice breaking with emotion. Lord Jaraadh plucked the clips from his hands and slid them on either side of his temples, gentle but firm, deep into his locks.

'And it is also about time, you started calling me, father...!' he retorted as Quinn broke Into a chuckle. He undid the centient bind at the nape of his neck, letting his locks fall free again. He ran his hand through them to straighten them out, placed then on either side, over the clips and kissed the top of his head.

He moved back around to face his adopted son, swishing some water out of the large flask nearby and into the air with his centient. He glazed it into a much-detailed, icy mirror in front of Quinn so he could admire his new clips.

'Well? What do you think?' inquired Lord Jaraadh, his brow raised. Quinza-foor glanced at the makeshift mirror in admiration. It reflected him perfectly but he wasn't looking at his reflection. The detailing on the mirror was exactly the same as his clips and ran all around the rim of it. He shook his head, grinning.

'...and the Princess and Lord Jaraadhrin think that I am the show-off?' he jested, his Lord could have just summoned a mirror from within his chambers behind him. He didn't have to glaze a mirror from water and it certainly didn't need to be that ornamental. His adoptive father laughed as he dissolved the mirror back into water and slid it into the flask. Quinn's mirth died suddenly as his eyes glazed auburn for a moment. His hand slid to his temple, inadvertently.

'Aaashh!....tsk ...tsk' Jaraadhrin murmured in a soft hum within Quinn's mind. *Maybe I should just try mediating more tincture.*

Lord Jaraadh shook his head and sighed.

'Is it your shimling's bedtime then? Time for you to coo him to sleep, I suppose.' he snorted as Quinn reddened. His adopted father was so attuned to him that he knew Quinn's every involuntary move. He swept over to him and placed his hand briefly against his adopted son's face, on his way out. 'Well, goodnight son. Make sure you rest too.' Quinn nodded with a quick a salute, his eyes moist as he watched his Lord leave, still chortling at his ridiculous sons. His visits brought back the one thing Quinn missed, more than anything else – the caring warmth and love of family.

He sighed and drew his harp from within his ribbons. He lay back on the chaise, balancing it against his midriff and arm. The soft breeze caught his hair and cloaks and swirled it around him. He closed his eyes as he slid his fingers across the strings, blazing auburn to amply the tunes over the palace. A soft sigh blew through his head as Jaraadhrin's silver mind, slipped to peace.

'*Thank you, Quinzafoor....*'

Quinn's finger snagged on a string as a sudden chuckle burst out of him. Lord Jaraadh's words flashed through his mind.

'Jaraadhrin is not a shimling, you know. He should be able to asleep without your lullabies'

The Cryslis Blossoms

Jaraadhrin jumped out of bed at the crack of dawn, well rested and bursting with energy. He dressed quickly, summoned an early breakfast as he wondered about Quinn. He was probably still asleep. He could hardly eat as he stared at the brightening dawn on his terrace. It was already quite warm and it was such a waste to spend it underground in the caverns. With luck, they would be able to finish up as soon as possible and head back out while the warmth prevailed.

He flew off towards his Princess, streaking through the beams of light, breaking between the clouds. It shone off his Lord Protector Alaqwa, held securely to his wavy hair by the silver centient bind as usual. It still wouldn't stay put without it! He landed on the King's terrace with his usual grace. Princess Saffrodel stood by the banister, smiling up at him as he landed. She wore pale blue robes like his own but over a tunic like the shimaras of the Martial Forces, usually wore. Her hair braided in intricate detail and high on her head, made her look taller. Her usual tiara glistened against the red gold of her hair.

'My Princess' Jaraadhrin sank into a quick salute.

'Dhrin. You are here early' She skipped over to him grinning and threw her arms around his neck, hugging him as she usually did when he sank into a salute. She took care not to pull his waves or dislodge his Alaqwa this time.

'I promised, my Princess.' He chuckled at her joy at the sight of him. Princess Saffrodel let go of him rather quickly, clearing her throat. She shot a sparkling, iridescent yishin back into the citadel.

'Would you summon Quinzafoor for me please? He may not recognise my yishin.' She requested, in rather a formal tone. Jaraadhrin stared at her in amazement.

My Princess wants Quinn here. Why? Was he supposed to accompany them? Of course, Quinn would recognise her yishin! There was no doubt of that!

'Er...Quinn?' he began as a shimara sailed in with another tiara in her hands. It was even more intricately shaped, made of Altheen, a metal that glowed a glittery gold. It had a large, heart-shaped stone in the middle with two dragons encasing it on either side, their wings spread high. The long chains hung down ending in little tear shaped jewels around her. The shimara swapped the tiaras on her Princess's head with deftness and pinned it down neatly.

Princess Saffrodel raised her right hand adjusting the tiara as the shimara worked with it. Jaraadhrin noticed a large ring on her middle finger. She wore the Alaqain! The Ring of the Royals, identical to the one worn by her mother and father. It was imbued with the Essence of Royals and can only be worn by a true Royal, An heir to the throne of Shimrah. The heir stones embedded within it would immobilise any unworthy to wear them. It allowed to focus those Shifrs reserved for Royalty and had a multitude of hidden practical uses, known only to them. It was usually presented at a lavish ceremony at the time of an ascend to the throne but here she was, wearing it already. He shook his head. Everything was rushed with his Princess!

The ring was exquisite. The dragon Alaq in gold Altheen, its body coiled all the way around her finger in five rings, dotted with its many wings and legs, swept snug around it. Its head with the heir stones, glistening within its horn and eyes, lay at the base of Princess Saffrodel's, slender little finger. The tail fanned on the tip of her nail in a gentle embrace. It was incredibly flexible and bent gracefully with her as she positioned her tiara.

Alaq snarled up at him! It looked like this particular dragon held some personal vendetta against him. It always snarled at him! From his dragon clip – Alaqwa, the medallion – Alaqath and now the Alaqain! Jaraadhrin sighed. His Princess looked up at him questioningly, raising a brow as he hesitated.

'Er...Yes, Princess' he said, smiling at her expression and bolted a yishin promptly. He was supposed to summon Quinn and he had almost forgotten as he stared at the Alaqain. Quinzafoor soared down in front of them within moments, sinking to a salute before his princess, blindfolded and eyes blazing behind it. He stayed down on his bent knee, waiting for his Princess to raise him. Jaraadhrin realised this was Quinn's first summon from a Royal. He frowned slightly.

What was Quinn doing blindfolded and eyes blazing, this early in the morning? Who was he fighting with? Why did he look rather apprehensive? He had glanced at the clearing on his way to the Princess. It had been empty. Quinn took no notice of him but held his salute, his face level with her. She stepped towards him, adjusting her tiara and gazed at the auburn blaze. Quinn's brow tensed, confusion clouding his fair face. Princess Saffrodel nodded.

'Have you anything to say to me, Quinzafoor?' She inquired, her voice gentle. Jaraadhrin stared in surprise at her tone.

What was going on? Quinn shook his head, almost as if he was clearing it, than as a response to her question.

'My Princess.... I was summoned...?' he whispered, confusion evident in his voice. Princess Saffrodel smiled at him, her face radiant.

'Rise Quinzafoor. You will accompany us to the armoury today.' She said. He rose slowly as she turned away from them, facing the many tiers. Jaraadhrin glanced at him.

What on Shimrah....? Quinn shook his head quickly before his question formed. Jaraadhrin sighed, turning to his Princess.

'Well Princess, let's be off then. If it pleases you....' he said, formal in his exasperation and holding out his palm for her to jump off of as she always did. She glanced up at him rather annoyed, her gaze dropped to his hand. She smiled up at him suddenly, dazzling him for a moment.

'What would I jump off of, if you weren't there, Dhrin?' She trilled, pirouetting up on the banister and soaring away from him as her cloaks fluttered around in a circlet, behind her. The tzars looked at each other in bewilderment for a moment then launched into the air after her. Quinn exhaled sharply beside him as they flew after their Princess.

Why on Shimrah wouldn't I be there? Jaraadhrin thought in chagrin.

'I can't read the Princess....' Quinn whispered, his voice almost inaudible in the wind.

What?

'I can't hear anything from her....' he repeated louder, puzzled. Quinn touched his golden clips on either side of his head. He had swapped the black Siyan clips, Lord Jaraadh had given as he dressed that morning. He felt they were too grand for everyday wear. Jaraadhrin's eyes narrowed.

The Princess changed her tiara just before you came.... maybe....? Quinn shook his head.

'No material can stop my Shifr. Lord Jaraadh and I have tested everything.

This isn't around the Princess's head but something within it. I would guess it's a Shield Shifr.' Jaraadhrin shook his head in some annoyance at how little he knew about Quinn's Shifr.

What are the darned clips for then? Ornamental headpieces….? You didn't strike me as vain…just a show-off but I may be wrong…! Quinn snickered at his thoughts.

'They can control the potency of others' thoughts, my Lord but I can still read anyone with them on. I need to focus more and that helps to weed out sense-less chatter. Most shimrans thoughts are rather needless. And you are quite wrong about me, my Lord… they didn't have to be this ornamental…I like decorative accessories too…. all shimrans do… not unlike your staff!'

Aaashh!!! groaned Jaraadhrin, rolling his eyes. All shimrans loved beauty and elegance whether it be a tzar or mara, though shimaras tastes were more exquisite. It was in every art. The therin of their clothes, the furniture, their architecture, their weapons, their day to day lives and in everything they said or did. It was just the way they were. They fell quiet as they followed their gliding Princess. Quinn chuckled suddenly and Jaraadhrin glanced at him in astonishment.

'The Princess has given this some thought; she saw through my Shifr at the clearing yesterday. She used some choice words to admonish me for my lazi-ness and commanded that I fight without it. She has accessed this Shield Shifr today and practiced. Summoned me to check if it works. Tsk…tsk! She is as intelligent as you say and certainly is a Mischievous Royal Little Imp!'

Quinzafoor! She is your Princess! Jaraadhrin thought sternly, amused and fight-ing back laughter.

'Pardon me, my Lord, it was your thoughts….' replied Quinn still chortling, he didn't look displeased at all, just impressed.

Exactly and I am allowed to THINK as her Mentor and Lord Protector, but you voiced…? Jaraadhrin rolled his eyes again. Quinn's mirth died suddenly in horror.

'Aaashh!!…Forgive my impudence my Lord…This does happen often…. the confusion between thought and speech… Aaashh!… I will apologize to the Princess….' he stuttered as Jaraadhrin snickered at his discomfort. It was a rare occurrence with calm, composed Quinn.

Forget it! I didn't hear anything….! Come, the Princess is too far in front!

Jaraadhrin and Quinn spun forward swiftly to either side of the Princess as she glided with ethereal grace towards the first tier. Jaraadhrin chuckled.

This mental communication with Quinn felt so natural. It needed less effort, at least on my part! I could just let Quinn do all the talking! He thought mischievously. Quinn snorted beside him, shaking his head and sending his brilliant bronze locks flying.

The soldiers on the fort walls cheered as they approached, shooting sparks and dust from their centients. The palace was still on high alert and the soldiers changed after long shifts. They looked tired as they had been standing guard all night but nothing could mar their happiness as they caught sight of their little Princess. She was much adored by inhabitants and the Martial Forces alike and they thrilled at the sight of her. It wasn't often that she left the citadel and when she did, it always caused a stir. A few hearts burst into the early morning sky, from the tier they were approaching.

Jaraadhrin and Quinn nearly crashed into their Princess in mid-air as she swerved and suspended herself suddenly, frowning at the tier. They pulled up behind her with gasps. She turned, smiling at them apologetically before twisting back to frown at the tier full of rejoicing Shimrans.

'Aaashh! Why do they do that? Why waste their centients like that? That's the collective energies of at least a century over the tiers!' She reproached. The tzars behind her, grinned.

'They adore you Princess; it's how they show it!' murmured Jaraadhrin, his voice tender as he glanced at the offending tier.

'It's one of the drawbacks of being a Princess, I suppose...?' Quinn supplied impishly. His Princess flashed him an annoyed look.

'You will inform them that I forbid it in my presence, in the future!' she commanded. Quinn chuckled as Jaraadhrin watched her little face with affection.

She is so considerate for a shimling!

'I cannot, my Princess, that is the main force. They are under Lord Jaraadh's command. There are inhabitants too' he replied. He quietened as he realised she was serious. Princess Saffrodel turned to face Jaraadhrin.

'Then you will inform your father of my wishes and stop this needless waste of Shimran centients!' she spoke to him in softer tones than those she used for Quinn but the authority in her tone was clear. He inclined his head.

'It is an age-old tradition, my Princess....' Jaraadhrin began. She waved her hand dismissively at him.

'I cannot speak for my parents' or ancestors and there are other ways to show one's devotion and fidelity! Less wasteful ways' she insisted.

Quinn made a soft noise that sounded very much like 'Aaashh!'. He was still very young and without any bond to the Princess, felt quite exasperated at her demands. He didn't have Jaraadhrin's immense patience for her and didn't know her well enough to understand her. Jaraadhrin frowned, warning him mentally. Quinn cleared his throat.

'How so Princess...?' he inquired, traces of disapproval still evident in his voice. She flashed him a glare and looked around her. Jaraadhrin sighed. How was he ever going to get them to sort out their differences? This was going to take a lot of work. How was he supposed to discharge his duties to the Princess effectively, if they annoyed each other so? How would he protect Quinn and train him? His Princess glanced into his eyes momentarily, twinkling at him and nodded.

'Send a yishin to all the tiers Dhrin, inform them of my wishes, not as an order. Let's see what happens.' She instructed him and pointed to an impenetrable growth of iridescent flowers growing thick and lush, along the banks of the Silverstreams. It stretched on both sides of the rivers and through the tiers. Jaraadhrin blinked in confusion as he bolted the yishins off and followed her finger.

The Cryslis blossoms were rather large flowers with transparent, glass like petals which scattered in to a million colours as the lights caught it. They held a small amount of energy which dissipated and absorbed into whoever touched them. The blooms disappeared in a haze as they released their centient and regrew back immediately. The lands by the Silverstreams were often referred to as healing grounds where Shimrans went to lay in, to replenish their cores and centients or just when they felt they needed to relax.

Princess Saffrodel dived down, signalling the tzars to follow her. She righted herself a few spaces above the thickly growing flowers, skimming along them. She used her centient to sever almost a whole field just below their heads and gathered them effortlessly above her. She lifted the massive field of flowers, swirling her fingers as she flashed to the first end turret, which housed the shield-maras for that tier. The blossom regrew immediately down in the fields as she sped past them.

The tzars exchanged stunned looks but quickly followed her example, gathering the flowers above them in large spirals and following her. Princess Saffrodel hovered high over the turret, she circled her hand forming a ring and flung them forward in a curve. The blossoms above her gathered in a large sphere, mimicking her movements and then rolled along swiftly, high above the tier wall and all the way to the other end. It rained the flowers down on the shimrans below, infusing them with its energies as it fell on them and refreshing their tired cores. The tier roared with awed cheers and the shimrans pirouetted up, waving and saluting in her direction. Not a single speck of centient dust shot in the air.

Princess Saffrodel smiled and nodded with satisfaction, directing her tzars to follow her example with the second and third tiers. They obliged, dumbstruck. Jaraadhrin, tender and affectionate, his face lifted in a smile of devotion. Quinn, grinning in admiration and respect at his Princess's ingenuity. Not only had she saved a hundred centient years but also added almost the same amount to the Shimrans below! Princess Saffrodel turned to face Quinn as he re-joined her and instructed haughtily.

'Inform the shield-maras to do that when I cross tiers. That would be my welcome. I will give, not take! I am sure you can instruct them'. Quinn's expression changed swiftly to exasperation as Jaraadhrin snorted with laughter. She smiled at her Lord Protector, her little face radiant with mischief as she taunted poor Quinn. He shot the yishins, shaking his head in annoyance at them.

They made their way over the cheering masses below, soaring over the tiers as the shield maras followed their Princess's instructions with immaculate accuracy. They gathered the Cryslis blooms and rained their tier walls in rolling spheres as she flew over each of them and the Shimrans below deafened them with their cheers. Jaraadhrin followed behind his gliding Princess still chuckling as Quinn glared blazing daggers at him, evident, even with his thin therin blindfold.

Blood, Blade and Bonds

They alighted on the walls of fifth tier whose fortresses housed the massive armouries. Their soldiers fell to their knees in salutation as they moved between them. Princess Saffrodel raised them elegantly with her little hands as she passed between the long line of kneeling, admiring Shimrans. They clapped as they rose, still cheering her resourcefulness with the blossoms. She was immensely popular.

A shimara raised a bunch of pretty pink flowers towards her Princess, her face beaming devotedly in admiration. Princess Saffrodel smiled at her, touched the shimara's face delicately to raise her and accepted the flowers with the same hand! All without any interruption in her elegant float towards the armoury entrance. Jaraadhrin inhaled, shaking his head. Words eluded him as he attempted to describe his Princess's grace and mannerisms.

The large doors to the armoury required three Water Shifr Shimrans to open, by placing three specifically shaped, ornate chips of ice, within the three slots simultaneously. They moved to open the door to the armoury as their Princess and Lords approached. Princess Saffrodel waved them away and studied the little slots intently. She stepped back, fashioning the three crystals with precision and forced them into the slots at the same time. The door clanked and clicked as the locks unbolted from within and they swung wide open. The soldiers clapped with admiration behind them.

Quinn rolled his eyes, sighing in vexation. The Princess was a Royal, she could open any boggling door in the citadel! Why was it so special? And she called him a show-off? Jaraadhrin glanced at him as he sighed, his irritation apparent in his usually merry face. He couldn't read Quinn's thoughts but the expressions were clear enough!

Did you just insult my Princess by calling her a show-off? He thought. Quinn groaned in frustration. Today was annoying him no end!

Princess Saffrodel giggled in front of them, a sweet shimling sound as she beckoned them in. They made their way down the long winding stairs, lighting the torches with their centients as they went.

'Aaashh! Stairs! So ungainly to navigate in robes!' Princess Saffrodel complained comically as she lifted a few spaces above and glided down them, held up by her centient. Jaraadhrin slid his hand over and down his face, pressing the back of it to his full lips. He had a hard time remaining stern and serious today. He was falling over himself laughing at her antics, both when she acted like shimling and mature. Seeing Quinn irritated and flustered wasn't helping either!

The stairs opened into deep, echoing caves under the citadel. They were natural formations but they had been used to mine for metals which were buried deep within them. The lands beside the Silverstream and Crystal Lake were bountiful in metals. They could hear Shimrans bustling around and wooshes of flames and water as they approached. It was very quiet for an armoury and weaponry. There were no loud sounds at all. They passed many empty caves with large holes in the ground, burrowed deep within its dirt floors. The earth was cracked and gashed open. They were spent caves where all possible metals have been mined from. They were abandoned. Princess Saffrodel stopped by one such cavern, frowning.

'Why aren't these holes closed off once they are done with it? Summon the head of weaponry, please Quinzafoor and someone with the Metallurgy Shifr as well.' Quinn saluted and sent a quick yishin. Jaraadhrin noticed that his Princes addressed most of her commands to Quinn than himself, even though he had more authority as her Lord Protector. He wondered why? Was his Princess still drilling Quinn for his daring hilarity at the clearing? He shook his head. Princess Saffrodel was not malicious, she had some other ulterior motive. A tzar joined them, sinking into a salute.

'Your Highness...?' he straightened and nodded at Jaraadhrin as Quinn introduced him.

'This is Dalfique, the head of weaponry and he also possesses the Shifr of Metallurgy' Princess Saffrodel glanced at him then waved her hand towards the spent cave.

'Why are these holes not closed off and these caves abandoned? Why have you not used them for something else? This is rather a waste of limited space under the citadel.' She inquired.

'They are spent and they have no more metals in them, Princess' Dalfique replied with respect. 'The caves down here are also extensive and leaving them in this state helps us distinguish them from the ones we haven't mined.' His

Princess frowned, shaking her head.

'That isn't....' she paused 'Show me around the entire place' she commanded. Jaraadhrin sighed behind her, that would take the whole day.

So much for finishing up and enjoying the sunshine. This is rapidly turning into an inspection tour than a weapon choosing. Dalfique bowed and led the way through the maze of caves. They passed many abandoned ones before they reached the main workplaces.

This cavern was very large in proportions indeed. It was also well lighted and had long tables of a glimmering black metal, all around and spaced evenly within the middle. They were probably made of Siyan, one of the most durable metal combinations of Shimrah. They were often used for homeware, kitchenware and furniture. One whole side of the cavern held large, black Siyan racks, stacked high with swords, shields, spears, staffs, daggers, bows, quivers full of arrows and every other kind of weapon imaginable.

The supple and elegant armour of the Shimran Martial Forces, flashed smartly in the dim light of the caves. They were made by infusing the colourless liquid therilium from the Therin Shifr shimrans with the metal itself, usually the Elmas, that gave them the almost liquid like movement and flexibility. Completely compliant and so strong that very few things can penetrate it.

Shimrans moved from table to table in various stages of weapon making as per their Shifrs. Caves led out of them, stretching for great distances around them, dark and dreary, lighted by torches. It was quiet except for the occasional clink and clatter of metal on the tables. The shimrans fell to their knees as they approached and Princess Saffrodel raised them swiftly so as not to disrupt them.

She glanced at a cave where the loudest sounds emanated, muffled by distance. She moved towards it and the tzars followed. Dalfique remained in the main cave instructing his workers to set out weapons for the Princess. They walked a short distance within the tunnels and it opened out into a cave much like the abandoned ones. But these were occupied by a few Shimrans who were extracting the metals from the earth.

Princess Saffrodel watched with interest as one particularly elegant mara, slid her hand in front of her as she walked along the far end, her fingers moving almost imperceptibly and eyes closed. She stopped at a specific spot, drew a sharp breath and swirled her hand gracefully over it. She lifted her upturned hand, fingers curled and above her waist in a gentle curve.

The earth at her feet ripped and gashes appeared around it in large, loud slits. She lifted away from the cracking ground, suspending herself in the air with her centient as they gashed deeper. Glimmering specs of dust and nuggets of the metal rose through them. They swirled in mid-air, siphoning off impurities and combined to a solid sphere as she circled her palms around and around them. She caught the globe within her hands and turned, facing them as she made her way out. The shimara was stunning and her robes immaculate even though she worked with the dirt all day. She froze, flushed red and sank in salutation. Princess Saffrodel smiled at her and raised her with an elegant wave of her little hand.

'That was very accomplished' she complimented. 'What would you do with it now?' The shimara bowed again and swished her hands around the sphere, suspending it between them. She slid her hands apart in a sudden motion as if she was releasing an arrow from a bow. The sphere rolled and liquified. It spun quickly as it elongated within her skilled hands. She twisted the wrist at her face, sharply. The spinning glob of metal fashioned itself into a brilliant silver staff, two pronged at the top with an ornate, circular head and long, embossed handle. Not too detailed and rather hazily designed but almost exactly the same as Jaraadhrin's staff! The shimara pursed her lips, blushing. She caught it deftly as it finished forming and twirled it with astonishing speed within her fingers, glancing covertly at Jaraadhrin between the twirls.

Princess Saffrodel giggled as Quinn snickered beside her, both shooting teasing glances at him. Jaraadhrin stared at the mara, the colour rising in his cheeks. He recognised her. She was one of the warriors from the clearing and she had sought his interest at least twice before. He cleared his throat, turning away hurriedly.

Aaashh! And in front of the shimling Princess too! How asinine! These accessory verbiages were so annoying. How many darned times do I have to tell them!

'Ahem....Princess maybe we should head back....? He whispered. She giggled up at him again, covering her lips delicately with her fingers. His Princess sobered and turned back to the shimara.

'I think you might want to try harder....' She made a slight gesture towards the staff '.... With the staff making I mean....' she said to the mara seriously as she turned away to follow them. Quinn howled with laughter, glancing down at his Princess and she twinkled up at him, sharing his moment of mirth. She had an amazing sense of humour, was very witty and still acted dignified. He couldn't but admire his little Princess. The shimara behind them giggled bashfully and Jaraadhrin shook his head in irritation at the lot of them. He swept away in front, red faced and his robes swishing around in the aura of his annoyance.

How many times do I have to show them that I am not interested! Aaashh! This happens every time I train my warrior shimaras at the clearing. There is always one or two who twirl their confounded weapons in the absolutely irritating lingos' of their many and widely, varied accessories! I cannot exactly feign ignorance either as I am supposed to be a master in them.

The privileges of a shimara were rather biased compared to the tzars. Shimaras were allowed to express their interest as many times and in any way, they wanted to. The tzars never asked more than once and they waited as long as it took for their interests to make up their minds. Tzars didn't fall for maras easily and once they did, it was for life. Once a tzar felt inclined to a particular shimara, they would do anything and everything for them. Protecting them, guiding them, just being there for them, even sacrificing themselves for their shimaras honour and lives.

The shimaras usually agreed at the end. Such bonds didn't form flippantly, shimaras knew it well and they were always true to it. They were just very careful and took time to accept their tzar. He knew many of his own soldiers waited for their shimaras, having asked just once. He chuckled. Tzars were just made that way. He probably wouldn't ask even once, if he felt the shimara wasn't interested. He had still to find one that interested him. Shimran bonds were permanent and sacred and the tzars took it very seriously indeed.

Quinn and his Princess followed him, still giggling away together. As they approached the opening, her expression turned thoughtful.

'Is that a regular occurrence down in the clearing....?' She wondered aloud.

'Oh yes, Princess. Lord Jaraadhrin is immensely popular with the shimaras....? He replied still chortling but trailed off as he glanced down at her face. He frowned.

What was she thinking? Why was she so serious all of a sudden? He couldn't read her and her expression let nothing on. He hated being this blind! She glanced up at him, smiling again and quickened her pace as they followed Jaraadhrin.

They caught up with him some ways away. He was still rather pink around his cheeks. They passed another low, tight cave that had a flurry of activity within. Princess Saffrodel stepped into it as they passed and the tzars backtracked to accompany her.

The cave was full of swishing sounds and a few shimrans moved gracefully around the rapidly growing trees. They were the Woodland Shifr shimrans who could control any material that came from a tree. They grew long shoots of green stems which layered in darker and darker sheets till they were a deep brown. The branches and leaves grazed the low cave and rustled against the stone ceiling. The shimrans rapidly sliced up the trunks into desired shapes and lengths and stacked them against the side with their centients. They separated the leaves and branches into piles. More shimrans moved the neatly segmented pieces via another tunnel back to the main weaponry room. Others transported the leaves and branches to other parts.

The shimrans used their centients forces a lot which is why all of them had such delicate figures and soft hands. There was no need to physically lift anything. Centient energy could be used to do basic everyday activities like moving things, changing temperatures and other basic actions. Most of the work didn't take too much power. Shimrans could lift large loads without much effort as long as they had adequate centient. Most never used their cores as their centient sufficed well for their daily chores.

Princess Saffrodel frowned as she stared at the ground of the cave. The roots remained within the earth. They were not being used to make anything but remained embedded in the dirt while the shimrans set to work, growing new trees from them again.

She shook her head. She knew warfare was relatively new to Shimrah but while there was a lot learned in the fairly short period of time, more could have been done in the many wider and complimenting areas. Most of the emphasis was placed on learning to fight. Shimran martial skills were lethal and they couldn't even defeat each other without very tiring and elongated fights. It was almost impossible when coupled with offensive Shifrs like Quinn's.

Princess Saffrodel appreciated the deadly proficiency of her Shimrans in martial arts but she still felt that there was much that could have been improved and altered to increase the efficiency of the systems already in place, that assisted that skill.

She sighed, turning back and out through the tunnels. She walked in silence, lost in thought as the tzars followed close behind her. Quinn still grinned and Jaraadhrin rolled his eyes at him. They emerged into the main cavern and Dalfique hurried over to them.

'Princess, would you like to try the weapons now?' he asked, respectfully. She nodded, moving over to the long tables on which were a multitude of weapons, laid in neat lines. She moved from one to another, picking up each, weighing them in her hands, twirling them, swishing them and flicking them. None seemed to please her. They were all exquisitely made with golden Altheen, glittery, rose Pembre, shining silver Gumoos and black Siyan inlays, set with jewels and crafted of glimmering, silver Elmas metal.

At the end of their table, shimaras minimised the finished weapons and pinned them on crimson ribbons for transport. They were the trinket ribbons which shimrans tied over their belts at the left side of their waists. Most wore one and others had a few depending on how many they needed and the number of items they carried within them.

Princess Saffrodel slid her fingers within her robes and ran her hands down the tassels of Jaraadhrin's hair, hanging at her waist. She smiled in content. Hers was so special, no one in Shimrah had one like it and her mother had told her exactly how she had come by it.

She glanced up at Jaraadhrin. He was bickering quietly with Quinn, his usually elegant, pale face, slightly tinged pink even though they had moved away from the subject of the shimara. The colour on his face made him look even more attractive. A long, wavy lock hanging by the side of his face, blew over his eyes. He moved it away delicately with his small finger, a soft tut of annoyance escaping his full lips. Principle Saffrodel giggled. Even his irritation was charming!

She sighed as she refocused on the weapons. None of them appealed to her. She slid down the table again, looking for the feather light sword with an expanding blade that she had noticed before. It was very intricately wrought silver Elmas, inlaid in shimmering rose-gold, Pembre flowers and black, Siyan vines, ferns and leaves. A small button within the handle, expanded it to nearly twice her height. She clicked it and watched the inner blade slide out swiftly. It disappeared with remarkable fluidity, within the first blade as she clicked it again.

'Excellent choice, My Princess' Jaraadhrin commended, behind her. She couldn't have chosen a better one. It was the cloaked blade of Menorak herself. The fiercest Queen in Shimran history. It was her original design. The sword hid seven secrets and only one has been discovered as yet – the expanding blade.

It will also help with my Princess's height currently as she can use the shorter blade now and the longer one later. He thought to himself with a smile. Princess Saffrodel shot him a glance and scoffed.

'I haven't decided on it but I shall probably take this as I don't like anything else.' She swung it a couple of times. It was certainly very light and shone, bright and silver. Princess Saffrodel set the pink flowers that the shimara on the parapet had given her, on the table as she scrutinised it with both hands. Quinn joined Jaraadhrin behind her and they watched intently as she examined it from every angle.

Princess Saffrodel sighed. She had to check if it was sharp enough. She drew a deep breath, infusing her finger with the century of centient, she had borrowed from the Queen that morning, just for the purpose. She coated the fair skin of her finger with the many layers of centient. She slid the index finger of her right hand quickly against the blade and it cut in deep, slicing through her century easily and spilling crimson.

'Princess....!!

'Saffrodel......!!!'

Jaraadhrin and Quinzafoor gasped, aghast and whirled to her sides. Quinn stood on one side of her, bending over to reach her hand and Jaraadhrin fell to his knees on the other, trying to grab it. She moved it away from their grasps as the blood slid down her hand and wrists, staining her blue robes. She frowned, distracted and stared into Jaraadhrin's agonised eyes, level with hers. It wasn't because he had called her by her name for the first time. It was his tone. The pain in it cut much deeper than the slice on her finger. It struck her heart, warm and cold, simultaneously. He grabbed her hand quickly. The Alaqain snarled up at him from around her middle finger.

'Aaashh! For the sake of the Crystal Depths, Princess!' Jaraadhrin trembled, his eyes and voice full of anguish. He raised her hand gently, shaking the therin off his other to heal her. Princess Saffrodel shook her head in confusion and ran a quick thumb over the long cut, on the inner length of her index finger. It healed and sealed shut with her centient.

What is all these overreactions for? This is how we test the sharpness of the weapons that we make, ever since they were invented. Nothing was more powerful than a century old Shimran centient. She thought, confused.

Jaraadhrin stared at her healed finger then into her glittering, green eyes. The agony in his, changed to outrage and disbelief as he sensed the century she had added and depleted.

How did I miss that? Have I been so busy dawdling around with Quinn, I didn't even noticed it? What an absolutely, disgraceful mentor I am! He shook his head.

'That was done on purpose...? he queried, his voice quiet. Princess Saffrodel nodded still rather confused

'Why would you even...? he began in anguish. His voice rising in exasperation.

121

'How else do you test the sharpness…' she questioned, shaking her head.

'Aaashh!' Jaraadhrin stood up swiftly in annoyance. He placed his palm on his forehead and turned away from her, exhaling in a loud gust. He gripped the belt at his waist with the other, for support.

'I don't know! Slash it at a rock or something…! He muttered still shaken and frustrated.

'That won't prove its efficacy against the Shimran centient ….' Princess Saffrodel tried to reason with him. She shook her head again, befuddled.

There was no need for so many emotions and reactions! Why did it hurt him so? It was a perfectly normal thing to do. Wasn't it? Why is my Lord Protector in so much pain and so shaken by a simple age-old blade test…?

'He means, you should have let one of us test it for you, my Princess….' Quinn interrupted quietly. He tensed, frowning against Jaraadhrin's pain, regret and torment as it flooded his mind. He placed his hand on his Lord's shoulder, squeezing it gently as he spoke. The extent of Jaraadhrin's agony surprised him. It was, after all, just a minor cut and it was how they tested swords. It almost felt like Jaraadhrin, himself had suffered a mortal injury. There must be something very strong in the Oath of a Lord Protector…

Princess Saffrodel nodded at Quinn, flicking her eyes in Jaraadhrin's direction and instructing him to stay with her Lord Protector, in silence. She could still feel the shudder of Jaraadhrin's core within her as he held her hand and watched the crimson spill down her wrist. She took a deep breath, clasping her hands behind her and turned back to Dalfique who was staring at everything in surprise and fear. He dropped his eyes as she turned.

'I will take the sword of Menorak, Dalfique. And a few changes if I may. Get the Woodland Shifr shimrans to use the abandoned caves I asked you about. They are large and cavernous, and the tree roots they grow would hold the dirt together. The height of the cave would also mean taller trees and so, more wood. The roots would help stabilise the caves under the citadel. If you continue this, it might collapse the citadel in a few hundred centuries. Do not enlarge the caves or dig more. Work within the natural formations. Make sure to use all abandoned caves in the future too' Princess Saffrodel instructed. Her orders spilled, swift and fluid as Dalfique gaped at his little Princess in surprise and shock. She was innovative and highly practical. He thought she was just a month old shimling?

'I know it might be difficult to bring them down here but you need more shimrans working too. Anyone can help with the conveyance back and forth; you don't need special Shifrs. Why are there so few even with the required Shifrs?' she inquired.

'Your highness, as you are aware, all these Shifrs were only regarded as domestic ones or for trade till very recently. The Metallurgy Shifrs for cookware, jewellery and ornaments. The Plant Shifrs for crockery, home and furniture. The Therin Shifrs for everyday clothing. There are very few who specialize into more martial fields.' Dalfique answered, his head bowed low and his voice teeming with respect.

Princess Saffrodel frowned, shaking her head thoughtfully. 'That tiny number isn't enough Dalfique, we must change with the times. Firstly, this place needs to be warmer and inviting. It is rather bare. Shimrans love beauty, they must hate working in such a bare, dank place. We infuse light into everything we touch and this place would actually darken a Shimran's moral, even their principal beings. The building of the citadel was begun five hundred years ago and the threat of the revolt emerged four hundred years ago. It should have been time enough to change over completely.' She paused for breath and glanced around.

'We live under a threat. The citadel itself is strong and we have strength in numbers of our soldiers. But we are complacent because of its protection. Without the citadel, our Shifrs and prowess means nothing! No matter. I will give this some thought and I will have my –' She glanced at Jaraadhrin and Quinn. They watched her in disbelief and amazement, Quinn's hand still on Jaraadhrin's left shoulder. She smiled at Jaraadhrin tentatively and drew a quick breath. ' – I will have Lord Jaraadh speak to you about the changes. For now, continue with variations I have advised you.' She finished.

Dalfique sank to his knee, saluting his astonishing little Princess. She raised him, gracious as ever and turned. She reached for the sword and grinned at Jaraadhrin's soft sound of warning. She looked up at him, pursing her lips in mischief. She tossed the sword smartly, caught it by the blade within two fingers, minimised it with a flourish and clipped it into her ribbon. All of which, she executed with perfect balance and precision, her eyes still on her Lord Protector's face. She made sure to keep her trinket ribbon and the tassels hidden from view. Quinn chuckled quietly as Jaraadhrin shook his head and closed his eyes with a soft sigh of exasperated amusement.

Princess Saffrodel nodded to Dalfique in parting and walked past Jaraadhrin and Quinn still gazing after her, their faces, a mixture of amazed wonder, mirth and annoyance. Jaraadhrin ran his fingers along his forehead and followed her some ways behind. Quinn turned to him.

'My Lord ...?' he queried in concern.

I am well, Quinn; I don't know what happened. The sight of all that blood on my little Princess's hand and sleeve just....

'I know...My Lord...'

Aaashh! Of all the Absurdities in Shimran History! The Princess is absolutely right. Why the dramatics?

'You couldn't help it, my Lord; it was a lot deeper than conscious thoughts and actions. It must be your Lord Protector Oath to the Princess – '

Aaashh! She must think I am irrational. Being unreasonable over a completely ordinary blade test...and however did I miss that century on her centient...? Quinn emitted a sudden chuckle.

'I can't tell you what Her Highness thinks about your irrationality... my Lord, but I couldn't see the century either until you held her hand and I read you. I do think it's her Shield Shifr. Its blocking everything about her.' Jaraadhrin's lips curved into a slight smile as he recovered his composure.

Ah yes... Thank you for confirming that I am irrational.

'Anytime, my Lord...and as often as you would like me to remind you...' Quinn drawled, his voice quiet, melodious and filled with mirth.

Jaraadhrin shook his head, snorting in amusement as they quickened their pace. Quinzafoor had a natural ability to neutralise any situation with his ever-present humour. His presence was always merry and jovial. Jaraadhrin was sure it was part of his Shifr. There was so much he still didn't know about the extent of it.

The Warrior Princess

Their Princess reached the stairs and soared round and around it, going up and through the large double doors and out into the late afternoon sun. They had been down in the caverns all morning and afternoon. No wonder they were ravenous. The soldiers had changed over and they sank into salutes as they emerged. Princess Saffrodel raised them elegantly. She sent a yishin with a careless flip of her wrist, towards the palace. With a final wave, she soared into the sky with Jaraadhrin and Quinn on either side.

The wind swept against their faces as they glided back up to the citadel at a leisurely pace. The Shield-maras rolling out the Cryslis flowers as they passed their respective tiers, amid deafening cheers. Quinn's mind whirled as he read Jaraadhrin's, reflecting the exact same turmoil as his. They were both equally impressed and bewildered by the Princess, her maturity, her antics, her innovativeness and her astuteness.

He ran through the recommendations his Princess had given to Dalfique. They made complete sense! Of course, Jaraadhrin knew her and it was not a rapid thing to digest in a short time as it was for him. His Princess was the most marvellous shimling, he had the fortune to meet. She was kind, considerate, loved her Shimrans, cared for them and was as wise as the Queen and as skilled at warfare as the King.

She was a little miracle. She wasn't the mindless little shimling he thought she was at the clearing yesterday. He frowned for a moment. Why was she shielding her thoughts from him? Why did she request his presence today? He hadn't done anything that Jaraadhrin couldn't do today. He suspected that his little Princess had an ulterior motive for summoning them together and it was still to come. A soft chuckle to his right, broke into his thoughts as he gazed after the Princess.

You are in awe of the Princess, Quinn; you finally see her through my eyes...well literally...!

Jaraadhrin grinned at him, his long locks whipping around in the wind. Quinn smiled back. His Lord may not have his Shifr but he did well enough, just by the looking at his face.

Hmmm, What a relief! Hopefully I will not need to put up with your shimling squabbles anymore! Jaraadhrin chortled.

Their Princess had already alighted on the banister of her terrace and was now gliding back and forth on the thin rails, completely at ease. Hand clasped behind her and head bowed. She looked very thoughtful and preoccupied. Jaraadhrin and Quinn soared over and landed lightly on the terrace behind her. She glanced up at them both, her lips lifted in a radiant smile.

'Will you join me for a late feast, my Shimratzars?' she said, curtsying to them. They grinned and bowed low, formal and exaggerated. Their long cloaks pooled around them and their bronze locks, fell over their shoulders as they thrilled to see her back to her shimling antics.

'If it pleases you, Your Highness!' they chuckled and she laughed at their fake formality. The table was already set in the terrace even as they spoke. It was probably why she sent the yishin ahead. It was still warm and the late afternoon glow illuminated the skies in brilliant golds, blues and pinks. They walked over and settled themselves around it. Jaraadhrin made sure his Princess was comfortable before taking a seat himself. They ate quickly, ravenous from the day's exploits. Jaraadhrin laughed and Quinn bantered as their Princess smiled at their jests. She was well at ease with them. Quinn often saw his Princess gaze, thoughtful and fond, at his Lord while he talked. The meal finished and their conversations lulled into a comfortable silence.

Princess Saffrodel reached for her drink and Jaraadhrin handed it to her. He froze suddenly as he noticed the crimson stains still on her hand and the sleeves of her robes. He replaced his glass and lifted her little hand off the table with a soft sigh. Jaraadhrin siphoned off the stains on the therin with a snap of his fingers and dipped a towel in water to wipe the ones off her skin, taking care not to touch the Alaqain. He ran a finger along the line where her cut had been. Princess Saffrodel gazed into his brilliant, blue eyes. They glittered with pain again. She blinked.

'I am sorry Dhrin...I didn't mean to....' She whispered, her voice soft and gentle. He shook his head.

'I overreacted Princess. You were right...but please do not ever harm yourself again, however slight' Jaraadhrin murmured as Quinn disappeared behind his drink. She nodded at him as he gazed back into her eyes. She withdrew her hand from him gently, tinging pink around her cheeks. She sighed, stood up and walked over to the banister.

She stood looking over at the citadels many tiers, deep in thought. Jaraadhrin and Quinn rose and moved to either side of their little princess. They could sense another spell of her maturity descending as she stood straight and tall, with her arms crossed at her waist.

'Princess, maybe you should rest? It has been rather a long day.' Jaraadhrin suggested. She shook her head.

'I am well, Dhrin' she replied. She took a deep breath as if bracing herself. 'How is Ashoora, Quinzafoor?' she queried without turning to him. Quinn bowed his head low, smiling as he thought of his beloved firehorn.

'She is well, my Princess, still rather wild but she has made the woods within the citadel, her home.' Princess Saffrodel sighed as she gripped the banisters with her little hands. She raised her head and stood taller.

'You might have to let her go soon, Quinn...' The tzars gasped at her in horrified shock. That wasn't even a possibility. Quinn had entwined with his firehorn! They were one and the same. Separating them would be akin to tearing Quinn in to two! It would cause them both much agony and heartache.

'My...my...Princess....?' Quinn stammered, his voice suddenly tremulous. His hand slid to his right shoulder instinctively defensive, and clutched it hard as it blazed auburn in reaction to his emotions and torment. It was where the Ashoora's jewel resided, embedded deep within his core and life force. The mere mention of a parting was wreaking havoc within Quinn's central being. The strength of the union of entwinement was immense and intense. His love and protectiveness for his firehorn, too profound and unfathomable to express. Icy shards erupted within his chest, piercing and sharp.

Jaraadhrin slid his hand to the small of Quinn's back, supporting him as he swayed imperceptibly. Quinn's warm, auburn essence, blazed a brilliant searing crimson within Jaraadhrin's mind and cut through his core in a flash of scorching flame. He inhaled sharply against it.

Patience, Quinzafoor! Hear the Princess out! She would never do anything to hurt a Shimran on purpose! You saw how she hated to waste something as trivial as their centients! I know it hurts but hold on!

Quinn nodded, trembling against his hand and biting his lip hard, drawing blood. If his Princess was to command him. He would have to obey it. It would rip him apart and probably kill his firehorn too. His core shivered at the thought and he drew a shuddering breath, trying to control the torment flooding his mind.

Princess Saffrodel leapt up on to the banister with a graceful whirl, turning towards them and level with Quinn's glowing blindfold. She inhaled sharply at the blaze on his shoulder and turned her gaze to his face, talking in quiet but quick and urgent tones.

'Ashoora is a wild unisus belonging to one of the strongest groups of unisi in existence – the Firehorns of the fiery Ashlands, the burning desserts of Southern Shimra. It is possible that the leaders of her herd are also known to the leaders and protectors of the other droves like the Silveroans, Gold-horns and Iceroans. I need her released so she may extend our protection and friendship to them. Shimrah is being engulfed by an unknown darkness. It is spreading from the murky ends of Southern Shimrah and we need to protect these powerful creatures.' She took a deep breath, tilting her gaze away from Quinn's ashen face as if she was unable to tolerate the agonised expression on it, anymore.

'The duty of Royals does not extend to just tzars and maras but every creature within our lands! The unisi are in much danger currently as is everyone, in all of Southern Shimrah! Their cores are light, like the Shimrans and they are immensely powerful. They might fall prey to the darkness. It might vaporise them or turn them dark. In any case they would need to be protected. We need them on our side, in the light and far away from the darkness as possible.' She blinked, then raised her eyes to his, gazing piercingly into his blazing therin blindfold.

'You and Ashoora are an example to show that shimrans could associate with them more. Only an unisus can deliver this message to their leaders as they might not look on kindly at a Shimran's interference in their herds, if we extended our assistance in person. Ashoora could relate her experience with you, Quinzafoor, and have a better chance of convincing her heads. If all Shimrans were to follow your example, it will make us stronger as we protect our unisi. We will have strength in unity, allegiance, devotion, love and the strength of Shimran pledge. Every Shimran should do what you have done. It will make protecting them easier. We divide the task effortlessly among us.' She finished with a nod. Her little face, gentle and mellow.

Jaraadhrin stared at her in incredulity. Where did this even come from? His Princess was absolutely right in every aspect that she had mentioned. He shook his head.

See Quinn, I told you…. I am pretty sure there is more descending on us….from wherever that came! Be prepared!

Princess Saffrodel raised her little hand to Quinn and he moved towards her still rather hesitant. She could still command him. Explanations didn't ease his pain. She placed it gently against the side of his face, much like the way Queen Debriar often did to Jaraadhrin. She slid her thumb against his lip, healing the cut with her centient. Her little shimling eyes glinted at him with love and compassion.

'I have seen what your firehorn can do and I have studied unisus lore. It isn't permanent, Quinzafoor. I know the bond you have and I would never inflict such pain on you unless it was absolutely necessary, for her kind and ours.' she soothed him, her voice comforting and kind, a soft breath of rain drenched spring breeze. Quinn sighed in relief, his heart lightening. The blaze on his shoulder diminished and the agony receded from his heart.

How wrong am I about my Princess! she had the gentlest, most caring heart and she loved her Shimrans - tzars, maras and beasts alike!

'This is not an order Quinzafoor and rest assured, this will never be one either. You may choose the time, whenever you are ready but I am requesting you....' Quinn fell to his knees with a strangled cry at her gracious words, nodding quickly. His heart swelled at her humility and love – a turmoil of emotions which he knew, he would never be able to express. She was a Princess, a Royal! She just needed to command him as her subject yet she treated him like he was her shimling, a brother, a friend. Her words struck too deep as he struggled to make sense of his raging centients and core.

Princess Saffrodel raised him by his chin as Jaraadhrin helped. She nodded as she blinked, rather surprised at how much her words affected this strong, young shimratzar. Jaraadhrin smiled at her, his face shining with his fondness for her as he held Quinn upright by the arm. Quinn shivered slightly, trying to regain his composure still battling against the swirling mass of his raging being. Jaraadhrin held him, he knew how disorienting that felt.

'Thank you Quinzafoor, I am grateful....' She murmured. Quinn swallowed hard, inclining his head in a salute, hand trembling at his heart. Jaraadhrin moved his palm to Quinn's back again, supporting him surreptitiously.

Princess Saffrodel blew a soft gust and shook her long braids out. She clasped her hands behind her and raised her chin high, much like Queen Debriar.

'There are many flaws in the way we think and act, my Shimratzars. We need to change before it's too late.' She said, her voice quiet and serious. They inclined their heads, listening intently. They knew by now that the Princess was no less intelligent and wise than the King or Queen. She was in fact a combination of both.

'We are gifted with much but being peaceful folk, we prefer to use our talents defensively. We never train with Shifrs, only with weapons and we have not taken any initiative to better ourselves and our Shifrs. We defend and that's all we do. That is no longer enough!' She explained.

'If I have read our Queen right, there is a lot more to this fear and uncertainty than what we know and what meets the eye. My mother is not always transparent. Some of her thoughts are hidden and they stay that way. There is something that she knows about our lands and future, that she would not disclose for some reason and I am sure she is right not to. My father, on the other hand' she paused, eyes twinkling 'is much freer with his knowledge and not that difficult to coax to divulge. But even His Majesty does not know somethings as his Queen is too protective of him.' She rolled her eyes good naturedly.

The tzars grinned at each other at the rapid changes from seriousness and mirth within her speech and expressions. Quinn still rather tremulous but recovering quickly.

Young shimaras! Highly changeable and volatile. Completely adorable though! This shimling will be the death of me one day! thought Jaraadhrin. Quinn tensed.

'Careful, my Lord, I have an inclination the Princess can read us like me....' Quinn whispered so quiet, it could have been a breath of wind. Jaraadhrin tensed, throwing him a quick glance of consternation.

You tell me this now? I think it's a bit too late!

Princess Saffrodel raised her brow at them questioningly.

'We do train to fight my Princess, we have weapons, the citadel and we do use our Shifrs as much as we can.' Quinn offered.

'For defence, defence and more defence. There is a fine line between attacking to defend and offensive training. It's simple enough. It's the mental approach.' Princess Saffrodel asserted. Jaraadhrin frowned, he had slight sense as to where this was going. She pursed her lips staring at them, thinking how best to explain.

'Quinzafoor try control Dhrin's mind to make him jump on the banister beside me.' She commanded. Quinn gazed at her in disbelief.

'My Shifr can do that, Princess?' she nodded, tapping her foot with impatience. Jaraadhrin closed his eyes, relaxing his mind with a soft chuckle.

Here we go again! You are in for a treat Quinn! Hopefully you can figure out your Shifr quicker than I have been able to.

'Try!' she repeated.

Quinzafoor closed his eyes, delving deep into Jaraadhrin's mind, trying to control it. It was a beautiful, glimmering silver as usual but now the mists dissipated effortlessly, letting him through with ease. It curved away as he approached, carving a path for him. Quinn's temples tensed and his eyes blazed brighter behind the thin, therin blindfold. They had been alight all day but now, burnt dazzling auburn with his efforts.

He pulled the clips off his head, frowning and concentrating harder. Quinn sunk even deeper till he could feel the collective mass of every tendril of the silver mist within his young Lord's being. He drew a deep breath as he requested it to move. Nothing happened. He tried again, concentrating harder and instructing the movement. Still nothing. Quinn inhaled sharply and clenched his teeth. His auburn essence fused with some the silver and he commanded the move.

Jaraadhrin took a step towards the banister and another. His eyes flew open in surprise. He was moving yet it was completely involuntary.

'Fight back, Dhrin! Use your Essence Shifr to block him!' His Princess ordered 'Take back your mind!' Jaraadhrin stared at her. He thought they were training Quinn? He closed his eyes quickly, trying find Quinn within his mind. Parts of his head glowed auburn among the silver. He concentrated, trying to disentangle his silver being from Quinn's auburn essence. A sharp slash of pain sliced through him as Quinn refused to let go. He gasped as he tried again to push Quinn's glow out of his silver being. He stepped back from the banister. Quinn huffed as he felt Jaraadhrin's backlash. The silver mists surged around him, attacking him and pushing him back brutally. He tried again, twirling the clips in his hands, faster.

Jaraadhrin gnashed his teeth against another slash of pain as he held his ground. Quinn's essence pushed further into his mind, viciously engulfing the silver with his blazing auburn flames. The soft silvers of his being, burned with icy white fire of its own as he retaliated and doused Quinn's flames in to swirling black shadow. They stood facing each other, eyes shut tight, trying to wrestle the other out.

'That's enough! Stop!' Princess Saffrodel ordered, her voice rather high. The tzars withdrew from each other, winded and breathless, hands on their heads. A dull ache split through their temples as they withdrew. They stared at her, eyes wide. Quinn replaced his clips hurriedly into his bronze locks.

'How do you feel?' she inquired anxiously; eyes tender with concern.

'Dull ache'

'Headache'

They replied, chuckling at each other. Princess Saffrodel didn't smile. She nodded, beckoning them closer. As they stepped towards her, she reached up to the sides of their faces and placed the tips of her fingers on their temples. The tzars bowed and closed their eyes as she touched them. She slid her thumb gently across each of their foreheads still holding the rest of her fingers against their temples.

Black shadow diffused out of their foreheads and coated her thumbs in a dark layer. Warmth streamed into their heads, dissipating the pain and calming their minds, from the rest of her sparkling opalescent fingers at their temples. She withdrew her hands, slower from Jaraadhrin than Quinn. Her fingers slid the length of Jaraadhrin's face tenderly, from his temple to his chin as she withdrew. The tzars snapped their eyes open in surprise as their discomfort ebbed.

'Mistress Afra…' she giggled at their unspoken question. Her little face turned grave again.

'You are in pain because you used your talents offensively. Those with offensive Shifrs need to be extra careful to stay in the Light' she flashed a quick glance at Quinn who tensed visibly. She lifted her blackened thumbs to show them and cleaned them with her centient. 'That is what happened to my darling uncles, their malicious intent made their minds dark. Their actions darkened their cores. When they used their Shifrs to act on their darkness, it tainted their cores irrevocably. Our Shifrs are an extension of our cores. How we use our Shifrs, effects our core.

'How did you –' Jaraadhrin began in admiration.

'I read a lot – 'she replied quickly, cutting him off.

'When? my Princess? Your days are –'

'I make time –'

'Then how do we practice Shifrs in an offensive manner with each other, my Princess? Would it not taint our cores?' Quinn interrupted, frowning. This was all very interesting to him and his Princess was rising higher and higher in his heart and mind, with every word she said.

'That is where your mental approach comes in, Dhrin and you were fine as long as he accepted and allowed you into his head. The moment he resisted, it caused you both pain. You can practice but with total submission to each other.' She explained patiently. 'You do need to keep in mind that if you are using your Shifrs on an enemy, it will be harder and you need complete control of your Shifrs. Our enemy will have darkness in his core and no fair Shimran can possibly be our enemy. His or her darkness will elevate your pain as long as your intentions remain righteous.'

'Quinn's is already an offensive Shifr. How does the rest of the Shimrans practice their domestic and trade Shifrs offensively...?' wondered Jaraadhrin, thinking hard. Princess Saffrodel smiled at him.

'Would you consider our centient powers offensive, Dhrin?' She asked quietly, a half-smile on her lips as she gazed into his eyes.

'Of course not...Princess'

Princess Saffrodel nodded and without looking away from his eyes, gathered her centient in a quick flip of her wrist, moved it around the large marble pillar on the right. She coated the pillar with her centient and with a swift movement, clenched her hand in to a tight fist. The pillar blasted into dust with a resonant crash!

The tzars whipped around gaping in shock at the place, the huge pillar had stood, completely obliterated and in its place was a cloud of dust. A few potted plants wobbled and teetered over the banister in the wake of the explosion. Princess Saffrodel flipped her hand rapidly, grabbed them with her centient and placed them back on the banisters.

'Oh my....' She quipped 'Mother would never forgive me if I destroyed her plants'

Jaraadhrin and Quinn turned back to her, their eyes wide in shock and their minds in an uproar at the completely different perspective of their beings. Even so they still couldn't hold back the bursts of laughter at her comical face.

'Aaashh! My Princess!' muttered Quinn 'And I am sure the Queen wouldn't mind you destroying her pillar though!' She snorted, nodding at them.

'Shimrans and their peaceful way of life has inhibited the search for the knowledge, pertaining to ourselves. We never bothered to find out how powerful we are, to the point that we accepted our talents as mundane, every-day aspects, that help us just live our lives and get by. That is not the case at all!' She took a deep breath, turning to gaze in to Jaraadhrin's eyes again.

'What are domestic and trade Shifrs, Dhrin? Woodland Shifr? Teach them to utilize anything wooden in their surroundings, to make arrows and fire them with the force of their centients. Fashion staffs and spears, set them on fire with their centient and fight in an emergency. Turn wooded places to strong holds by setting traps when and where needed.' she raised an eyebrow at Quinn.

'Water Shifr? Train those Shimrans to fashion blades of ice and to use them. Train them to shoot sharp spikes of ice from their hands. Teach them to blast scalding hot steam. Element Shifr Shimrans can retain the nature of the elements they produce for long periods of time. We can also con-trol temperature with our centients, combine it with your Shifr to make it offensive. Change the approach! Every Shifr can be turned offensive and for-midable! Even those of the Shimrans who serve us within the palace, can be transformed into something deadly!' She looked at them thoughtfully as they gazed back at her, flabbergasted at their little Princess's notions and strategies.

'The Therin makers in particular, can turn their Shifr very aggressive. They use the water droplets, the weightlessness of clouds, the colour of the light reflecting off of them and combine them with their colourless liquid ther-ilium. They make beautiful therin from their Shifrs for our martial gear. So light that it can aid us to fly, harness wind and in wonderous colours too....' Jaraadhrin listened intently. It was an art that interested him and he was amazed at how much she knew about it.

'They need something saturated with water to make their Shifrs work... leaves, petals, even the metal, Elmas for our amour! What if they could com-bine just the water itself...? Water from the Crystal Depths... perhaps?'

The tzars gasped in horror at her suggestion. The waters of the Depths were enchanted, the extent of their potency was still to be gauged. They dissolved Shimrans at the end of their cores, sedimented the energies of the dead and vaporised anything dark, disintegrating them with agony, a horrifying death. That would be one formidable piece of clothing, indeed! Princess Saffrodel smiled benignly at their expressions of shock.

'It is our way forward. If the threat that we face is as dire as my mother believes, then we will need all the help we can get. We are too complacent behind our citadel and our Martial Force. That isn't enough at all.' Princess Saffrodel warned, worry crossing her fair face for the first time.

Complacent behind our citadel? Quinn thought frowning. *Why do I feel this applies to me too? Is it similar in my case? Am I too complacent because of my Shifr? Would I be able to fight just as well and with such ease without it? Maybe I should try push it away and fight without it as the Princess commanded at the clearing?* Princess Saffrodel glanced at him briefly before nodding.

'It works both ways. All Shimrans need to know martial arts, it needs to be taught in the schools as a basic art like flight. All Shimrans are taught flight for transport not as a basis of martial arts. This needs to change. Their Shifrs need to be analysed in depth and they need to be taught to be creative with them, by combining their centients with their Shifrs. They need to be educated of the dangers of turning their Shifrs offensive and instructed in the path of the light. It is a dangerous road and one that takes responsibility and dedication but it is also the only way forward.' She paused, taking a deep breath.

'We have to weaponize our Shifrs and ourselves or perish!' Princess Saffrodel's voice rang, loud and clear. The Ring of Command almost unbearable. Two fiery crescents appeared between her fair brows and blazed bright, momentarily.

Jaraadhrin and Quinn sank to their knees, heads inclined in salutation. Their minds churned and their hearts flooded with raging emotions at their little Princess's words. Her reasoning, the way she had explained via the experiment, her forethought, her strategies, her courage, her resourcefulness but above all her infinite love and concern for the Shimran folk. How much thought had gone in to all this? How long had she been thinking about all this? It was uncanny how such a tiny little shimling could be all of this at the same time and still enchant them with her mischief.

Princess Saffrodel felt a shoot of discomfort and a flash of warmth between her eyes. She ran her finger between her brows and rubbed it gently. It was darker and the shadows lengthened on the terrace. It had been such a long day and her Lord Protector and Quinn must be as exhausted as she was. Princess Saffrodel smiled down at them tenderly.

'Quinzafoor, I think you should take your leave now. Your soldiers in the clearing and Ashoora must be missing you very much. Practice well and remember what I said.' She reminded him. Quinn nodded, rising slowly as the Command released. He stepped towards the banister to her left. He had to do something to show her how much he had changed this day. He felt such intense reverence and fealty to his Princess, that it was almost tangible. His respect and affection for his little shimling Princess, pulsed within him to the rhythm of his very heartbeat. He wasn't sure if she could read his mind but he certainly wished she could at that moment. His attitude towards her had changed drastically from their last meeting at the clearing.

How could I possibly let my Princess know how I feel?

Quinn twirled his hand over the white marble. The large, black Siyan ring on his finger flashed in the fading light. The auburn mist of his centient swirled around his hand and solidified into the bunch of pink flowers within his grasp. The very ones that the warrior shimara on the parapets had gifted his Princess. She had left it forgotten on the table in the commotion of the blade test. But they now had a few Cryslis blossoms wedged between them, supported by the stalks of the pink flowers. He placed them gently at her feet touching one of the blooms to her shoe so it disappeared in a soft haze, releasing its force into her.

He raised his head to glance at her sweet, little face through the thin, pale blue covering of his eyes. She didn't look down at him but blinked slowly, her lips curved in a slight smile and she nodded.

Quinn lowered his head in a quick salute again, grinning widely, his dimples etched in. His Princess knew and she could read him! He leapt off the banisters and soared away, his heart singing!

Princess Saffrodel slid off the banister as she picked up the flowers. The Cryslis blossoms released their energy into her at her touch. She placed the rest in between the buttons of her tunic by her heart. Jaraadhrin felt a stab of annoyance.

So, she approves of Quinn now? Maybe I should get her some flowers too? She giggled at him.

'Why do you not rise, Dhrin?' she said, rather puzzled as he stayed down on one knee, hand over his heart and held in his salute.

'You haven't released me Princess, you used the Ring of Command...? She frowned at him, perplexed. She strode over and sat down in front of him. She pushed her palm against his chest roughly and Jaraadhrin chuckled as he lost his balance yet slid back cross-legged, exceedingly elegantly as the Command released.

'What Ring of Command? She inquired with interest. Jaraadhrin laughed.

'After all you have done and said today, Princess, I do find it rather amusing that you do not know this.' She shook her head.

'Tsk...tsk...I can't know everything old tzar. Now stop being annoying and tell me!' she retorted.

'It's a Shifr that only Royals have. If you order a Shimran whether it be a tzar, mara or intelligent beast, they have no choice but to obey. They sink in salutes and cannot move till you release them, verbally or by action as you just did to me. Very unceremoniously, I might add.' He chortled. Princess Saffrodel frowned.

'There is no formality between you and me Dhrin, that disappeared when you held me as a day old shimling. But this is very crude! How do I know if I had used it? That time was indeed involuntary!' she cried, rather troubled at the thought of binding Shimrans against their will to her command. Jaraadhrin smiled with tender affinity at her distress.

'There is no need to be distraught Princess, it's part of being a Royal. Some-times leaders must make harsh decisions and this ensures compliance. You should have felt a pain and warmth between your eyes. We did see the blazing, fiery half crescents between your brows. It wasn't a fully intertwined mark yet, just two crescents so it was not too potent. That and if the Shimran you commanded cannot rise, of course' he chuckled at her. She nodded, thinking hard.

'I thought I was tired...erm... How do I refrain from using it then?' She asked expectantly. Jaraadhrin shook his head.

'The Ring of Command requires belief. You meant what you said Princess. It cannot be refrained from and it isn't a bad thing. You just need to release them as soon as you issue the orders, Princess, so they can action on it. This is ancient Shimran enchantments too. The Alaqain helps with the focus of such commands. They are imbued to help with Shifrs and enchantments reserved for Royalty.' He chuckled again as Princess Saffrodel slid the Alaqain swiftly off her finger and clipped it to her ribbon.

'That will not help, my Princess. The Alaqain will work as long as it is any-where on your person or in your vicinity, once you have accepted it. You have been wearing it all day in the light of the sun so you have accepted it and it is yours. There is no returning that now.' He explained quietly. Princess Saffrodel nodded, replacing it back on her finger. Jaraadhrin gazed at his little princess, his eyes twinkling down at her.

'No Royal had ever misused it, no Royal ever will. Certainly not my Princess who is so devoted to her Shimrans, that she prevents them using their centients to welcome her.' He whispered, looking in to her charming shimling face. She smiled shyly, gazing up at him.

'Will you come earlier tomorrow, Dhrin? We had more time today and it would be pleasant.'

'Of course, I promise, my Princess' he agreed.

'You know old tzar, you made a promise that you haven't fulfilled yet!' Jaraadhrin gazed at her sudden comment, in surprise. She giggled up at him, more her shimling self than she had been the whole day.

'What is that Princess? I usually keep my promises, tzars never break them if they can help it' he wondered in dismay. Had he forgotten something? Princess Saffrodel stood up, slightly pink in the face and started walking towards her chambers.

'Princess....?' Called Jaraadhrin as he made to follow her.

'I mastered flight, now it's your turn, old tzar. You made a promise to fan dance with me if I mastered flight. Remember?' she giggled again. Jaraadhrin stared at her in vexation.

Aaashh! That! And I thought she had forgotten it!

'I will prepare the fans for tomorrow.... Goodnight Dhrin. Make sure you practice well. I am not dancing with a graceless tzar!' she trilled impishly and skipped away, laughing at the look on Jaraadhrin's face.

Jadheedhath

T hat night, Jaraadhrin sat cross-legged outside on the lush cushions laid on his terrace, deep in thought. It was a cool night and the breeze was fresh and stiff, blowing his long tresses behind him. He was trying hard to make sense of Princess Saffrodel's words.

'Fight back, Dhrin! Use your Essence Shifr to block him.' She had said.

Essence Shifr? He remembered how he had been able to sense his father's essence as the unisus approached. The different colours of the soldiers' essences, pain glowing crimson and other colours for different emotions, over their base essence shades. He had sensed Quinzafoor brilliant, auburn essence the other day at the farewell ceremony for the fallen soldiers and then again today, burning crimson with his agony. Jaraadhrin shuddered as he remembered it. Could this latent talent be a proper Shifr? If so, how could it possibly combat against Quinzafoor massively potent one? He still didn't know how lethal Quinn's Shifr was in the first place.

Jaraadhrin knew the ornate clips on Quinn's head, served a greater purpose other than decorations to either restrict or increase his powers. He had no idea why the blind fold was necessary or the reason for the blaze behind it, when he fought. Quinn could obviously read another person's thoughts. His reactions and replies to Jaraadhrin's thoughts had proved that time and time again. He was a master potionist, able to whip up tinctures with ease which means he must have other powers, related to intelligence and the mind.

The control of his being and transmission of his core was beyond normal. He was precise and expert at core power extraction and didn't even need to mediate it as he has had to every night. Quinn was a master melodist who was able to transform the tune of melodies to heal as per the situation required. He could also control another Shimran's mind to make them do what he willed as the Princess made him demonstrate today. Jaraadhrin sighed. How on Shimrah does Princess Saffrodel expect him to be equal that? It was impossible.

A soft blue glowed behind him as he sat pondering.

Father. He opened his eyes and turned around smiling, Lord Jaraadh grinned at him.

'That Shifr of yours is quite pronounced now.' Jaraadhrin frowned. 'Yes, so Princess Saffrodel says' he grimaced.

'The Princess?' Lord Jaraadh raised his eyebrows as he sat down beside his son on the cushions. Jaraadhrin recounted everything that had happened the last few days. His father nodded, wise and thoughtful.

'I have already been instructed by the King on the armoury décor, weaponry changes and the proposed alterations of the Princess. I must say her little Highness is a combination of her mother and father in every aspect. I was astonished as I heard the amendments the Princess proposed. Her characteristics amazes me. Shimran Royalty can access any Shifr they want but they usually chose ten to fifteen and practise them. No one has used more than that, at any time, in all of Shimran history. The Princess seems to be wielding a vast number, currently. She is in complete control with most of them and she also has a shield Shifr on today which blocked me from getting anything else' said Lord Jaraadh with a pained expression on his face. Jaraadhrin roared with laughter at his aggrieved words.

'Quinn figured as much and it annoyed him no end. He was totally blind because of it and my Princess seemed to have managed to get you irritated as well, my Lord! Her Highness is immensely intelligent as she is mischievous!' Lord Jaraadh chuckled, joining in his son's mirth. Jaraadhrin sobered, sighing.

'I can't figure out, for the life of me, how mine could be as potent as Quinn's as the Princess says' he mused.

'Shifrs need to be figured out by the owner or it will not work for them, this is old Shimran tradition and the magic of the ancients' Lord Jaraadh replied, still chuckling. 'You will get there' Jaraadhrin nodded. Father and son sat in silence as they gazed up the brilliant moon, hanging low in the sky.

'Have you heard anything more about Ifreeth or the kind of attack he is amassing?' inquired Jaraadhrin, his tone rather hesitant. He didn't wish to pry on matters of the state or those that may be regarded as confidential. His father sighed and shook his head.

'There is no news at all, Ifreeth seemed to have disappeared off Shimrah along with his brother Ibreeth and his nephew Nibrath. They are obviously hiding but we have no idea where. It's like they never existed.' Lord Jaraadh pressed his hands against either side of his head wearily. Jaraadhrin stood up and kneeled behind his father. With a swift motion, he slid back his long sleeves, imbued his fingers with his centient and placed them against his father's temples as he massaged it in lightly. He increased the flow for warmth. His father exhaled as his worries dissipated in the wake of his son's centients, flooding his mind.

'Where did you learn that? That's refreshing' He murmured.

'Mistress Afra, she is forever getting others to do it for her' Jaraadhrin chortled as he thought of his beloved Mistress. 'Apparently her head is too full of unnecessary thoughts and it helps her organise and forget the ones she doesn't want to remember. It is supposedly an issue if you live for thousands of years' Lord Jaraadh chuckled and sighed as he closed his eyes. His slim figure relaxed as the tensions flowed out of him.

'The main problem is' he continued. 'There is this talk, rumours if you will, of a dark type of creature or creatures in the murky forests of Southern Shimrah. So far, six of our spies have disappeared with no trace. Only their essence can be found splashed in random spaces. No bodies or auras, just their essence contaminated with another sinister, bloodcurdling, dark essence. A Demonesque Essence.' Jaraadhrin frowned.

'Demonesque? It might be useful for me to know this essence, father' he said thoughtfully. Lord Jaraadh snapped his eyes open, turning around to face him. He shook his head and spoke in the stern tones of the Lord Protector of Shimrah.

'No Jaraadhrin. Your duty is to the Princess, besides the essence in itself is deadly and we think it's what caused these Shimrans to go missing. I have never heard of such darkness in Shimrah.' He sighed again. Jaraadhrin sat back down, cross-legged facing him and listened intently.

'The Decoran woods line the Southern end of the Shimran Kingdom. A dark and dank place. It has been gathering this darkness ever since Ibreeth and Ifreeth turned against the throne. We have reasons to believe that it hides their fortress.' Lord Jaraadh continued. 'The creatures come out at night and are impossible to detect. They have some kind of concealment. Many Shimran folk had disappeared from nearby villages and we have evacuated everyone to North Shimrah. It is all we can do for now till we know more of what we are dealing with.' Lord Jaraadh finished, shaking his head. He looked very weary.

'Rest, father' Jaraadhrin comforted. 'You have been working continuously for a while now and your centient is very low, you might need to replenish it.

The soldiers, Quinn and I have been training very hard. You do have a backup Martial Force if you require it. We are ready, father' Lord Jaraadh smiled and nodded.

'I know, I have seen you two put on quite a dramatic spectacle, every morning.' He grinned at his son, his blue eyes lighting up in mischief. 'I have often wondered why it needed to be that sensational. If I hadn't known better, I would be rather inclined to believe that they were solely for the benefit of our warrior shimaras.' Jaraadhrin snorted and his father roared with laughter at his expression. He sobered and sighed. 'I suppose your right, I should turn in'

'Hmm.... hmm...' Jaraadhrin chuckled as his father stood up. He patted his son's head and made his way back to his chambers.

Jaraadhrin sighed and closed his eyes again. Concentrating on the essences of things around him. Living essences were easier to see, stationary and non-living ones, more difficult. The darkness helped. He hummed quietly to himself as he reached out with his senses, other than his eyes and ears. He swayed in the gentle breeze as it lifted his long locks and blew them over his face.

Suddenly, he felt a blazing bolt of heat zoom from behind him! He frowned without opening his eyes. Where did that come from? He moved down defensively, bending flat at his waist without a conscious thought, his waves arcing high over him. Jaraadhrin leapt to his feet, facing the direction it had come from. It was a fire bolt and it had crashed on the banister behind him. Another zoomed from his left, along with a third aimed at his head. He concentrated on the direction of the bolts and his tall, lithe frame moved defensively, shifting him away from the path of danger.

More and more bolts started firing, ricocheting off the banisters, the marble floors and walls. Jaraadhrin's body whirled into action, dodging, spinning, twirling and turning. His martial arts kicked in, without any conscious thought, in an intuitive action of protecting himself. His feet stepped light and nimble, back and forth, around and about, in a graceful dance as he avoided being blasted to smithereens by the bolts. His core spun powerfully inside him, physically contorting him to impossible positions as he danced away from the threats, cartwheeling and somersaulting him away from harm.

His staff zoomed out from his ribbon and he slashed at the firebolts, breaking them apart and scattering them in all directions as his being moved him fluidly. The last bolt crackled overhead and Jaraadhrin split it in to two with a quick spin of his staff. It crashed with ear-splitting sounds behind him. He straightened, his long, white night robes settling around him as he became stationary. The essences of everything shone brighter than it had ever been as the blood rushed through his head and heart, throwing everything into sharp relief. He turned slowly as he took in his brightly blazing surroundings.

A shimmering of cool blue and silver, magnified, towering over him and a chortle, made Jaraadhrin's eyes fly open. He gasped in awe and amazement. His father stood leaning lazily against the doorway. Coiled around him, gigantic and serpentine, was his silver blue dragon! Its huge, blue horn glimmered in the moonlight between its curved prongs, the sapphire within flashing brilliantly. The sharp, white fangs under its long snout, glittered, menacing and ominous. The scales on its body and the beautiful, thin crystal-like wings behind its neck and on its back, sparkled, throwing flashes of light as it moved.

Lord Jaraadh had summoned it and it was staring at him with its tongue out and head tilted to the side. It looked as if it was giggling at him too. It opened its huge mouth, manifested a firebolt from its massive, dragonesque core with indolent idleness and shot it at Jaraadhrin who instinctively deflected it. It made another snickering noise and brought its huge tail wing to its snout, fanning itself lightly with it and dispersing the smoke at its nostrils. Its actions were far too elegant for a dragon and contrasted sharply with its form. The gestures seemed oddly familiar too. The tilted head.... the fanning....?

Lord Jaraadh grinned up at it

'Enough Jade' he said. 'You made your point, I think young Jaraadhrin here, got it now'. The dragon gazed down at him affectionately, nudged the top of his head, lopped its tongue at Jaraadhrin and whooshed back into his father in a rush of blue and silver. Its essence struck deep in to Jaraadhrin's heart, warm, powerful and familiar.

He shook himself, stunned. That was the first time he had ever seen a real dragon and it quaked him to his core! The majesty and beauty of them! What truly enchanting creatures!

'You are not supposed to summon your dragon unless in a crisis, father' he said faintly, still in shock. Lord Jaraadh shrugged.

'She wanted to. She can be very impatient. Jade says that you are too composed and a shock now and then, would do you good!'

Jaraadhrin stared at his father in disbelief as a memory surfaced into his mind, from some faraway, forgotten space, swamped in the agony of loss. He was two or three moons then. Mistress Afra had been complaining to his mother that her son was unlike any shimling his age. Always studious, never playing around, always serious and unperturbed. Yet he took no effort to master his Shifr of Projection. His mother had nodded wisely at his Mistress and had taken him on a longer route home, than she usually did.

They had spent the day in and around the Goldhorn forest, a beautiful woodland to the southeast of Northern Shimrah. The home of the Goldhorn unisi. It was filled with cone shaped trees, that blazed gold in the sun during the early mornings and late evenings. They had swum in its pretty little streams, played with the Goldhorn foals, flown among its trees and had a lovely picnic.

He could still remember her stunning, floor length, thick red hair, drying in the sun. He had arranged the strands in intricate swirls and patterns on the ground around her as she sat, her charming face beaming with laughter at his antics. Her loving arms encircled him in hugs, every time he sat down beside her. It was a very warm day and she had been fanning herself with her silver-blue fan, making the locks fly back as she did. He had been very tired and had fallen asleep beside his mother as he watched the sunset. When he had awoken later that night, cold and hungry, he had been alone. All he could find was his mother's fan beside him.

He had been deathly scared and worried for his mother's safety. He had run and flown high over the forests, screaming and shouting for her until finally exhausted, he had returned to the stream where they had sat. The grief and the shock had blossomed his Projection Shifr and he had split himself into a full five replicas, sending them helter-skelter into every corner of the forest looking for her.

His mother had then flown down from the tops of the trees where she had been watching and protecting him, all that time. Jaraadhrin had rushed to her, hugging her tightly, sobbing into her robes as his projections flew back into him. He had been so angry at her, raged at her for putting him through that. She had smiled down at him with her head tilted as she usually did. Her brilliant, green eyes glittered with wisdom as she hugged him tightly and kissed him between his brows. She had patted his head as she murmured...

'You are too composed, my darling shimling. A shock now and then would do you good...'

'Ja...Jade as in .... Jadheedhath?' Jaraadhrin stammered, his brilliant blue eyes wide, swimming in tears as he said his mother's name for the first time in years. His father blinked at him slowly, nodding. He had always felt that his father was very good at hiding his grief for his wife but now he knew. She was right their inside him! Jaraadhrin had never felt her loss as a devastating weight in his heart either. He had thought it was because of the closeness of his father. But no. His mother had been with him too. Right their beside them both, protecting and watching over them. She never left.

Of course, Lord Jaraadh never had a dragon till after his wife's demise, it had always been a sore point with him. He had come home with it, a few months after his mother's untimely passing. It all made sense!

Lord Jaraadh smiled tenderly, his eyes soft with the reflected emotions of his son's. He regained his composure.

'Well that was a fiery revelation …. have a good night, son. Tomorrow's match would be historic, indeed' he said chuckling. He placed his hand on his heart, kissed it, touched it to his eyes and waved it at him, sending a warming glow of centient towards him. It floated to Jaraadhrin and diffused between his brows. He drew a deep breath, closing his eyes. He could feel his mother's love and his father's blessings radiating within him. Lord Jaraadh smiled at his expression and slid away quietly.

Jaraadhrin stood stunned and still as it finally dawned on him. He wasn't thinking of his defensive moves when the firebolts started shooting from his mother. His Shifr had moved him instinctively and defensively, removing him from harms path. He was merely concentrating on sourcing the direction of the attack. If Quinzafoor was attacking him instead of the firebolts as he used his Essence Shifr, then he would only see the mirror of his attack in Jaraadhrin's mind and not his defence as there was no conscious, defensive thought.

His mother had helped him realize it, just as she had helped him realize the extent of his Projection Shifr. She had shocked it out of him just as she had done on that day by the stream, at the Goldhorn forest. She had guided him, protected him and would always be with them. The reason his father often channelled her endearments and the extraordinarily close relationship, Jaraadhrin shared with him was because Lord Jaraadh was actually both his parents! They were one and the same.

He exhaled in a soft gust, sitting back down as his mind whirled with his thoughts and emotions. His heart, lighter and happier than it had been for many years. He closed his slanted eyes again, smiling slightly as all the essences around him blazed in sharp glows and flames. It was beautiful and bewildering at the same time. He didn't even have to concentrate anymore to see the glows of different creatures in his vision. He gazed after the brilliant green of a flying moth as it zoomed across.

'Tomorrow's match would be historic indeed!' his father's voice echoed in his ears. Quinn's face flashed in his mind, comical, puzzled. Jaraadhrin lips stretched in a mischievous smile and his howl of triumphant laughter echoed off of the palace walls.

Incareth

Jaraadhrin awoke with start. It was just before dawn and still dark outside. The shadows within his chambers, threw sinister shapes against the walls. The wind from the open terrace doors, breezed his rustling draperies in. It played with the fringes of his magnificently ornate four poster bed. The tassel bells of his bed screen ties, tinkled. The therin of its hangings so thin and light that it flew over his face and figure as he lay warm and comfortable under the richly worked sheets.

Jaraadhrin folded back his covers quietly. He felt a presence but couldn't see anyone or anything. He lay still sweeping his room with half closed eyes. Nothing at all. Jaraadhrin closed his eyes completely and summoned his Shifr, his heart racing. The darkness blazed into different essences and he swept the room once again. Nothing! What had woken him?

He turned on his side and slid soundless, to the very edge of his bed, his robes and sheets, rustling around him. His Shifr skimmed across the room once more and rested on the door leading to the vinery. It was ajar! He never left it open. He liked to keep the scents of the many salts and incenses within it. As he gazed at it in surprised through his Essence Shifr, a very familiar, pale cream aura drifted out of it, carrying what looked like towels.

Incareth?

He frowned, opening his eyes slightly. There was no one there! He shut his eyes again.

No, she is certainly here. He thought as her essence blazed, warm and caring. *Why can't I see her with my eyes then?*

He pretended to awake and sat up. He swung his legs down on to the steps of his massive bed, eyes closed, still watching her. Incareth turned away and slid back against the walls, melting into the rich tapestry. She stood still, her head bowed low and motionless. He opened his eyes again in amazement, gazing at the place where he had seen her essence. Jaraadhrin still couldn't see her! He moved away the rich drapes around the posts and shook his head.

How very strange?

He slid off his bed and stood up. Jaraadhrin lighted the torches in his chambers with a quick bolt of his centient. The light flooded the corner where she stood. All he could see was the wall adorned with the tapestry. He sat down on a nearby chair and pulled his robes straight and secure, facing her. He leaned forward with one elbow on his knee as he gazed at the place where he sensed her essence, frowning and deep in thought. No wonder he never saw her. She couldn't be seen normally.

How was this even possible?

'Incareth?' he queried, his voice low and tolerant, so as not to startle her. A shocked gasp sounded from where she stood and a slight disturbance shook the air as she promptly dropped the towels she held. They materialised as they left her hand. Jaraadhrin caught them with his centient and placed them on the pedestal next to her in a neat fold.

'My Lord...You can see me?' She quivered, still turned away from him.

'Come here, Incareth.' Jaraadhrin called. Her aura was very young indeed, barely sixteen. He had imagined it to be quite old. Her essence turned around and glided to him, head still bowed. The air rippled as she moved but otherwise she was completely invisible to his eyes.

'Why can't I see you?' he questioned, puzzled. Her essence lifted its head, baffled.

'I thought you could see me, my Lord...?' she whispered in dismay. Jaraadhrin shook his head, rather amused.

'I can see you with my Shifr but not my eyes.' he explained patiently 'Tell me why.' Incareth's essence nodded.

'Lord Jaraadh did warn me that this would happen one day, young Lord. It is an Vanish Shifr. Most of us have it.' she revealed. Princess Saffrodel's voice rang in Jaraadhrin's ear as he gazed at her in astonishment and incredulity.

'Every Shifr can be turned offensive and formidable. Even those of the Shimrans who serve us within the palace, can be transformed into something deadly!'

'Most of you...?' He inquired.

'Most of the Shimrans servers, my Lord. It helps us fulfil our duties without irritating and disturbing our Masters and Mistresses...'

'Aaashh! How crude and distressing! Show yourself at once.' Jaraadhrin commanded. Incareth hesitated then moved her trembling hand over her face. She glimmered cream and solidified before him. Jaraadhrin's eyes softened. She looked terrified, her eyes shut tight and shivering.

'Come sit here, Incareth' he sighed, pointing to a chair near him. She shook her head but quickly obliged as he made a soft sound of annoyance.

'My Lord, we are bound by our Oath of Honour. We do not enter unless we are sure you are presentable. We cannot look at you unless you are anyway. We cannot hear anything you would consider personal. The Oath guides us so we do not intrude on your privacy. Even now I can't open my eyes because you are probably in your night clothes –' Incareth reeled off in a rush of words still shuddering.

'Aaashh! Shush for a moment mara...' Jaraadhrin interrupted. He sprang up, reaching for his robes and pulling them on hurriedly. He fastened the belt on to make himself more presentable. He slid his locks back swiftly tying them with his centient. He wasn't sure how presentable he had to be to release poor Incareth from her bind. Did she need him in outdoor clothes?

'I am sure I look decent enough in my night robes but still...' he sat back down in front of her and Incareth opened her eyes, looking up at him terrified as the oath released her. Jaraadhrin smiled down at her and her gaze lit up in awe. She shook her head and lowered it again with a soft gasp.

'Don't be afraid, I am not angry' he reassured her. He kept his voice low and calm. She looked so timid that he was rather concerned she would faint if he raised his voice 'But, I have seen you around the palace. You are not always invisible?' He said thoughtfully.

'We only use our Shifr when we feel it is necessary not to disturb you, my Lord. We are guided by the oath –'

'I know about the Oath but I didn't know that it binds you so or about the Shifr that most of you have. It took me by surprise. Shimrans trust each other with their lives. The honour of a shimratzar or shimara is impeccable. I always wondered why there was a need for such an oath?' he frowned 'It seems so unpolished and sparks doubt, doesn't it?'

'But my Lord, you did say it was crude and distressing...? She whispered, puzzled. Jaraadhrin glanced at her, smiling benevolently at her misunderstanding.

'The fact that you think you need to remain unseen as you serve us, as you assist us with everything, every day. The fact that you think we would take offense at seeing you, is crude and distressing' He explained. Incareth beamed at his warmhearted words.

'The oath wasn't created by those we serve my Lord. We invented it out of our loyalty and devotion to the Masters and Mistresses we serve. No one makes us take it. We do it of our own free will. It is a gift of honour and commitment to our Lords and Ladies.' She replied quietly, flushing pink.

Jaraadhrin sighed, closing his eyes and shaking his head. He couldn't object to that. He loved every aspect of Shimrah and its folk. He was Shimran but he still learned such astonishing truths about their characters, their beings and their lives that impressed him.

'I still think it's a little too much to bind yourself like that...' he disagreed. Incareth giggled suddenly, his expression amused her. Jaraadhrin glanced up at her, smiling. Her laugh made him happy.

'One could say the same about your devotion too, my Lord. To the King, to the Queen, to the Princess, to your friends, to your soldiers and the kingdom in general.' She ticked off as she became timid once more 'All loyalty is the same, the difference lies in how we express it. What we can do is very limited. We can't protect them, fight for them or lay down our lives for them in glorious sacrifice like you could and you have, My Lord. We do not have many ways to express it, so we choose this path.' She explained, flushing redder.

Jaraadhrin stared at her, stunned. She was right, there was nothing he wouldn't do for his King, Queen or Princess. He understood her well. He sighed again as he smiled down at her innocent, little face.

'You need not use your Shifr around me anymore if you wish, Incareth and you may come and go as you please. I would like to talk to you as you do your duties. It would be a welcome change.' He said. Incareth nodded, beaming. She stood up and curtsied.

'Your bath for the morning is ready, my Lord. I have infused it with the scent you are partial to. Your martial robes and fresh towels have been prepared and beside it. If it pleases you my Lord, I would like to get back to my other chores, now.' She requested. Jaraadhrin nodded and she bowed. She gathered up the towels, placed them neatly on the shelves and moved towards the door to his chambers.

'Oh.... and... Incareth' he stopped her. She turned quickly to him, her hand on the door. He stood up, inclined his head with his hand on his heart. 'Thank you for everything you do for myself and my father. We wouldn't be able to get by without you.'

She sank to her knee in a salute, her slender hands clasped to her heart. Her eyes swam with tears and with a soft sniffle, she fled through the door! Jaraadhrin shook his head and sighed, touched by her humility and devotion.

Jaraadhrin couldn't sleep after Incareth left. He turned restlessly on his bed as he lay fully clothed. He gave up trying to sleep after a while and slid off. He strode over to the corner of his room by the terrace doors and sat down at his work desk. It was made of ornate Siyan with curving legs and held many little drawers. He flipped the booklet his father had given him for a bit, making sure he still remembered it. He nodded contended. Everything was still etched in his mind.

He slid a decorative box out from one of the draws and opened it. A large nugget of glittering, rose gold Pembre lay within it in a silken cushion. He had acquired it yesterday from Dalfique during the armoury visit. Jaraadhrin did not possess the Shifr of Metallurgy but the Pembre was a lovely colour and he had wanted it as a souvenir. He shifted it within his fingers thoughtfully as he mulled over the happenings of the past day and his beloved princess's words.

'We have to weaponize ourselves and our Shifrs...'

He shook his head as he recalled her suggestions. *Shoot spikes of ice? Blast scalding steam? Cloaks made of the waters of the Crystal Depths. Weapons of ice and fire? Aaashh! Where did all that come from? Then the matter with Ashoora and Quinn. What ingenuity!*

Jaraadhrin inhaled sharply as Quinzafoor's agonised face, flashed before his eyes. His lip cut and bleeding crimson where he had bitten into it, in his torment. He had swayed and nearly lost consciousness. It was the first time he had seen such anguish on Quinn's usually merry face and it rattled him. Quinzafoor's torment cut deep into him at the memory. Jaraadhrin clenched his hand around the nugget, his centient heating it rapidly as it flowed into his palm with the extent of his emotions. He dropped it in shock on his desk as it liquified within his grasp, scorching him.

'Aaashh!' he exclaimed as he healed his hand and stared at it the melting mass on his desk in amazement. That took no effort at all. He raised the now molten mass of metal carefully with his centient, trying to hold it together. He rotated his fingers and it curved into a glowing sphere, much like the one, that imp of a shimara in the caves had made. He cooled it right down and it solidified it to glittering ball. Jaraadhrin picked it up and rolled it between his slender fingers in amazement, deep in thought. Pembre was rather a soft metal with a low melting point but it was still very much higher than normal everyday heating ranges of Shimran activities. Would he be able to melt Elmas with his centient?

Metallurgy Shifr Shimrans could detect the metals deep underground and extract them. Did they also shape them and make weapons with their Shifrs or did they just use their centients? Were they already combining their centients with their Shifrs like his princess had suggested? If that was the case, any Shimran with some skill could fashion a blade if they had the metal. Couldn't they?

He slid his staff from his ribbon and studied it intently, enlarging it just enough to see all its many details. He placed the sphere of Pembre back on his desk. Jaraadhrin closed his eyes and concentrated hard, on the design of his staff. He moved his fingers as he lifted the Pembre and coated it with his heated centient. It spun swiftly and elongated into the shape of his staff. Jaraadhrin opened his eyes, clipped his actual staff back on the ribbon and focussed on moulding the Pembre into an exact replica of his staff.

His eyes narrowed in concentration as he melted and merged the metal into the flowing, ornate design of his weapon. He chipped and smoothed away the grooves and ridges neatly and fashioned in the many winding lines of the Gumoos inlay with the Pembre itself. He gave it a final twirl and cooled it down rapidly. He gazed at it in wonder as it lay against the black of his desk. The stunning, glittery pink staff – an exact replica of his but much smaller.

He nodded to himself as he picked it up and twirled it between his fingers. It was probably easier to make a bigger version of it than smaller. That amount of detail would be simpler to etch in a larger version. His princess was right, they needed to study their own beings in more detail and ascertain their strengths and weaknesses at its fullest.

Jaraadhrin sighed and glanced out to his terrace as the first light of dawn broke over the horizons. He shook himself and set the little Pembre staff back on his desk. It was rather long, almost the length and a half of his hand. He couldn't use it as a weapon as it was too small. Weapons were made large and diminished for storage. This Pembre staff was made miniaturised so it couldn't be expanded.

He tapped it as he searched for a use, for it. it looked too ornamental to discard. Jaraadhrin moved his fingers over it again and the two prongs fed out the Pembre in a long chain from its tips as it shortened. It could be now worn as a necklace.... except the staff was still a little too long. He tutted in some frustration. He should probably get ready, he had promised his little princess an early start. He would find a use for the staff later.

He stood up to prepare for his day. Today was going to be so lively. He needed to be with his Princess first for the fan dance! Ugh! He groaned at the thought of it. He wanted to get it done and behind him before he had an audience. He felt thrilled at being with his Princess this early though. His days were so full of things he had to get done, that it was very appealing to him, to spend more of his hectic days with her. His limited time with his Princess, in her childhood was cherished and it was already vanishing rapidly.

Then he would go down with her to the clearing. She would be so surprised and Quinzafoor....? Jaraadhrin crowed with silent laughter. Quinn would be shocked. He would probably know the plan beforehand but that would still not help him win. They would probably still be just as evenly matched again. Quinn would just anticipate the moves based on his own attacks but at least, the tables would be turned today. He would be fighting Quinn's skill alone with both his Shifr and his skill as his beloved Princess had suggested.

The sweet, scented bath Incareth had prepared for him was still steaming. She had covered it with her centient to keep the heat in as she always did. Jaraadhrin hummed as he washed and dressed. He swung the layers of his robes more elegantly around himself and twirled in each of them. His core sang with his mood. His tall frame danced involuntarily as he prepared for the big day head. He pulled up his wavy locks in a slightly different way to his usual, letting more hang down to frame his face. It glistened a brilliant bronze against his pale skin.

Jaraadhrin tied on his red ribbon, adding his gold, ornate fans to it from another of his work desk drawers. They were not really dance fans, they were actually weapons, with a hidden dagger as the grip and sharp, spiked, blade thin edges in the fan rims. They were made entirely of Siyan with the exception of the rims and daggers. These were fashioned out of Elmas. Every surface of the fans have been intricately inlaid with elaborate decorations of Altheen, so thick that the fans looked gold.

Yes, they were highly ornate weapons, deadly and dangerous but one could dance with them too. Maybe he should use them to fight Quinn? He had been practicing a variation of an obscure martial arts which involved the moves of a very charismatic fan dance, when Queen Debriar had watched over him with her visions. He was sure Quinn didn't know this particular variation of combat. It involved many light spirals, elegant wrist and finger movements, high leaps and sure-footed agility. Jaraadhrin chuckled as he clipped a sword, a pair of draggers and an axe to his trinket ribbon as well. He really was looking forward to that match.

Jaraadhrin glanced at himself in the mirror one last time, making sure he looked good enough, both to dance and fight. Still in his Lord Protector blue therin, he looked both elegant and formidable. Not even his hair annoyed him today. He walked swiftly to the terrace and skipped off of it, his heart soaring with his robes behind him.

What a beautiful day it was. Brilliant sunshine and the wind soft on his face as he glided towards his Princess. The trees whirled below him, full of blossoms and the waters ran clear and sparkling. The green grass carpets, dotted with vivid colours as the blossoms burst forth in bunches, here and there. He swooped down and grabbed a bunch of red flowers, skimmed a few spaces above the ground then rose quickly. The sky stretched blue and gold with slightly pink tinged clouds, scurrying above him. Jaraadhrin sighed softly. Such peace was bliss.

He landed on the King's terrace with an extra turn, just because he felt like it. His little Princess sat on the white marble banister, her tiny hands on her cheeks facing away from him, deep in thought. Even as she sat, dangling her legs over the side, the pale green of her robes swirling around them, Jaraadhrin could tell she had grown slightly taller overnight. She whirled off the banister as she heard him land and walked swiftly over to him with her arms outstretched.

'Dhrin....! She exclaimed 'You came early....!' Jaraadhrin laughed, sinking to his knee as fast as he could.

'Of course Princess, I promised' He replied, smiling at her and holding out his arms too, the flowers he had brought her still within his grasp.

Princess Saffrodel stopped herself suddenly and dropped her arms spaces from him, looking awkward and pink in the face. Jaraadhrin tilted his head gazing at her in surprise. She would normally just put her little arms around his neck and hug him hard, pulling his hair loose for good measure. Something about her was different and it wasn't just her height. Princess Saffrodel smiled radiantly and sat down in front of him, cross legged on the cushions. Jaraadhrin dropped his hands and sat down too, wonderingly. She glanced at the flowers and giggled. Jaraadhrin followed her gaze to his hand. He cleared his throat and handed them to her.

'Ahem.... For you, my Princess.' He said with a quick flourish and chuckle. She giggled again and took them from him. She removed a few off the bunch and slid them neatly into the braids at the back of her head. She then slipped the rest of them between the buttons on her tunic by her heart as she had done with Quinn's.

Jaraadhrin smiled down at her. The flowers matched the red gold of her hair perfectly.

'Where are your fans then, Princess? Let's get it done before we have an audience' he said grinning. Princess Saffrodel's smile vanished and she became serious.

'That dance is important to me, Dhrin' she muttered, her voice grave. Jaraadhrin tensed at the tone of her voice and words.

'It is to me too, My Princess, that is why I want it to be private....' He said, swiping at her little button nose with his finger, grinning and trying to lighten her mood. She moved away from his touch, her cheeks pinking over again. What was wrong with his Princess today? She looked like she usually would but her behaviour was off. Something was annoying her and she was worrying about something else too, that much he could tell.

'Is everything alright, my Princess?' Jaraadhrin leaned forward, peering into her little face 'Is there something you want to tell me?' She sighed and looked up. She started at seeing his face so close to hers and leapt, whirling away from him. Jaraadhrin stood up slowly, frowning. How strange! Was she angry at him for something? Princess Saffrodel smiled up at him again.

'I am grumpy in the mornings. Its early Dhrin, you have never seen me at dawn,' she lilted. Jaraadhrin stared at her. What was with her words and the way she said it. He nodded.

'So, you don't want to dance now...?' He inquired. He felt disappointed and realised that he had actually been looking forward to it. He couldn't remember the last time she had been impartial to dance, she shook her head, infuriated.

'I am not tall enough to dance with you, we wouldn't cut a graceful picture' she ranted. 'But we will dance tonight at the palace gardens. Right now, teach me to fight!' Jaraadhrin eyes snapped to hers in surprise.

'What?' he faltered, incredulous. Something was very wrong with his Princess. Why was she asking to be taught to fight so suddenly? Where was her adorable cheeky antics and manner? Yesterday's events ran through his mind as he tried to find a cause for her actions today. She had been normal, a lot mature and in control when she had advised Dalfique and them of her strategies but otherwise just her sweet little self. What had changed overnight? He shook himself, collecting his composure and taking it in one at a time.

'Firstly, you will be the same height tonight, Princess, as you are now, so it really wouldn't make any difference. Two, you would cut a graceful picture for both of us! Three, you shouldn't be roaming the palace gardens at night and four, if you are not tall enough to dance with me, then you certainly are not tall enough to fight me, Your Highness!' he reasoned, ticking them off on his fingers.

He inclined his head to her in a salute, hand on his heart and bronze locks sliding around his face as he bent. His brilliant eyes twinkled down at his little Princess as his full lips parted in a dazzling smile. Princess Saffrodel gazed at him for moment. She lifted her little hand up to his face, entranced then clutched it into a fist and withdrew.

'Aaashh! Of all the Senseless Shimaras in existence...!' she fumed as she dropped her hand, her voice quiet in anger. She rolled her eyes in annoyance and turned away from him. Jaraadhrin straightened out of his salute, utterly confused.

What did my Princess say...? Who is she talking about? May be one of the servers had antagonised her? It was very unlikely, she loved her shimrans too much for that.

Princess Saffrodel clasped her hands behind her back and raised her chin high in a striking resemblance to Queen Debriar.

'I won't be alone in the palace gardens; you will escort me there from the terrace. I will wait for you here.' she whirled back to face him and Jaraadhrin took a step back, incredulous at the look of authority and royal command in her little face. 'I know I am not tall enough and I am working on it' she snapped, irritation evident in her voice. Her hand moved inside her robes at her waist. 'For now, as my mentor, you will find a way to teach me to fight!' she commanded, her fingers flashed out and the massive blade of the sword of Menorak, expanded in her hand. The point stopped a hair's breadth from Jaraadhrin's neck, the hilt held gracefully in her slightly turned wrist.

Jaraadhrin raised his hands, palm towards her and moved his head back slightly, away from the sharp sword. He stared into her face; she was deadly serious. He stepped back and cleared his throat, nodding and trying to collect his thoughts. He tilted his head, studying her posture. She stood tall and straight and held the sword with ease and confidence. The blade was so long it was twice her height.

She had practised. He realised.

Princess Saffrodel scoffed, leapt into air to make room for the sword to twirl free under her and spun it around. She arched it over her head, upright and behind her back. It slashed to a stop, pointed straight up as she slipped in to her one-foot flight stance. Only it wasn't amiable anymore. It looked threatening and radiated power. She straightened her head, looking him in the eye and flipped her free wrist. The sharply positioned fingers, slipped free of her sleeve and she aimed it at him, palm up in his own classic martial stance. Her eyes flashed cold and deadly. Jaraadhrin's core trembled faintly at the changes in her expression as he expanded his staff off of his ribbon.

'Aaashh! Of all the Miracles in Shimrah! And here I was ready to dance.... Ugh' he murmured under his breath. His eyes widened and he flew back, gasping as Princess Saffrodel swung her sword high over her, bringing it down in a flash on his head. He raised his staff rapidly and blocked the blow which landed with a resounding crash in a mid-air. He gazed into her eyes as she hovered over him for a moment. It flashed cold steel.

Tsk...tsk...whatever did I do to cross this little warrior Princess of mine? He thought chuckling.

She spun away from him and slashed again, this time aiming for his neck. Her movements so swift, he barely had time to block them. He kept meeting her eyes inadvertently, every time he blocked her swift attacks. He was distracted, unable to concentrate and barely defended himself. She flew up again spinning, her cloaks slashing through the air. All her attacks were from the air, to compensate for her lack of height. She kept twirling around him, attacking him fast and ferociously, every time she leapt. Jaraadhrin's tall, lithe figure coiled away, defending himself as her sword slashes rained on him. He twirled his staff as he spun around her, his robes soaring. Princess Saffrodel spiralled high into the air, pointed her sword at his face and drove down on him swiftly.

'Fight back, Dhrin!' she raged. Long stands of fiery, crackling red hair flew free from her many gold clips as she raced down towards him. The corner of his lips curled in a smile as he watched her small frame shoot down. He lowered his staff.

This is getting out of hand! He thought.

Princess Saffrodel's eyes widened as she realised that he wasn't going to block her this time. She diminished the sword mid-flight and flipped away from him. Her sleeves spun rapidly as she sheathed and caught Jaraadhrin in the corner of his eye. He shut them instinctively, blocking her palm as it slashed towards his neck. A vivid memory flickered in his mind. Him sheathing his staff as Quinn blocked his wrists in the clearing.

She hadn't practiced at all! He realised in awe. *She learnt it all by watching me and Quinn in the clearing.*

Princess Saffrodel's little wrists flipped and flashed. Jaraadhrin blocked them with fluidity as his Shifr took over and moved him instinctively, his eyes still closed. His Princess's aura glowed brilliant colours but it was breaking and melting together like fracturing crystals around her, her emotions raging out of control.

'Young shimaras are volatile....' His father's voice echoed from far away. Her centient years were no longer at two, it was around fifty! Jaraadhrin's temples tensed. Where had that come from? Why hadn't he noticed it straight away? Princess Saffrodel was using her slender legs to fight as well. Her kicks so fluidly serpentine and strong that Jaraadhrin had a hard time seeing them. Without his Shifr and some training she could easily beat him!

He grinned in sudden amusement as he spun around his little Princess. This was a moon old Princess and she could beat him...?! He was supposed to be her mentor. He must be going soft. How delightfully ironic. Momentarily distracted, he missed Princess Saffrodel's last move as she spun rapidly towards him, her foot aimed at his chest. He slid low and blocked it at the last moment, crossing his hands at the wrists. He didn't use enough force and her toe made the slightest touch on his chest.

An explosion of blue-white erupted from the point of impact, blasting Jaraadhrin back as he slid several spaces. He planted his feet on the ground trying to stop the backward slide. His Princess had flown across with the blast and spiralled down as lightly as a feather, facing him.

Jaraadhrin sank to one knee. He felt weak and shivery. A cold shudder passed through him as he coughed up blood which slid down from the corner of his mouth. He placed a hand on his chest, astonished. His core felt raw. He stared up at his Princess in wonder as his vison blurred and hazed over into shadow.

Shimling to Shimara

Princess Saffrodel's face had been cold and emotionless but changed in a flash as she saw the blood. She flashed to his side swiftly. Jaraadhrin gasped. She had literally vanished and reappeared in front of him, her eyes wide with horror yet her face cool and collected, level with his own. Her aura was centuries old, tinged with silver under the breaking colours. He drew a shuddering breath. It was the Lightening Foot Shifr in less than one tenth of its potency! It had almost depleted his core, vacuuming his years into her.

'I am alright Princess; We just need to get help...' he clenched his teeth as his core split with the effort, spilling more crimson from his lips. He shuddered, more worried about the effect of his overwhelming centient within her and its consequences on his little princess's central being.

'Stay still Dhrin....and shut up!' Princess Saffrodel's voice was tender but firm and rang with command. She moved her arms swiftly, spinning and stamping her right foot, mid manoeuvre to refocus her centient. With a rapid flash, she transferred it with ease to her left hand, glowing in a swirling globe of iridescence and afloat in a silver mist. She grasped him by the left shoulder with her other hand, holding him steady as he swayed. She turned her left hand with the centient sphere towards his right shoulder and drove in the forces, pulsing colourful from her hand to pure silver as it entered him. She let her palm hover without touching his right shoulder, moving her fingers gently to keep the forces flowing.

Princess Saffrodel's face reddened and she averted her eyes from his, looking away. Jaraadhrin squeezed his shut, gritting his teeth against the agony. He felt his core stitch up and the rifts healed within him with alarming rapidity. His central being filled up and the centient years added on faster and faster as his core brimmed. He groaned.

'Princess.... no....stop.... I can't store them without... meditation...' he huffed as his centre bubbled up and over with the extra centients that she was propelling into him. Princess Saffrodel's eyes snapped back to him. She removed her palm from above his right shoulder hastily. She crossed her hands at the wrists, swirling them around each other before slapping one on his chest and placing the other cautiously on the side of his head. Her fingers glowed iridescent against his temples.

She reddened, even more from the heat of the powers spinning around them and looked away again. Her hand on his heart glowed lustrous and shimmery as she worked within his central being. She held the position for few more moments as Jaraadhrin's core quieted down. The centuries sedimented effortlessly within his body. His inner being felt unusually spacious, enough to accommodate a few more life spans. He sighed softly as the pain subsided and his core cooled to normal.

Princess Saffrodel moved back from him, withdrawing her hands from his chest and his flushed face. She gazed at him intently, watching for signs of distress with her fair forehead, slightly furrowed. Jaraadhrin inhaled, he felt strong and solid within. He sat back on his heel and raised his eyes to his little Princess. He couldn't make sense of his emotions raging within him but above everything else, all he could name was the admiration and wonder, he felt for this tiny, shimling warrior Princess.

Yesterday she was strategizing and advising. A Princess, A Leader, a Mentor and a Councillor! Today she was a Fierce Warrior, A Healer and A Mistress of the Shimran Being! He exhaled in a quiet gust, gazing at her, half exasperated and half amused but completely in awe, still at eye level with him. She returned his gaze with a tentative smile, scrunched up her nose and mouth and pulled at her ears delicately with her hands.

'Sorry!' she mouthed. He chuckled at the look on her face. The coldness, the anger and command were gone. She was his Princess again. His mirth turned to a cry for reasons unknown to him. He drew her gently but swiftly to him by the back of her neck and hugged her tight. His long robes folded around her tiny frame, enveloping her in them and close to his heart. Princess Saffrodel gasped as her little form stiffened in his sudden and unexpected embrace. Her breath racked, wild and shallow against his left ear as he patted her brilliant red-gold locks. He repositioned the loose flowers on her hair delicately. Her locks, too thick and long, fell out of her braids, unable to stay still within its flimsy clips with the ferocity of all her recent movement.

'You saved my life!' he cried, his voice shuddering. She swallowed hard, trembling slightly against him and cleared her throat. She held her arms stiff and straight under his. They didn't fold over behind him.

'I almost killed you too, Dhrin, so....' She replied, her voice tremulous.

Jaraadhrin chuckled and let her go, sitting back on his heel. Her face was red as ever! He frowned.

'Why are you so flushed all the time, my Princess? Do you feel well?'

'I.... erm...that took a lot of effort!' she exclaimed with her hands on her cheeks. She flew over to the banister and sat down, gazing at him. Jaraadhrin stood up, lifting a few spaces into the air with a sprightliness of his core. He did a quick whirl in mid-air amazed at the strength and stability of his centre. He laughed, it felt like a brand-new core. He sat down beside his Princess and gazed at her.

'I am finding it really difficult to understand who is mentoring who and what is even being learned?' he said, feigning a sigh of confusion. Princess Saffrodel giggled and said nothing.

'Well, your foot work in sword play is excellent but you might need more practice with the wrist movements' he said still gazing at her in admiration. She was a Royal! She had access to any Shifr. She was bursting with Shifrs and he could no longer tell them apart. No wonder she was angry and irritable. She was growing faster than any shimling, assimilating and using all her Shifrs in one go.

How difficult it must be for a month old shimling to do so much in such a little period of time. This many Shifrs could drive her mad. His gaze changed to that of concern.

'Aaashh! Of all the Absurdities in Shimrah, Dhrin!' Princess Saffrodel exclaimed. She jumped off the banister and whirled around to face him, her hand on her hips and her expression annoyed again. 'You have got it all wrong!' she raged. Jaraadhrin stared at her in shock.

What? She could read him! Quinn was right! Princess Saffrodel threw her hands in the air.

'You old tzar! Sooooo, irritating in your concerns for me!' she said in exasperation as she rolled her eyes. She took a deep breath, calming herself. 'It's a Mirror Shifr.' She informed him. 'Yes, I am a Royal and I can access any that takes my fancy. But why would I take so many on and go mad when one could give me everything I could ever want? I could Mirror every Shifr in the entire kingdom with just one Shifr! Of course it will not be the potent version of the original Shimran but it is enough. I have been manifesting it a while now, to learn. My mother feels I should learn everything as soon as possible. She is concerned about something she doesn't want to tell anyone, I told you yesterday. How else do you think I could know so much information and be the shimara I was born to be? My mother seems to think that I am some Saviour of the Shimran folk. I don't know how or why but I have been trying hard for my mother and the Shimrans!' She paused and exhaled.

'Mistress Afra's healing abilities, my mother's vision, my father's memories, the sword strokes of the tzars and maras in the clearing, every one of their Shifrs, your staff strokes, Quinn's powers of the mind, his practical ability to sediment excess centient into himself, your Essence Shifrs voluntary reflexes, all your martial styles' she said ticking them off on her slender little fingers 'It's one Shifr, Dhrin!' Jaraadhrin nodded, dumbstruck.

'Ah...I see yes...that's very clever' he murmured, brimming with admiration and pride. He frowned suddenly. 'So, you emptied my core on purpose?' Princess Saffrodel sighed again, incensed

'That was mistake. I lost control there. I was angry and you wouldn't fight back. It was the Lightening Foot but it has metamorphosed from the standard. Usually, when someone uses it, it depletes the user's core and those of the opponents. Mine channels everyone's back into me so I ended up with yours too. My father's heritage and blood affect our Shifrs and abilities in unpredictable ways. I just have to roll with it as it presents itself. Fortunately, I can understand what happened immediately and that helps me counteract any negativity' Jaraadhrin nodded, that made some sense.

'Core sharing is a learned trait, core extraction from Quinn, centient-core sedimentation within the being like that, especially in another body than your own? Is that Quinn's too?' He wondered, thinking hard. She shook her head.

'You have a Core Shifr too, Dhrin. Its dormant. All three is from you! Quinn's isn't a Shifr, it's a learnt and practised skill, years of it' he stared at her, assimilating what she had said.

Aaashh! And I have been mediating Javnoon for hours on end! Was it this dormant Shifr I used on the King? So why couldn't I mediate it immediately after?

'You exhausted your inner strength tapping in to an undeveloped Shifr, so you needed help then. You should be fine with practice' she answered him, swiftly.

'And no, the Shifr detection one is Lord Jaraadh's, your father's' she replied to his half-formed question. 'He visits sometimes and I think I managed to annoy him a bit with my shield Shifr. It wasn't for his benefit; I didn't want Quinn to read me yesterday. It is from one of your warriors shimaras and my mother. That's how the Queen shields thoughts she doesn't want me to read.

It takes practice to slide back and forth from the mind. Your father wants to see you fight Quinn. I do too. Quinzafoor needs to be taught and trained. He is a good tzar but very young and content behind his Shifr!' she declared.

Jaraadhrin chuckled; half startled. His Princess was a month old shimling who called a fourteen-year-old tzar, young! She thought of training Quinn and was concerned about his ineptitudes, just like Jaraadhrin was. So yesterday was indeed planned. Princess Saffrodel sighed and moved beside him.

'Quinn's training wasn't. Just the armoury tour and the issue around the unisi. I heard your thoughts when we were bickering over the centient welcome and I decided to help, but yes, I do care about my soldiers and Quinn in particular. He is a good tzar and he revers you.' Jaraadhrin's lips curved in an impish smile.

That's why Quinn's attitude changed quickly. My Princess took the initiative to change it because Quinn revered me. And by just being herself with him? What a prodigy she is! Tzars had a hard time saying no to maras in general. Poor Quinn didn't stand a chance against a Royal shimling!

'Aaashh! It's not like that...!' Princess Saffrodel glanced at him, annoyed. 'You know it's not like that at all! Do not even jest in your mind about things like that! It is against my honour! No shimara would ever misuse her power over the tzars like that and I am no different!' she sighed, shaking her head as he chortled at her outrage.

Dhrin knows this well enough! He is just antagonising me! He really is very mischievous indeed under all that fake sternness! She thought to herself in amused vexation.

'I can read you too, you know. I know your concerns and they are true. His Shifr is lethal and presents opportunities to stray, especially with his past and the spreading darkness in Shimrah.' She continued, her fair brows furrowed in concern.

What happened to Quinn....? thought Jaraadhrin frowning. His father had said something about Quinn's difficult past too. His Princess shook her head.

'That is for him to tell you when he is ready' she replied to his thoughts. 'He needs Shimrans by his side to help him see light, should he step away from the right path. You know...to guide him back. I...er...well...I wanted to be one of them... that's all...' her voice trailed away. Jaraadhrin gazed at her affectionately. Words eluded him and his heart swelled with warmth for his Princess. She worried incessantly over the wellbeing of all Shimrans whether she knew them or not. Of course, she cared for Quinn. She knew him personally. She loved and respected him. All that and she was only a moon old shimling!

Princess Saffrodel placed her hands on the banister gripping it, just like her mother often did. She looked up at him and slipped the therin over her fingers. His Princess reached up on her toes and wiped the crimson off of his lips and chin. She smiled at him.

'I am completely well. I can deal with my Shifrs, the education and everything else that is happening. I have one other Shifr that helps me manage everything perfectly and kindly stop referring to me as a month old shimling' Jaraadhrin chuckled again. 'I have a fifty-year centient equal to two Shimran or core years as you had noticed. That makes me a grownup shimara essentially.'

Jaraadhrin smiled at her, at a loss for words. He couldn't think straight. *How amazing is she. What is her other Shifr and how did she get that centient? Tinctures increased centient years but she certainly hadn't used any.* Princess Saffrodel shook her head again.

'That's for tonight, I will tell you then' she said.

'What's tonight?' he asked, distracted, his mind still overcome in wonder. Princess Saffrodel sighed, tapping her foot with impatience.

'The fan dance!' she reminded him huffily. Jaraadhrin grinned, he wouldn't miss it for anything. He stepped down, he had to do something. He wasn't used to feeling such overwhelming admiration, tenderness, affection and a whole host of other emotions he couldn't even begin to name, for anyone.

'You are a perfect little, warrior Princess but we do need to get that wrist movement right' he said as he gathered his composure. 'Let me show you?' he extended his hand to her, his brow raised. She smiled, unclipped her sword and handed it to him. It was very light indeed and well made.

Jaraadhrin stepped as lightly and gracefully as the wind, the sword slashed vehemently around him as he showed her the wrist movements. The therin of his mantle, furled and unfurled, caught in the relentless wind under his heels. He spun around, his cloaks and sleeves followed his nimble steps as it fluttered in the soft breeze. His tall frame, straight and elegant, swayed with the force of his blade's strokes. His long tresses lifted, spread and swirled, around him in immaculate bronze waves as his sword ripped, precise and swift.

His handsome face, stern with concentration and his glittering, blue eyes focused on the strokes. He leapt up in mid-air, rotated the sword effortlessly around his wrist and caught it deftly as he floated to the ground. His wraps settled in clouds around his long legs, his blade pointed in Princess Saffrodel's direction, who sat on the banister gazing at him in admiration. Her face in her hands and her eyes, glazed. Jaraadhrin tossed the sword in the air. He caught it by the blade delicately between two fingers and handed her the hilt.

'Did you get the moves, Princess?' he said, smiling at her expression. She nodded.

'I think so' She took it from him, clicked it and the blade decreased in length. She frowned in concentration, turning it around slowly, unsurely. Princess Saffrodel stopped.

'Can you show me once more, Dhrin?' she requested, smiling up at him pleasantly.

'Hmm...' he wondered, taking her sword from her, lengthening the blade and tapping his chin. 'There is still the height issue' Princess Saffrodel glared up at him. 'No matter, no matter' he said hastily. He held up his left arm in front of his slim waist, the long sleeves flowing off of it. 'Jump on and sit facing front.' Princess Saffrodel flushed red again.

'On your arm?' she questioned, her voice hardly audible. Jaraadhrin tensed, confused.

'What happens to be the quandary now? You had no squirms swinging off my arm in mid-flight the other day and sliding around my shoulders in front of the entire...'

'Alright! Alright!' She muttered and leapt up. She sat herself self-consciously on his arm. He handed her the sword back and swished the therin off of his feet.

'Observe the footwork as well if you can, Princess' He said as he slid lower, in to the first stance.

Jaraadhrin pulled his arm back, supporting her frame against his chest and held the sword over her arm and hand. She stiffened and gasped quietly. He tilted his head, looking at her face sideways in concern as his locks slid over her shoulders.

'My Princess...?'

'Aaashh!...Of all the....Just show me, Dhrin!' she said her voice tense. He sighed, shaking his head. He would never understand his Princess.

Jaraadhrin swirled around and slashed the long blade to his right, then stepped smartly to his left. He crossed and uncrossed his legs as he followed the graceful spins of his wrist. He re-enacted the movements from before but this time holding her hand over the sword and her legs tightly with his up-turned palm as she sat on his forearm. He swished the sword around them in lithe, powerful strokes as they spun in circles. His long tresses whipped around against her with the ferocity of his movements. His handsome face moved close to hers and swung away as their sword arms spun together, twirling her around with him.

He pulled their arms in a large sweeping circle over them as he bent back-wards. Princess Saffrodel leaned back against his chest with the sudden twist, her cheek resting on his right shoulder as she turned to follow the arc of their sword arms. A sudden warmth blazed against her skin through his robes.

She trembled violently and drew a quick quaking breath. She pulled her hand free from under his, on the sword and pirouetted off of him, landing by the banister. She stood, turned away from him. Her hands shook on the white marble and her long red hair slid off its clips, more tousled than before. Her whole form trembled as she breathed hard. Jaraadhrin halted in surprise.

'Princess?' He called, concerned. A slight silver glow on his right shoulder, dis-tracted him and he looked down to see it emanating through his robes.

That is new. What now? The last time it did this was when I absorbed the eons from the king. I am not brimming over with centients at the moment. In fact, thanks to my little Princess, my core has never felt more organised and in sync with my being than right now. Maybe it blazed when overwhelmed by emotions too? He certainly was filled with a lot of those right now. He felt so astonished at the prowess of his shimling Princess. He frowned, pulling another layer of therin over it and turn-ing back to his Princess.

'I think I have learned enough for today, Dhrin' she said, her voice rather higher than usual.

'My Princess, are you...!' queried Jaraadhrin, rather troubled.

'I am well... I just need to rest... I feel rather... spent' Princess Saffrodel straightened with a deep breath. She turned to face him 'I will see you to-night. You should go beat Quinn now' She smiled radiantly at him. 'I am sorry I can't be there but come tell me the good news tonight and make sure you rehearse for that dance' She added. Jaraadhrin smiled down at her affection-ately as he inclined his head and saluted.

'As you command, Your Highness' he jested. His Princess smiled up at him shyly and rustled away as quickly as she could, her locks finally flowing free of the flimsy clips as they clattered on the marble in her wake. The Pembre staff on his desk flashed in Jaraadhrin mind as he gazed after her. If he could sharpen the base of the little staff, it would hold up his princess's locks more efficiently....

The Victory

Jaraadhrin made his way to his terrace, ravenous. What a morning it had been! No wonder he felt this hungry. Incareth had already set the table for him within his chambers, keeping it warm with a sliver of her centient. She was such a thoughtful little shimara. He washed and sat down to it. He noticed a little yishin sphere beside his plate. It was a glimmering cream in colour. He slid the crystal sheet from within it.

'I made your favourite dishes today, My lord. I heard it was a special day. I will have a scented bath ready for you before you meet the Princess. Please take it before you leave. Pardon me for not being there to serve you, your meal.'

He smiled tenderly. Sweet, gentle Incareth. How did she know he was going to see the Princess tonight? He himself had known it just this morning. Jaraadhrin ate, his mind elsewhere.

He still hadn't gone to the clearing. He had wanted to bring his Princess down with him, to see him fight Quinn but her wishes came first. He sipped at his drink, his mind turning to Quinn. Jaraadhrin had seen him in the clearing as he had coasted back. Quinn had waved as usual from the top of the pedestal, where he had been watching the other tzars fight. He hadn't been fighting for a change but leaned back lazily, strumming at his harp, placed in the crook of his bent knee and with the other stretched out. His posture splayed his cloaks in a wide arc and they shimmered in the sun.

A group of warrior shimaras had sat some ways from him, glancing at him every so often and giggling. He had often seen that but hadn't made the con- nection till lately. Jaraadhrin chuckled, even from a distance, doing absolutely nothing, Quinzafoor was an impressive figure. He was undeniably, the most elegant tzar, Jaraadhrin had the fortune to meet and it was obvious that the shimaras found him so too. But Quinn never had a thought for them as far as he could see, much like himself.

Jaraadhrin finished and stood up, straightening the therin of his stoles and his tresses. He moved his fingers in a circlet and a silver yishin sphere, carrying his gratitude to Incareth, floated beside his plate where hers had been. It was such an ingenious and welcoming gesture. He would make sure he left one for her every time.

He checked his crimson belt for all the weapons. He didn't really plan to use most of them. They were there just in case. His core soared and he smiled. Thanks to his Princess, he felt powerful and invincible. He was sure Quinn would adapt quickly enough but what if he lost to Jaraadhrin? It may be his first loss against anyone in his whole life. Jaraadhrin frowned, he wouldn't want to make Quinzafoor loose face before him and his soldiers. He was the commander of his entire Martial Force in the hierarchy next to him and the soldiers needed to give him that respect and superiority. Jaraadhrin pondered for a moment more, remembering his father's words.

'I need you to train as hard as you can with Quinzafoor. I had a word with him, and I feel he is exactly right to be by your side. You will both need to be by the Princess' Lord Jaraadh had said 'But be warned, Quinzafoor is immensely powerful, very young and he has had a hard past. He will need work and patience on your end. You will be his closest. Your Shifrs are the only ones that can match him and even manage him...'

Jaraadhrin had scoffed at his words. His Princess's words broke through within his mind as he chuckled.

'You can but you won't, you are too soft with him! You are all paternal and odd with him!.... He is a good tzar but very young and content behind his Shifr!

Jaraadhrin drew a deep breath; his Princess and his father were right. Quinn was too dependent on his Shifr and somewhat complacent. Shimran Shifr magic could be counteracted, changed and mutated so much by other forms as his Princess had proved to him today. Quinn needed to understand this if he was going to stand by him and help protect the Princess. Only then would he be able to deal with every eventuality.

Jaraadhrin would make sure he fought Quinn with humour and mirth. He would teach his second-in-command in the language he understood best. Wit and hilarity. He would probably have to dispel his sternness for a while and be himself. He might probably make a spectacle of himself too but he had to try for Quinn's sake! The way he would take this match would be a good indication of his character and his adaptability to situations.

Jaraadhrin leapt off of his terrace and soared to the clearing. Most of the soldiers had left for their meals. A few sat around nibbling and drinking around the pedestals in relaxed conversations. Quinn sat with a few tzars, drinking from little cups, lazing in the petal shaped chairs that were set around the marble plinths. He hoped it wasn't anything too strong. He didn't want Quinn's senses impaired; it wasn't like him to drink midday either. He looked as if he had just eaten too. As Jaraadhrin approached, Quinn leapt off the tables, blind folding himself quickly and jumped down to the clearing. He was ready and rearing to go.

'You are little late, my Lord' he grinned. 'We were expecting you this morning.'

'Quinn was expecting you, my Lord' Someone called from behind Quinn 'He wouldn't fight anyone today. He has been sulking' Quinn turned quickly to face the soldier who called out, his expression changing from a grin to a glare, deadly even with his blindfold as he quelled the tzar. He turned back to his Lord, genial again. Jaraadhrin alighted gracefully into the clearing.

'I had a prior engagement with a very important little shimling' he replied. Quinn's full lips curved up in amusement as the flashes of Jaraadhrin's morning reached him.

'Eventful? Wasn't it?' He observed, his grin widening.

'You would be exhausted just thinking about it!' Jaraadhrin quipped, tilting his head 'So let's try keep your abnormally meddlesome mind out of it, shall we...?' Quinzafoor chuckled as the soldiers joined in the mirth. They loved their leaders and was always happy to see their skills, both martial and humour, matched so evenly. Jaraadhrin slid two fingers across his eyes and a centient blindfold appeared over them. Unlike Quinn's, it was thick and ensured his Lord couldn't see at all. Quinzafoor frowned, a puzzled look on his face.

'I don't think that's.... Oh!' he began, before his face changed into a look of surprise and shocked amazement as he read the Shifr in his Lord's head. Jaraadhrin chortled. The expression on Quinn's glowing auburn essence was just as satisfying as he had imagined. Quinn grinned again, reading everything including his Princess's and Jaraadhrin's concerns, his sense of responsibility and his Lord's need to protect him. He nodded, thickening his own blindfold with centient so he couldn't see either.

'So today we are even' Quinn speculated.

'No... ' Jaraadhrin replied, smiling. 'I have an unfair advantage over you as you have had in every contest before this' The soldiers fell quiet, gazing from one to another, watching the exchange in confused silence.

'I can fight with that' Quinn answered him, his face breaking into his infectious smile again. He had given much thought to everything that had happened yesterday and he was of the same mind as his Princess and Lord. He knew their thoughts; they were on his side and they cared. He would try hard and make them proud of him. He just didn't expect the opportunity to present itself this soon.

'Good, that's what I like to hear' Jaraadhrin unclipped his staff and whirled it lazily in his hand, concentrating on Quinn's brilliant auburn essence in front of him and letting his Shifr take over. Quinzafoor pursed his full lips. All he could see was himself in Jaraadhrin's mind, twirling his double daggers as a brilliant auburn glow. He drew a deep breath, pushing his Shifr off focus and reaching out with his other senses. He would be fighting with his martial skill alone, robbed of his Shifr and dependent on his hearing, smell, skin and instincts. How right they were. He was too reliant on it. He felt completely blind and off his depth.

Well, that changes today! He thought grimly.

The wind displaced from Jaraadhrin's whirling staff, wafted his scent down to him and he could tell roughly where his Lord was. He adored that scent, it reminded him of the freshness's of hill tops and early morning fog. The breeze and his hearing would be his best bet at not losing to Jaraadhrin today. He couldn't even consider winning.

Quinn's handsome, laughing face tensed; his brow furrowed in concentration as he felt a thick draft of wind on his left. He blocked with his daggers instinctively and met Jaraadhrin's staff. He stepped back as he felt the staff withdraw. He blocked again as Jaraadhrin swished his staff at him, this time on the right.

It was getting easier with every blow to anticipate Jaraadhrin's attack. He could do this with practice. His martial skill was lethal enough to compensate for the lack of his Shifr. The fresh scent wafted down to him on his left and Quinzafoor slashed his daggers at it, attacking this time. He grinned as they met Jaraadhrin staff with a resounding crash.

Oh, well done, Quinn! He heard Jaraadhrin's relieved whisper, quiet in admiration, within his mind. *Now concentrate, forget the Shifr.* Quinn nodded, strengthened by the fact that his Lord was happy for him and that he favoured him enough to train him personally. He drew a deep breath, reaching out and started participating more fully, employing his senses at full capacity.

The soldiers had started gathering around them. Word had spread that their young Lord Protector had finally joined them and that he was blindfolded. The match was turning out to be as sensational as Jaraadhrin's father had predicted. Both tzars blindfolded, clashing with each other with lethal weapons, using just their skills and a deadly new Shifr, they knew nothing about.

The crowd gasped and shrieked as the fight intensified. The roles were reversed, however. Quinzafoor was no longer lazy and relaxed. He swirled over and under Jaraadhrin's swift staff strokes, blocking and attacking as fluidly as ever but his face tensed in concentration while Jaraadhrin pirouetted around him, relaxed and almost indolent.

If my Princess could see me now, she would probably give me a good talking to. Maybe call me a show-off and a few other choice words thrown in the mix. Jaraadhrin thought, grinning to himself.

Quinzafoor chuckled as the thoughts streamed to him from Jaraadhrin. His Lord had the most amusing head, he had ever been in. Even the silver of his youthful being, infused with its shimratzarry merriment, tickled his mind. Jaraadhrin looked so stern and cold all the time but he had the most humorous head and the gentlest of hearts.

Concentrate Quinn, you absurd little whelp...! Jaraadhrin commanded in exasperation as his staff nearly blasted Quinzafoor off of his feet. *Stop eavesdropping into my mind! You are not supposed to use the Shifr for anything when we fight.* Quinn leapt up, spinning at the last moment, his toes missing the flashing staff by a hair's breadth. He dodged another whirl of his Lord's staff and spun away from him, chuckling.

'It isn't a choice my Lord. I can't block it at will and trust me when I say, I wish I could! It could help ease the massive cramps on my sides from laughing at your thoughts so much. Your entertaining mind is constantly busy thinking up hilarious remarks' he replied, snickering.

Aaashh! That was supposed to be a secret. You puny, senseless, little imp! Stop airing my head to everyone! Jaraadhrin grinned at him good naturedly.

Quinzafoor doubled up, spinning further away from him, his dimples flashing as he fought to stop his mirth. Their soldiers watched, sniggering with laughter at them. They could only hear some of it but it was enough to guess the rest. Jaraadhrin sheathed his staff and pulled out a pair of fans from his ribbon.

'Clearly the staff twirls are making too much sound and a stiff breeze which you are blowing away on, Quinzafoor' he said chuckling in mischief, referring to the fact that Quinn kept spinning away from him in his mirth. 'Shall we try something that doesn't give you a hurricane indication as to where I am? he jested. Quinzafoor snorted as the tzars in the crowd burst into laughter at his gold fans. They loved this side of Jaraadhrin. The softer, gentler side, full of laughter and witticisms. Jaraadhrin raised his brows at them in comical sternness.

'What?' he said, pretending to misunderstand. 'Do you think them too entertaining? More for the shimaras, perhaps?' He teased, inclining his head respectfully at where he knew a group of shimaras sat. They cheered him loudly, shooting hearts and flowers with their centients.

'Never underestimate the accessories and powers of the shimaras, my good shimratzars!' He bantered, his lips curving in a grin as he posed with the fans with exquisite elegance. The tzars roared with laughter as the cheer from the maras grew deafening and colourful dust sparked into the air. Jaraadhrin felt the warm centients of the warrior shimaras falling around him as their flowers, hearts and sparkles, rained on him.

Oh my! For the Love of Shimrah! I might as well go to the Crystal Depths and lay myself down in its waters! If the Princess saw all that wasted centients, I am surely dead!

Quinzafoor nearly fell to the ground, chortling away, clutching at his sides. Jaraadhrin gazed at his auburn essence in frustrated amusement.

Aaashh! This meddlesome scamp of a tzar...! I can't even think in peace with him around....! Anyway....

Jaraadhrin flipped the fans open and spun them rapidly around his slim wrists. He crossed them and sent them spinning around the edges of the clearing. They slashed though the entirety of it, in a wide circle, from both sides before boomeranging back to his wrists. As he caught them deftly between two fingers of each hand, crossed at the wrists and the fans fully open, branches leaves and even whole trees crashed around the edges, littering the clearing.

The soldiers fell silent in awe then started clapping and shrieking in admiration at his grace and the deadly skill he used. Jaraadhrin raised his chin high, fanning himself with sophistication, his expression hilariously haughty. Summoning his centient, he swished away the debris with his other hand, the fan closed. Quinzafoor roared with laughter, unable to hold it in any longer. His face red and tears of mirth soaking his blindfold. He could read Jaraadhrin's posture, expressions and actions in the minds of the watching soldiers as he heard the crashes around him.

He tried to see through their heads to fight Jaraadhrin but they were too excited, their attention skipping between Jaraadhrin and himself for a steady sight. Quinzafoor refocussed on his senses.

The fans disturbed the wind less but it also provides me with two targets and you are probably in between them, my Lord! he thought, grinning. His forehead furrowed as he concentrated harder. He slashed his daggers at the subtle changes in the breeze and the scent of mountain freshness. His daggers met Jaraadhrin's fans every time.

Jaraadhrin blocked his advances, quick but idle as his Shifr moved him around Quinzafoor without much effort. The obscure martial form he had practiced many years ago, resurfaced instinctively within his current postures and fighting methods. He spun his fans around Quinzafoor's head, leaving just enough room so they wouldn't touch him. The crowd gasped as Quinn crossed his wrists, deflecting them away from his ears with the tips of his daggers. The long tresses at the sides of his face, flew in the breeze of the spinning fans. He chuckled as Jaraadhrin caught them again with a mock yawn.

Jaraadhrin grinned. He wanted to see what other weapons, Quinzafoor would try against his fans. He dove in swiftly, spinning his fans around Quinzafoor's daggers, loosening his grip on them. He flashed his fans apart, the daggers caught in their rims. They flew off and rammed themselves into trees on either side of the clearing with echoing thuds. A stream of flames poured from the dark edge of the clearing, followed by a soft neigh as Ashoora showed her appreciation. She sat on her folded front legs as she watched with interest. She usually supported Quinn but today, seemed to be quite impressed with Jaraadhrin. This was the very first time anyone had disarmed her powerful master.

Quinzafoor leapt back, unclipped a pair of swords from his ribbon and attacked him again. Jaraadhrin moved away, blowing the repeated strikes of the sharp blades aside with ease, fluid and nimble with quick flips of his wrists. He twirled around at the last double stroke, slapped Quinzafoor's wrists and rotated his fans rapidly around the hilts in Quinn's hands. He used the spinning momentum within his fans to grip the hilts and blasted them into trees as well, chortling. The crowd roared, cheering as he unarmed Quinn the second time. Ashoora stood up and cantered about excitedly. She shot more flames from her horn, as sparked as the crowd.

Quinzafoor tensed with concentration. He somersaulted back and expanded sharp, metal stars from within his fanning robes, in mid-air. He slung them with both hands even before he alighted, his wrists snapping swiftly as they whizzed towards Jaraadhrin's head and chest.

His Lord soared high in an elevated spin and using the advancing stars as steppingstones, spiralled light-footed from star to star, touching each with the tip of his toes. He crossed the distance of the clearing between him and Quinn with incredible agility. As he launched the last star, Jaraadhrin jumped on it and stepped lightly on to Quinn's outstretched hand. He pattered along Quinn's arm and over the back of his shoulders with lightening swiftness as his Princess often did. The crowd shrieked, going wild over Jaraadhrin crazy manoeuvres.

He skipped down behind Quinn, pinning his arms tightly at his sides with his left arm still holding the closed fan in his hand. He flipped the other fan around, clicked open the dagger within the handle and placed the blade flush against the robes on Quinn's right shoulder!

The soldiers shrieked in awe, clapping and whistling, the maras flying high into the air, twirling their skirts and shooting stars at his victory. Ashoora whinnied loud and victorious, hoofs high in the air as her wings bristled up behind her and shot a great plume of fire. She was enjoying herself today. The shimaras screamed at her reactions in mirth.

Startled, Quinn moved his head abruptly to the right in shock. His sharp nose bumped into the ridge of Jaraadhrin high cheekbone. He flinched away, spun the fan around, flipped it open in mid-air and fanned them both with sophisticated style. The long tendrils of their tresses, framing their faces, flew back in the breeze.

'We are done, Quinzafoor' Jaraadhrin chuckled. 'Time to cool off' He removed his centient blindfold. Quinn's handsome face broke into a smile as Jaraadhrin loosened his grip. He turned with astonishing swiftness as his central being moved him, driven by his emotions. Quinn threw an arm around Jaraadhrin's shoulders, pulling his Lord against himself, in a quick, one-armed hug and tapped a gentle fist on his Lord's back.

'It was an honour, my Lord' He glowed. He moved away hastily from his spontaneous embrace, horrified at his impudence and sank into a salute as the crowd roared around them. Jaraadhrin rolled his eyes and lifted his second-in-command up by his chin, level with him. He touched the ridge of his reddening cheekbone gently.

Aaashh!' exclaimed Jaraadhrin, twisting his fair face in mock vexation. 'Any sharper and you could use that nose of yours as a weapon!'

Quinzafoor threw back his head, laughing as all his pent-up mirth exploded out of him. His long tresses flew behind him in the aura of his hilarity and the soldiers joined in. Quinn's laugh was too infectious and just hearing him was usually enough to get everyone to join in. Quinn removed the thicker sentient from his eyes so he could see again. He summoned his scattered weapons from around the clearing and stored them away in his ribbon, still roaring away. His firehorn trotted over to him, sank into quick bow in front of Jaraadhrin then rose and nudged Quinn's head. He turned to her, grinning widely.

'Turncoat!' Quinn teased and Ashoora snickered, cantering around and around her beloved Master. The soldiers were now clapping excitedly as they replayed their young Lord's final martial moves to each other.

Jaraadhrin smiled, his eyes tender as he gazed at Quinn's slender face and endearing dimples, handsome in their mirth. He placed his hand on his shoulder, squeezing it. He was such a decent tzar, taking the first loss of his life in his stride so casually. Quinn smiled at him, his eyes ablaze behind their blindfold.

'But of course! You are my Lord, my superior and I am thrilled that we were able to prove that today to the soldiers' he answered Jaraadhrin. 'Besides, how could I possibly be angry or annoyed, knowing of your fatherly and protective sentiments for me?' Quinn wriggled his brows at him. Jaraadhrin frowned in amused irritation.

Aaashh! Those were the Princess's words; you should know better. It's more of a brotherly protectiveness Quinzafoor, I am not such an old tzar and you are no shimling, so stop acting like one, you little urchin!

'And.... Here we go, once again...! Quinzafoor chortled. Jaraadhrin shook his head smiling and reached up to pat Ashoora as she nudged him. He sighed.

'As much as I would like another contest, I have to be off now and get ready for tonight.'

'I would rather think not, my Lord' sniggered Quinn, glancing around. 'I don't think your soldiers can take any more of your heroics today. Bless their poor hearts, especially our warrior shimaras' he smirked, gazing up at a group of shimaras who were chattering away, flushed and excited. He glanced up as he read more in Jaraadhrin's head.

'A dance arrangement? He raised his brow mischievously. Jaraadhrin exhaled as he shook his head in resignation.

'With an extremely, angry warrior Princess if I am late' he replied.

'Oooh, I understand the need for the fans now. You were practising! The Princess said she wouldn't dance with a graceless tzar!' Quinn snorted again, his dimples flashing in and out of his cheeks. Jaraadhrin rolled his eyes and diminished his fans. Seriously, his head wasn't his anymore. He was like an open book being read left and right. He gave Ashoora a final pat and turned away from them.

Aaashh! This had to stop. He thought as he dove into the air with a wave towards his soldiers. They saluted as Quinzafoor bowed to him. Quinn's smile vanished as Jaraadhrin glided further away. His face turned tender with his overwhelming affection for his Lord as he watched him soar off towards the palace. He sighed softly.

You need not have worried at all about being a graceless tzar, Jaraadhrin...I have yet to meet another shimratzar, deadlier and more elegant than yourself....

The Mystery Shifr

J araadhrin felt nervous as he made his way back to his Princesses' terrace, the light fading in pinks and auburns. Incareth had had his bath ready for him as she had promised, warm and steaming, with pink petals in them. It also had some healing salts of blue mixed in it. She had really outdone herself today. He had emerged from it, perfumed with the fresh ocean winds. She had also laid out his best white robes, embossed in silvery threads of light. It was nice to come home to a shimara's presence but it was nicer when you knew who the shimara was.

He soared quickly through the darkening evening towards the King's terrace. It was a first and he had no idea what to say or do. He never really cared about his clothing before the Princess came into his life. It wasn't necessary. He was a tzar, Shimrans always looked well-dressed no matter what they wore. It was in their nature.

He alighted lightly on the empty terrace. His Princess wasn't there yet. The warm night air blew soft and sweet, carrying with it the scents of the fading day. He breathed deep, rolling the little fans on his crimson ribbon between his long fingers. He remembered the beautiful movements of the fan dance and he knew his Princess would be exceptionally stunning and graceful performing it. He smiled to himself as he pictured her sweet little face.

The palace gardens below, lit up suddenly with hundreds of tiny, sparkly centient lights, hanging suspended in mid-air. Little lanterns graced the trees and sparkles poured over the bubbling waters in the fountain. The waters ran a brilliant blue and reflected the moon. The spiralling sculptures shone and glittered in the lights and a beautifully decorated table had been arranged, bearing many dishes. Their scents wafted up to him aromatic and delicious. The queen's own lilac centient covered the food, keeping it warm. The grass gleamed slightly as the blades caught the lights, glimmering in the trees. It was as if it had been enchanted. Jaraadhrin stared down from the terrace in surprise. He hadn't arranged any of that.

'Do you like the decorations, Jaraadhrin?' Queen Debriar's voice floated from behind him. Jaraadhrin spun around and sank into a salute in surprise. King Dunyazer and Queen Debriar approached him, holding Princess Saffrodel's hands between them. 'Oh my.... Doesn't he look handsome!' said Queen Debriar, her voice soft in admiration. King Dunyazer chuckled.

'I hear you are taking my daughter for a stroll in the gardens tonight.' He said, grinning at Jaraadhrin. He blushed delicately at his King's words.

'If it pleases you, my Liege and Your Highness' He mumbled. Queen Debriar's laugh tinkled as Princess Saffrodel glided to him. She was dressed in rich, midnight blue therin, embossed in gold. It glistened in spirals and curls as she moved. An ornate gold tiara nestled within her beautiful braids at her forehead and a matching belt shone at her slim waist. The tassels of his tresses hung, long and bronze against her cloaks, on their red ribbon.

'Now that won't do! Will it, my Queen? said King Dunyazer, pretending to stare disapprovingly at the pale contrast of his white robes as he stood beside his Princess. Queen Debriar shook her head, her face serious then broke into giggles. She snapped her fingers and his robes changed into a matching set to his Princess's. Midnight blue with gold threading around it. The richness of his belt glimmered with its own light as he moved. An ornate gold headpiece flew into his hair, lifted his locks away from his face and settled high against his forehead. It was a tzar's version of the one his Princess wore and it glimmered almost identical in its curves and spirals.

He stared down at his floaty robes. These had all been made for him. Queen Debriar had just swapped his clothes. No one could magic things out of thin air. How long had these been planned? No wonder Incareth knew about the visit to his Princess that evening. All the servers probably knew. They would have helped with the clothes, the food and the decorations of the palace gardens.

Jaraadhrin lifted his hands in surprise as the cloudy therin flowed from them. This was the first time he had worn such a dark colour and his skin glimmered pale against it. He could see his reflection on a large mirror already set up for him, some ways away. He touched the elegant crown on his head. The gold shone brightly between his bronze waves, enhancing them. It was the first time his annoying hair had looked good. He could hardly recognise himself. He looked so very different from his usual self. He looked like Royalty!

'There!' said Queen Debriar. 'Now you will cut a graceful picture together' she said, her laugh tinkling as she winked at her daughter. Princess Saffrodel giggled beside Jaraadhrin. He stole a quick glance at her.

Didn't the Princess say something like that this morning? Queen Debriar was in on it. Looks like a lot of planning had gone in to tonight!

'My Queen' He whispered, 'It is beautiful and I am...' He bowed low to them. He was staggered. His King and Queen loved him so. He didn't know what he did to deserve their affection.

'Off you go, then' said King Dunyazer 'I think we will retire early today as our little Princess is in capable hands.' He twinkled at Jaraadhrin who inclined his head again, still a little flushed.

Queen Debriar glided over to them. She placed her hands on her heart, palm on palm, kissed the tips of her fingers, touched them to her eyes and placed them gently on the sides of their cheeks. She smiled radiantly at them, eyes tender as she stroked their faces. She turned to Jaraadhrin.

'Watch over her well, young Lord Jaraadhrin' Queen Debriar murmured. He nodded, eyes moist. He didn't trust himself to speak. She smiled then with a nod, re-joined her King. They turned away from them with a final wave and disappeared swiftly, chuckling to themselves. Jaraadhrin turned to Princess Saffrodel as she gazed up at him.

'That was...very unexpected' he remarked as he blinked down at his little Princess. She looked rather dazed as she stared up at him, eyes glazed and wide. Her little lips parted slightly and her head tilted to the side. He raised his brow at her expression and she giggled suddenly, looking away.

'You look like a Prince. Dhrin' she said, 'It's strange but it suits you so well at the same time' Jaraadhrin chuckled at her words.

'After you, my Princess' he said with a flourish, bowing low to her. He held his palm out just in case she wanted to leap off of it. Princess Saffrodel smiled at it, raised her little hand and held the therin just under his wrist as it flowed off his hand. Jaraadhrin shook his head in amusement at her antics, she could have just held his hand.

They leapt off the terrace together, soaring side by side as the wind swirled their matching robes around them. They landed lightly on the gleaming grass. It was a beautiful sight up close and Jaraadhrin wondered at the exquisiteness of it. It must have taken quite a lot of effort to get this much done in such a short time. When had they started? After he had left that afternoon? They walked in silence till they reached the water fountain which bubbled and tinkled. Princess Saffrodel sat down on the rim and Jaraadhrin followed suit. The therin of their robes rustled quietly around them. It was thicker than their normal ones but felt soft and luxurious. A familiar essence caught his eye. Pale cream centient boats, filled with flowers, floated within the fountain's tinkling blue waters. Incareth. No wonder she was too busy to serve him his meal. He smiled down at them.

'I want to try something,' Princess Saffrodel whispered, rather preoccupied. Jaraadhrin turned to her attentively, gazing down at her. She looked stunning in her blue therin. He smiled at her in admiration. She was undoubtfully the most adorable little shimling he had ever had the fortune to meet. The wind blew a long strand of his tresses over his eyes and she reached up to move it.

'Aaashh!' She hissed in quiet annoyance as she couldn't quite reach the top of his head. She withdrew her hand and sighed. Jaraadhrin bent his head down closer to her so she could reach, grinning at her sudden irritation.

'For a shimling, you do get annoyed by the smallest things, my little Princess' he chuckled. She stared up at him indignantly.

'Did it occur to you, Dhrin that I didn't need to ask you to show me the sword play again with my Mirror Shifr and while I was reading your mind with Quinn's, this afternoon?' Jaraadhrin frowned.

That is true. My Princess didn't have to ask me for a replay and there was no way she missed it the first time with the Mirror Shifr. Even if that had failed, she could have just picked the moves from my mind. So why did she feign ignorance?

'Because I wanted to see you do it again' Princess Saffrodel answered his thoughts 'You were so elegant and graceful, yet formidable and regal. I wanted to imagine how you would look when you danced. I didn't expect you to offer to help me learn and then... couldn't turn you down either' she added, looking down at her hands clasped in her lap.

Jaraadhrin nodded slightly, remaining silent and trying to empty his thoughts. She was still using her Shifrs and though he felt flattered at how well she thought of him, he was worried he may trigger her anger again. She was already dealing with so much; he wanted this night to be a happy memory for his little Princess. She sighed tenderly, closing her eyes.

'I am not angry at you, Dhrin. I cannot possibly be.... I am angry at myself' she explained. Her voice quiet with emotion 'I am angry and irritated because of a very childish reason' she grinned up at him again. 'It isn't something that can be helped except, maybe temporarily but I am just impatient and just want things to happen overnight which isn't always the case' Jaraadhrin shook his head, trying to make sense of what she was saying. His mind was as confused as ever which was quite often these days, especially around his little Princess.

'I am not growing physically as fast as my mind, Dhrin' she whispered looking away from his face, her cheeks pinking over. 'Apparently, I will grow at the Shimran pace. I am essentially a young shimara stuck in the physique of a shimling' she paused. 'With the intelligence, emotions, thoughts.... and desires of a shimara, not a shimling' she added, so quiet that it could have been a breath of wind.

Jaraadhrin stared at her, his eyes widening in horror as the meaning of her words sunk in.

Everything makes sense now. My Princess's maturity, her words, her anger and irritation. Her reluctance to touch me and the way she moved away when I did. The pink flushes and blushes! Her responses when she lay against my chest during the sword training, my hand over hers. The blaze on my shoulder! Aaashh! Shimran central beings detected core and mental maturity not physical ones. Then right after she revived my core... in a rage of unrestrained emotions... when I...when I had....when I hugged her....! His face flushed and he swallowed hard, his hand clenched to a fist against his full lips, distraught at his own actions!

Princess Saffrodel moved away from him awkwardly as if the distance between them could help.

'Maybe I should try subdue the Mirror Shifr and not read you mind for now' she murmured. Jaraadhrin choked as he tried to speak.

'My Princess...I....' *What could I possibly say to my Princess? I didn't know.... I have always looked at her and treated her as a shimling, she is my shimling Princess and yet she isn't so little.... I have tortured her inadvertently...transgressed on her honour!*

'I know.... not ...of course not' she mumbled, trying to keep up with his rapid thoughts. She stood up self-consciously and turned away from him. 'That's why I want to try something now but I will need your help.'

'Anything, your Highness....' He said quickly. 'Anything to redeem my inexcusable behaviour. I crave nothing but your forgiveness at my ignorance and lack of judgement, my Princess.' He stood up behind her, inclining his head in a salute, hand on his heart. He shook his head, vexed at his ridiculousness and idiocy in not realizing this as a possibility.

'Don't do this, Dhrin! There is no need for redemption. There is nothing to forgive and you couldn't have possibly known. If anyone needs to ask for forgiveness, its myself' Princess Saffrodel sighed 'You didn't know and I didn't tell you till now. You crossed no lines. I may have… I didn't know… how to….'

'My Princess…' Jaraadhrin began. She shook her head quickly and spoke faster.

'I didn't realize what it was all about till that day in the armoury. When I saw how shaken you were. How much you cared after the blade test…. Till then I was as you saw me but after that…I… have been battling with myself trying to understand and… I am not sure if I understand even now….

'My Princess…?' he whispered. It hurt him to see his Princess like this. Worried, unsure, agonising over things and fighting with herself. He knew how fighting with one's being felt from experience. It was unbearably draining, even for a cool headed tzar. He could only imagine how intolerable it was for a shimara. He was still rather confused as to what her fault in all this was.

What is my Princess talking about? What is she battling? What didn't she understand? This isn't her fault! It is all mine…! Princess Saffrodel drew a deep breath, steadying herself.

'This is a very complicated Shifr and it can deplete my core quite rapidly,' she rushed. 'I need you to watch over me. I have been practising but not quite so much'

'My Princess, if it would harm you, maybe we shouldn't…' Jaraadhrin disagreed.

'I want to' she affirmed, her voice ringing with authority. 'Be ready.' Before Jaraadhrin could argue again, she swished her hands in a rapid circlet and slapped her palms together as her sparking rainbow core expanded swiftly between them. She ripped it apart with abrupt force, rotating them around each other as if she carried something very heavy within. Thunder flashed above them and the aura between her hands expanded with alarming rapidity, enveloping her little form and nearly blasting Jaraadhrin away from her.

He stood his ground; his hand crossed over his eyes, protecting them from the brilliant flashes as he reached in with his other, to get a hold of his little Princess. This was a very powerful Shifr indeed! Cloud like smoke, rolled around on top of them and lightning flashes and crashing sounds streaked through the air to the ground, encasing them in a fiery white cage.

Princess Saffrodel's aura expanded higher and higher till it was almost level with his shoulders. He could see her outline within the sparkling shimmering haze, her long red-gold hair on fire. He closed his eyes reaching into the aura with his Essence Shifr, deathly scared for his little Princess. He could sense her clearly but her form was now as high as the tip of his chin and her core drained with deadly swiftness.

'Princess! No...!'

Jaraadhrin pushed through the blazing mist, his sleeves singeing in the fiery rage and grabbed his Princess firmly around her waist, pressing her to him as she swayed and trembled.

'Princess...Princess Saffrodel....!' He summoned his centients and placed it gingerly on the back of her left shoulder streaming it into her, replenishing her core as it kept depleting. He lost count of how many years he had streamed. He didn't care either! He was just immensely thankful that he had enough.

The blaze brightened to an unmanageable glare as the ferocity of the thunder and lightning increased and his Princess trembled, shuddering hard against him. A soft gasp escaped her lips as she clutched his hand at her waist. She was in pain. It was hurting her!

'Saffrodel... Saffrah...Saffrah...please!' he cried, almost out of his mind with fear for her wellbeing, shaking her anxiously. *What is it doing to her? What is she doing to herself? Why was it necessary to take such a risk?*

She exhaled as the blaze began to lessen around them, slowly but surely. The thunder and lightning overhead slowed and the glimmering rainbow mists dissolved. Jaraadhrin doubled the flow as the now taller Princess, swayed forward. He held her firm as he replenished her and added the fifty years she had had. Princess Saffrodel sighed, removing her hand over his on her waist and trying to free herself from it. Jaraadhrin didn't notice as his concern for her wellbeing, raged out of control.

'Aaashh! Of all the Absurdity in Shimran History, my Princess!' exclaimed Jaraadhrin incensed. 'You nearly killed yourself...! And for what? To become taller...?! You were never to hurt yourself after the blade test. What absolute....'

'Jaraadhrin....' murmured Princess Saffrodel melodiously, her voice quiet as the gentle rain pattering on the marble. He stopped short, enchanted and amazed by the difference in that voice. This was the first time she had called him by his name in full but it was the tone that slashed through his heart with its warmth and tenderness. He withdrew his hand from her waist quickly and stepped back. 'It isn't to become taller....and it's a minor discomfort in comparison...' The voice pattered around him, drenching him and soaking through to his very being. She turned to face him with the grace of pink petals in a spring breeze 'It's my second Shifr Jaraadhrin .... it's time.... To age physically...' She whispered, raising her eyes to his which was glittering blue in anger and anguish.

Jaraadhrin gasped and stepped back in shock. The backs of his legs grazed the rim of the fountain and he nearly lost his balance in his surprise. She caught him by the sleeves of his arms, steadying him as her full pink lips, parted subtly in a nervous smile. His eyes widened and his heart raced as he gazed down at her, stunned. His centients thundered in a surging roar within him, crashing wave over wave of pure energy as he stood, dazed to his core. She was the most beautiful shimara he had ever seen! It wasn't just that either, something else about her made him breathless and lightheaded. It dazzled him, overwhelmed him and held him in a vice like grip of pure light, unable to blink or turn away.

She looked much like her mother, Queen Debriar, but her eyes were a more brilliant green, flecked with glimmering gold specks. The long lashes feathered her beautiful eyes, delicate and thick. The pink of her cheeks streamed darker at her lips, revealing sparkling white pearls as she smiled. Her button nose was gone and in its place was this gentle slide, bridging the ridges of her delicately curving cheekbones. Her face lifted and flowed in the most gracious of features. The glistening red and gold hair embraced her dainty, heart-shaped face in its gossamer softness, playing with the breeze on her smooth forehead and temples.

Jaraadhrin raised his fingers unintentionally, to brush away the tendrils from her forehead, entranced by her glittering eyes. She cleared her throat, soft and quiet. Her eyes flashed to his fingers, almost at her temples, before dropping to the floor. She released the robes at his arms and stepped back from him gracefully. Jaraadhrin shook himself, drawing a shivering breath and trying to steady his being as the horror flooded him again.

What on Shimrah am I doing? He thought in chagrin. *How dare I?! She is my Princess! I am her Protector, her mentor, nothing else! What is wrong with me?!*

He turned away from her and sat down on the rim of the fountain, his handsome face, red and livid. He dropped his head into his shaking hands. He took a deep breath, his long locks crackling with the aura of his anger, his frame trembled as he fought his being.

'I am sorry, Jaraadhrin...' Princess Saffrodel whispered, shaken as his emotions flooded her 'I didn't mean to spring this on you like that' she sat down some distance away from him. Jaraadhrin choked back an infuriated laugh.

What is my Princess apologizing for? It is all me, I am such dreadful, vulgar tzar who doesn't know how to behave with a shimara! How dare I touch her?! Especially after she just explained everything? How did I become so dishonourable!?

'Hardly……you are being irrationally' she murmured, blushing 'At least you now know how I felt all morning….' He looked up at her words, breathing deeply and trying to steady his core and composure.

My Princess felt like this? She certainly did a better job of dealing with it!

'We are not supposed to feel like this, Princess' he admonished, more to himself than her. 'I have a duty to protect you with my life and that's all! Anything else is…is just….' '

This is irrational and I can't make sense of this! I have never even felt the need to look at a shimara and now…' He stiffened, his long fingers pressed to his forehead, grimacing against another roaring wave of deafening centient as he recalled her radiant features.

Even as a shimling those eyes have haunted every waking moment and my dreams! He thought desperately. *I always thought it was my sense of duty to my* Princess *but after tonight…. Aaashh!* he exclaimed again, shivering silently. He squeezed his eyes shut as Princess Saffrodel's feather lashed, shimara eyes, burned behind his lids. Her innocent shimling ones were gone. All he could see were the thick lashed, emerald brilliance from the moment she had turned to face him. He inhaled sharply as the image triggered another crashing wave of torment over his core.

What is wrong with me? How did I become so uncouth and discourteous? Shimran bonds were pure and sacred, irreversible for life. Tzars protected their shimaras honour with their very beings, no matter how and what they felt. They waited for their shimaras to accept them! Those who were wedded had eyes only for their wives and the unwedded shimrans, guarded their honour until a pledge was made. Why have I changed so drastically? Why on Shimrah am I racked with such powerful emotions? Maybe I am tainted by something dark unknowingly? I have heard that darkness amplifies normal emotions making them irrepressible and overpowering! The Princess is entrusted to me! What will I say to my King and Queen! I deserve to be tried for treason! There must certainly be something very dark in me…!

Princess Saffrodel stood up suddenly with a painful gasp. The sharp edge of his agony pierced her heart and she knew she had to do something to set his mind at ease. She had been quiet, unsure of what to do as Jaraadhrin's tortured thoughts roared in her mind. His guilt, remorse, desires and anguish, thundered around her, paralysing her into inaction but how could he even think he was tainted by the dark? He honestly thought it was a possibility! How could any darkness even survive in his pure silver-misted being? It was incomprehensible!

'How irrefutably ridiculous are you, Jaraadhrin?!' Princess Saffrodel exclaimed, clenching her hands to fists at her sides. 'That Mistress Afra. Why couldn't she find the time?! She had all the time in Shimrah.' she muttered in annoyance. His Princess walked swiftly over and knelt in front him. Jaraadhrin flinched violently away from her, almost falling into blue waters of the bubbling fountain.

'Princess!' he exclaimed in anguish at her nearness.

'Aaashh!... Shush, You old tzar!' She said in exasperation. 'Don't make this any harder than it already is. You are tormented because you are fighting destiny. No one can do that!' She flipped her sleeves off her long fingers and placed them quickly at his temples. His gaze drifted to her eyes in surprise, unwilling as he tried to fight it. A bolt of warmth flowed into his forehead, glazing them as Princess Saffrodel looked away from him. She smiled bashfully, incapable of looking into his brilliant blue eyes without reddening.

Flashes of memory illuminated his mind. At the swearing-in ceremony, Jaraadhrin kissing Princess Saffrodel's little fists as she held his long fingers, surrounded by thick gold mist... unable to break free from her eyes as it swirled silkily around them... His face stern yet his eyes churning with emotions, reflecting his raging core...Princess Saffrodel sleeping with her cheek resting on the tassels made of his hair every night, her face tear stained after Jaraadhrin left... Of her admiring him fighting with Quinn every morning before he arrived... Him balancing on Quinzafoor's shoulders, his fans open majestically this afternoon as the shimaras cheered behind him... a stab of annoyance tinging it... Another flash of Queen Debriar gazing at the shimling princess as she murmured....

'Was that...?' And Mistress Afra's reply...

'That was...! The Soul-Light crossfire.... yes! It has to be Marshadath or Ashaqath. With the mist that thick. I would say it's a combination of both Crossfires and which would fit as Jaraadhrin is the Princess's mentor! It's incredibly rare and it is for all eternity...It's the oldest and strongest of Shimran destiny magic...!'

Jaraadhrin inhaled sharply as Princess Saffrodel moved her fingers off his temples, breaking the connection. The flashes of memory darkened and he blinked, breathing in quick shuddering breaths. He stared at her in pure incredulity. They had crossed? The Soul-Light Crossfire? The Marshadath and the Ashaqath? At once? No wonder he felt this shaken. He had read about it as a shimling and often wondered how it felt, now he knew. But with the Princess? With Royalty? He would never have imagined it in his wildest dreams. And everyone knew except him? Aaashh!

Everything made sense now. His obsession with his Princess, the incessant worrying, Queen Debriar's and King Dunyazer unshakeable trust in him, their acceptance of him! How did they even accept him? He was just a noble. One destined to guard and protect them for ever. How gracious were they to accept this so unquestioningly?

His head spun as he remembered and made sense of memories and words that had puzzled him at the time, trying hard not to think of his rejoicing core! He felt hypocritical and it was betraying him. True, he had never thought of his Princess in such a manner until he had seen her as a grownup shimara, gazing up into his eyes as they reflected everything he felt but he had been asking for her forgiveness moments before, for inadvertently acting the way he just did. He shook his head trying to make sense of it all.

He gazed into her eyes again and she promptly dropped hers. His princess flushed and focussed on his singed sleeves. She smiled radiantly as she felt his core quiet down and his centients calming. Jaraadhrin wasn't fighting it anymore and his centre made peace with his being. He couldn't fight against ancient Shimran pledges...nor can he fight against destiny...

'My mother's visions....and mine.... Congratulations on this afternoon. It was very well handled indeed and no.... I could never think undesirably of you, Jaraadhrin. I wouldn't be able to....' she whispered as she waved her hands above his sleeves. The therin mended itself around his wrists and arms where it had singed in the fiery cage of the Time Shifr. Her voice changed to sternness and sudden amusement.

'And you're overthinking again. Old tzar! Its Shimran destiny magic, it's not to make sense of and none has any say in it but to accept it. Unless, you don't want to, of course... Jaraadhrin...?' she teased him. His name rolling off her lips pleasantly, warming his heart. A tender smile lifted the corner of his lips as he gazed down at her.

Didn't want to? That would be the most absurd thing that could happen and today has been so full of absurdities, it was beyond belief!

Princess Saffrodel giggled quietly, traces of her shimling self still evident in her laughter. She reached into his mind, careful and tentative. It burned a brilliant silver as the doubts, the torment and agony emptied from it in rapid succession. His thoughts were pure and honourable as it had always been. His confusion cleared, leaving peace and hope in its wake. It calmed with accept- ance and relief at her explanations.

A melody surged from among the trees, beginning gentle and soft and in- creasing in volume. Princess Saffrodel glanced towards the music in some confusion.

'I didn't arrange that' she said distracted.

'I did' replied Jaraadhrin as she looked up, gazing at him with her eyes half closed in embarrassment. 'I was supposed to dance with you tonight, my Princess' he reminded her 'May be the timing isn't -'

'It's just right, I think' murmured his Princess, lowering her lashes. Jaraadhrin's face brightened into a smile.

'In that case, my Princess' he said, reaching into his robes for the tiny, ornate fans and offering them to her 'May I have this dance' he asked tenderly, his eyes glimmering.

'Oh my' Princess Saffrodel exclaimed, her long fingers over her lips as she as gazed up at him in dismay. 'I forgot my fans!' Jaraadhrin's laughter echoed around the gardens as he helped her up and handed her his fan which promptly expanded in her slender fingers.

Jaraadhrin spread his arms on either side, flipping his fan open and posi- tioned himself with extreme daintiness behind her. His Princess giggled, mimicking him. He moved slowly and smoothly as a silver stream. Their arms and long sleeves, parallel to each other, their robes swishing and billow- ing behind them as they stepped in sync with their movements. The wind rippled around the floaty blue and gold therin of their robes and lifted their hair in gentle rivulets of gossamer as they twirled elegantly behind each other as one, surpassing one another in refinement and loveliness.

The music swelled and the tempo increased as they spiralled into the air and back down repeatedly, their arms flowing in delicate arcs and curves around each other. Never truly touching and never truly apart. The fans clicked open and closed, spinning in their long-fingered hands as they flowed smoothly in the wake of the melodies. Jaraadhrin leaned forward to gaze at his Princess's face and their eyes sealed over her shoulder as they continued to twirl around each other. Golden mists glimmered around them as they spun together, caught in a magical moment of love and bliss.

The Night of a Thousand Moons

High above them on the terrace, King Dunyazer gazed down at them tenderly with his arm wrapped around his Queen. She laid her head on his shoulder, their hearts warm and content. Queen Debriar sighed softly against him.

'She did it' she whispered. King Dunyazer nodded, his eyes moist. He was grateful to fate, destiny or whatever it was. It had given his daughter such a strong and honourable young shimratzar, to protect and cherish her. At that moment, he didn't care much for anything else. She had him and he had her, just like his Queen and himself, had each other. That was enough. They could stand against the whole of Shimrah together and overcome whatever it threw their way.

The music bubbled high in a concluding, glorious melody as Princess Saffrodel and Lord Jaraadhrin spun to face each other in a final flourish. Their elegant faces spaces from each other and their tresses trailing behind them in the wind. They swished their fan arms and closed them simultaneously as they gazed into the other's eyes. Their breathing quieted as their movements ceased and their cloaks floated to a halt around them. Jaraadhrin gazed down into her radiant eyes as his breath caught in his chest.

Hours of martial training has no effect and one short dance with this enchanting Princess, does this to me?

A petal floated down from the trees above them and landed, soft and light, on Princess Saffrodel's face. Jaraadhrin lifted his fingers to her it, hesitantly. She didn't move away this time but closed her alluring eyes as he lifted the petal off of her forehead. The tips of his fingers grazed the line of her brow. The skin of her face gleamed in the moonlight, all roses and cream. Jaraadhrin leaned closer, enchanted by the shimmering smoothness of it as her scent wafted up to him of Spring blossoms and Summer fruits. He sighed, soft and content.

His Princess's cheeks tinged pink as she felt his warm breath so close to her lips and drifted away from him, smiling bashfully. Jaraadhrin chuckled and followed her as the spell waned. They walked side by side, the therin trailing behind them, content in each other's company as their minds and hearts found peace. Rejoicing in a future together.

Jaraadhrin smiled down at his Princess as they walked. She was no longer the irritable little shimling, changing between various faces of her personality. Her behaviour finally suited her stature.

'How long does this last then Princess' Jaraadhrin wondered.

'A quarter of a day, sometimes less' she replied 'The reversal is not that dramatic. I tire easily in this form and fall asleep for a long time, after. It happens when I am asleep. I cannot be woken till the effects wear off. It needs the sun's rays to break. Mistress Afra was worried to death the first time.' Princess Saffrodel answered him as they walked. Jaraadhrin inhaled sharply as an icy shard slid through his heart. He knew how that felt. He tested her aura, it felt strong and solid but her centient was now at seventy-five. He glanced at her in surprise. Princess Saffrodel laughed.

'Aging adds years, I had accrued about fifty when practicing, that's what I had this morning. Tonight, I aged a year which is twenty-five centient years' she explained. Jaraadhrin shook his head. He would need to study this Time Shifr in detail. At this rate she would soon have a core older than his and more centients too! Princess Saffrodel's laughter peeled like bells across the gardens.

'And that's what worries you...?' she giggled to his thoughts. Jaraadhrin chuckled.

'Come now, Princess. Out of my head, then' he teased. She flipped her fan open and fanned herself coyly but slid Quinn's Shifr off of her mind so she could no longer read him.

'No' she said grinning up at him, traces of her impish, shimling self, resurfacing in her gracious features. She looked down at the fan in her hand, suddenly interested. It was the one Jaraadhrin had used to fight Quinn in the clearing. 'This isn't a dancing fan, it's the one you used to fight this afternoon' she observed as she turned it over, examining it intently. The dagger flashed out from the handle and the rim glistened sharp.

'They are weapons, yes, of my own design. Dalfique made them for me when I was four moons old. You met him yesterday, Princess. He was one of the first shimrans to martialize his Shifr.' Princess Saffrodel nodded as she replayed the way Jaraadhrin used them with Quinn that afternoon, within her mind. She spread the fan wide, holding it elegantly within her fingers, crossed it before her and swung it away. It flashed, circling the fountain and zoomed back. She caught it, precise and neat, as it sped past her. It slid to a stop between her two fingers, fully opened and glittering deadly. She flipped her wrist, spinning it around it with blurring swiftness and tossed it high. Princess Saffrodel caught it by the handle, half opened and fanned herself with extreme daintiness.

She gazed up at Jaraadhrin with her feathered lids, half closed. He pursed his lips in a smile and shook his head in awe. His princess handled them with even more sophistication and skill than himself.

'I think I have finally found my weapons, Jaraadhrin.' she murmured as she gazed up into his eyes, shy and bashful. He nodded, chuckling at her face. He diminished the one he held in his hand and reached down to her waist. She gasped at the swiftness of his movements as he bent and pinned his fan on to her crimson ribbon. He smiled up timorously at her expression and moved away with haste.

'Erm...Pardon me Princess, that was...er... out of habit' He cleared his throat, awkward but recovering. 'They are yours, now' he said, his voice tender. Princess Saffrodel looked up at him from behind the half open fan, distracted and rested its sharp rim and spikes against her lips.

Jaraadhrin flushed red and turned away from her, his long fingers over his own. His other hand gripped at his belt, holding it tight for support. His core roared as it rejoiced and he hastened to quieten it as fast as he could. It didn't do that when the other shimaras had used these languages. It had always growled at them in annoyance. Accessory verbiages was the last thing on his Princess's mind right now. A smile played around the corners of his eyes and lips.

'Ahem...erm...Princess? You do know accessory semantics, don't you?'

'Hmmm...? she stared at him, confused. Jaraadhrin cleared his throat again still turned away from her.

'Er.... fan language...? Did you...' His voice quietened as his central being roared, sudden and passionate at his own words. '...want me to...?'

Princess Saffrodel looked down at the half-open fan resting against her lips and diminished it hurriedly, clipping it away into her ribbon.

'I... erm.... I wasn't...Aaashh! No...of course not!' she flushed as crimson as her hair, whirled around and leapt into the air, gliding away from him, her hands over her cheeks. Jaraadhrin followed her, chortling at the expression on her face. His Princess flitted from treetop to glimmering treetop in her mortification. Jaraadhrin's core grumbled down and settled at his mirth as he soared after her, roaring with laughter. Princess Saffrodel slid Quinn's Shifr back on. She needed to stay vigilant around him. Jaraadhrin was so mischievous. She didn't know this side of this mysterious shimratzar. She turned and crunched up her nose and lips at him as she flew further away from him.

Princess Saffrodel alighted, light-footed at the far end of the palace gardens beside another massive fountain. Marble chaises scattered around it furnished with gold cushions. She sat down on one of them and sighed, still rather red. Jaraadhrin slid down beside her, taking in her beautiful features, illuminated in all its radiance against the darkness of the night as he memorised them. She looked rather tired already. The night was cool and the breeze soothed them as they gazed up at the stars. It blew at the therin of their cloaks. Jaraadhrin leaned forward, moving his outer cloak off his legs as he rested his elbow on a knee. His red ribbon slid out and lay between them on the seat, over the cushions. Princess Saffrodel slid a little white box off her own tasselled ribbon.

'I have something for you.' She whispered. She handed the box to him. Jaraadhrin smiled down at her.

'Your first gift to me?....is it a tassel made from a lock of your lovely red-gold hair then?' He teased, taking it from her. It was luxuriously made and intricately designed with inlays of silver Gumoos. Princess Saffrodel giggled at him. She shook her head, her face serious again.

'Our first gift to you....' She replied quietly. He glanced at her puzzled as he made to open it.

'Our....?' He repeated as Princess Saffrodel took it from him hurriedly and clipped it to his ribbon which lay between them. She bound it down with her core. He tensed. *Why core and not centient? I wouldn't be able to release that till my princess wants me to.* He thought.

'Not now...at daybreak in the sunlight and yes, you cannot remove it till then either. That way you cannot say no or return it and must accept it' she explained, grinning up at him impishly. Jaraadhrin gazed at her, half dazed as her radiance sprinkled over him. It was another Shimran tradition. Gifts given cannot be returned if they have been touched by the light of the sun and in the hands of the receiver.

But why on Shimrah would I return a gift from my beloved Princess? Her first ever gift to me too? What could she give me that would warrant such ingratitude and rudeness from me? I wouldn't dare hurt my Princess in such a manner. Especially hurt her core by trying to prise it off and open it earlier. How horrifying! She could have just ordered me. I would rather swallow it whole than disobey her commands or return it! Princess Saffrodel shook her head, tinkling with laughter.

'You do have the most ridiculous thoughts Jaraadhrin. Quinn is right! You have the most humorous mind. When you are not being utterly frustrating and preposterous that is!' she paused, smiling tenderly as he chuckled 'It's very...endearing.' she flushed delicately again and lowered her eyes. Jaraadhrin gazed at her entranced. The red gold of a stray lock of her tresses, curled against the pink of her lips as the wind blew it and it was strangely appealing. The memory from a moment ago flashed in his mind. His Princess resting the golden fan against her....

She cleared her throat in discomfiture, sliding the lock away from her lips, swift in her haste. He grinned, abashed and tinging pink himself as he looked away.

Aaashh! I really needed to keep my thoughts in check! He slid his ribbon back into his robes, caressing the box as he did. Princess Saffrodel sighed and leaned back against the cushions. She looked tired and sleepy.

'I am exactly a moon today' she said, her eyes closing wearily against the brilliant glow of the moon, gleaming down on to her face.

'Jaraadhrin...?' she whispered.

'Hmmm...? He answered as he gazed up at the moon.

'When I turn back to my shimling form, don't forget this night....' She said, her voice trailing lower.

His Princess looked half asleep already and as Jaraadhrin turned to her, her head slid gently on to his left shoulder. He drew a long, sharp breath as her sparkly aura, scent and essence embraced him, circling around him a misty swirl. This was the nearest she had been to him tonight and his core tremored at the proximity. He raised his hand and caught a long tendril of her hair, breezing over her closing, thick lashed lids, trying hard not to touch her and disturb her.

'How could I, my Princess' he murmured, his voice soft and a slight shiver of passion tinging it as he slid the glistening lock behind her ear. 'This is akin to my Night of a Thousand Moons!'

Princess Saffrodel's lips lifted in a chaste smile as her cheeks tinged a deep rose. A quiver ran down her graceful figure against his, at his words. The beautiful Shimran expression meant something entirely different to this night. It signified something more blessed, pure and sacred. A period of Spring that would bind her to him for eternity but she knew what he meant. Jaraadhrin was the happiest, the most content he had ever been in his short life. It was all because of her and he revered this time they had had together!

'Saffrah ...' She whispered

'Hmmm...?

'Saffrah...You have said it before... I heard you...I like it.' she opened her sleepy eyes with difficulty. The memory flashed behind his lids; he had been out of his mind with concern as she aged within the blazing, lightening cage. Jaraadhrin smiled down at her.

'Princess... I...'

'Remember what you said to Quinn. Intimacy voids titles' she whispered gazing into his brilliant blue eyes. He blinked slowly, dazed.

'You pry too much, Princess' he drawled, transfixed deep within her dazzling emerald gaze.

'Saffrah... Saffrah...Saffrah' she whispered, her voice trailing away, her heavy feathered lids, sliding closed. Jaraadhrin gazed down at her delicate features. He sighed, smiling tenderly.

'Saffrah...Saffrah...Saffrah... Saffrah....' he repeated, his voice quiet and melodious. His breath fanned her face with the sweet scent of mountain freshness as his enchanting voice brimmed with his many emotions for her. Princess Saffrodel's lips lifted in a contented smile.

'I like that very much....' she murmured as she sighed away to sleep.

A warm colourful mist enveloped her as she shrunk back into her tiny shimling form, sliding against him. Jaraadhrin caught her quickly and held her shimmering figure against the blue robes of his chest. He gazed down at her fondly, staggered at the way his emotions changed with her form and features to that of protectiveness and adoring warmth for a shimling.

Jaraadhrin didn't know how long he held his little Princess against his heart. The silver moon drenched them in its soft light. The sparkly aura around her subsided back into her form and she moved closer to him in her sleep, sighing peacefully. He drew his long sleeves over her, enveloping her in its warmth and luxury as he stared at her pale little features. He touched her little button nose with the tip of his finger, chuckling as he remembered how she scrunched it up at him, sticking out her tongue. She smiled at his touch, slipping her little fingers deeper into the frontal folds of his robes as she had done ever since Queen Debriar had placed her in his arms, the very first time.

He sighed; it would be another eight moons before he would see that enchanting young shimara by the fountain again. He wasn't going to let her use her Time Shifr anymore. It was too dangerous and too draining. It wasn't worth it. He couldn't wait for tomorrow when he could spend the day with her. There were no more secrets between them, everything had been laid bare. He understood her perfectly and he would make sure he behaved appropriately, considering her emotions. She was just a shimling to him again but it wasn't the same for his Princess. He knew that now. He exhaled; it was midnight. He would have to return the Princess to the King and Queen soon. They might worry about her.

Jaraadhrin sighed again, shaking his head. He didn't want to move. If only he could just hold her as she slept this night...today... forever... knowing she was safe and well. He sat up straighter; He was Jaraadhrin, The Lord Protector of Shimrah, Third in command of the entire Royal Martial Force and the Mentor and Protector of his Princess! He will do that duty first. He rose with a soft rustling of therin, trying not to jolt his Princess. He knew she wouldn't wake till the first light of the day but he was careful anyway. He leapt lightly into the air and made his way to the terrace.

Queen Debriar and Mistress Afra sat at the ornate table at the far end of the terrace as he landed, even more light-footed than usual on the cool marble. They glanced up at him, beaming as he walked over to them.

'About time! Its past midnight! Well after the princess's bedtime.' Mistress Afra bustled over to him. 'We thought you had flown off with her' she said. Jaraadhrin handed the Princess gently to her. As he tried to move away, his robes pulled where she still held them. One little fist deep within the folds and another clasping the edge. Jaraadhrin raised his fingers to stop Mistress Afra.

'Don't cut that off too, now! Those are perfectly good wraps. Very unfortunate about the locks though.' she whispered mischievously. Jaraadhrin shook his head at her, rather annoyed. He still hadn't forgiven her for not telling him about the Soul-Light Crossfire. She could have spared him much torment and self-doubt. He ran his fingers down the section of his mane which Quinn had repaired, with a brow raised, to show her how trivial she was being.

'Thank you for not telling me....' he grimaced, his countenance changing swiftly as he bent down to his Princess. Mistress Afra giggled at his expression. Jaraadhrin pressed the little fist at the edge of his robes to his lips tenderly. 'Let go, my Princess. I will come find you in the morning.' He whispered.

Princess Saffrodel smiled, sighed and withdrew her wrist from inside the folds of his robes as well. Clutched tight within it was his Pembre staff on its long chain. He had swept it off his desk, almost involuntarily as he passed it and slipped it around his neck. He had tucked it within his white robes in his haste to visit his princess that evening.

Mistress Afra stared at it in wonder as Jaraadhrin sharpened the base of his staff with his centient. He worked rapidly and carefully so as not burn his little princess by accident. He unclasped the chain from around his neck and slid it over her head, careful not to wake her.

'Is that your staff...' Mistress Afra began, her eyes fond and mellow. Jaraadhrin nodded, glancing up at her with a quick smile. It was impossible for a tzar to stay angry at a shimara for too long. It was just the way they were.

'It's an exact imitation of my staff...yes...made of Pembre and I have fashioned it so it can be worn as a necklace or a hair stick. The Princess's locks are too thick for her clips.... They unravelled when she fought this morning....' His voice trailed as his little princess's giggled quietly in her sleep. She loosened her hold on the staff and Mistress Afra tucked it within her robes.

'How considerate... Lord Jaraadhrin...' Mistress Afra placed her fingers on her heart, kissed them, placed them on her eyes and laid them lightly against his cheek. Her eyes brimmed with tears and her face affectionate. Jaraadhrin smiled warmly down at her, patting her hand on his face. She had always loved him like his mother had.

'Tsk...tsk...look what you done...you made me cry...Aaashh! You senseless tzar...off with you...' she murmured as she wiped away her tears. She turned on her heel and glided back into the chamber as Jaraadhrin chuckled. His hands free, he saluted his Queen and she smiled up at him.

'She told you....' Queen Debriar questioned. Jaraadhrin nodded, self-consciously. She raised her hand and he strode to her, sitting on his heel in front of her. She laid a gentle hand on his head. Jaraadhrin inhaled sharply as he closed his eyes. Pale lilac and glimmering green streamed from her into him – His King's and Queen's blessings and love.

'I stayed up to tell you...' She whispered, her smile radiant as she gazed at him. 'That you have your King's and my blessings, Jaraadhrin. We cannot possibly ask for a more noble companion for the Princess.' He nodded, speechless. His Queen was infinitely gracious. He was always speechless in front of her affection and gentleness.

Jaraadhrin drew a deep breath, opening his eyes as she slid the hand on his head, down the slide of his cheek to his chin and raised his face to hers. He gazed at her gracious features in admiration. Another, more stunning set of features flashed before him, closely resembling that of his Queen.

'My Princess looks very much like you, my Queen' he murmured, gazing at her in awe. She smiled down at him. 'And the nose...? It is mine too, isn't it...?

Jaraadhrin's chuckles and his Queen's tinkling laughter echoed over the terrace and into the cool night air.

The Quest of the unisus

Mistress Afra handed the fussing bundle to the bright eyed shimara beaming with happiness.

'It's a shimling tzar, my darling, Nuri. You did very well indeed.' Nuri smiled. She glanced down at her shimling as he gazed up at her, bright eyed and adorable. She pressed her lips to his forehead. The shimling gurgled and raised his little fists to her cheeks, tapping them and staring into his mother's eyes lovingly.

'His aura is a little off and the core is rather unbalanced. Just feed him the tinctures I prescribed and make sure you position the crystals around him when he is asleep. He should be hale and hearty in a few days. You have to meditate and rest up as much as you can too, my darling. Don't strain for at least three moons. It was rather a rough birth. Your core was almost depleted when you came in. Why did you summon me so late?'

Nuri shook her head as her eyes clouded with tears. Mistress Afra rushed to her side at once and held her close. She wept silently against her as the Mistress poured in her eons into Nuri, gentle and caring as always. She wiped her tears and smiled up again.

'I am alright Mistress… now that he is here' she glanced towards her little son. ' I lost my shimratzar in the war and haven't been myself since.' She explained, her voice quiet and racked with grief.

'Oh… my darling, I am so sorry ….' Mistress Afra hugged her tight again as she stroked the shimara's long hair. She was so young maybe around twenty Shimran years. What a calamity this was. How many young, expectant shimaras were left unaided after the war. How were they coping? She made up her mind to speak Queen Debriar about it. Her Queen would ensure they were all well cared for. They needed to secure these vulnerable shimrans immediately. Mistress Afra expanded a tincture from her many ribbons and handed it to her.

'This is a calming draught. It will help. You have to focus on your shimling my darling. He needs you.' Nuri nodded as she regained her composure and sipped at the tincture. She grimaced at the bitterness of it but her aura calmed significantly around her. She sighed and glanced out of the window as a soft rush of wind breezed through it. An expression of surprise and astonishment crossed her fair, tired face.

Mistress Afra followed her gaze and gasped in amazement. A firehorn soared outside, tossing its long, fiery mane with blazing impatience. She sent a quick yishin to Leilimma, another healer, including detailed instructions on how to take care of Nuri and moved to the window.

'Ashoora? What's wrong? Does something distress you? You should be at the creature Shifr Shimrans then' Ashoora neighed loudly and tossed her head again. She lowered it with a shake and a glow emanated from her fiery horn. It solidified in to the shaped of tzar with glistening gold clips on either sides of his head.

'Quinzafoor? Oh no....Did something happen to him?' Mistress Afra inquired, her eyes widening in horror. Ashoora neighed in agony and pranced away from her, her wings flapping wildly and urging the Mistress to follow her. Mistress Afra turned to Nuri just as another healer entered. She was almost as old as the Mistress and was her first and senior disciple. She glanced at Ashoora, fluttering outside.

'Is Quinzafoor well, why is Ashoora here?' Leilimma inquired, concerned. Mistress Afra shook her head and turned to Nuri.

'I have to be off, my darling. Leilimma here will take good care of you. You have to stay with us for a few days.' She advised. Nuri nodded as her healer leapt to the sill and soared off behind the prancing unisus.

'Mistress Afra! Send me a yishin if you need anything and tell Quinzafoor I asked.' Leilimma shouted after her. She shook her head smiling as she focussed on Nuri. Her Mistress would drop everything and rush to Quinzafoor's side if he needed her. So would every other the healer within the citadel. Quinn was such a proficient healer himself and he rarely needed them. It was an honour to be summoned by him. Most of the healers had either taught him or were taught by him.

Mistress Afra spun as fast as she could after the firehorn. What happened to Quinn to get Ashoora in such a state? Quinn had one of the most powerful Shifrs in the citadel which rarely required her care. However, his experiences of life had had direct effects on his mind and its Shifr, that at times, it could incapacitate him rather severely. Quinn would send her yishin if he felt poorly. He knew the dangers of ignoring his discomfort. Why was Ashoora here? It could only mean one thing, Quinn was too far gone to send for help himself and she needed to be at her youngling's side at once.

Ashoora flew as straight as arrow to Quinn's terrace and Mistress Afra huffed in surprise as she tried to keep up. Unisi flew much faster than Shimrans, how astonishing. Such speed was an advantage when she needed to be beside her Shimrans in emergencies. Maybe she should look for one of her own.

Mistress Afra's heart raced in fear and apprehension as she spun rapidly behind Ashoora. They were almost at his terrace and she could just make out Quinn lying on his front on the luxurious cushions and carpets that usually adorned it. Her centre tremored at the sight of this strong, young shimratzar, inert and vulnerable. Mistress Afra landed, almost falling over herself in her haste to reach her beloved disciple.

'Oh my.... Quinzafoor.... What happened, my little one? Is your mind congested again? What ails you? Are you well?' She cried as she turned him gently over on to his back. Quinn's brows were tense and his eyes shut tight but his handsome face relaxed as Mistress Afra sat down beside him and pulled him up on to her lap.

'I will be... now that you are here, my Mistress' Quinn sighed. Mistress Afra slid her hand over his chest, checking his core, centient and for other ailments. She could find none. He was as well as ever, physically. She glanced up at the empty carafes and bottles littering the low plinth beside which he lay. Ashoora pawed anxiously, sending them flying in all directions.

'How many tinctures did you take?' she demanded as she slid her hands to his head. She winced as the gold clips, blazed fiery and scorched her. She slid them off with her centient and placed her hands where they had been, controlling the surging, seething mass within.

'A few....' He murmured, a slight smile lifting his lips through his agony. Mistress Afra shook her head in exasperation.

'More like fifty...you senseless little one!' she exclaimed 'Why didn't you just send for me?' She slid her hands to his temples, siphoning off the swirling thoughts within his sodden mind. Quinn's head surrounded in flashes of hazy auburn, turning pink as it dissipated within her hands. She frowned, she knew Shifrs evolved and strengthened over time but Quinn's was moving forward, faster than normal. It felt different to the last time she had checked. There was something else clogging his mind than just random, unnecessary thoughts. He chuckled, quiet and soft.

'I thought I could manage a headache... till you were a little less preoccupied.... Your services were more urgently needed elsewhere.... I am glad that
Nuri and the shimling are well....My head may be too heavy... but my heart
is lighter....My Nuri has gone through too much.... to suffer more....' he whispered, pausing often as he fought against the pain within his head. Mistress
Afra stared at him in surprise. *Quinn knows the shimara I was tending to? How
did he know her?*

'She was one of my servers... My mistress. I let her go as soon as I found out...
she was with a shimling... but I have been looking after her. She lives alone...
as you know' he replied to her unspoken thoughts. Mistress Afra choked as
she blinked back the tears, her heart tender. Even in this state of utter debili-
tation, Quinn was selfless and acted the honourable shimratzar he was. Her
little one never failed to astonish her, both with his prowess and the essence
of his being. She increased the flow of her centient to his head and he sighed
softly in relief.

'What happened today? Tell me about your day. I am trying to understand
what is clogging your mind so. They are not thoughts anymore, I have siphoned them all of but there's is still too much here.' puzzled Mistress Afra as
she tried to dredge out the churning, bubbling mass within his warm, auburn
mind. Quinn chuckled his eyes still shut tight. Ashoora let out a soft whinny
and settled down on her crossed hoofs beside them. Her master's laugh
calmed her, he will be alright now. Quinn raised his hand and ran it through
her mane comfortingly.

'We had a truly extraordinary contest today...erm... I lost to Lord Jaraadhrin.
He disarmed me twice.... within a space of moments and... eventually won.
You should have seen his martial skill.... my Mistress! I have yet to see a tzar....
that proficiently lethal and yet so graceful. My Lord is.... something else entirely' Quinn's lips curved into an admiring smile as he recounted, still pausing often as he winced at the sharp blasts of agony within his mind. Mistress
Afra frowned, Quinn was not displeased and had no negativity at all so why
was his head this clouded.

'And you are not displeased at the first loss of your life, little one?' she inquired quietly. Quinn's smile saddened and he sighed.

'This isn't my first loss... my Mistress.... I lost everything.... when I was a
three-moon old shimling.... and I have no one to blame for it but...myself' he
replied, his voice quiet and agonised, worsened as he flinched. Mistress Afra
gasped at his torment as it infiltrated her pink centient, through her hands

on his head. She rapped his forehead with her knuckle and it furrowed at the physical shoot of discomfort. He chuckled at her maternal rebukes.

'Again with that irrationality! Stop it. You cannot be accountable if it has been willed so. Trust in the Light, little one! It will not lead you astray.' She chided him. 'So what else happened?' Quinn's admiring smile returned as he answered her.

'Well, the soldiers went wild of course.... It was a first... The whole clearing exploded with.... awe and mirth at Lord Jaraadhrin's....antics and his skills. Aaashh!' He shuddered. 'The shimaras thoughts were rather insufferable.... I had a hard time tuning them out.... They kept it up for so long after my Lord left.... The tzars tried to imitate his skill but not one... could get any of his moves right... some of the shimaras came rather close though.... They were well applauded and the whole clearing was... bursting with Shimrans till quite late still rejoicing.... and too excited to settle down. I slipped away as the sky darkened... with a rather an achy head. For all I know they may still be there....It might have been their loudness... they were very lively.'

'Hmmmm...' murmured Mistress Afra as she slid deeper into his swirling auburn misted mind. She changed the position of her hands on his temples slightly and siphoned off emotions instead of his thought. If she was right, Quinn's head was congested with sentiments of his soldiers in the clearing and not thoughts. His Shifr must also be channelling feelings and emotions as well. Quinn inhaled, long and deep as the agony ebbed and his fist, clenched around the fringes of his cushions, relaxed. He slid his hand to her knee as he lay on it and squeezed it. Quinn opened his eyes, gazing into her brilliant green ones.

'Thank you, my Mistress. That feels better' he breathed, his voice soft in relief. She nodded. She slid a tincture off her ribbon and raised him against her as she helped him drink it. He obliged. Quinn's mind was still rather tremulous. Mistress Afra slid away the potion and dabbed the extra moisture off his full lips with the therin of her sleeve. He tried to sit up but she held him down.

'Not yet. Tell me what you are reading from me' said Mistress Afra. Quinn shook his head in confusion. She knew he could read her, why did she need him to say it?

'You are concerned and you think I am channelling sentiments as well as thoughts. You have just siphoned off extra emotions. I think you may be right, my Mistress.' he acknowledged. Mistress Afra smiled down at him and shook her head.

'Tell me what I am feeling? Can you channel my emotions? I need to know the extent of this new development and how it will affect you. It might incapacitate you worse than before' she explained, her eyes clouding in worry. Quinn gazed into his Mistress's eyes as he tried to follow her instructions. He inhaled, sharp and shaky, surprised at the strength of her emotions flooding him in a gush. His face softened with his own overwhelming affection and fondness for her.

Quinn closed his eyes, drew a deep breath and turned towards her midriff. He slid his arms around her slender waist and buried his face deep within her robes, snuggling closer to her.

'You love and care for me just as much as my own mother did....' he murmured against her. Mistress Afra stifled an abrupt, irrational giggle at the sudden, shimling embrace from this strong, young shimratzar. She gathered him closer to her with a soft sigh. 'Maybe even more...I don't know....I don't remember....' He continued. The last time he had hugged her like that was when he had been seven moons. It was a similar situation too. Quinn had been left weak and incapacitated by the violent ravages of his Shifr on his mind. She patted his head, deep in thought.

'We need to find another way to siphon off these extra thoughts and emotions off of your head, my youngling' said Mistress Afra 'Preferable a way in which you could do this yourself. I may not always be around. There is much uncertainty in the air. You should try practise this extraction as well. You have never needed it before this because it was only thoughts. Emotions are much more potent, especially if you channel them off of shimaras. Your shimratzarry mind might not be able to handle them' Quinn snorted against her and she smiled at his mirth. 'There was an ancient book on it, in the old annals under the citadel. I will find it for you.' Quinn nodded still holding her tight.

'Sleep it off now, little one. I will stay by you for a while.' Mistress Afra slid his harp off his ribbon, expanded it and set it beside his head. She skimmed her centient over its strings, playing it with slight movements of one hand as she controlled it. It was similar to the tunes Quinn often played for his Lord Jaraadhrin. Mistress Afra picked up the now, cooled clips and slid them back into his satin bronze locks. she hummed quietly and in tune to her melody as she stroked his head.

Quinn sighed against her as his mind relaxed further with the melodies and his Mistress's sweet and enchanting voice. Yes, he had lost much but he had gained more. He still had loving and caring Shimrans who rushed to his aid when he needed them. They never left him alone and would always check in on him. Queen Debriar, Mistress Afra, Lord Jaraadh and his gentle Nuri had always taken care of him in every way, they possibly could, along with half the shimaras and shimratzars of the citadel.

Today he had realised he had two more Shimrans that he loved and revered who stood beside him. Strong, powerful Shimrans whose affection for him burned fiery with a scorching edge of protectiveness. His beloved little Princess and his Lord Jaraadhrin. Quinn smiled, calm and content as his mind slipped into blissful dreams. His arms loosened from around Mistress Afra's waist and slid serenely on to the cushions. There wasn't anything he wouldn't do for them either.

Quinzafoor stirred with the wind as it blew around him. It was cold against his face but he was very warm and comfortable indeed. *How long have I been asleep?* He opened his eyes to the darkened skies with a full moon hanging low. It wasn't midnight yet. He hadn't been asleep too long at all but he felt rested and refreshed. His mind clear and alert as usual. Something soft and warm slid over him and a pleasant little voice murmured in his mind.

Are you awake, my Master? Are you well? Quinn moved his head slightly, glancing behind him. He lay against the long, fiery, thick mane of Ashoora. Mistress Afra must have left after he had fallen asleep and his beloved firehorn had taken her place. She had covered him with her blazing wings and tail, over his own sheets to keep him warm. He slid upright, swinging back his locks as he ran his hands through her mane.

I am well Ash, do not worry about me. He replied to her within his head.

You should probably have something to eat and get your strength back.... She advised. Quinn Shook his head.

I am still too full of those tinctures, ugh. They still taste bitter...

Well, now you know how I feel when you give me those disgusting Shimran foods....

Quinn chuckled. He loved talking to Ashoora. The mental communication took no effort at all. He stood up and glided over to the banisters, stretching his arms above him in astonishing grace as he went. He placed his hands on the banister, wide apart and stared over the beautiful Shimran landscapes, breathing in the cool night air. He wasn't going to be able to sleep tonight. Not after all the tinctures and melodies. He was too full of energy.

How are Shimrans so very light-footed and elegant? Wondered Ashoora behind him. Quinn glanced back at her in surprise.

Hmmm?

You know. You, Lord Jaraadhrin, all the shimratzars and the shimaras in the clearing. You all either float, glide, soar or just move around really smoothly.' Quinn grinned at her in amusement. He turned around and faced her, leaning against the banisters with his elbows resting on it.

What a strange thing to say, Ash. Are unisi graceless? I thought you were quiet elegant yourself. Ashoora tossed her head as she sat.

No, we are not. We are only agile in the air and water. We like to jog and canter around. We like to run with the wind. We like abrupt movements, we like rolling in fields of flowers and frolicking around the trees. I have yet to see a Shimran who is as carefree as we are. You are all so composed and just tediously dull. Quinn roared with laughter.

Well, we are not horses... for one....' He managed to think within his mirth. Ashoora often made such ridiculous comments. She was immensely interested in the Shimran way of life and admired them no end. She loved learning every possible little detail about them.

It's nothing to do with being a horse...and I am a unisus ...thank you very much. She harrumphed indignantly. *Shimran folk move like they have been filled with air and light. You even 'curved' to the floor with such grace, when you fell on the terrace, incapacitated with all that agony from your ridiculous Shifr. It flooded my mind and I could hardly see to fly straight, for help.'* She snorted, her thoughts tinged with exasperated amusement and concern for Quinn. Her words in his mind lilted with her expressive eyes. Quinn quieted his hilarity but couldn't wipe the grin off of his face completely.

I am sorry Ashoora, I don't know how I can stop that from infiltrating you. Tell me if you know how. He replied, his mind voice, soft and tender.

Oooof! Tsk... Tsk... She exclaimed in annoyance as she stood up. *I don't mind that and I am not complaining.* She cantered over to him and tossed her head as if to prod him with her horn. Quinn slid it away from him with a quick, wide sweep.

See? All elegant and graceful. You can't even swat away my horn... you 'slide' it away. She demonstrated. Quinn chortled. Ashoora was so strange. She had him in stitches most of time or shaking in irritation at others. He turned away from her still grinning. She prodded him on the back this time.

Aaashh! Ashoora, enough. What's wrong with you today.' Quinn exclaimed in amused annoyance.

'I am going to find out if you are capable of abrupt or clumsy movements.' she neighed as she prodded him yet again. *You even fight like you are dancing. We fight hard unlike you fragile Shimrans.*

You fight? How? Quinn inquired as he slid her horn away from him, gazing up at her in surprise.

Draw your daggers, I will show you. She neighed

Tsk... tsk...tsk quit playing around Ash, I don't want to hurt you. Quinn groaned, his mirth ebbing to irritation. Ashoora stepped away from him and stamped her right hoof hard, twice against the marble. A flash of flame engulfed her horn and it elongated to many times its length. The glow spread around her and enveloped her whole body in a shimmering haze. It looked thick, impenetrable and delicate, all at the same time.

Hurt me? She crowed. *Try if you can...!* Ashoora slashed her horn hard towards him. Quinn whirled away, his eyebrows raised and chuckling.

Stop it. you puerile mare! What has gotten into you? Aaashh! I just recovered from a bad bout of my Shifr's negative effects. He grinned. Ashoora snickered at him, she knew he was perfectly well. She rose high above him, her wings bristled up and brought her horn down on his head with immense force.

Quinn's ribbon whipped as he zoomed out a sword and blocked her horn instinctively. The clash rang, loud and echoing over the terrace. Quinn tilted his head to gaze into her fiery eyes, twinkling with mirth. His own widened in shocked amazement.

Aaashh! Ashoora!

She tossed her head, bringing her horn down on him and Quinn blocked her again, his face breaking into a smile of exhilaration. Ashoora knew how to fight alright. Quinn slashed his sword at her front hooves and she lifted up high on her hind ones. He slid under her quickly and between them as she made to place her front hooves, squarely on his chest.

I will see how fast you can turn around to face me and slash that confounded horn at me again. He thought competitively.

Ashoora didn't turn around. she flapped her enormous fan like wings in one quick blast and it sent him soaring away from her. She flipped her long tail, curled in one thick, plumed rope and elongating rapidly towards him, even as he soared away. It caught him quickly and wrapped itself around and around his waist, many times over. She raised him high still enshrouded and flipped him carelessly into the air.

Quinn shot free with the momentum of the unravelling tail and spun uncontrollable. He caught his balance and sheathed his sword in mid-air as his began to fall back. He swished his white night robes, harnessing the wind and spiralled delicately back to the terrace. He laid himself along the length of one side of his body, his head propped up on a bent elbow on the thin rim of the banister. He bent his leg, placing the foot on his straight knee and slid his palm on the bent one. He snickered at Ashoora, wiggling his eyebrows at her frustration as his robes fluttered down around him in shimmering clouds of therin.

Done yet? He teased her. She tossed her head, mane and tail, crackling in frustrated annoyance at the stunning refinement of his landing. The glow receded from around her body and diffused back into her now shorter horn.

Bah! Still wholly smooth and sophisticated! Oooof! And still completely dull! she muttered as Quinn chortled.

Maybe we are just made that way? You do fight very well though. That tail trick took me by surprise. You would be formidable in a real fight. I assume the glow around you is a shield. Amazing! Quinn straightened, pivoting around on the banister in a complete turn and stopped, sitting on it with his legs dangling over it and facing the many tiers.

Ashoora let out another infuriated snort at the flawless fluidity in which he changed positions and cantered over to him. She laid her muzzle against his shoulder. Quinn jerked away from her.

I hope you are not trying to push me off the banister now, to catch me in a clumsy move? He jested. She snickered and nudged him. 'Come now, let me enjoy the moonlight and the night breeze in peace.

Humph, you do need some air and given your way of getting it, it will never be enough. Ashoora retorted. Quinn rolled his eyes at her and splayed his arms in a wide arc.

I am on my terrace and there is a stiff breeze and I wouldn't get enough air? Very well, how would you get it then? He challenged.

I could show you? she murmured as she moved away from him. Quinn glanced behind him. Ashoora had sat down facing away with her wings folded neatly back. She turned her magnificent head to him and gestured slightly to her back.

A flash of howling, racing winds, whipping Ashoora's long mane and tail back violently, glimmered in his mind. A memory of her wings, flapping together behind her like colossal fans and she, propelling forward at great speeds at every blast of them, illuminated in flashing recollections. Ashoora, neighing with exhilaration and triumph and her rush of excitement gushed through him. Her emotions sharp and strong, flooded him as if it were his own, nearly knocking his breath away.

'Woah....What on Shimrah...!' he exclaimed as he spiralled back to face her and skipped off. *You want me to ride you?* she snickered at his reaction to her thoughts and emotions as she blinked at him. He stared at her in amazement. *I though unisi were these proud, wild creatures who didn't offer rides to us humble Shimrans.* Ashoora had once complained about King Dunyazer and Lord Jaraadh riding her and had been very miffed. She tossed her mane in a careless shrug.

Meh... I thought I would make an exception for one senseless Shimran... you know... just because I am feeling generous. Quinn snorted as he slid his hand down her sleek back.

I don't know.... He hesitated as he remembered the racing, howling speed of the winds *My night robes aren't as wide as my morning....*

Ashoora's horn slashed against the sides of his nightrobes in rapid succession, ripping long slits down them from his waist and exposing his white clad legs underneath.

*There... that should let you ride....*Quinn stared down at himself in frustrated amusement. He shook his head, drew a deep breath and leapt up over her back in one fluid motion. His ripped robes moved away around his frame as he sat across.

'Aaashh! Ashoora! Did you have to ruin...' Quinn began as Ashoora rose swiftly and leapt into the air. She flapped her colossal fan shaped wings once.

'....my roooooooooooooobes!' Quinn yelled as she shot forward with immense swiftness, spinning around and round rapidly with massive speeds as he held on to her mane for dear life.

Ashoora flew off and over the citadel towards the lake and waterfalls behind them, whizzing through the winds as Quinn held on. She was very fast indeed. Quinn's long hair and ruined robes whipped behind him and he closed his eyes against the rush of wind. He could see through her eyes and wonder flooded his mind at how high they were. They soared over the treacherous ice spike mountains which stretched for a great distance before it ended abruptly in steep precipices and glimmering blue waters.

Ashoora twisted around, sharp and abrupt, and headed back to the citadel, spinning rapidly as she soared.

Aaashh! why is it necessary to spin so? He complained as he sunk lower and deeper into her flaming mane. She righted herself and he straightened hesitantly. His tresses whipped back, smooth and silky, flowing behind in a wave. Ashoora peaked back at him.

How is this even possible? Not a single silly lock of hair tousled? she grimaced. She shook her mane in frustration.

Aaashh!.... Quinn growled, vexed as she flung herself down headlong in a nosedive over the Crystal Lake

'Ashoooooooooraaaaaah!' he yelled as she dove. He entwined his fingers within her slippery, fiery mane and gripped her tight with his legs. His roguish unisus righted herself just before they splashed into the waters of the Crystal Lake. She skimmed smoothly along it, their reflections glittering in the clear waters.

She flew level and swift once, twice, thrice around it. Quinn sighed. Ashoora was so playful and impulsive. His Shifr couldn't keep up with her rapid reflexes when she didn't want him to. He gazed around him. It was breathtaking. The snow-capped Ice spikes range, the frothing cascade of the Ice falls, the magnificent citadel with its fourteen forts and the scintillating crystal-clear waters of the lake. He sighed as he leaned forward against Ashoora's mane to run his hand through the cool water below them.

A soft snicker sounded within his mind and before he could reach into his impish scallywag of a unisi's head, she swung around in rapid pivot, dislodging him from her back and into the water. He tutted in frustration as he reharnessed the wind and spun away rapidly across the waters in a horizontal whirl. His locks and robes dipped in and skimmed across the surface, soaking his clothes and drenching his tresses. He slapped his palms down against the tensed surface of the liquid to prevent himself from taking a very cold, unintended bath.

Ashoora groaned, slid through the water and rose up from under him as he sped to the shores. He slid over her back again and she rose higher, away from the waters. Her skin and mane blazed warm, drying his robes and hair quickly as he lay against them.

'Well? Was that clumsy enough for you?' snapped Quinn, irritated at her persistent attempts to catch him graceless. They were closer to the shores and the Cryslis blooms grew thick and lush on the high banks. Ashoora sniggered.

Not even close, still extremely skilful and nimble. You should have just splashed into the lake and clunked to the bottom like a stone! she answered him. She flew low over the Cryslis blooms, her hoofs touching them as she skimmed and they released their energies into her.

'Aaashh! Of all the Annoying Creatures in the Whole of Shimrah, Ashoora! You have to be the worst! Could you possibly be any rougher and more brutal' he exclaimed.

'Now that you mention it, my Master....Yes!' Ashoora spiralled rapidly, throwing him with the force of a hundred arrows shooting away together, headlong into the field of Cryslis blossoms.

Quinn gasped at the strength and speed of her throw and spun, swift and supple, away from her. She couldn't rise up to him from beneath him now, he would have to right himself. He dipped low to the ground and slapped his palms, hard against the earth. He flew up, cleaning his dirt covered hands and righted himself. He glided away, found a thick part of the fields and floated down into the flowers. He sank deep within them as they released their centients into him, regrowing repeatedly. He couldn't help it, his martial skill, kicked in instinctively. He just couldn't be clumsy or awkward even if he tried.

Ashoora soared around and around above him. She looked truly maddened and fully irritated with him. Quinn crossed his ankles and slid his arms behind his head as she glided down to him in circles. She alighted, towering over him, blazing fiery flames against the dark sheen of her skin and scorching eyes, intense and furious. She would be formidable and intimidating in true anger. She let out an elongated neigh at the look on his face and stamped her right hoof hard as if she was a shimling throwing a tantrum.

Alright! I give up! You cannot possible be awkward, it's what you are! Whatever! Be darned elegant and graceful! Still absolutely, outrageously, ludicrously and ridiculously absurd! Dreary and dull as well!' she stamped her hoof again as Quinn roared with laughter at her thoughts and actions. She gazed at his face for a moment and shook her massive mane out. She folded herself beside him with a soft whinny and nudged his face, gentle and tender, her anger dissolving in his mirth.

'Oh, Ashoora, You absurd mare, you...you will be the death of me' stammered Quinn clutching at his sides as he shook with laughter. She snorted and laid her heavy head on his chest. He sighed, closing his eyes against her warm blaze and running his hands through the fiery flames at her neck. Princess Saffrodel was right. What magnificent creatures they were, so powerful and full of light. He couldn't possibly let any darkness rob their light and innocence. His firehorn was like a little shimling, sometimes exasperating but still an adorable little shimling. Ashoora nudged him again.

You keep thinking of it but you will not send me away, Master. She whispered within his head. *I think the princess is right, she has it figured immaculately. Why don't you just send me. It's just an errand, I will be back as soon as I can. My kind can't go against the Entwinements either. Besides, I could bring back my friends and we could start what the princess suggested. It would also be nice not to be the only unisus in the citadel.* Quinn exhaled

I think you know the answer to that too, Ash. I am too used to seeing you at the clearing in the mornings.

So? I would still be in the clearing at the break of dawn if I left tonight. I could get there and back as you sleep. You would not have time to miss me. Quinn opened his eyes and gazed at her in amazement.

The Ashlands are all the way in Southern Shimrah and you need time to speak to the leaders... Quinn reasoned. Ashoora shook her mane and flipped her tail carelessly.

I could be there and back before the sun rises and I don't think I need an audience to speak to my father.... Quinn sat up, stunned.

Your father....? Is the leader of the ....? He stuttered, his eyes widening in shock. *You are a Princess...?* Ashoora chortled at him, she slid a leaf off his locks with quick flick of her muzzle

Now that's more like it... a little less composed and with a leaf in your hair...

'Ashoora...!' Quinn exclaimed as she sniggered.

It's not like that. We are not like Shimrans. The leader of the herd is the great father of pretty much half the herd. He has some twenty-eight other foals, twenty older than me, eight younger. I am sort of a rebel but he would see me immediately. I could send him a message as soon as I cross the border of the Ashlands and he will see me at once' Quinn nodded.

Still a princess to me.... he murmured as she rested her muzzle lightly over his shoulder and he slid his arms around her neck. He sighed. *Go tonight and hurry back to me then... its almost midnight, I should probably take the rest of the*

tinctures and turn in soon.

May I give you a ride back to the terrace...' Quinn grinned. He knew she was stalling.

I think I can find my way there but if you insist....and promise to be gentle with me.... He chortled as he mounted and she flew off. She soared, slow and calm without jolting him at all this time. She took a longer route back, flying over the lake and ice spikes and meandering around the fourteen forts. She even alighted and cantered through the woods behind the citadel for a while before soaring back into the air. Too soon they were over his terrace and they alighted. Quinn dismounted and slid his arms around her neck again as she turned away from him.

'Hurry back to me Ash, I will await for you in the clearing at dawn' He whispered. Ashoora nudged him, whinnying quiet and low.

Don't let concern haunt you, My Master, I will be back to annoy you again, sooner than you may want me to.... she replied, her thought tenors, impish as ever. Quinn chuckled. She stepped away from him and with a final toss of her flaming head, leapt into the air. She flapped her wings and shot forward in a great surge of speed. Ashoora turned back to look at her beloved Master one more time.

Quinn had moved to the edge of the banister and was watching her leave. His right shoulder, where her jewel and life force lay, blazed a flaming auburn even from such a distance. She could feel his sadness flood her as she flew. He raised his hand and waved, his long sleeves floating and locks flowing behind him in the wind. Graceful and elegant as ever.

Ashoora snorted, there wasn't much she could do for her beloved Master. He was a proficient and lethal tzar, self-sufficient in every respect. He would never need her except as his companion perhaps. At the least, he wasn't even ungainly so she could watch over him. She could do nothing for him. This quest was the one thing she could offer him, even if it caused them agony to be apart. She knew it was very important to her Master. Ashoora tossed her mane and sped ahead. She would make good time and surprise him on his terrace again before daybreak, instead of in the clearing the next day.

Quinn sighed and made his way back into his chamber as Ashoora vanished from sight. He would probably need a bath before he turned in, what with all the antics he had been forced to perform because of his senseless little mare. He noticed a little book on his work desk and picked it up. It was the book on thought and emotion self-extraction that Mistress Afra had had promised to find for him. She must have left it there when he was out. He removed the ribbon off his waist and clipped the book on it. Quinn placed it carefully on his work desk arranging the many trinkets neatly. The ribbon was almost full. He would need to acquire another soon.

He made his way to the vinnerry and disrobed. His servers, efficient as ever already had his bath ready. He chuckled at his ruined robes as it fell to the floor around him. They were no use now. He doubted if the therin could be mended when they had been slashed by unisus magic, he didn't want them mended either. He picked them up, folded them neatly and placed them on a shelf with a yishin to his servers, instructing them to have it cleaned and returned to him. They were now a souvenir. A reminder of their first flight together and their first parting, however brief.

He would probably have to instruct the therin makers on altering his martial robes to be fit for riding. His day robes were floaty and wide to aid with harnessing the wind but adding waist length slits at the sides to each layer would make them more comfortable to ride in.

They would also be breezier, floatier, more graceful and annoy Ashoora no end! Quinn sniggered. *Well, She can't blame me, it was her design....*

He slid into the warm waters and lay back. He was still too full of energy to be able to sleep but he did need to rest and replenish if he was going to be at his best tomorrow. Lord Jaraadhrin would expect him to fight without his Shifr again and he did need to control it better if he was channelling emotions as well now.

He sighed and sank deeper within the waters, letting it soothe him. It was very warm and relaxing. His thick lashed lids, closed gently over his eyes as the steam rose in long, misty tendrils around him. He wasn't tired but it was very comfortable indeed.

A soft whoosh sounded, followed by a flash of silver and accompanied by a waft of mountain freshness as Quinn snapped his eyes open.

Jaraadhrin

It was a silver yishin from his Lord. Why was he still up? It was well past midnight. Quinn reached for it, his heart filled with dread. Had something happened to his Lord? His eyes widened as he read it quickly and spiralled out of his bath with such force, that the waters sloshed out of it in a whirlpool as he reached for his robes.

The Remedy

Jaraadhrin soared towards his chambers, his heart singing as he spiralled gracefully round and round in mid-air. The wind swirled around him, celebrating with him as it spun him high. He landed on terrace after darkened terrace and twirled the length of each one of them, replicating the fan dance with his Princess, before leaping back into the air and making his way to his own. He caught sight of the great dragon Alaq, standing magnificently with its many wings tiered over each other. He glided over to it and alighted on the tip of its massive horn. He balanced on the toe of one foot with the other behind the crook of his knee, his hands clasped behind him as he gazed over of expanse of the beautiful planes of Shimrah, cloaked in a velvety darkness.

He breathed in the cool air of the night. He felt on top of the world. The citadel was quiet, it was well after midnight. The lights glimmered below him reflecting in the waters of the moats. The many flags rustled quietly as the wind blew at it. He sighed with happiness and contentment. He pirouetted on the tip of the horn and swirled off of it. Jaraadhrin sat down on the dragon's snout and lay his head against its horn, an elbow resting against one bent knee. His midnight blue robes splayed in a wide arc around to the other. He closed his eyes as the beautiful memories of the night flooded his mind, ending in his Princess's stunning, feathered eyes at the moment they had turned to face him. He sighed contentedly.

He could feel the essences of everything around him in brilliant colours. The trees, the flowers, the water, the stars and the moon. Everything was so bright and glowed like his mood and being. He could see the shimmering shields, silver grey, enveloping each tier as they merged seamlessly above him, powered by the massive cores of the shield-maras in the forts. He opened his eyes and stared up at the starry sky. It was blissful and calming up here.

Jaraadhrin snapped straight suddenly, recalling something strange. He closed his eyes and zoomed in on the shields. What was it that was different about them? He focussed from tier to tier trying to recall what had alerted him. His temples tensed as he focused harder. His vision sped back and forth, his Shifr concentrating on each essence one after the other, swiftly. What was it that caught his attention?

There it is! A dark blotch far beyond the outermost shields! A few dark blotches! What was it? Jaraadhrin flew over to the parapet edge, eyes still closed. Did the shield have holes in it? He took a deep breath, confused. His Essence Shifr usually worked in colours. What was these spots of black? It wasn't even a black. It looked like the colour had been sucked away from the place it hovered. He stared at the dark patches. They were not on the shields but beyond the shields itself. His eyes widened as he realised that they were slowly growing larger!

Jaraadhrin sprang into action. He bolted yishins to the shield-maras to fortify the shields even more and another to the Shimrans in charge of maze and moat formations. He needed the Denisthar and Drystwitch again. They were the most formidable and their details existed only in his King's private martial strategy annals and the minds of very few Shimrans. The walls, turrets, towers, forts and moats spun almost immediately with deafening crashes, rumbles and thuds. Torches blazed high along the walls, illuminating the entire eight tiers of the citadel and water gushed through into the moat sections as Jaraadhrin specified. He flipped another yishin off to Quinzafoor to join him and alerted the frontline defences of archers and blade shimrans. He hesitated for a moment.

Should I alert the King and my father? I don't know what I am dealing with yet. He shook his head and flashed them yishins. *Better a silly mistake now than a grave one later!* he thought, still trying to see the black dots beyond the shield.

His and Quinzafoor Martial Force were already amassing in the second and the third tiers looking up at him in confusion and some admiration at his princely appearance, especially the shimaras. Jaraadhrin sent them yishins with quick explanations and they sprang into action. Their segment leaders barked orders as they arranged into groups and lines in their respective battle formations. He could hear Quinzafoor whizzing high above him already, trying to see what it was that Jaraadhrin had summoned him about. He landed swiftly beside his Lord in full martial gear. Quinn flashed him a quick glance, a brow raised as he took in the rich midnight robes and golden crown at Jaraadhrin's forehead. He turned back to stare down at the eight tiers.

Has my Lord robed up for the occasion then? His yishin did say it was an emergency? Maybe it was an attire emergency? Maybe I should have robed up too. He thought, drily

'I can't see anything, my Lord. What is it? I can't hear anything either!' said

Quinn confused, turning his attention back to the threat at hand.

'Read me' Jaraadhrin replied. He closed his eyes and focussed on the black dots beyond the outer shields. They were growing steadily bigger as if they were rushing towards them.

'What on Shimrah...?' Quinn scowled; he wasn't used to being blind. 'I can't hear them... still...' He jumped up. Jaraadhrin caught his hand as he made to glide off.

'Stay behind the shields and feed back to me' he said urgently, his voice ringing with command, his eyes still closed, focused on the black holes. 'Don't make me send my projections after you...!' Quinn chuckled.

'Don't you dare, Jaraadhrin' he answered, his voice almost matching his Lord's ring of authority. 'I will be right back!' Jaraadhrin nodded. Quinn was ready. The match had done him good.

The black spots were growing larger. They hovered just above the ground. *Flying!* Jaraadhrin realised in shock. What was it that approached them in such a sinister fashion with no indication and with such camouflage? His father's words echoed in his mind.

'The creatures come out of the night and are impossible to detect. They have some kind of concealment. Many Shimran folk had disappeared from nearby villages and we have evacuated everyone to Northern Shimrah...!' Could these be them? What were they doing here? Quinzafoor flashed back to him.

'No comprehensible thoughts. Just sinister, ominous whispers! Feels very, very dark. Not like the light of Shimran folk. No auras, no cores, definitely not Shimran.' Quinzafoor spoke in short, abrupt sentences as he had done that night, long ago when they had watched the approach of the firehorn. He shivered involuntarily beside him. Jaraadhrin placed a hand on his shoulder still trying to penetrate the darkness of the spots. He was only getting the black, beside him Quinn glowed warm and auburn, blazing at the eyes. More soft rustles and King Dunyazer, Queen Debriar and Lord Jaraadh landed lightly behind them. His father made a soft sound of admiration as he took in his son's princely appearance.

'What happened, Jaraadhrin? We couldn't see anything....?' King Dunyazer queried. Quinn filled them in as Jaraadhrin tensed, trying harder to reach them.

'My Queen... the Princess...?' he whispered through gritted teeth as he focussed.

'With Afra, still asleep... maybe you should go to her side –?' Queen Debriar replied. Quinn interrupted her.

'He is the only one who can see...I can barely hear them...a very low ominous murmur...we are unsighted without him' Something about Quinn's voice alerted Jaraadhrin.

Quinn? he thought questioningly. Quinn shook his head. *Tell me now, this isn't the time for mind games!* Jaraadhrin commanded in his head. Quinn hesitated.

'I am not sure but the whispers feel obsessed with the citadel and.... shimrans...er... Shimran light cores and life forces... to be exact...a few hundred thousand at least......!' Quinn replied. He shivered again and drew a deep shuddering breath. Jaraadhrin tightened his hand on his shoulder in concern. Quinn was the bravest tzar he knew. He wasn't afraid of anything. Why was he shivering? Was something wrong with him?

Are you well? he thought concerned. *Why do you shudder?* Quinn nodded again.

'Their whispers are cold and dark; they are freezing my mind' he muttered, tightening the gold clips on the sides of his head, flush against his hair. Shimran Shifrs were powerful but they were also an inlet to a shimran's core. Jaraadhrin nodded.

'Try tune them out. If they are not capable of intelligent thoughts then there is no point -' he replied.

The citadels alarms rang loud and clear into the night and a flurry of activity ensued as Lord Jaraadh shot more yishins to the main Martial Force under his command. Pale blue robed figures poured out of all the many dwellings within the citadel and soared over the tiers as they took their places within the defences.

'No Shifrs, my Liege' Lord Jaraadh reported beside them 'I am drawing a blank' Queen Debriar moved beside Jaraadhrin closing her eyes trying to focus a vision of them. She gasped, snapping them open. She shook her head as she stepped back.

'Solid blackness and freezing cold, I am blind' she recounted 'This is it! This is Ibreeth and Ifreeth, we cannot see them, their auras, cores or Shifrs. My senseless brothers thought of everything except Jaraadhrin and Quinzafoor's Shifrs which they didn't know of.' She gasped again. Her eyes clouded over in pale lilac as she swayed. King Dunyazer flashed to her, holding her steady and

Lord Jaraadh moved to their side protectively. Dark visions were very drain-ing and it took a while for the Queen to lapse out of their effects. Quinn tensed beside Jaraadhrin.

'Vision....? he inquired silently. Quinn shook his head.

'A flash and the Shield Shifr...I guess we now know where the Princess got that from' he replied to Jaraadhrin's thoughts dryly.

'Flood every moat with the waters of the Crystal Depths' Jaraadhrin said in his normal voice as he focussed. 'They are dark, they will incinerate over it.' Lord Jaraadh shook his head behind him.

'That won't help, my Lord.' He replied quietly still focused on his Queen. 'The powers of the waters will not extend beyond the light shields. They are made of the Shimran core. The water will not detect the darkness beyond it.' Quinn chuckled at the title. It sounded strange as Jaraadhrin was Lord Jaraadh's son but they were currently in full martial mode and relationships took second place. There was only the King and kingdom in their minds now.

Quinn stiffened beside his young Lord in a swift sudden motion. He shook his head and trembled. His right shoulder and eyes blazed,

brilliant auburn. He sighed, soft and tender. It sounded agonised. Jaraadhrin glanced at him in concern.

Quinzafoor? He questioned again. There was too much going on and he needed to know everything Quinn knew. They had to be on the same footing if they were to work together. The situation was rapidly turning very serious indeed. Quinn nodded wincing.

'I let Ashoora go to her herd leaders tonight as the Princess requested. She is far away in Southern Shimrah over the Ashlands but she wants to turn back and be by my side. She can see this through my eyes. I forbade her to come to me. I...er...I bound her away from me against her will and with her own jewel. She is fighting it and it causes us both anguish.' Quinn paused abruptly, draw-ing a sharp breath of agony as his shoulder blazed brighter.

'Aaashh! Ashoora! Stop it!' He trembled again, more violently this time. I am sorry...you leave me no choice. I will...Aaashh! I will come find you...or just wait for the sun....' he stuttered as he instructed through the pain. He winced again and his usually merry face, hardened.

Quinn shut his eyes tight as the thin therin of his blindfold dampened. He slid his hands in front of him and moved them in a rapid set of flips and twists. His centient gathered within his palms, raging and thundery. He encased it within his hands and raised it to his right shoulder. He forced it into the blaze and his frame jolted, violent and brutal. He quaked, eyes shut tight in agony behind their thin blindfold and his slender neck arched backwards.

'Quinzafoor!'

Jaraadhrin eyes widened in horror and he slipped his arm around the back of Quinn's waist, supporting him. Quinn's expression and his physical response alarmed him. His auburn aura blazed red with agony and sorrow, many times more potent than the previous episode. The last time he had felt Quinn this tortured was when his Princess had suggested, he send Ashoora away. What did he do to Ashoora? What did he do to himself?

'Open your eyes, Ashoora!' Quinn gasped in pain as the blaze in his shoulder dimmed. He raised his hand quickly, still glowing auburn. He moved it in front of him as if he was catching something gently within his fingers then lowered it. He opened his fingers and slid his palm off to the side as if he had laid whatever he had caught on an invisible surface. He sighed inaudibly as the blaze on his shoulder, flickered and went out. He straightened wincing and nodded at Jaraadhrin.

'I am well, my Lord, I had to render Ashoora unconscious. I will not be able to concentrate here as long as she fights it. She is deathly worried for me and her return will only make things worse. It's for the best. I cannot risk her coming back with this darkness around us and if this is indeed Ifreeth and Ibreeth, then her quest is even more important. She will be all right' he nodded again as if to reassure himself.

Jaraadhrin gazed at him in amazement. Quinn's and Ashoora's bond had grown very powerful indeed and he could hardly imagine the torment they had just gone through. Quinn had probably knocked Ashoora out when she was in the air, on her way back to him and he had been able to guide her back down to the ground safety from here! How incredulous was the power of the Unisi and the strength of their pledge? And Quinn...what strength and courage resided within this tzar and yet how gentle was he? Quinn was practical and sensible and his affection for his firehorn knew no bounds. He would rather torture himself than have anyone hurt her. It said a lot about his character.

'Oh Quinn...' Jaraadhrin exhaled quietly as he closed his eyes and refocussed on the threat before them. He patted Quinn on his back. Quinn's locks hung wet behind him and Jaraadhrin siphoned off the moisture quickly with his centient. He had probably rushed to his side with much haste. He straightened them out and withdrew his arm. Quinn sighed at his Lord's thoughts and his touch. 'She is safe for now.... that's what matters...' Jaraadhrin consoled his second-in-command.

The black blotches were a lot larger, closer and Jaraadhrin reached out to the largest one in the middle. He felt a slight change in its essence, He stepped closer to the ramparts and leaned forward pressing his temples hard, his locks flying out behind him in the aura of his concentration. There was something streaming out of it like black ink, pouring and being reabsorbed. He reached out tentatively. It reeked.

Queen Debriar straightened, fully recovered from her vision as her King glanced up at Jaraadhrin's sudden movement towards the parapets. He nudged Lord Jaraadh swiftly who was still gazing at the Queen in concern. It took longer for his Queen to recover from visions than usual. She was a Royal and powerful but she was still rather frail from the shocks to her being and the birth just a month ago. Quinn Debriar had insisted that she accompany them as they had hurried to Jaraadhrin's side.

'No Jaraadhrin...pull away... Jaraadh?' King Dunyazer called, urgently as he moved forward and placed his hand on Jaraadhrin's shoulder. His Essence Shifr made contact with the outermost edge of the flowing inks at that exact moment. An icy shard crackled through his core and blasted him back against his King. Quinn rushing to his side and his father on the other. Pain rippled through his chest as he tried to breath and a pair of brilliant green eyes burned the back of his lids.

'Jaraadhrin!' They cried in dismay.

'Stay still!' commanded his Queen as she knelt beside him and placed her glowing hand over his chest.

Jaraadhrin coughed, turned and heaved a huge amount of blood. His lips reddening threateningly compared to the pallor of his skin. He shut his and gritted his teeth against the icy shard in his core. Lord Jaraadh and Quinn gasped beside him as King Dunyazer pulled him higher up against himself, his arm wrapped tightly around Jaraadhrin chest.

'Essence is...poisonous...hurts Shimran... c..c..central....being' he choked as he tried to inform them. 'it's....'

'Demonesque....' said Quinn and Jaraadhrin together. Quinn glanced at Lord Jaraadh. He nodded anxious and pale.

'It's the creatures...!' Jaraadhrin inhaled, sharp and trembled as agony racked through him again. 'I am here son; it hasn't touched you...it cannot hurt you...' he whispered in a tortured voice. Queen Debriar moved her hands swiftly over his chest, her face grim.

'His life force is bleeding out.... he touched it with his Shifr.... its lodged itself in his core.... bleeding him from the inside' she reeled off as the King moved his arm from Jaraadhrin chest to let his Queen work.

'No!' she stopped him, her voice firm and urgent 'Your aura and essence. It is the only thing keeping his core intact!' she stared up at him, incredulous. 'I don't know how.... or why... yet!' Her eyes flew back to Jaraadhrin as he coughed again, sending another splatter of crimson over his chin.

'Quinn! Keep up with me' she frowned. Her eyes glittered with concern but were clear and intelligent. Jaraadhrin groaned as Quinn placed his hands on his chest over the King's and replenished his draining core. He throttled in the King's essence and aura combined with his own centients, deep into Jaraadhrin's centre.

'My Queen....' Quinn's voice shook as she followed his gaze, a silvery shimmer was pouring out of Jaraadhrin's body. It flowed out of him in rapid seeping mists. It was his essence and life force!

'Halt it with as many years as you can spare' she ordered. Quinn whirled up as Lord Jaraadh took over replenishing his son's core. Quinn moved his hand rapidly, summoned a large, auburn centient bolt and enveloped it around Jaraadhrin. He encased the flowing silver and pulled tighter around his Lord's slim frame, forcing the silver back in. It wasn't working! He tensed, eyes shut tight behind his blindfold. His fair forehead furrowed with the effort of holding Jaraadhrin's being together and his heart iced over at the thought of losing his Lord. Queen Debriar gnashed her teeth as she worked over him.

'I need your blood, my King' she said, her voice trembling. She loosened his golden belt and wrenched the robes off Jaraadhrin right shoulder, exposing the glistening, intricate, silver design which was rapidly fading on his pale skin. Lord Jaraadh averted his eyes with a shocked gasped.

'No!' He moaned 'He can't....'

'He won't....' Queen Debriar replied, her voice grim. She glanced at King Dunyazer 'It's the only way I see...!'

King Dunyazer had already slit his hand on his dagger. He never questioned his Queen. Especially not in such situations. She held it over Jaraadhrin's silverine and let her King's blood flow freely on to it. It pooled crimson over the silver mark then drained into it as it gleamed a faint silver. The King squeezed his hand to let more flow.

Jaraadhrin coughed again expulsing another bout of blood, shuddered and fell back lifeless against his King. The crimson crystalized into shards and turned an unholy black. It incinerated in a cloud of black smoke and red sparks against Jaraadhrin's pale chest. King Dunyazer glanced at his Queen, she nodded without looking up. Her delicate hands glowed lilac as they flipped and flashed over him. Jaraadhrin silverine absorbed the flowing blood faster as the silver mists around him seeped back into his slender frame. Quinn drew a trembling breath almost spent as Lord Jaraadh kissed his son forehead above his glittering crown.

Queen Debriar healed the King's hand, holding it tight in hers and kissing it. She waited for the last drops of his blood to drain in to Jaraadhrin. It cleared over his shoulder without a trace, leaving his skin smooth and unblemished. The silver mark glowed brilliant and intricate once more. Queen Debriar pulled his robes closed and straight, fastening his belt tight around his waist as fast as she could. It wasn't the best idea to expose his life force entry way with such creatures around. Quinn nodded at her unspoken command and removed his centient from Jaraadhrin with some hesitation. There was no silver mist seeping out of him anymore.

Queen Debriar spun her fingers on Jaraadhrin's chest and shot a bolt into his heart and another against his head, rotating inwards. Jaraadhrin gasped, his eyes flew open as he drew a deep breath. He looked up at them dazed as his aura strengthened around him. His Queen sat back on her heels with a soft sigh of relief. Lord Jaraadh buried his face in his son's hair with a silent sob. He had almost lost his son and he shivered at the thought. Quinn quivered behind his Queen in relief, his slender fingers over his face. King Dunyazer shook his head and glanced at her.

'What just happened?' he wondered. His Queen smiled up at him. 'Something about you is an antidote to this demonesque essence, my King. I don't know what exactly. Jaraadhrin should have died and released his being as soon as he touched it but he fell against you. Your aura enveloped him and held his core in. It gave me some time to work.' she explained, her words tumbling out low and rapid. 'Apparently something in humans can withstand these creatures, Shimrans cannot' she looked into his eyes piercingly. Quinn stifled a gasp behind them as he read the unspoken communications between his King and Queen before the Shield Shifr descended.

Nothing in Shimrah is ever a coincidence! It is always penned with purpose.... A destiny.... A plan by some higher force we know nothing of! King Dunyazer nodded, holding his hand out to Lord Jaraadh.

'Quinzafoor' he called, his voice quiet. He spun to Jaraadhrin's side immediately. Lord Jaraadh unclipped his Lord Protector medallion and handed it to the King, bursting with pride as he gazed at his adopted son. His king promptly clipped it to Quinn's waist, twirling his sceptre in a flash and expanding it out of his ribbon simultaneously. Quinzafoor huffed as the heat shot into his heart, a scorching burn which seared through from the medallion as Alaq pranced around on it.

'I appoint you Quinzafoor, son of Zhafoor as the Lord Protector of Shimrah, to Lord Jaraadhrin and to his Princess Saffrodel, future Queen of Shimrah' he said. Quinn's eyes widened as he looked up at his King, the auburn blaze vanishing in his shock and amazement. The words of the pledge jarred. Quinn couldn't reach his king's mind. Queen Debriar's Shield Shifr seemed to be covering him too. All he could gauge was that it was premeditated.

What is the need for a second Lord Protector for the Princess when Jaraadhrin already is one? Why am I the Lord Protector for Jaraadhrin? Shimran Lord Protectors had a second-in-command, not another Lord Protector. Quinn shook his head. It didn't matter. It was just a title. He was already too devoted to the Princess and his young Lord for a title to make any difference. He would see it through.

King Dunyazer slid his sceptre over Quinn's head and tapped his right shoulder thrice. A brilliant green glow glittered around the ornate head of the sceptre and seeped into Quinn. He inhaled sharply as the warmth of it, slid through him combining with that of the medallion.

'Don't you dare leave their side!' finished the King grimly. Quinn nodded. He leaned over Jaraadhrin, lifted his pale right hand in both of his and pressed it hard against his eyes. Quinn's heart raced. His core and centients seethed and brimmed as his reactions to the forces of the binds racked him. His central being quaked with the extent of his tumultuous emotions. Another tremor rattled through him as he fought to regain his composure.

'Don't you ever scare me like that again!' he whispered fiercely. His hands around Jaraadhrin's, shook and his voice so quiet only his young Lord heard him. Jaraadhrin chuckled, weak and shivery, but still rather stunned and amazed at the King's decision. The impromptu swearing-in-ceremony took him by surprise. What was the need for it at a moment like this?

Was it planned beforehand? It certainly feels like it. He thought.

'I accept and Congratulations!' Jaraadhrin whispered as Quinn answered his question with a nod, his hand still pressed to his eyes. Quinn gripped his fingers tightly, unable to or unwilling to let him go, just yet. Queen Debriar raised her hand behind her to the huge dragon, her sleeves flying. She shot an enormous blast of her core at its chest to trigger it. The great Alaq shook its wings out and roared as majestic as ever, just as it had done for Jaraadhrin.

It shot a huge plume but this time, it showered Quinn in gold and red sparks! It roared again and the next plume of centient from its gigantic snout, covered all eight tiers of the citadel. Queen Debriar promptly misted some of it into a Royal banner announcing his swearing-in and suspended it high above the dragon's great wings for all to see.

The Shimran soldiers in the eight tiers spun in astonishment as the dragon roared high above them, fearing a death which might necessitate a new swearing in. They broke into a deafening cheer as they caught sight of the vast lilac banners. They whirled down immediately into salutes, graceful and in sync as ever, their robes and locks flying around them as they swore their allegiance to Quinzafoor in a loud chorus.

Long Live, Lord Quinzafoor, Son of Lord Zhafoor, Lord Protector of the King, Queen, Lord Jaraadhrin and the Princess of Shimrah. We bow before you, Our Lord! We swear Fidelity to the King and Kingdom in immortality and death. Accept our sword and service, My Lord!

Quinzafoor stood up, pulled off his blindfold and raised his hand at them. He looked stunned and moved as if in a dream. Shocked and core quivering, he still managed to look imposing and elegant as ever. His eyes blazed fiery auburn without its usual thin therin covering.

Even under the dire circumstances they were in, laughter and rejoicings rose as the soldiers shot colourful stars and mists from their centients. Having robbed of the opportunity to activate the dragon for him, they were dispensing it in any way they saw fit! The tiers flashed and burst with their elation; They had another leader they could look up to, in these times of dire uncertainty.

The streams from the second and third tiers were particularly thick and interesting. Those were their own band of soldiers with whom they always practiced and trained. Quinzafoor was immensely popular among this crowd. The air was thick with hearts and flowers above the two tiers below them. The hearts were definitely from the many warrior shimaras who often gathered around, gazing and giggling as he practiced. Jaraadhrin chuckled again as they helped him up.

'That would be the freshness of my eyes then' he said, grinning widely 'Alaq was very creative but not as much as the warrior shimaras from the clearing!' Quinn rolled his eyes and narrowed it quickly as he refocussed on the ominous spots of blackness. They were much bigger and was almost at the eighth-tier shields.

'Talking about shimaras, you had to think of one's eyes even at death's door, my Lord.' He paused, tilting his head as he recalled them. 'In all fairness.... I can't say I blame you, they are the prettiest and the most stunning, I have ever seen too' he chuckled as Jaraadhrin gazed at the back of his head in some confusion.

What is Quinn on about?

King Dunyazer slid the ornate crown studded with numerous jewels off of his head and held out his hand for his Queen's dragon shaped one. She slipped it of promptly and handed it to him. He placed them base to base and they fused in a flash of gold. They spun rapidly and shrunk within his hands to the size of finger rings. The crowns of Shimrah were infused with ancient magic and were deadly when touched by any who was not of Royal blood. They usually froze the wearer solid by icing their cores over temporarily. They made an unworthy wearer immobile till their treason could be punished or whatever other action the situation warranted.

King Dunyazer reached into Jaraadhrin's robes, pulled out his red ribbon and clipped them on it. He chuckled at his astonished expression.

'For safe keeping' he explained. 'It is embedded with the heir stones to the thrones of Shimrah, lethal in the wrong hands'. King Dunyazer turned away from him. He embraced his Queen as Lord Jaraadh slid his arms around Jaraadhrin's and Quinzafoor's shoulders, pulling them to him in a tight, warm hug.

Quinn choked, stiffening in his adopted father's sudden embrace. Lord Jaraadh's thoughts had emptied, His King's and Queen's minds were cloaked in Shield Shifrs. A tremor ran through his being. This felt ominous. His father's figure shook slightly against him and it sent roaring waves of agony through his being.

'Father...?' Quinzafoor mumbled, eyes shut tight against Lord Jaraadh's neck, holding back the tears threatening to spill out of them. Why did he feel so shaken all of a sudden? He could remember feeling like this just once before, long ago.... His father drew a sharp, rattling breath.

'You call me that now?....you little urchin! Aaashh!' exclaimed Lord Jaraadh in a strangled whisper. Beside Quinn, Jaraadhrin's mind raced ahead in tortured thoughts as he tried to make sense of the situation. Jaraadhrin slipped his arm around Quinn's back, pulling him closer to himself and their father.

'No matter what happens....Protect the Princess and Stay in the Light!' Lord Jaraadh's voice broke as he whispered into his sons' ears. He kissed them hard on their cheeks. He didn't wait for their reply but turned away in one swift motion, eyes glittering wet. He slid to his knees before his Queen as King Dunyazer released her. He reached for his Queen's hand and kissed it as he held it within both of his. Queen Debriar raised him swiftly.

'No....Lord Jaraadh, my brother....' Queen Debriar reached up on her toes, her hands against the sides of his face and pressed her lips to his forehead. 'Be safe....' He nodded speechless and slid to his beloved King's side.

'It's time......' said King Dunyazer, his hand still stretched towards his Queen. 'Guard the Princess at all costs' his gaze flashed to Jaraadhrin and Quinn who sank into salutes. Queen Debriar eyes moistened over as her King flew up with Lord Jaraadh, their hands reaching for each other till they flew out of range. Queen Debriar lowered her hand as if in a trance still gazing after them as they flew under the shields to the lowest tiers, to hold the defence. Jaraadhrin shook his head, drawing shivery breaths as wave after wave of sharp anguish raced through his already vulnerable core.

Why did all this feel like a farewell? He agonised as he gazed after his father and the King.

'Because it probably is!' Quinn grimaced through gnashed teeth, trembling through his own torment beside him as Queen Debriar shot him a warning glance.

The Shimran Dragons

What? *Quinzafoor* – Jaraadhrin turned to Quinn, stunned.

'Feel you core' Queen Debriar interrupted him.

'It's stronger my Queen, the ice shard is gone' he replied, distracted. 'Thank you, Your Highness'

'I forbid you to touch it gain with your Shifr! You will not be this lucky next time'. She warned him. He nodded anxiously. The dark blotches were over them now, swarming around in long elongated pins, flowing like shadows over the shields. Thicker and rounder at one end and pointy tailed in the other, waving and flowing. Lord Jaraadh's yishins sparkled everywhere as he commanded their martial forces. A thick explosion of blue stars burst into the air and the archers lifted their bows high, raining arrows through the shields at Lord Jaraadh's command.

Queen Debriar unclipped her bow and shot a few arrows at the black flying masses over them. Though her aim was true, the shapes merely dissolved into a menacing black shadow as the arrows made contact, letting them pass through before solidifying again.

'As I thought! We cannot harm them with weapons.' She observed.

'What did you mean by....' Jaraadhrin began turning to Quinn who promptly raised his hand between them, hiding his face with the length of the therin sleeves of his robes.

'Don't look at my eyes, my Lord' he grimaced, staring intently at a shape zooming in closer and closer to the shield above them. His eyes blazed auburn through the therin of his sleeves. Jaraadhrin made an exasperated noise.

'Why ever not...!'

228

At that moment, the outline above them made contact with the shield and shrieked in agony. The darkness enveloping it split in long, black hair, coarse and matted. It flew off its body, blowing furiously behind it and exposing the creature within, in all of its foulness.

It was the most despicable being the Shimrans had ever seen. Its skin mottled blue with blood red lips and blind silver eyes. Its bare body merged with wings on either side of it, stretching from the tips of its red taloned, fingers all the way to its tail. The edges of its wings, sharp and claws protruding at every curved ridge. Its legs fused together ending in an elongated, serpentine tail which swished and slashed, sharp and deadly. It snarled and shrieked, baring at its fangs at them, contorting its face in repulsive grimaces.

It slashed the shield with its talons and huge tears appeared in it, re-healing immediately as the shield-maras reinforced it. Quinn whirled in front of Jaraadhrin and his Queen, shooting bolt after blazing, auburn bolt of fiery centient fireballs from his eyes!

'Ten...thirty...fifty...ninety...about ninety-eight!'. He counted under his breath as the creature shuddered. It shrieked as the bolts hit it and incinerated in cloud of black smoke and red sparks. He drew a quick breath and tilted his head toward Jaraadhrin.

'That's why! ...can't always control it!' he replied to his Lord's question, grinning as Jaraadhrin stared at the place where the creature had incinerated in awe.

'I don't believe it! Oh Ibreeth, Ifreeth, what have you done?!' Queen Debriar groaned 'How far have you strayed off the light in your ambitions and desires for the throne?' Quinn and Jaraadhrin spun towards her questioningly. Her face whitened in the glow of the grey silver shields.

'Tlumods of the Delcrum!' She answered, her face ashen 'What have you unleashed on Shimrah?' she gasped suddenly as she grabbed Quinn by the arm. 'Your eyebolts are made of your centients. We have to fight them with Shimran centients and cores? Only the life-forces of a Shimran can kill them? Nearly hundred centient years to kill one?...And there's thousands...?' Queen Debriar whispered as Quinn nodded grimly, his eyes closed against the blaze.

Jaraadhrin frowned. What were they? The words were unfamiliar to him. A glance at Quinn showed him that he didn't know either. The citadel didn't stand a chance if it depended only on the Shimrans' lifeforces. This wasn't a battle, it was massacre! His shimling princess's words echoed within his head.

'Would you consider our centient powers offensive, Dhrin...? We have to weaponize our Shifrs and ourselves or perish!'

Princess Saffrodel was right. We were too slow to change and it is already too late. He shook his head hard. *It doesn't matter, I will see it through. No matter the odds. Today we teeter at the edge of a precipice but even at the brink of the impossible, I promise you, my Princess! I-will-see-it-through.'* He pledged. Quinn nodded beside him, a slight smile on his grim face as he registered Jaraadhrin's thoughts.

'We will see it through, Jaraadhrin!' he hissed.

The incineration of the first seemed to have started a chain reaction and the creatures, swarming everywhere, were beginning to reveal themselves. Slamming at the shields, screeching and slashing at them with their talons. The shields ripped and healed as the shield-maras fought to keep them together in the fourteen towers behind the citadel. They were the most protected but in a way, they were also the most vulnerable as their centres were usually attacked first, by everything and anything that attacked the shields.

Jaraadhrin and Quinn bolted yishins to Lord Jaraadh and to their Martial Force in the two tiers below them, instructing the command leaders on how to kill them but they knew it was no use. Shimran soldiers only had a few thousand centient years each over their cores. It would weaken them and they wouldn't be able to hold the attack. Queen Debriar snapped her fingers, enclosing Jaraadhrin and Quinzafoor in the shining armour of the Lord Protectors of Shimrah as they summoned their massive cores.

The Queen, Jaraadhrin and Quinzafoor shot colossal, century old centient bolts at the swarming creatures rapidly. The Queen had eons but Quinzafoor and Jaraadhrin had only mediated to few thousands as the Lords of Shimrah. Their cores expanded out of their slender frames, separated in to seven rings and circled them in brilliant loops of blazing colours. It spiralled around them, protecting them as they positioned two fingers of each hand in front of their chests, slinging out bolts with quick snaps of their wrists.

They drew sphere after sphere of flaming power from their rings to shoot the shapes above them in rapid succession. Their lilac, silver, and auburn corebolts flashed around the screeching creatures, incinerating them at contact at every blow, their aim true and precise every time. Their soldiers on the second and third tiers, roared with anticipation. They followed their leaders and summoned their cores into visible rings around them, shooting rapidly, their centient bolts lethal and accurate.

The lower tiers flashed with multicolour rings and bolts as all Shimrans in the main Martial Force who can spare any, flashed their firebolts at the black blotches. They shot down many, incinerated some as others swerved and flew out of range. The numbers of the main martial force were greatly reduced and many were still recovering from the war. They would be the first to fall if the shields failed. Jaraadhrin could see his father's cool blue rings, spinning around himself and another golden-haired figure as great beams of pure light poured out from around them. He was sharing his centre, protecting the King as he had done these many years.

Lord Jaraadh's centre was eons old, almost like Royalty as he had to be to protect his human King in war. It was an incredibly difficult task for nobility to undertake. Royalty was more powerful than nobility. His father had trained and nurtured his being in the desserts of Southern Shimrah, the snow-capped peaks of the Icy Spikes and deep within the crystal waters of the arms of the Silverstream, where supreme centient powers gathered. He had meditated for years, without food or water and sometimes even without air or conscious thought, to attain this level of supremacy. It had taken him centuries and many hardships to reach that state. All that to protect his King and Queen with everything he had! Jaraadhrin felt a sudden rush of respect and affection for his father and his mother within him. Their loyalty to the crown knew no bounds. They lived and breathed for their beloved King and Kingdom and he, their son, would do the same!

The slashed shields glimmered silver grey at the slits, quickly replenished by the massive cores of the shield-maras but for how much longer can they withstand it? It was the only barrier between them and the creatures. Demon-esque essence was poisonous to a Shimran's core. What if it poisoned them? What if it tainted their cores as they held the shields? Their Shifrs were so rare that even the loss of one weakened the citadel greatly. If the creatures were to touch them, they would splatter their essence and vanish just like those poor villagers in Southern Shimrah and he had nearly done, moments before. He felt an overwhelming gratitude to his Queen and her astuteness.

The middle tier glistened suddenly, brightening with brilliant shards and flashes as Lord Jaraadh's glittering blue sparks flashed across the skies.

'The dragons! They are summoning the dragons!' The yell went up, repeated excitedly, especially among the second and third tiers of soldiers who were under sixteen Shimran years and hadn't entwined yet. They, like Jaraadhrin, hadn't seen dragons either. That was until his mother had made an appearance for him! The dragons were only summoned as a last resort and at the end of a Shimran's tether. Lord Jaraadh was summoning them early to try finish this before it could get any worse and before his soldiers used up too much of their core, to be able to summon them.

The main Martial Force of the King had suffered heavy losses. Of the few hundred soldiers who had returned from the war, very few had returned with their dragons intact, a hundred or so. True, dragons were immensely power-ful and could help vaporise these foul beings but they were still weak from all the fighting they had already done.

The natures and powers of Shimrans were very particular. Violence weakened Shimrans. Peace and love strengthened them. War had bred hate and revenge in many of the fair folk of Shimrah, negative emotions that weakened their cores and centients even if they were rightly placed. It was a difficult situ-ation. They needed to defend and fight but they also needed to do it without any form of negativity or they risk losing themselves to the darkness. It was a narrow and difficult path to walk.

The soldiers shrieked in awe as the dragon bearers crossed their wrists in sync. They spun around in a swirl of robes and gathered their cores. Their arms whirled around in specific motions as they summoned their huge dragons out of them. The majestic creatures burst above them, in differ-ent colours and shapes, blazing against the night sky. They shot through the shields, roaring deafeningly, their large snouts open, breathing massive plumes of flames that disintegrated the tlumods immediately in hundreds.

Jaraadhrin could see Jade, his mother, glide swiftly out of his father as she soared high, curling her huge tail in graceful coils. Her long, slender, scaly body and wings, flashing colour as it caught the light around it. She shot a plume of blue hearts enveloped in a silver mist in his direction before shoot-ing through the shields to join the others. Jaraadhrin smiled, his eyes tender, he could guess what that meant. Quinn sighed beside him, his face saddened still throwing bolts of fire.

'Your mother says you look very handsome and Princely, Jaraadhrin. She loves the crown. She wanted me to say that you have her blessings and she is very proud of you!' Jaraadhrin whipped to face him in amazement and Quinn raised his sleeve rapidly, mid fire, with an exasperated 'Aaashh!'

'You speak dragon? Since when do you speak dragon?' Jaraadhrin inquired incredulously.

'No, my Lord...I READ dragons... and any other intelligent creature with a Shimran core!' Quinn replied through his teeth and in amused frustration 'And please! For the Love of Shimrah, my Lord! Could you remember not to look at my face unless you want to be incinerated along with these pesky creatures!' He swished his hand down, swift and sharp, as he shot a snarling tlumod. 'I do need my hands to fight!' Jaraadhrin turned away from him in feigned indignation.

'Yes…well it's not like I miss the sight of it, anyway!' he grumbled, grinning widely as his eyes twinkled.

Queen Debriar chuckled at the good-natured quibbling of her young Lords. That felt like typical tzars! Kind, caring, good natured and level-headed. But they were far from conventional tzars. Jaraadhrin and Quinn were very special. It was nothing to do with their deadly Shifrs, skills and abilities. It was the essence of their very being. There was a reason Jaraadhrin's hair was wavy rather than straight like the rest. There were a reason Quinn's eyes where the brightest blue-green different from the piercing blue of the other tzars. They were perceptive, compassionate and complex, much more diverse than others. The extent of that difference was still to be learned. Hardly anything perturbed them and their bickering in the middle of such a situation was refreshing.

Queen Debriar moved her hands in a graceful circlet and swished her own dragon off to join the excitement. It blasted out of her, gigantic and lilac, bigger than all the others. A huge amethyst jewel glimmered inside its horn. Jaraadhrin and Quinn stared at it in awe. It glided up higher than everyone else's and blasted a plume of fiery flames in a great arc at a huge cluster of tlumods which promptly burst into flames. It settled on its folded legs sitting in mid-air, purring with endearing indolence as it lopped its tongue out. The rest of the dragons soared majestic and bright moving with extreme grace, flashing their wings and tails just above the shields.

Their Queen's dragon looked as if it was sticking its tongue out at the enemy. King Dunyazer and Lord Jaraadh glanced up, chuckling as the Shimrans below burst into loud hilarity at their Queens' humour, boosting their morale. The tiers echoed with cheers and claps of triumph as their dragons cantered above them, sending the tlumods fleeing back to the dark depths, far away in front of the citadel. It looked as if they could turn this around after all.

Jaraadhrin and Quinn chuckled, staring up at the dragons as the shields strengthened. There wasn't a single tlumods in sight. They had all retreated as soon as the dragons appeared and diminished their numbers down by almost a few thousands. Queen Debriar stood behind them frowning slightly as Quinn's face sobered to seriousness.

'You are right my Queen, this doesn't seem right, we should be vigilant.' Jaraadhrin had already closed his eyes. He knew what his Queen thought for he was of the same mind. Ifreeth knew about the dragons and if the tlumods could be so easily beaten by them, why send them alone? He had chosen this creature to combat the light of the Shimran core, their Shifrs, their citadel's defences and their shields. He would have indeed factored in the dragons. The tlumods retreat was an ominous sign that something else was afoot.

'Jaraadhrin' warned Queen Debriar 'Be careful what you touch with your Shifr, the next wave could be more deadly.' He nodded. He needed no reminders. He had to be as strong as he possibly could be to fight them. He couldn't see anything yet, just the dark mass faraway where the tlumods hovered, waiting for something. The moments passed by as the dragon bearers held their dragons aloof. Their gigantic beasts settled down around the Queen's great lilac one. They were glad to be summoned by their Masters and to see some action.

The silence stretched as the soldiers below held their positions. It dawned on each of them that it couldn't be over just yet or that quickly. Jaraadhrin tensed, reaching out further and further, nearer to the dark mass as Quinn removed an ornate clip from the side of his head, eyes closed in concentration. They stiffened suddenly on either side of the Queen.

'Slithering, dark, serpentine shapes, about a hundred, heading straight for the dragons through the air'

'Murderous hisses and murmurs focused on the Dragonlight'

Jaraadhrin and Quinn reported, simultaneously, their voices urgent and low.

'Call back the dragons, now!' commanded Queen Debriar as a yishin shot out of Quinn to Lord Jaraadh with the order, even before the sentence was completed. He usually sent yishins as he could read an order before it was spoken and it made the process faster. Queen Debriar swung her arms in a wide circle as the great lilac beast above them, jumped up over the smaller ones around her, shielding and protecting them from the incoming threat. it roared up, blowing a great plume of lilac fire in a wide half circle.

The soldiers below gasped as the flare illuminated the serpentine creatures, dark as night, slithering rapidly towards their dragons. They had the faces and bodies of a female till the midriff and a long, scaly, winding tails that slashed and curved with three spikes at the end. They were covered in black scales, their eyes and fangs flashing silver as they snarled down through the shields at the dragons and their owners. The blood red lips stretched in an ugly sneer as they reached through the shields for them with their long thin arms, ending in gigantic snake heads. They screeched as they burned an angry red on the light of the Shimran shields. They did not disintegrate.

The dragon bearers pulled back their dragons as fast as possible on Lord Jaraadh's command as Queen Debriar lilac beast stood guard, blazing plume after plume of fire as the creatures circled her. They scorched in her fires as they neared her, screeching and howling and glowed red with the burns. The foul creatures slithered in and out, trying to find an opening to attack her. She was being surrounded as more and more closed in!

'Hurry!' she huffed, breathless with the effort of keeping her dragon float. Queen Debriar was still vulnerable after all she had been through. Dragons placed much pressure on the Shimran central being. Any Shimran with their centient powers exhausted and below their core levels, cannot summon them. That was why Lord Jaraadh had ordered them summoned early but now these creatures were intent on their Dragonlight. It was a threat to the very Shimran being as well as their dragons. Not only could they kill the dragon with its massive central being but they could deplete the Shimran cores to a minimum depending on the strength of their bind with their dragons. Entwined soldiers shared a pledge a thousand times stronger than that of Quinn and Ashoora. It was sacred and lethal to break and extremely dangerous when destroyed forcibly. It usually meant the end of both the dragon and their Shimran.

Most of the brightly coloured dragons had already disappeared into their bearers as Queen Debriar stood guard against the few still being pulled back. Jade pranced back and forth across the queen, to either side of her and protecting her. Queen Debriar's dragon glanced back at her for a moment, roaring an order to get the rest of them to safety. Jade nodded her large snout and ushered the beasts through the shields.

In the moment the lilac, dragonesque beast looked away, a host of the serpentine creatures swirled in around her, snarling. Black liquid poured out of their foul mouths drenching the Queen's dragon from all sides. It gave a great roar before curling back in though the shields as the last of the smaller dragons flipped down. It fell around Queen Debriar, coiling lifeless round and round her as she sank to her knees. It glimmered lilac, unresponsive and shimmered away in a soft breeze.

The soldiers thundered as their Queen's dragon descended, inert and limp. They yelled in horror and anger as they jumped up to fort walls, summoned their cores and blasted powerful fireballs at the loathsome serpents. The Meinedders retreated rapidly, their part was done. Queen Debriar moaned and stood up, helped by her Lord Protectors.

'He is alright' she choked, referring to her dragon. 'That venom paralysed him, took away some thousand years. He will need to recover but not for a few days though. We can't use dragons anymore, not with the Meinedders. They would kill them and the Shimrans with it'. She raised her hand swiftly, flashing lilac sparks to indicate that she was alright and yishin to Lord Jaraadh informing him. The dragons who have been hovering just below the shields, disappeared roaring as they were pulled back into their bearers, when the command delivered. Jaraadhrin sighed with relief. A thousand years was nothing to a dragon, it had eons. Somewhere deep in his mind, his father's words echoed,

'There is a darkness to Ifreeth's army, their blades were black and they paralysed our dragons...' Could they have been imbued with these creatures' venom?

'Meinedders?' Quinn shook his head. *Where is this foulness coming from?* Queen Debriar sighed.

'There was a book in the archives of the great annals under the citadel, very old and very dark. It was sealed initially but I found a way to break in and read from the black book of Queen Thiloket. It was named Delcrum. I thought it was fiction when I was very young. It was lost over the years and I never bothered anymore. Seeing these creatures today leads me to think that there is more to it than scary stories.' She paused abruptly. *Could my brothers have found it?* She thought in dismay. Quinn nodded grimly.

'Certainly looks like it, Your Majesty.' Queen Debriar gazed at him. thoughtful. She flipped her hand in a circle, her palms facing each other as if holding something between them. She closed her eyes, her fair brows furrowed. Lilac mists surrounded her head, streamed out and collected within her hands. It solidified into a shining lavender book, immensely thick. She held it a while longer as the streams of lilac subsided and handed it to Quinn.

'Everything I ever read in that book would be in here. Whether I remember them today or not. It should have all the unconscious facts I read or noticed. They will be quite comprehensive but they may also have much missing. I am afraid I never read it as knowledge, just as a hobby.' Queen Debriar explained. Quinn took the book from her. He placed it against his brow, his eyes closed. An auburn glow emanated from his mind, encircling the book for a brief moment then disappeared back into his forehead. He inclined his head to his Queen, his face pale and his eyes cast down. He clipped it to his ribbon.

'There is much darkness within these pages, my Queen. Let's hope Ifreeth doesn't empty all of them on us! Jaraadhrin gazed at him in astonishment. He rolled his eyes in some annoyance and amusement. His father's words surfaced in his mind.

'Here... Learn and memorise that as soon as possible, guard it well. Quinzafoor has already done it and you should know it too'

Lord Jaraadh had said as he handed him the booklet containing the huge, vault maps. The confounded booklet that he had poured over for nights on end to learn and memorise!

Did you knock the darned booklet on your head to memorise it too? No wonder you are an expert potionist, melodist and healer! What more can you do with that boggling Shifr of yours? Its high time you gave me a full revelation of your abilities, you mysterious little whelp! thought Jaraadhrin as he shook his head in chagrin. Quinn chuckled momentarily then frowned.

'But how did Ifreeth get these creatures in to Shimrah? We are surrounded by the magical waters of the Crystal Depths and the Ice Spikes. Darkness cannot cross it, under, over or through. They would incinerate over the waters...unless they never crossed the waters...?' He pondered.

The tlumods were swishing over them again, strengthened by the Meinedders attack on their dragons. They screeched with laughter and agony as they attacked the shields again with vengeance. The soldiers tensed, their cores spinning, ready for any to approach or break into the shields. Ibreeth and Ifreeth had been very clever, counteracting everything that may stand in the way of their victory and no one knew what more creatures he intended to use from his arsenal before the night was out.

The Nightmare

Jaraadhrin sat down beside his princess as she stared into the tinkling waters of the fountain, his long white robes, floating gently in the wind. He grinned down at her. His brilliant blue eyes, sparkling between his thick lashes.

'Tsk...tsk...Saffrah....' He tutted gazing at her elflocked red hair. She had been training with her fans and her thick locks kept unravelling out of their clips as they breezed in the wind of her spinning weapons. Jaraadhrin waved his finger delicately at the front of her robes, pulling out the miniature staff on the Pembre chain with his centient as it hung around her neck. It slid out from within the folds and over her head. Princess Saffrodel inhaled sharply, drawing her shoulders in as his centient grazed against her. He smiled down at her.

'This should hold your tresses more firmly, my Princess. It can be used as a hair stick too...didn't Mistress Afra tell you?' She blushed, smiling up at his tender face as he gazed down at her.

'She didn't have to Jaraadhrin, I heard you' She whispered. Princess Saffrodel sighed. Sitting here, beside him, on this moonlit night was bliss. She watched its white light breaking in to a million little orbs as it reflected in the tinkling waters of the fountain. His silver aura glistened around her, enveloping her with its affection as he sat tall and straight, his bronze locks framing his elegant face. She reached down to the waters and her tresses slid off her shoulders. It floated for a moment before sinking within blue of the fountain.

'Aaashh...' he murmured '... you will get chills if you keep this up...' Jaraadhrin caught the Pembre staff hovering beside him and placed it between his pursed lips. He summoned his centient over both hands to lift her long locks out of the water and dry them. Princess Saffrodel turned away from him so he could reach her locks with ease. She could see his reflection in the waters of the fountain. She stilled the waves covertly with a swift slide of her fingers so she could see him better. He had his slender hands on either side of her dripping locks, palms straight. His warmed centient flowed between them as it dried her wet tresses. They snaked and wound around in the air, siphoning off the moisture.

Jaraadhrin's fair forehead tensed and his eyes narrowed in concentration as he shaped her now dry hair, in to intricate braids with slight movement of his fingers. He rolled them up, secure and stable, to the back of her head, shaping and curling with his centients. He let some of it hang gracefully down to her waist. He tilted his head to the side as if trying find a flaw in his perfectly accomplished creation and nodded in satisfaction. Princess Saffrodel giggled at his expression. He glanced at her reflection on the stilled waters and raised his brow, his lips curling into a smile around the staff. He slipped it of his mouth with another wave of his fingers and slid it deep within the intricately braided mass on her head. He moved his hand in a quick spiral and the long chain wound around it, holding everything in place, firm and secure.

'There.' he said with satisfaction as she giggled again. He looked so content with his achievement. His eyes shot to her face as she turned to glance up at him. He wiggled his brows at her comically and snapped back away with a chuckle as their eyes met.

He was so playful and amusing under all that sternness. It was adorable. Hardly anyone knew the gentle and jovial Jaraadhrin under all that ice and the few who did, cherished it. Princess Saffrodel stood up and walked away. Jaraadhrin moved swiftly beside her. She only reached to just over his shoulder.

Maybe I would grow taller if I aged more. It isn't likely, Shimrans reached their permanent frame in about nine months but I have aged a year today. She thought as she walked by him.

The breeze picked up, stiff and cool as they moved, swirling the pink petals around them in gentle streams. Princess Saffrodel folded her arms at her waist.

'Are you cold, my Princess?' he inquired, his enchanting voice breezing down with his warm breath. She shook her head, thought for a bit, then nodded. Jaraadhrin chuckled at the indecision. He swung his long sleeves, well over his fingers and swirled it around her, laying the therin neatly on her shoulders. He held his arm behind her and away from her so the floaty sleeve stayed put. She smiled. He was such a moral tzar and yet he had berated himself in the worst possible manner at the fountains!

Their heads snapped up as a burst of light lit the dark sky, disturbing the peace with a bang. Jaraadhrin frowned.

239

'What was that? Fireworks? Were we celebrating something?' He glanced at her questioningly as she shook her head. More flashes and bangs and the sky rent with roars and screeches. Quinzafoor came soaring down through flashes of light, blindfolded and his eyes blazing.

'My Lord, we are under attack, Ifreeth's armies are finally here!' he informed, his voice low and urgent. Jaraadhrin slipped his sleeve off Princess Saffrodel. Turning to her, he whispered, his voice fond but firm.

'Go into the citadel and wait for me there, my Princess. I will come find you!' He made to follow Quinn who stood some ways away from them.

'But...' He spun back to her again, hurriedly. 'Just be safe...' Princess Saffrodel said as she stalled him.

'Hmm' he nodded, turning back to Quinn.

'Don't get too close to them...' Jaraadhrin stopped mid turn,

'Hmmmm...' he said facing her, his lips lifted slightly at the corners.

'Don't use your projections....'

'Hmmmm...'

'Come find me as soon as possible...'

'Hmmmm...hmmmm...' hummed Jaraadhrin, nodding at her again, amusement on his face and eyes tender as he watched his princess struggle with the farewell.

'Princess, I will be alright, you need not concern yourself – '

Jaraadhrin inhaled sharply and jolted backwards as his tall frame stiffened. He shut his eyes tight against the deafening roar of his being. His long locks crackled back and lifted in a fanning blaze of sudden passion as Princess Saffrodel threw her arms around his waist! She lay her head on his left shoulder, hugging him tightly as she had often done as a shimling. Only, it felt very different now.

I don't need to grow any taller, this is just right. she thought, smiling against him. Quinzafoor whirled away from them, facing in the other direction, chuckling.

Jaraadhrin exhaled, a slight shiver in his warm, quiet breath. He opened his eyes as if in a dream. His frame relaxed as he recovered his composure and quieted his thundering core with difficulty. His lips curved into a tender smile as he folded his strong arms around her shoulders and slender waist, bringing his Princess in against him, delicately. He tilted down his face as she raised hers, her smooth brows and nose nestling against the chiselled slide of his cheek, graceful and natural, as the distance closed. Her whole petite frame melted within his arms and long sleeves, warm and comforting. He sighed. His warm breath fanned down to her. The wavy, bronze curls at the side of his face, caressed her pink cheeks.

'How would I ever leave now… Saffrah…? He breathed. Princess Saffrodel giggled as she patted the small of his back over his still crackling, long, wavy tresses and pulled away from him, red in the face and abashed. Jaraadhrin gazed down at her, still rather dazed. She giggled again at his expression, her slender fingers over her full lips.

Why do shimaras have such power over the tzars. I didn't mean to incapacitate him so. It was entirely involuntary, stemming from a completely impulsive action. Nevertheless, it is there and it is hard for him to deal with! She thought in chagrin. Jaraadhrin smiled at her guilty, little face.

'I will find you….' he murmured, blinking away the daze. He nodded and moved away from her, his hand still stretched towards her.

Princess Saffrodel gazed after them in tender fondness as they flew off into the dark night, flashing and bursting with colour. Quinzafoor held out an arm protectively behind Jaraadhrin. She smiled. It didn't matter that she had initially disapproved of Quinzafoor. He was still a wonderfully, loyal soldier and she knew he would look out for her Dhrin. She could feel the sync of their auras as they flew off. She was glad that Quinzafoor accompanied him. Quinn was undeniably a lethal tzar to cross.

Princess Saffrodel made her way back into the citadel which was bustling with activity, her Shifr would wear off and she would need to lie down. What a time to have used her Time Shifr. She would be completely unable to defend herself if the worst came to pass. She felt drained and sleepy already. She slid into a chair and laid her heavy head against the cushions. It was quieter here at the back of the palace overlooking the lake. She closed her eyes sighing as her thoughts turned to a tall handsome someone with bronze waves. She smiled as she slipped in and out of sleep. She could feel the healers visit her often as they made sure, she was well.

Princess Saffrodel frowned suddenly. The sounds of the battle outside were getting louder and louder. The citadel itself seethed with activity, something was wrong. She tried to jolt herself awake but the Time Shifrs effects were too deep to shake off. The yells and shouts were deafening and the flashes brightened alarmingly against her closed lids.

'The great dragon has fallen....... We are losing!'

Princess Saffrodel tensed. *Did they mean the great Alaq? Where is Jaraadhrin? Is he well?* she pondered as a creeping cold reached her from above. It felt dark and very murky. The darkness spun around her making it difficult to breath. It rattled and snarled around in icy winds, slithered and hissed ominously, screeched and howled in a whirlwind around her. She shuddered. *What on Shimrah was happening?* She was helpless. She couldn't move! Had they forgotten her in all the commotion and the fact that she couldn't wake up till the sun rose again?

A brilliant silver glimmered far, far above her, flashing and blazing. A beacon of light and hope. *Jaraadhrin!* He was alive, well and pulsed with power, stronger than she had ever known him to be.

I need to go to him; he would protect me! He would make this dreadful darkness and scary sounds go away but how could I go to him? Princess Saffrodel felt livid with anger. *Why didn't I go with him to fight by his side? Why did I just let him go and cause this dreadful separation between us?*

'I will find you...' he had said before he left. *Why isn't he by my side yet? What was he doing high up above there, all alone? Where is Quinn? He was supposed to protect my Dhrin. I need to wake up and go to him.... I belong at his side.... I need to join him.... I need to fight beside him...! I need to go to him now!*

The Fury of Shimratzars

Jaraadhrin frowned, his heart sinking as he thought hard. *There must be a way.*

'Quinn' he called. Quinn tilted his head in his direction still flashing huge, auburn spheres into the sky and bolts raging from his eyes.

'Remember the tincture? Javnoon? Have you anymore?' Quinn nodded as he read his Lord.

'A whole chamber full of them' he replied, chuckling. He swished his hands between firing and summoned sixteen vials of glimmering auburn liquid.

'My Queen' he said, handing fifteen to her 'The shield-maras, for their cores and yours'. Queen Debriar nodded. She slipped them on to her ribbon, placed the tips of her fingers behind their shoulders and shot in a few thousand years into them.

'Use that up quick, so you don't have to mediate. Be right back' She whispered and flew off to the forts, swift as a bird. She flashed in and out of the fourteen forts, delivering the vials to them. The extra centients would help them strengthen their shields. Shield-maras were able to mediate eons in moments and right now they needed those shields more than anything else. Barely a few moments passed and the shields glimmered. They blazed gold from the silver grey they had been. They had been strengthened and refurbished. The colour indicated the next level of shield strength.

'So how does that work then? The Javnoon? Is it a part of the Shifr too?' inquired Jaraadhrin as he blasted tlumods to oblivion. Quinzafoor chuckled.

'I wish' he said. 'They take months to make and my supply has matured for ten years.' He shot an eyebolt at snarling tlumod right in its face. 'The Shifr is just to summon it from a known place and return it back, over short distances. Like the Princess's flowers and my weapons which you unceremoniously scattered around the clearing this afternoon, my Lord' he explained, grinning. Jaraadhrin shook his head.

Was that this afternoon? It feels like years ago.

'Hmm... hmm....' Jaraadhrin acknowledged, deep in thought.

So where is this chamber full of Javnoon then? I would certainly have noticed a hall full of flasks of fiery liquid in the palace in my fifteen years of wondering around in it! Quinn rolled his eyes, snickering.

'I wouldn't keep something that precious and forbidden in plain sight. It is in my private collection, my Lord. It is personal!'

Ah yes. Personal? Is it, you imp? And nothing in my head is, I suppose? Scoffed Jaraadhrin good-naturedly. Quinn chortled.

The creatures screeched as the shields burned them, scorching them as they neared it. They howled and snarled at the Shimrans below, hovering menacingly and baring their teeth. By the time Queen Debriar returned to the shimratzars sides, they had already used up her loan of centuries. The creatures now hovered just out of shot. Quinn raised his vial to drink, glancing at Jaraadhrin's waist to make sure he had his. Jaraadhrin felt his glance and chuckled.

A couple of unmediated sips of that nearly killed me and you fly around downing vialfuls! Brilliant! He thought and Quinn grinned.

'Your health, my Lord' he said and emptied it in one go adding, a few hundred thousand years to his centient. The vial vanished and he performed the six-point core stabilizing movement rapidly to sediment the extra eons, he had consumed. A fiery blaze enveloped him, lifting him a few spaces above the ground as the centuries sedimented within him with his quick movements.

'That will not stay in long without proper meditation' Queen Debriar warned him still gazing at the skies for a renewed attack. 'You better use that up quick.' Quinn nodded.

'I will need to get closer.'

'No!' said Jaraadhrin 'You can burn up on those shields too.' Queen Debriar leapt into the air conjuring her own shield of lilac, protecting them against the fiery haze of the Shimran shields.

'Come' she commanded. They leapt in the air, moving as close to the main shields as possible. Jaraadhrin aimed at the closest tlumod and spun a bolt at it. He barely swung out of the way as it ricocheted back to him, bouncing off the gold shields. The fireball hit the stone parapets and glanced back out, this time making through the main shields but falling short of the creatures. Queen Debriar shook her head as they alighted back down.

'The shields are too strong. You can't shoot through them at short range but we need to bring those numbers down quickly.' She twirled her hands in a quick spiral, enveloping Quinn and Jaraadhrin in lilac shield bubbles of her centient, around their own spinning rings of power.

'I am propelling you out of the shields, try not to get splattered!' she lifted her hands and thrusted them out before they could object.

Jaraadhrin and Quinn focused their centient as they emerged through the gold Shimran defences. They spun quickly within their rings and shot the centient bolts in rapid circles as the creatures closed in on them, screeching and howling. They incinerated in clouds of black and red, so fast and thick that it obscured the tzars from view. Jaraadhrin's centients exhausted faster than Quinn's as he shot centuries out of himself. His core growled within him still fragile in its newly recovered state.

They felt a sudden jolt around the lilac shields, the Queen was pouring in more of her eons into them. She clenched her teeth. Even her massive core was draining rapidly, without her dragon and with all the power she was expending. The lilac shields depleting more of her centients as she struggled to keep the tlumods demonesque essence off of her young Lord Protectors.

The creatures still swarmed over the shields out of shooting range. They no longer slashed at the shields but hovered snarling, circling menacingly and looking for an inlet, a weakening. The tzars shot more and more bolts, destroying a few hundred more as the Queen's shields thinned. She gasped and pulled them back through the Shimran shields as she sank to the ground on her knees. Jaraadhrin flashed to her side. He undid the vial at her ribbon and handing it to her. Quinn stood guard, his auburn core rings still spinning, swift and powerful, around him.

'My Queen' he whispered. 'You cannot exhaust yourself like this. We will find another way'

'There is no time, Jaraadhrin' she replied as she emptied the vial and her core bubbled up 'We need to get this under control before sun rises.' He stared at her, confused.

The sun? Maybe these creatures hated the sun? So why do we need to win this before the sun rose? We could use its power. It was only a few of hours to daybreak any-way. He shook his head. *The Queen, in her infinite wisdom had her reasons. No one questioned it. If she needed this finished before the sun rose then I will follow through or die trying.*

The gold shield above them quivered. A massive shriek emanated as about ten of the tlumods crashed into the shield directly on top of them. They were combining their demon essences at one point of the shield to break through to them. They screamed in agony and disappeared in a blaze of black shadow. The shields quivered again but held as another attack ensued. A larger assem-bly of tlumods crashed on the shields this time. It shook and trembled but still stood, glimmering gold. Jaraadhrin sprang to his feet in front of the Queen, summoning his core into power rings again as another horde collected. Quinn, ready by his side, eyes ablaze. This cluster was much bigger than be-fore, almost twenty-five to thirty of them.

The shimratzars braced, their cloaks and locks flying around them in the crackle of their rings and the extent of their anger. Queen Debriar's concerned face, broke into a smile as she gazed at them before her. Lightening crackles whipped their long tresses back. It trailed in circlets along their manes. She could feel the heat emanating from them as they blew fiercely back towards her.

She had heard of this happening to tzars when they were very angry but had never seen it till now. Shimratzars were usually calm and rarely angered for anything. They were natural protectors of shimaras and shimlings and were patient, kindly beings. They fought with mirth and humour and were extremely cool headed. The young tzars shielding her were beyond furious! Emotions usually reduced the powers of a tzar. It was a natural protective mechanism for themselves and those they protect. It had a very deep sig-nificance in Shimrah. However, those emotions could provide the opposite effect with one catalyst. Righteousness. There were very few emotions that enhanced the powers of the cores of a tzar, one of them was anger. Roaring Righteous Rage!

The creatures crashed with a resounding screech and the shield splintered letting one through. It incinerated promptly as Quinn shot fire with both his eyes and palms, mixed with Jaraadhrin's. They could see another, more mas-sive cluster, rushing behind the dissipating shadow of the last one. Cluster after cluster crashed into their shield, occasionally letting a couple through as Jaraadhrin and Quinn blasted them to shadow. They seemed to be intent on getting in at that point. They had become the main targets. The foul creatures seem to have realized that this tier presented the most threat to them and was even ready to sacrifice their massive numbers to take them out. These crea-tures were either intelligent or they had someone ruthless instructing them.

It all made the situation deadlier.

A loud yell went up in the tiers below theirs, among Jaraadhrin's and Quinn's own soldiers. They turned as one and rained fireballs at the approaching tlumods. Groups of the more powerful shimaras flew up on to the fort walls, defending them fiercely from the sudden concentrated attacks on their Queen and young Lords. They were terrifying in their rage as their spinning rings blazed through the darkness, their brilliant red locks on fire and trailing behind them in fiery plumes.

A hundred of the tlumods sped at the shields at once and crashed with a massive explosion, their talons spread as they reached in. It was the largest horde yet and the shield splintered! A huge slit rent it apart and twenty of the tlumods slid in simultaneously. Jaraadhrin and Quinn whirled around as they slashed them with their firebolts, burning them up left and right. They drew their weapons and used them as spinning shields to fend off the creatures' attacks as they blasted them back to the hell, they had escaped from.

The air crackled and flashed in a swirl of brilliant, blinding light and shadows, making it harder to see. Jaraadhrin closed his eyes, letting his Shifr take over as he slashed at the foul creatures. He could feel their demonesque essence more strongly. The black, reeking ink swelled around them as they attacked. He twirled his staff, imbuing it with his core. It blazed silver, dissipating the shadows as it spun within his fingers. He lifted his head up to feel the blackness of one screeching towards Quinn, its talons outstretched. Quinn hadn't noticed… he was fighting three at once.

'Quinn…!' Jaraadhrin yelled as he leapt into the air, pulling Quinn under him. He vaulted over and faced the creature full on. It slashed its talons against his face and the back of his hand as he raised it. Angry red welts appeared on the side of his face and hands as silver glimmered deep within them. Jaraadhrin gasped and drove the prongs of his staff, blazing silver with his core, straight into the creature's midriff. It screeched, its foul fangs, a hair's breadth from his face before disappearing a in a cloud of splintering red sparks and shadow. He staggered back as the red welts deepened and his silver essence surged out.

Quinn caught him and slashed his other hand forcefully against the three creatures still hovering around within the rapidly mending shields, triggering a fiery plume of fire. He roared in rage and stamped his feet hard against the white marble floor. A blazing auburn glow expanded out of his slender frame turning the creatures and everything else it touched on the tower to dust. Queen Debriar swiftly shielded herself and Jaraadhrin with the lilac shimmer of her powerful armour. Quinn's auburn fury pulsed some distance within the tier, vaporising everything alive and covering anything else with grey ash! The trees and flowers shrivelled and shrunk, the waters misted into vapour and the white marble greyed over with ash as the glow spread over them, before dying down to a crackle.

The Shimran shield above them closed completely and glowed a brilliant crimson as the shield-maras strengthened their tier to the maximum. Any successful attempt at breaching the red shields would be the death of the Shield-mara who conjured it. They were taking the major risk of sacrificing themselves for their Queen and Lords. A roar of cheer rang from the lower tiers as their soldiers turned away swiftly, refocusing on other areas, happy with their temporary victory.

'Aaashh! You senseless little...!' Quinn whirled around to him in fear and rage as Jaraadhrin groaned and pulled himself upright. The angry red ridges dissipated from his face and hands as the silver surged from deep within them, like water and sealed them shut. Quinn grabbed his arm staring at it in incredulity. Queen Debriar laughed in triumph, behind them.

'It worked; he has some protection against this evil!' she said, glancing up as the lull in the attacks, deafened them with their silence. Jaraadhrin gazed at his arm and touched his face, thinking hard.

'The archers! Infuse the arrows with their centients, that will wound them!' he said as the Queen shot a yishin to the commanders, nodding. His Princess's strategies resurfaced in his mind. Every part of this battle seems to be following some semblance of her plan. He squinted at Quinn who had turned away in a huff.

Tsk...tsk...Aaashh! Quinzafoor! Did you have to destroy half the tier to save me? And a senseless little what exactly.... My Lord Protector....? He thought, chortling with mirth as Quinn scoffed loudly. He was truly exasperated and Jaraadhrin found it hysterical.

A bevy of arrows, flashing with coloured sentients, flew off through the shields as the archers were finally able to release them. They struck the creatures, amid agonised shrieks, wounding them as they flew high and away from the scorching arrows.

The archers roared in triumph as they let fly, wave after wave of colourful arrows at the snarling blackness. The unused arrows clattered back among the tiers, releasing their centients into the nearest Shimrans. The tlumods withdrew and flew higher and further away from the range of the arrows as it rained on them.

They seem to be soaring high over them and away from the shields. They weren't retreating, just flying higher over the citadel. What were they up to now? The solders gazed up in astonishment, wondering if they had won as the creatures withdrew into nothingness, cloaking themselves with their long, matted, disgusting locks.

Jaraadhrin and Quinzafoor leapt up on to the parapets. The very ones on which Quinn had once held Jaraadhrin as he prevented his Lord's fall. Tonight they stood beside each other as their silver weapons reeled within their hands. Tall and majestic shimratzars, leading a stand against the foulest creatures in Shimran History!

'Hold your positions, this isn't over yet! Jaraadhrin commanded stern and cold, his voice amplified with his centient. His gold crown flashed at his forehead. Jaraadhrin's rich midnight blue and gold robes bellowed in the wind beside Quinzafoor's pale blue- gold ones. Their long, brilliant, bronze locks still blazing with auburn and silver crackles, lifted in a fan behind them in their fury, one straight and the other, wavy. The soldiers below gazed at their young Lords in admiration and amazement. Their armour glinted in the moonlight as they towered above them.

Lord Jaraadh glanced up at the highest tier as he turned to stare at the diminishing black blotches. He caught sight of his sons' standing tall and stately, side by side, defending the palace so efficiently that his face broke into a smile. They stood, regal and formidable. They were proud young shimratzars, Lords of Shimrah, capable and lethal. His King and himself had nothing to worry. King Dunyazer caught the pride in Lord Jaraadh's face and followed his eyes to the tower. He smiled tenderly.

'That was us some centuries ago' he reminisced. Lord Jaraadh turned back to his King, his brow raised in mock horror.

'Are you implying that we are old tzars now, my Liege? I think we still look like that... well except for the tresses of course...yours is gold, my King....and straight!' he said grinning. King Dunyazer chuckled.

'Dear Jaraadh! Always the jester – ' he stopped suddenly as the gold shields quivered. There was a disturbance somewhere.

Hand in hand, they flew up to the seventh-tier turret. Lord Jaraadh spun his core rings around both of their slender forms. The tlumods were moving in large clusters to the front of the citadel, the outermost gates of the eighth tier. Their numbers were still huge and they seemed to be focusing on the tier with the least number of bolts expending out of it, this time. They retreated some ways away and in large, thick clouds were approaching the eighth shields as if to crash into it. Lord Jaraadh shot yishins, yelling commands to his martial force to cover it quickly. A surge of soldiers soared over to hold the defences, flashing their bolts as the creatures rushed headlong at the shields.

High above them, Jaraadhrin stared at the rush, frowning. He was sure there was a lot more than that. He felt he was missing something. Quinn made to fly off to help his King and Lord Jaraadh, hold the defences in the lowest tiers.

'Wait....' he stopped Quinn. 'That's not right. There was a lot more when we flew out' Quinn glanced at the mass in front. Jaraadhrin was right. Where was the rest?

'Spread our Martial Force off the second tier among the rest of them, concentrating on the last.' He instructed as Quinn shot a yishin down to the commanders under him before his Lord finished his sentence as usual.

'That amount can breach the shield' Queen Debriar muttered behind him. Jaraadhrin frowned as he shot a yishin to the shield-maras informing them. The eighth tier glowed red just like their own.

'My Queen I need to see, something isn't right, these things or Ifreeth is intelligent. I have a feeling this is a ploy!' She nodded. Queen Debriar enveloped him in her own shield and propelling him out of the red one above them.

Quinn, be ready! Jaraadhrin thought as he cleared the shields. *Read me and keep your focus on the front of the citadel as well.*

Nothing attacked him as he soared above and the skies were clear. All the tlumods were concentrated in the front of the eighth tier still moving towards the glowing red shield. Jaraadhrin spun in mid-air, eyes closed as he tried to find where the rest of the creatures seem to have disappeared to. He couldn't see them anywhere but he did know, deep in his core, that the large wave approaching the main gates weren't all there were. His central being was rarely wrong, it had never let him down yet. Had they killed off that many with the dragons, bolts and arrows? It wasn't possible. He spun once more and froze as his Shifr picked up something far above them and behind the citadel.

Quinn glared up suddenly at his spinning figure from below him as he read his Lord's rapid mental commands, his face whitening. He pulled the gold clips off the sides of his head, letting them fall to the marble with a clatter. His loose hair flew, long and thundery in a bronze fan around his head as his eyes blazed in fiery flames. He nodded grimly.

Quinn's wrists spun yishins around him, his lips curling in anger. The lower tiers emptied. Shimrans flew and soared in through the mazes back into the citadel. They poured up the tiers and in to the first level, disappearing into the main palace. They weren't all soldiers but Shimran inhabitants and it looked like they were fleeing deep within the citadels. A large cluster of soldiers from the second tier rose as one. They soared over the great Alaq to the back of the palace. They divided swiftly in to fourteen groups and flashed away to the forts.

A few dozen sped down to the King and Lord Jaraadh. They surrounded their King and Lord while the rest spread out even more between the tiers. The soldier number evened and their cores spun rapidly on high alert. Blade Shimran glided to concentrate within the lowest tier. They positioned in long lines around the circle of the tier walls, their blades flashing colour as they saturated them with their centients. All shields glowed gold momentarily before burning a brilliant crimson – at its highest and most lethal forte.

The essence of the King

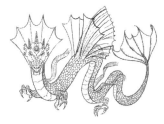

Queen Debriar stepped closer to the banister. She moved her fingers slightly as she swept Quinn's blazing locks, high behind his head and off his furious face. She bound it quickly with her centient and slid a Lord Protector clip, identical to Jaraadhrin's at the back of his head. Alaq snarled as he moved. The heat from the clip blended through the crackling flames of his hair. Quinn didn't even notice in his concentration. Queen Debriar peered down and around at the whirlwind of activity below them. She knew he was following Jaraadhrin's mental orders.

What on Shimra has made Quinn this livid? She raised her brow and tapped him on the shoulder.

'My Queen.' he said inclining his head towards her over his shoulder, his face grim. Quinn was too busy reading Jaraadhrin, to read her.

'Erm…captions please?' she jested. Quinn chuckled. His face mellowed at her humour and returned to an angry sneer almost immediately.

'Ifreeth, Ibreeth and his son Nibrath with a handful of Shimrans, far beyond the large line of those foul creatures in front, on unisi and cores tainted dark. Behind them another few thousand tlumods. This lot split in two and the rest are at the back, high above the shield turrets and ready to attack. They know the shields are our last chance. The ones in front were meant to be a distraction. They are willing to sacrifice as many of those foul things as it takes to bring us down'

He clenched his teeth, his locks burning fiery in his anger; He flashed his palm and another mass of vials appeared which he propelled out to Jaraadhrin above them, enclosed in an auburn shield. Jaraadhrin grabbed them, shook away from the Queen's lilac shield, summoned his own and soared off towards the back of the citadel.

'Ifreeth is furious that we put up such a fight already, he didn't count on a fight! It was supposed to be a smooth and silent carnage.' Quinn's lips twisted in scorn. 'He lost much of his number but he has much more behind him and at his call if he wanted it. He is confident in that. He figured out Jaraadhrin's Shifr and protection against his creatures. My Lord is the newest target!' Quinn's voice quieted, his anger deadly. 'Ifreeth wants Lord Jaraadhrin desperately! I can read them......the vile filth!' he spat. Queen Debriar's gasped.

'No....' she whispered in distress. Quinn drew a deep breath.

'My Lord has ordered a complete evacuation of everyone except soldiers with over half their core. They are to make their way through the roads under the lake and take refuge in the vaults, beyond the ice spikes and behind the waterfall. Soldiers have divided to protect the King and those that were sent to the shield-maras will join Lord Jaraadhrin in the defence. You, my Queen, should take the Princess in to the vaults and guard the rest of the Shimrans, seeking refuge there. Royals are the only ones who can seal the gateway behind them.' Queen Debriar shook her head in amazement.

'How did he know about the vaults and...' She began

'Lord Jaraadh and he has also guessed your visions, my Queen, just from your unspoken communications and expressions. He knows the citadel falls tonight before the sun rises' Quinn scoffed 'The odds are too great and even if we win this wave, we cannot win the next beyond those filth of Shimrah. Ifreeth has emptied hell on Shimrah and he is confident in the knowledge that he can summon more if needed! But do not worry, my Queen. Lord Jaraadhrin is not one to give up in the face of overwhelming odds or even let a glimmer of doubt or dismay enter his mind or heart. He will fight to death for his Kingdom and his Princess! And I with him!' Quinn growled. 'Go, my Queen... for the Princess. We fight another day; I have to hold it here.' Queen Debriar hesitated.

'I...'

A sudden shrieking and howling followed by resounding crashes, burst at the front of the eighth tier. At the same moment, the shields shimmered with the disturbance at the back of the citadel. Tlumods flew around, throwing themselves at the fourteen forts, behind them, furiously. Large bolts of colour flashed at their rear as the soldiers and Jaraadhrin protected the shield-maras. Queen Debriar could see Jaraadhrin, his rings spinning silver at their head as he fired liquid spheres of power, bursting the tlumods to flames. His rage blazed icy white in the silver of his core rings. The lowest tier flamed red and black, the crimson shields flickering as the incessant mass of tlumods rammed at it again.

It flashed a brilliant red once more and then went out suddenly, falling in crimson dust around them! Quinn zoomed down to the mid tiers, gnashing his teeth. The two shield-maras who held that shield on either side would have died for their kingdom as the creatures breached them. They were the first to sacrifice their lives today and it would only be a matter of moments before more followed them. They were gone and it shot a flash of pain within his heart. The absence of the shield exposed the lowest tier where the King and Lord Jaraadh fought with the concentration of their soldiers.

The tlumods directly above the moats, exploded with shrieks of agony as the enchanted waters of the Crystal Depths vapourised their darkness. The blade Shimrans sprang forward valiantly, slashing their centient infused weapons at the creatures as they surrounded them. Coloured arrows rained thick and fast as the tlumods bursts in to clouds around them. The proximity of the tlumods allowed the Shimran combat soldiers to engage more fully and their lethal martial skill saw the end of many of the foul beings of hell. But the ceaseless use of their limited centients were bound to exhaust them. They couldn't keep this up indefinitely, not against an inexhaustible dark force like Ifreeth's.

Lord Jaraadh yelled for the soldiers to retreat within the next shield level. They were too exposed fighting without them but it was too late. The tlumods screeched and zoomed down, slashing through the ranks as they flew. Their long talons had but to touch the Shimran folk and they vapourised immediately. Their fair essences scattering where they stood, their beings bursting in clouds of colour. The tlumods fed on their energies, growing bigger, blacker and more menacing. The screams and yells of the retreating Shimrans rent the air as they fled to take cover in the next level, still fighting for their lives with their weapons and raining fire bolts at the foul creatures. The mere closeness of the tlumods seem to ice the Shimran cores over. They attacked them relentlessly, clawing and slashing even as they withdrew.

Lord Jaraadh whirled fiery beams of blue light, still defending his King at the back of the retreating Shimrans along with his soldiers and protecting them as they took shelter. His javelin glowed a brilliant blue as he spun it rapidly. He shielded them as his fierce centient beams incinerated multiple tlumods in one go. He turned to bolt a quick yishin to flood all the moats with the waters of the Crystal Depths as the shields were already falling. It may help slow the rapid assault of the tlumods as they slashed through the ranks of his Martial Force.

They were mere spaces away from the seventh level shields, when one of the largest creatures lunged and grabbed King Dunyazer from the back and its talons emerged from the front of his chest. It scorched in Lord Jaraadh's power rings as it tried to lift him away and slashed its talons across the King's face in its agony.

'My Liege…!' Lord Jaraadh thundered as he spun rapidly back to his King, his eyes furious with rage, his hair, blazing blue. He propelled his javelin and a massive bolt furiously into the tlumod's foul neck. It screeched as it started bursting into shadow. It reared its head high and sank its fangs deep in to his hand which held his javelin within it as it disappeared.

Lord Jaraadh's weapon clattered to the floor and he shuddered as the darkness coursed through him, burning the light of his fair being in a black haze. King Dunyazer threw his arms around his Lord Protector, free from the talons which had burst into shadow at his chest. Their retreating soldiers turned as one and dragged them back in to the crimson shields. They yelled furiously and used up most of their cores in a concentrated and final attempt to save their King and Lord. They shot huge bursts of bolts with their hands covered in their centients protruding out of the crimson shields as they protected them. King Dunyazer collapsed among his beloved Shimrans still holding his Lord protector, tight against his chest.

'My King…' Lord Jaraadh's voice trembled as he felt his essence leave him, slowed by the Kings embrace. Their soldiers rushed to them, trying to revive them.

'Do it now, I don't have long!' rasped King Dunyazer. He pressed the therin of his sleeves to his neck where the creature had slashed him, trying to stem the flow of crimson within it. The Ring of Command burned fiery on his smooth brow, the circlets entwined and intricate, blazed in a solid flame. 'We do not have long….' Lord Jaraadh nodded grimly, tears sliding down at the corners of his eyes as his King released him, to action on his command with a tightening of his arms.

'Goodbye, my King and may we meet again at the Crystal Depths' He spun his hands using up everything he had within his core, they trembled as his centient enveloped them with its shimmering blue haze. King Dunyazer closed his eyes and inhaled deeply. He pressed his lips to Lord Jaraadh's head as his figure hazed over and murmured against his Lord Protector's locks.

'I will wait for you there, My Friend, My Brother, My Protector, My Kin…'

Quinzafoor thundered furiously as he spun from tier to tier to try to get to them. He flashed past Shimrans, tlumods and firebolts, weaving in and out of them as they obstructed his path. A blue and gold blurry whirlwind joined him on his side, spiralling and speeding with him.

'Jaraadhrin!' He gasped as he turned to look at his Lord, aghast. His face was cold and hard. Fury pulsed in every feature as his eyes glittered in icy blue rage. Quinn's core trembled in fear at the sight of it as they flashed together passed the many tiers to their King's and father's side.

King Dunyazer dissolved in a brilliant green and red mist within Lord Jaraadh's blue centient shield. He shimmered down to vials beside his Lord Protector while the soldiers withdrew from them in shocked horror. They choked with grief and knelt, their hands on their hearts in a final parting salute to their great King and Lord. Their heads bowed in torment, their breath quivering out of them in the extent of their anguish.

Lord Jaraadh's life force seeped out quicker without the King's aura and essence to hold his in. He raised his hand and shot the vials, enclosed within a gleaming blue shield, to the higher tiers with the last vestiges of his core. His body shimmered down to an essence and dissipated among the kneeling soldiers just as Jaraadhrin and Quinnzafoor landed beside them. They sank to their knees in salutes, their fists clenched at their hearts, their chests heaving and eyes flashing fire. They were too late.

The tlumods circled around and above them, shrieking in laughter and triumph as they soared. Their wings outstretched, they bared their fangs at them, derisive in their victory and just out of firing range. Quinn's head snapped up as he read Ifreeth's evil thoughts. He was celebrating his triumph. Quinn stood up swiftly to fly out to him as Jaraadhrin caught his sleeve.

'Where do you think you are going? He hissed. Frozen blades of ice, slashed in his voice.

'To drain that filth, dry of his core!' Quinn trembled in his rage, locks blazing as brilliantly as his eyes.

'You will head the defence here and fall back as we lose shields' Jaraadhrin ordered, His voice sliced through Quinn like icy shards, commanding him, binding him in. 'We will fight to the last! We will not concede defeat!' He rose. *And you will act as the Lord you are!* Commanded Jaraadhrin in his head. Quinn nodded, teeth gritted and eyes closed tight against the blaze. He swallowed hard trying to get a grip on his fury.

Jaraadhrin raised his hand, slowly and delicately. He lifted the waters of the nearby moat and laid it against the essences of his father and the traces of his King. He dissolved them in it and shaped it with his centient. It solidified to ice in the way they had last been. His father against his King's shoulder who held him tightly as Lord Jaraadh gazed up at him in devotion. His King holding his bosom friend as their lives parted. The soldiers clasped their hands to their hearts, head bowed. Quinn fashioned the crystal farewell boat on the moat's waters. It surpassed in splendour and the icy Shimran insignia flew high in the water flag. Jaraadhrin floated the figures of their King and father on to it together. They had been inseparable in life and so they shall be in death.

'Open that moat's gates to the Silverstream. The boat will find the Crystal Depths.' Quinn directed, his voice racked with grief. Jaraadhrin, Quinn and the soldiers touched their shoulders, palm on palm with both hands, pressed them hard against their lips and eyes as one. Centient flowers streamed thick from their already depleted cores through their hands as they waved their love to their King and Lord. The movement completed the final action of the Shimran farewell as the boat slid away along the moat.

They fell to their knees as it passed them horizontally down the tier, tears running down the corners of their eyes. The tiers above them, thickened with the centient flowers from the rest of the citadel as the Shimrans slid to their knees and paid their last respects to their beloved King and Lord as they floated away, smoothly together on their final journey.

Quinn shuddered suddenly, gasping for breath as he clutched the front of his robes. His heart rent with overpowering grief and the agony of a rapidly draining core.

It isn't my own! He realised as his head snapped up, gazing at the higher tiers in dismay. Jaraadhrin grabbed him by the arm and steadied him as he swayed. His eyes widened in shock at the sudden torment on Quinn's fair face.

'The Queen!' He mumbled, shaking with the intensity of her emotions. Jaraadhrin nodded. The uncontained sentiments raging in the tzars at the moment was bound to amplify Quinn's Shifr even more. It looked like his Lord protector was channelling a lot more than just thoughts.

Tune out of it, Quinn! Focus here! Jaraadhrin commanded as he leapt into the air and shot off to his Queen. He left a shivering Quinzafoor, battling with his Shifr and in charge of the defence against the tlumods as they screeched above them.

Queen Debriar leaned over the stone walls of the parapet as he alighted beside her. She straightened, breathing hard. Her pale lilac essence writhed crimson in her anguish.

'My Queen' he began, unable to face her and shuddering as her agony cut through to his core.

'I know Jaraadhrin.' She quivered. 'I saw... it was beautiful' She nodded. Her brilliant green eyes swam with tears, the corners red and bloodshot. He sank to his knees in front of her.

'I have failed you, my Queen!' he whispered, his voice racked with grief and anger. She raised him by his chin and gazed into his eyes, warm and piercing.

'You did no such thing; We made a stand because of you, Lord Jaraadhrin! No one can fight Destiny and it will always favour the Righteous in the end. No matter how hard it is now as it takes its course. I need you to understand this more than anything and remember it to the Crystal Depths! Have faith in it and place hope in it. Never let this falter!' Jaraadhrin nodded as he stared into her emerald, green gaze full of conviction. Her words etched itself into his heart. 'Nothing in Shimrah is ever a coincidence.... It is always penned with purpose.... A destiny....'

Queen Debriar lifted the vials of green and red shimmer and pressed them to her heart. Her elegant features tensed in grief as she kissed them and touched them to her brow. She grabbed his hands and placed them in to his. They glittered in the slight light. They were already minimised and had scrolls tied to them. Jaraadhrin could sense his father's essence around them and his King's within.

'This is the King's Essence and blood' she whispered. They will help find an antidote to this darkness and evil. They are the key to restoring Shimrah back to its fair and light past and to get rid of the darkness that has besieged it. Guard it well'

'My Queen' Jaraadhrin's eyes shot up to hers frowning, his voice trembled as he clipped the vials to his ribbon hurriedly. He could feel the rapid drain of her core as she touched him. He flipped his hand and summoned his own to replenish her. Queen Debriar shook her head.

'No Jaraadhrin' she stopped him, her eyes tender and her smile gentle. 'It will never replenish. Those in a Crossfire will lose their powers with their soulmate. Their Shifrs, their centients, their dragons, everything. I have lost the King permanently this time. My core will drain to its minimum, only to survive for the Princess. She will hold me in for a while. I will have no more powers and cannot access any Shifrs or my dragon anymore. It's the disadvantage of a Crossfire' She sighed. 'The King and I are connected on an unfathomable level, that is too strong and old to define. I will cease to exist, once my sense of responsibility to Saffrodel ceases to exist or if I am....' She shook her head, drained and weary.

'My Queen' Jaraadhrin repeated, his voice quivering. His eyes flooded and his heart iced over as the healers swarmed around his Queen to escort her to the vaults. Ever since he had lost his mother, Queen Debriar had watched over him, looked out for him and today, he couldn't do anything for his Queen. She raised her head, her chin high.

'Retreat, Lord Jaraadhrin. We have proved to my brothers that we are deadly even without our weapons, citadel and Shifrs! We will protect the Princess and secure her and we will bring them down another day. Send Quinn to me to help with the evacuation and bring the rest of the Martial Force in with minimal loss of life. Save the shield-maras, they are irreplaceable and they are also necessary to seal the vaults.' She commanded, her voice ringing with authority one last time. She smiled tenderly into his teeming eyes.

'Come back to us safe, son.' She murmured, placing her hand on the side of his face for a brief moment as she walked away from him.

The Silver Seraph

Jaraadhrin bowed his head as he turned towards the tiers below him. He sent Quinn a quick yishin with Queen's orders. The tlumods had started attacking again and Quinn and the soldiers were vehemently striking back. His fair face darkened and his brilliant blue eyes blazed as the images of his King, his father and his Queen flashed over them. His Princess's green eyes burned behind his lids as he slammed his hand against the stone parapet in his anger. It cracked and giant gashes ripped through the stones with the force of his wrath. He reached into his robes, pulled out the almost full vial of Javnoon and emptied it in one go.

His core churned and bubbled as the eons added rapidly. It seethed around him, silver and icy cold, driven by his fury and anguish. Jaraadhrin closed his eyes as he felt his latent Core Shifr blossom within him. It reared up and devoured the many eons he had added with blazing swiftness, regimenting them efficiently within his body. His core twisted and raged with his fury. It roared out of him in a solid sheath of silver and encased every part his figure, his locks and his robes. He drew out his staff in a rapid twirl and the sheath extended over it, infusing it with the power of his centre. His long bronze hair, coated in silver, cackled and snapped in the wind as he lifted a few spaces off the ground. He soared on the pure aura of his massive centre.

He would retreat alright as his Queen ordered but not before he took down as many of these foul creatures as he could and Ifreeth as well. His form glistened and glimmered. It pulsed around him like a raging creature as he leapt off the parapets towards the shield-maras.

He spun rapidly to the fourteen forts, blasting bolts with his staff at the creatures around them. He burned them up so fast with his slashes that they didn't even have time to screech in agony. He flashed in and out, twirling his staff in mid-air, slashing furiously with all the anger raging within him. His deep blue robes billowed, contrasting sharply with the silver lining of his power. The silver pulsed out of his form in large blasts as he soared around them, vaporising them left and right. He alighted in one of the forts.

'Wait till Quinzafoor and the Martial Forces are within the citadel. Drop all shields at once and flee to the vaults. Do not try to shield or protect me' Jaraadhrin snapped at the shield-maras and his soldiers protecting them. 'I will cover you.' They fell into salutes, redoubling the shields on the six tiers. Two had already fallen killing four shield-maras.

Jaraadhrin swung his staff and soared to the sixth tier. He sprang over the final shield in front of Quinn and his soldiers, still battling the foul beings of hell, ferociously. He slashed his staff with vehemence in a wide circle, vaporising the screeching creatures with one massive, flaming plume of icy, white fire! An avenging silver seraph of death and destruction! Quinn huffed sharply as he stared up at Jaraadhrin's shining silver form in astonishment and reverence. That bolt was eons strong and it had incinerated at least a few hundred tlumods in one go!

'Get to the vaults with the soldiers. Now, Quinzafoor!' he ordered. A fiery mark blazed between his brows, circlets woven in an intricate pattern. Quinn gasped, clutching his head as the reverberating Ring of Command, shot physical pain through his head. 'Shields will fall as soon as you reach the citadel. Escort the shield-maras to safety. I will hold till then and join you.' There was no arguing with that. Quinn sank into quick salute as Jaraadhrin raised them rapidly with a wave of his hand.

How did Jaraadhrin used the Ring of Command? It is a Shifr of Royalty? Quinn puzzled. He shook his head against the pain as he shepherded his soldiers to safety.

Jaraadhrin twirled and spun in mid-air as his staff whistled against wave after wave of screeching tlumods. His anger twisting his handsome features in a scornful sneer as the second army of tlumods behind Ifreeth, leapt into the air. The numbers of the first wave diminished rapidly, falling prey to his fury and his brilliant silver staff, in quick succession. His form dazzled silver in the middle of the murky black shadows and incinerating red sparks of Ifreeth's dying dark minions. He could feel Ifreeth's fear and shock in his soiled essence as he gazed up at him, hidden in the shadows like the coward that he was. Jaraadhrin threw back his head, laughing derisively and bolted him a yishin, blazing silver.

'I am coming for you...!'

Quinn and the soldiers retreated, breathless with admiration and awe as plume after thundery plume of blazing silver fire, emanated from their young Lord. Jaraadhrin hovered over them, single-handedly defending their entire regiment as their King and Queen had done. A true leader of Shimrah. Shim-ratzars and Shimaras who existed for their Kingdoms and their subjects.

They were safely within the citadel and the shields' fell swiftly as the second wave rushed at him but they gave him a wide berth and aimed for the flee-ing shield-maras. Jaraadhrin soared over to them. His staff blasted them to shadow as he roared up behind them, protecting the shield-maras as they flew into the citadel. His staff throbbed and pulsed in his hand as his anger found an outlet. The silver beats travelled great distances around him, dis-persing the foulness with its brilliant, intense light.

He twisted around to face the rest of the tlumods. He would dissolve every one of those creatures as long as he had such power, even if Ifreeth had a hell full of them, backing him up.

Jaraadhrin paused suddenly as an auburn yishin shot up to him. He plucked it and read, his face twisting in horror. It was Quinn's and the Princess was missing! They were searching for her. Jaraadhrin closed him eyes as he zoomed over the citadel trying to find the sparkling aura of the Princess. He vaporised the tlumods that dared to near him reflexively, in his fear and fury. She was in the healing rooms at the back of the palace by the forts but he could no longer feel her rainbow aura in any of them. Ifreeth was riding to-wards the citadel flanked by his minions.

Jaraadhrin flashed his arms around him, brought his palms in and ripped them apart forcefully. He tore himself to ten projections with ease. His terror and ire so great, it took no effort at all! They sped away from him, search-ing and feeding back to him. They twirled their many staffs, incinerating tlumods as they combed through the landscape. He could feel his core groan with the strain of them as he fought to maintain them.

The Shimrans gathered, brightly colourful within the citadel and below the lakes, making their way to the Ice spikes behind the waterfalls. Quinzafoor flashed around in the woods on the far left of the citadel. His essence blazed auburn with dread and rage as he searched for his Princess. The Queen and the healers were within the palace. They flitted around from chamber to chamber desperately in search of his princess, flanked by soldiers and healers. Tlumods kept sweeping in and out as they searched, being blasted by the heal-ers and soldiers as they protected their Queen.

Where was his princess? Dread chilled his heart as he sought for her essence, flying low with his eyes closed and frantic. She would not wake till after the sun rose due to the effects of the Time Shifr so she couldn't have gone off on her own accord. His heart hammered and throbbed as he glided over, trying to keep the dark thoughts off his mind. What would he do if he failed her too tonight? He had already failed his King, his Queen, his father and now... his Princess? If something happened to her, he would not live after that. He scoffed at himself, livid with anger at his failures. At least he wouldn't need to, it wasn't a choice! His core would drain rapidly, agonizingly and he would cease to exist too. it was a fitting retribution and it was welcome compared to the torment of living without her.

He rushed down as he caught a slight crackle of rainbow between the trees. That was definitely his Princess. He sighed in relief as he pulled his projections back into his destabilizing core. They whooshed back to him in streams of silver. His princess's aura pulsed around her, healthy and strong but what was she doing behind the palace, deep in the woods by the water's edge? He bolted a yishin to the Queen, informing her that he had seen his Princess and zoomed down. He nearly crashed in to a tlumod in his haste. He swerved rapidly to avoid it and blasted it to shadow. He turned his eyes back to his Princess's aura. It had swerved out of the trees, mimicking his movements just below him and he could now see her between them.

Jaraadhrin frowned. She was still asleep. Her tiny figure was still wrapped in her rich blankets. Her floor length, red-gold hair flew free between the sleeves of her white night robes as it hung down on either side of her. She floated a few spaces above the ground. Her face was troubled and a frown furrowed her fair forehead. Jaraadhrin swerved again, slashing at another creature and Princess Saffrodel moved gracefully below him. She was attracted to his aura. She was asleep but subconsciously drawn to him. She had used her Shifrs without conscious thought before and now she must have sensed the dangers and the darkness surrounding her. Unable to break free from the Time Shifr's draining sleep, she must be reaching out for the one person sworn to protect her, himself! The sacred pledge of the Crossfire and that of a Lord Protector!

Jaraadhrin uttered a cry of dismay as she floated higher towards him. She cannot come to him now, not when he was fought these hellish minions of Ifreeth. He could see the shield-maras and the soldiers who protected them, were safe within the citadel and the fort towers empty. He spun sending wave after wave of flashing, pulsing bolts as his robes flew off his legs. They fanned around him with the force of his rotations as he blasted the tlumods out of existence.

I have to finish this quickly and go down to my princess...

Sharp skittering's, slithering and threatening hisses drew his eyes up quickly.

Aaashh! Not these dastardly things again! He thought. Despair descending over him in a thick cloud as he whirled around to face them. He was deathly worried for his little Princess still floating up to him as he fought against the more dangerous Meinedders. He rotated furiously within a cloud of flashing talons, slithering scaly tails, snarling fangs, jagged wings and long, black matted hair as Ifreeth concentrated all the remaining creatures on bringing him down!

Silver lightning bolts hurtled around him as he twirled his staff. The creatures continued to swarm around him, black shadow and red sparks adding to the thickness of their foul bodies. Jaraadhrin reached out to his Princess, frantic and panic stricken. How far below was she from him?

He gasped as he felt a pale lilac aura flash up, embrace his Princess's sparkly one and floated back down to the water's edge. He sighed with relief as he redoubled his efforts. His Queen had his Princess, they could make their way to the vaults and be safe. His heart lightened as he redirected his attention to the creatures around him. The refocus of his wrath reverberated with thundery crashes along with flashes of his silver light strikes.

He could sense Ifreeth's foul aura moving faster on its unisus below him. He probably wanted to be there to see Jaraadhrin fall. His tainted essence glowed red in anger and revenge. Jaraadhrin scoffed.

Aaashh! Looks like I have managed to make my Queen's darling elder brother very angry indeed! Meh! I am sure she wouldn't mind! He thought sarcastically, sniggering at Ifreeth's wrath.

Queen Debriar's core faded even more as she grabbed Princess Saffrodel and alighted beside the water's edge. She moved her hand over her daughter's head, setting her mind at ease and severing the unconscious link with Jaraadhrin. She had to stop her daughter from flying back up to him. Queen Debriar stared up in horror and amazement as their young Lord Protector fought in the middle of the cloud of darkness and silver gashes illuminated his slender, shiny sheathed form. The twisting staff above his head moved so fast that it was a solid circle of brilliance and his long bronze tresses burned white fire beneath it. His figure radiated pure energy in his rapid, fluid movements and wrath.

She turned quickly to escort the Princess back to the vaults and stopped dead as she saw Ifreeth racing towards her, his face turned up to the battle in the air. Her way to the palace was blocked by his approach. She glanced in panic at the Princess in her arms, he cannot know about her. She looked around desperately. Behind her the lake expanded and in front of her Ifreeth approached. She wouldn't last long with her minimal core within the waters of the Crystal Lake. It would dissolve her as she was already dying.

She turned swiftly and crafted a farewell boat of ice, much like the one used for fallen soldiers but with the splendour for Royalty. She kissed Princess

Saffrodel's brow and laid her within it, bound down to the boat with her core and pushed it off into the cool waters. No one disturbed the boats of the dead till they reached the Crystal Depths and the Crystallites never harmed the living. Her Princess would be safe and escape unnoticed until she or Jaraadhrin could recover her.

She spun around to face Ifreeth, the blade of her long sword flashing towards his right shoulder as he reigned in his unisus viciously. It neighed loudly in agony, raising itself high on its hind legs, its front hooves soaring above her and its wings outstretched. Ifreeth dismounted and faced her.

He was a tall tzar and was once very graceful, handsome and elegant but now he reeked of foulness, his face twisted in a permanent sneer. The lines of his forehead and sunken cheeks etched in and the glittering blue of his once warm eyes were cold, pale and almost transparent. The bronze of his locks streaked and matted in filth. He no longer held the Shimran light in his essence or core.

'Hello sister' he gravelled. 'Saying goodbye to your filthy human King's remains I see' he said, glancing at the tiny boat, floating away behind her. 'I heard my pets slashed him to bits!' He scoffed. 'I am surprised you could find enough of him, to fit in to that boat!'

'You have no right to talk about the King, you vile piece of filth!' She said, her voice quiet and disgust dripping from it. 'If Shimrans were so pure, how come your core is so dark and tainted? You emptied hell on Shimrah, robbing its light with your darkness. How many had died to serve your twisted purpose? The King may be human but he protected his Kingdom and its Shimrans till the end! As did every other shimratzar and shimara before him! Unlike you!' He threw back his head laughing loudly and scornfully at her.

'The Shimrans! The Shimrans! Who cares about those pitiful little lives? They live to serve the King, slaves of the higher order!' Queen Debriar scoffed at him.

'That is where you are wrong brother and that is exactly why our father, the great King Dheriyadhar, bestowed me the throne even though I was younger than both of you. Our people are entrusted to us to protect and cherish, not to misuse and abuse! You have gone against everything Shimran Royalty stands for! They entrust us with their lives, their loyalty and devotion and we would sacrifice ourselves willingly for their trust. Apart from a title we are one, brothers and sisters of the same kin.' She drew a long breath.

'Today you betrayed Shimrah but rest assured, brother. Its light will resurface and have its revenge against the darkness you brought!' she declared, her voice ringing deadly as her eyes flashed daggers. She stood straight and tall, her face stern and cold, a true Queen! Ifreeth moved closer, chuckling evilly.

'No, I freed Shimrah from the weakness of the light, I have made it stronger.' Ifreeth raised his sword against hers. 'Are you going to fight me, little sister? Sacrifice yourself for the Shimrans you love? Where are they now, when you need them? With the state of your core, I doubt very much if you can win...' he bared his blackened teeth at her as he taunted her. Queen Debriar knew he was right; she wouldn't last a single stroke of his, powerful, in the seething darkness within him. Queen Debriar gazed into his eyes, searching for some last vestige of their brother-sister bond. Some flicker of light in his dark core.

'If it wasn't for the throne, brother' she murmured 'Would you have felt inclined to kill me....?' Ifreeth paused. He moved closer to her, looking into her eyes. His sword flashed up suddenly as he growled.

'Yes! You and your filthy King would always be a threat to us' He raised it high, aiming at her left shoulder as a silver bolt of lightning struck it from above him. It hauled it away from her as Queen Debriar raised her own blade to shield herself. Her delicate fingers trembled with her depleting core. The bolt blasted Ifreeth off his feet, some ways from the Queen.

Jaraadhrin wrenched Ifreeth's sword away with his centient with one hand as he twirled the staff in the other. It landed some ways away from Ifreeth. He was still defending himself from the foul mass around him, still fighting the ever-increasing numbers of creatures. Jaraadhrin coughed crimson, his core weakened more and more as he fought harder and harder. He was frantic to fly down to his Queen and his floating Princess, moving further and further away from him, down the river. He sped around trying to find a way out, terrified for his Queen and Princess but the creatures held him in a deathly circle of ripping talons and gushing black venom. He barely kept them from tearing him apart as his eons depleted and his centients drained with alarming swiftness.

Ifreeth stood up, dusting his robes. He picked up his sword and cleaned its blade with a black rag. He glanced up at Jaraadhrin.

'Is that the next Lord Protector? Powerful and handsome young tzar he is, isn't he? Where is the other?' he inquired with interest. 'Tsk...tsk...What powerful Shifrs! Almost stumped me tonight, both of them. I was wondering why you had two at the same time?' he inclined his head, grinning evilly at her. 'Rather a big break from traditions isn't it, little sister? Is there anything you are hiding from me?' Queen Debriar glared at him, her eyes flashing.

'Leave them out of this, they are not Royals!' Ifreeth turned back to look at

Jaraadhrin again as he whirled lightning and thunder. He snapped his fingers, summoning a few hundred more of his serpentine pets.

'No! Stop! Call them off!' Queen Debriar shouted. She gazed up fearfully as Jaraadhrin's slashes of silver, dimmed in the thickening mass of foulness.

'Oh, don't worry' he sneered. 'My pets are not going to harm him. They will bring him to me once he cannot fight anymore and I will use his Shifrs! Turn him dark and powerful with my demonesque essence and he will serve to make me stronger! As will your other Lord Protector, the one with the blazing eyes.'

Queen Debriar gritted her teeth and glared at him in disgust. A fate worse than death, lay in wait for her young sons. Ifreeth's mouth twisted in an awful leer at the look of utter horror on her face. He moved closer, reeking, enjoying the reaction his words had caused. His leer vanished from his face suddenly as his eyes caught something beyond her on the lake, they glinted in astonishment that changed to rage in moments.

The first rays of the brilliant sun broke over the frozen caps of the ice spikes and fell over the lakes in glittering beams. It danced off the waters and over the boat as it floated Princess Saffrodel away. She stirred as the beams fell on her little face, the effects of the Time Shifr finally leaving her. She yawned and opened her eyes, her dreams had been vivid and scary. She wouldn't be at peace till she was with her Dhrin again. She started, puzzled as the huge mountain ranges and the palace walls slid around her. She could hardly move; she was bound to this iciness under her.

A corebind? Why? She felt her mother's warm essence in it. Her eyes widened in shock as she realised she was in a farewell boat for fallen soldiers. Was she dead then? Why would her mother bind her to a farewell boat when she was still alive? Why a corebind instead of a centient bind? Her mother wouldn't use her core unless it needed to be very strong or unless... she had no centients left? That would mean she was in grave danger! Princess Saffrodel undid the binding around her, still dazed with the effects of the Time Shifr. Her body felt heavy and cumbersome as she turned. She raised her dazed eyes cautiously over the side of the boat.

'What?!... You have an heir! A daughter!' Ifreeth screeched as he caught sight of Princess Saffrodel's shimling eyes peering, dazed and fearful. Queen Debriar spun her sword high, sinking it deep into Ifreeth's right shoulder as her core surged with fear for her daughter's wellbeing. He shrieked, his vile locks flying behind him in wrath. He slashed his sword deep into her left, blasting her away from him with the force of the thrust.

He turned to the Princess, summoning the darkness of his foul centre as his wretched life ebbed. He pulled his hands together combining the darkness with his core and shot a murky cursebolt at her. Queen Debriar gasped, heaved his sword from her shoulder and slashed it vehemently at his neck. It severed free of his body as the cursebolt left his hands.

The creatures around Jaraadhrin disappeared in a howl of rage as Ifreeth's head plunged into the enchanted waters of the lake, vaporising in black smoke and red sparks immediately. He glanced down in horror as despair flooded his exhausted core. His Queen was mortally hurt and Ifreeth's darkbolt raced to his Princess. He flashed Quinn a yishin as he sped off to shield his Princess from Ifreeth's darkness.

The Queen moved her trembling hand as she tried to draw back Ifreeth's curse. Her core was almost exhausted and her essence ebbed from the mortal injury, she had suffered at her brother's hand. She released her centient bolt to counteract it. It flashed pale lilac behind Ifreeth's darkness as she fought to hold her strength.

'Saffrah...! Jaraadhrin yelled in terror and she turned to him, her eyes wide in fear. The darkness of Ifreeth's cursebolt hit her hard as she turned, glancing off her brilliant green eyes and straight at him as he sped towards her. His Princess's little figure coiled against the side of the boat, her long locks curved high in an arc behind her and landed in the water.

The ricochet hit Jaraadhrin squarely between his brows. He shuddered and gasped as agony raced through his head, burning up every particle of light within his fair being in a fiery black blaze. He gritted his teeth as he tried to control his fall, rapidly losing awareness as the darkness swirled around inside him and thickened. It swallowed him as he catapulted, limp and lifeless to the ground.

'Jaraadhrin.... Saffrodel' murmured the Queen as she sank to her knees in the waters of the lake, her legs already hazing swiftly in the soothing liquid. She enveloped her daughter in her lilac centient as the full rays of the sun flashed on her tiny body, trying again to lift the curse off of the Princess. Her little head lay on the side of the boat and her long red hair, trailed in the waters as it rapidly turned silver-white.

'No.... Queen Thiloket...your prophesy held true... now I hold you to your promise...!' Queen Debriar moaned, drawing a deep breath, her last. She harnessed the power of the rising sun as she strengthened the lilac haze around Princess Saffrodel. She couldn't lift the dark bolt's curse. She wasn't strong enough.

She twisted her fingers sharply and locked the curse deep within her daughter. She buried it, making it as latent as possible with the sun. The boat disappeared down the curve of the Silverstream and Queen Debriar's slender fingers, slid lifeless into the glimmering waters of the lake.

The pledge

Quinn spun through the trees at his young Lord's yishin. It was ominous in its wording.

'Lake!'

Yishins didn't take long to send, especially martial ones. They were a quick translation of thought at the time of sending and usually interpreted to few sentences. Jaraadhrin must be in dire danger if he couldn't even transfer a yishin with a cohesive thought. He could not hear or feel anything from his young Lord. He had been focusing on his Princess with such concentration, that he had tuned out everyone and everything else.

He had concentrated on his Princess's impish thought tenors or a Shield Shifr. It had been easy to tune out everything when he had been racked with such worry for her. He spun through the trees, clearing them within moments. He emerged on the western end of the lake, blazing auburn in his haste. His eyes flashed to the eastern parapets where Jaraadhrin's slender figure curved gracefully, unconscious and in an uncontrolled fall. His core was almost empty as he hurled to the ground.

Quinn gasped and sped forward. He caught his Lord in his arms and drove a massive bolt of his core into Jaraadhrin, in mid-air. He spun around trying to understand what happened. His breath caught in his chest, shooting a jolt of agony as he saw the last mists of his Queen's essence, diffuse in a lilac haze into the enchanted waters of the lake. His eyes clouded with tears as the anguish ripped through his heart. He alighted and laid his Lord gently on the grass, hidden behind large boulders.

'Jaraadhrin…Jaraadhrin…Dhrin!' Quinn's voice trembled as he called his Lord's name again and again. His core was still depleting. He grabbed Jaraadhrin's right shoulder with the hand under him as he lay on it, pumping his auburn centients in and shaking him hard with the other. Quinn inhaled sharply. There was something very dark within Jaraadhrin and it pushed back against him as he propelled his centients. Quinn gritted his teeth at the resistance.

Jaraadhrin stirred, groaning, his face whitened in pain. Quinn shook him, breathing hard. *How could I have let this happen? Where was I when my Queen and my Lord needed me the most? And where oh where is my Princess?* He hadn't been able to find her anywhere either.

'Jaraadhrin... look at me...please awake!' Quinn cried, his face twisted in pain, spaces from his dying Lord's. Jaraadhrin stirred again.

'My Princess...gone...! He murmured.

'What? The Princess? Where is she...?

Jaraadhrin opened his eyes, too weak, too drained. They widened slightly as he stared into Quinn's piercing, bright blue-green eyes for the very first time. They blazed and glittered, shining with tears as he agonised for his Lord, his Queen and his Princess.

'You said... once... blue-green? ... more... stunning...' he mumbled as he exhaled with agony. Quinn reached into his mind swiftly as he tried to read what his Lord had wanted to say about the Princess. Jaraadhrin's mind was unhinging, his thoughts muddled.

'Dhrin...' Quinn stared at him as the corner of Jaraadhrin's lips lifted in a weak smile. Something was very wrong. Jaraadhrin's mind hazed and heaved illegibly, clouding over with something he couldn't place. Quinn shook him again, gazing deep into his brilliant blue eyes as he tried to dissipate the confusion enough to read him. Their colour changed, the blue obscured with flecks of gold that seem to mist out of it and around them as he held his Lord's gaze, unable to break free.

Quinn's core seethed and bubbled with fear as he stared and the gold mists around them thickened. The expression in Jaraadhrin's eyes shook his very being and his fidelity to his Lord, reared its head like an immense dragon. It roared thunderously within him. It filled his being, brimmed over, churned and bubbled inside him to unmanageable proportions. Quinn quivered. He tried to steady himself as his core racked his very being. The flames of his auburn centre reared, engulfing him in scorching fires. He pressed his hand against his racing heart as he drew quick, shuddering breaths trying to steady himself.

What is happening to me? Why can't I look away? Is Jaraadhrin doing this to me? is it an unconscious Shifr?

271

Quinn reached into his mind again tentatively and gasped. Jaraadhrin's was in turmoil but at its forefront, it mirrored his own. The sentiments enhanced than his own, with a fiercely protective edge to it but then, Jaraadhrin had always been like that to him. His Lord's thick lashed lids lowered.

No....! Quinn thought, desperately. He shook his Lord again and his eyes snapped open. *I will not let it happen...not as my Lord ....* Jaraadhrin wasn't going anywhere without him. He would be by his side as his Protector, his Guardian, his Friend, his Brother, Anyone and Everyone his Lord wanted him to be. Quinn's core roared deafeningly in his ears as it churned and shook within him, his mind hazed over in the pure force of its surge as it drowned in the gush of thoughts.

He held Jaraadhrin tightly, still driving his centients into his Lord. He trembled against his overwhelming emotions and the resistance of the forces, trying to stop him from streaming. He leaned forward unable to bear the weight of it all and involuntarily touched his forehead to Jaraadhrin's brows. Their minds flashed in pure gold light at the contact and their eyes glazed over, shimmering and glowing as the Pledge sealed.

Quinn blinked against the haze, drawing back. The connection waned as he sensed the severe disturbances in Jaraadhrin's mind. His blue-green eyes flashed to Jaraadhrin's face. His Lord's smile faded with rapidity. Darkness surged within his gentle, silver misted mind, spilling over into the brilliant blue of his eyes. It thickened and streamed, obscuring all of the stunning sea brilliance. The long bronze waves at his hairline, crackled and sizzled, burning Quinn's arm as he held Jaraadhrin under his shoulders. The splendid bronze of the curling waves, leached out in a blaze of scorching ice as the white flash crackled drown the strands of his tresses, leaving them straight and silver.

Jaraadhrin's slender hands flew to his temples, teeth gnashed in agony. He threw back his head in anguish against Quinn's shoulder as a low groan escaped his lips. Quinn inhaled sharply and huffed as the pain infiltrated his head too. He fumbled in his robes for his clips to block his Lords thoughts and suffering. He didn't have them; he had dropped them during the battle.

The torment sliced his mind, shooting lethally and slashing in black blazes. Again and again, it attacked as he fought to control it in his and within Jaraadhrin's mind. Quinn panted as he tried to reduce it, to infiltrate to the source of whatever was causing it. His centients drained rapidly with the effort. He unclipped a vial of Javnoon and downed it through the pain. He couldn't mediate it with his Lord in his arms but it didn't matter. His core was draining too fast for the tincture's many years to build up as he fought it and core shared with his Lord. He didn't know where this was going but of one thing, he was sure. He was going with Jaraadhrin, wherever it took him!

The silver of Jaraadhrin's head, tainted with the darkness, swarmed grey within their minds. It swirled thick and heavy, smothering them with its weight and obscuring everything from their consciousness. Quinzafoor bent forward, his brow pressed against Jaraadhrin hair as he held him tight to his chest. He clutched his locks at the side of his head with his other; eyes shut tight, shuddering and groaning through gnashed teeth. Wave over wave of dark agony racked through them as they fought to stay within the Light of their Shimran cores.

Quinn lost track of how long he held his Lord, completely debilitated and fighting what felt like a battle, they were steadily losing. The innocent silver mists of Jaraadhrin's mind, writhed and thrashed as the darkness attacked it relentlessly. The murkiness whirled and whipped in his Lord's head, till the pure silver was all burnt in a blaze of black. The agony ebbed slowly but surely and the drain on their cores slowed. All the silver of Jaraadhrin's mind had been replaced with a swirling mass of dreary grey.

The torment within them subsided to a dull ache as Quinzafoor lifted his head to look at Jaraadhrin's face, utterly exhausted and swaying weakly. His Lord looked at the end of his tether too. Jaraadhrin's hair was completely white and straight! Brilliant, blazing silver-white. His eyes glistened black, deep dusky wells of darkness. He stared up into Quinn's vivid blue-green eyes for a brief moment. A sharp blast of pain, a flash of dazzling emerald and Jaraadhrin's thick lashed lids, slipped over his gaze and his mind slid into a void.

Quinzafoor gasped in shock and caught his Lord's wrist quickly as it fell off the side his head, limp and lifeless. Cold shards of torment pierced his heart as Quinn's eyes shut in his own exhaustion. He slid to the ground beside his Lord, shuddering violently as his mind slipped into oblivion. It wasn't the pain, the flash of green eyes or his young Lord's strange appearance that tortured him. It was the look in Jaraadhrin's eyes as they had closed. His Lord's mind had blanked and he didn't recognise Quinn!

Lord Jaraadhrin no longer knew Quinzafoor!

Not far from where they lay, a tiny icy boat curved into the western arm of the Silverstream, trailing long silver locks as brightly white and straight as Jaraadhrin's, on its way to the Crystal Depths...the final resting place of the Shimran folk...

To be continued.............

Dear Reader! You may now throw the book at your least favourite thing to help ease your frustration...! I promise the second book in the series will be available soon as it is already underway. Thank you for your support!

Glossary

A

Alaq – The Shimran insignia. The first dragon to have entwined with a Shimran and it has now been adapted as the sign of the Shimran Kingdom. It is used in many items of power like The Alaqain – the Ring of the Royals, The Alaqwa - the Lord Protector clips and The Alaqath – the medallion brooch of the Lord Protectors of Shimrah. The power of the dragon transfers to its sculptures when fashioned and it binds Shimrans to oaths and pledges made in its name.

Alaqath – Lord Protector medallion brooch featuring the Shimran court of arms and the dragon Alaq. It is bestowed to the Lord Protectors of Shimrah and is imbued with the enchantments of the ancient dragon itself. The sculpture of Alaq moves when first worn and can gauge the depth of the pledge or bind of the wearer by the reaction of their central being.

Alaqwa – Lord Protector dragon clip. It is bestowed to the Lord Protectors of Shimrah and is imbued with the enchantments of the ancient dragon itself. The sculpture of Alaq moves when first worn and can gauge the depth of the pledge or bind of the wearer by the reaction of their central being.

Alaqain – The Ring of the Royals portraying the dragon Alaq. Helps royalty focus their Royal Shifrs. Can only be worn by a true Royal and carries hazardous coincidences if touched by an unworthy Shimran.

Altheen – A golden metal, previously used for jewelry making in Shimrah. It is now also used to decorate inlays in weapons.

Ashaqath – A type of Soul-Light Crossfire of love. It binds romantic soulmates together and is usually indicated by thick gold mists.

Aura – combination of certain aspects of core, centient and essences. Usually felt than seen unless you focus and meditate to see it. Outermost layer of a Shimran being.

C

Centient powers – a bubble of energy measured in years which resides over the core of the Shimrans and fuels day to day life. Can be added by a variety of methods and given away by a few trained Shimrans. Certain Shifrs can access these in wider forms of application.

Centient years – Twenty-five years added to every core year of a Shimran. Directly proportional to a human's physical years. Also known as centient powers or energies.

Center – Shimran core and centients powers

Central being – Core and Centients of a Shimran

Core Shifr - A talent which allows the Shimrans to manage their central being and the sedimentation of energies. Full potential unknown

Core years – Number of years of life of a Shimran

Core powers – The center of a Shimran being is immensely powerful. It corresponds to each Shimran year lived which equals twenty-five centient years.

Crystal Depths – A large lake of blue waters found between the two land masses of Shimrah where the Shimrans go in death. The waters can dissolve the shimrans cores, centients, auras and essences. They are also imbued with many ancient enchantments and their full potency remains a mystery, even to the Shimran folk.

Crystallites – Also known as soul keepers are the water nymphs of the Crystal Depths. Their exact function is unknown. They do escort dead Shimrans away from Shimrah.

Cryslis – Iridescent blossoms of power capable of releasing a small amount of energy to the Shimran who touches it. They can sediment on the cores and centients of Shimrans.

Cursebolt – A darkbolt containing a curse to harm or kill a Shimran

D

Dhawasath – A type of Soul-Light Crossfire which is that of friendship and indicated by red mists.

Denisthar – A moat defense layout of the citadel.

Drystwitch – A maze defense layout of the citadel.

Dragonlight – The jewel that resides in the tip of the ornate horn of the Shimran dragons. It is the lifeforce of the dragon.

Dragonlight Entwinement – A sacred and private ritual which occurs between Shimrans and their dragons essentially, but it can also occur with other intelligent creatures of light like unisi. Dragonlight entwinements occur in the year after a Shimran's fifteenth year of birth. It involves the dragon choosing his Shimran and pledging itself to its Shimran by giving up the Dragonlight in its ornate horn. The process requires the dragon to pierce a Shimran's silverine to lodge the Dragonlight deep in their core. Some discomfort normally but the threshold of pain can be influenced by other factors. This enables the beast and Shimran to share their powers. The dragon disappears within the core of the Shimran and have a deep and complicated relationship with their owner. This often gives them a split personality.

Darkbolt – A bolt of centient or core powers from a tainted Shimran being

E

Elmas – The hardest metal in Shimrah. Silver in color.

Essence - is the combination of aspects of the core, centient and conscious thoughts, emotions, scents, characteristics etc. of the Shimran. Not all shimrans can see them. Often manifests to those who can see them, as light and scent.

Essence Shifr - A type of talent that enables a Shimran to see theire essences and lends additional powers of empathy and compassion. Full potential unknown.

F

Firehorn – A type of unisus which is black with horn, hooves, mane, wings, and tail of fire, found in the volcanic Ashlands, deep within the desserts of Southern Shimrah.

G

Goldhorn – A type of unisus which is white with horn, mane, hooves, wings, and tail of molten metallic gold. Found in the Goldhorn forests of Northern Shimrah.

Gumoos – A silver metal in Shimrah often used for jewelry and now used for decorative inlays on weapons.

I

Iceroans – A type of unisus which is white with horn, hooves, wings, mane, and tails of liquid ice.

J

Javnoon – An incredibly strong elixir which can add eons of centient and core years to the drinker's central being. Normally need to be mediated to sediment within the Shimran beings. Too much of central powers can make Shimrans explode out of their bodies.

Jafath – A type of Soul-Light Crossfire which binds a Shimran to his or her twin. They must be of the same gender and is characterized by gold mists. This type occurs when they were one and the same person or two characters of the same person in a past life. It is indicated by gold mists.

Javaahath – a type of Soul-Light Crossfire of siblings It binds Shimrans destined to be siblings who were siblings in a past life together and is usually indicated by thick blue mists.

M

Mara – Girl, woman

Marshadath – A type of Soul-Light Crossfire which binds a mentor to his or her student and is usually indicated by gold mists.

Meinedders – A type of venomous creature that barfs poison from its mouth and has snake hands that can immobilize and even kill dragons. Their venom can destroy the Dragonlight in large quantities.

Metallurgy Shifr - Ability of some Shimrans to detect and extract Shimran metals from the earth. Full potential unknown.

Mirror Shifr - A type of duplication talent whch allows the Shimrans to mirror any shifr in the kingdom but at less than the potency of the original version. Full potential unknown.

P

Pembre – Rose gold metal usually used for jewelry making and now for inlays in weapons.

Principle being – Shimran core and centients.

S

Shifr – Special gifts of Shimran folk emerging from their cores. The use of which requires centient powers. Some Shifrs can be more complicated and require more power than the centients and hence might draw on the core of a Shimran. Other Shifrs can destabilize the cores and wreak having in the Shimran being due to their immense power. Royalty can access a many shifrs as required, nobility and the martial forces around ten and normal inhabitants of Shimrah can access three at most.

Shimrans – The fair folk of Shimrah

Shimrah – A world where a better version of humanity lives. A version we may attain one day if we tried.

Shimara – Lady or gentlewoman, Madam – very respectful word for a female Shimran

Shimratzar – Gentleman, Sir, Master – a very respectful; word for a Shimran male

Shimling – A baby Shimran

Soul-Light Crossfire – An ancient Shimran enchantment that recognizes and binds soulmates to each other should they have the fortune to meet in their lifetimes. The Shimrans must have eye contact for it to work and a physical touch to seal the pledge which often occurs involuntarily after the eye contact. They are immensely powerful lifetime pledges that will incline Shimrans in the most extreme sense to the other. Shimrans in such Crossfires share a love so deep for each other that they would willingly sacrifice anything and everything they have for the other. Even themselves.

Warning – Crossfires alter the essences and auras of Shimrans. They wreak havoc within the Shimran being and those caught in it, will need to rest for a recommended period of three days and not engage in strenuous activity. If strain is placed on the Shimran being before recovery, it could destabilize their cores and cause internal injuries. It misaligns their center and they would need to be tended with the healers. Those in a Crossfire end together unless there is something else which ties them to life such as a shimling. In which case, they can exist as a minimal being till their purpose is fulfilled.

Silveroan – A type of Unisus which is black with silver horn, hooves, mane, wings and tail of molte metallic silver.

Silverine – Intricate colored mark on the left shoulder for a shimara and on the right shoulder of the shimratzars. Very elaborate and the design and colour defers from Shimran to Shimran and reflects their internal beings and essences. The life force entryway of Shimran folk and often used in every entwinement. It is very private and personal part of the Shimran being.

Siyan – Black metal found in Shimrah and is very strong. Also used in weapon making.

Shield Shifr - An ability of Shimran folk to cloak their minds or those of others against intrusion by certain other shifr's like Quinn's Mind Shifr. Full extent unknown.

T

Tzar – Man, boy, gentleman

Therin – Shimran fabric. They can be made from anything saturated or immersed in water and is made by combining a colorless liquid therilium only found in Therin Shifr shimrans.

Therilium – The colorless liquids that therin Shifr shimrans can extract from their beings by transforming their centients. It is combined with other materials to make therin which are the fabrics of Shimrah.

Therin Shifr - Shimrans who can produce therillium from their centients which can combine to form fabrics with any material saturated or immersed in water. Full potential unknown.

Tlumods – A type of dark creature which can explode Shimrans with a touch and absorb most of their energies.

U

Unisus – A type of alicorn with completely different placement of wings than traditional ones.

V

Vanish Shifr - An ability of some Shimrams to become invisible. Full extent unknown

Vinnery – The set chambers housing the spa, bathrooms, and toilets. Shimrans love peaceful private times and often make time to relax and gather their beings together. This time is important for their central being to function appropriately as peace strengthens them.

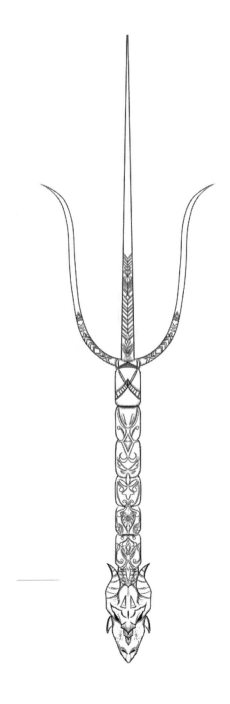

Fan Language

"Come talk to me" - Carry fan in left hand.

"I wish to speak to you" - Touch tip of fan with finger.

"You have won my heart" - Hold shut fan to the heart.

"Do not betray our secret" - Covering left ear with open fan.

"Follow me" - Carry fan in right hand in front of face

"We are being watched" - Twirl fan in left hand.

"I am married" - Fan slowly.

"I am engaged" - Fan quickly.

"I am sorry" - Draw fan across eye.

"You have changed" - Draw fan across forehead.

"I hate you" - Draw fan through hand.

"Do you love me?" - Present fan shut with both hands.

"I fancy you" - Draw fan across right cheek.

"I love another" - Twirl fan in right hand.

"You are cruel" - Open and shut fan.

"Yes" - Rest fan on right cheek.

"No" - Rest fan on left cheek.

"Kiss me" - Hold fan half closed against lips.